Neal Asher started writing SF and fantasy at the age of sixteen and has since had many novels published. Married, he now divides his time between Essex and a home in Crete. He is currently working on his next Polity novel.

# NEAL ASHER

## THE GABBLE

### and other stories

**TOR**

First published 2008 by Tor

First published in paperback 2009 by Tor
an imprint of Pan Macmillan Ltd
Pan Macmillan, 20 New Wharf Road, London N1 9RR
Basingstoke and Oxford
Associated companies throughout the world
www.panmacmillan.com

ISBN 978-0-330-45759-0

Visit **www.panmacmillan.com** to read more about all our books
and to buy them. You will also find features, author interviews and
news of any author events, and you can sign up for e-newsletters
so that you're always first to hear about our new releases.

*For*
*Peter Lavery and his scary pencil.*
*Happy retirement!*

# Contents

# Acknowledgements

Thanks to those who first grabbed and published these stories: Gardner Dozois, Sheila Williams, Andy Cox, David Pringle, Chris Roberson, and Paul Fraser. My best wishes to those whose work at Macmillan brings this book to the shelves: Peter Lavery, Rebecca Saunders, Emma Giacon, Steve Rawlings, Liz Cowen, Neil Lang, and many others besides. And thanks as always to my wife Caroline for not objecting too strongly to being a word-processor widow.

# 1

# SOFTLY SPOKE
# THE GABBLEDUCK

Lost in some perverse fantasy, Tameera lovingly inspected the displays of her Optek rifle. For me, what happened next proceeded with the unstoppable nightmare slowness of an accident. She brought the butt of the rifle up to her shoulder, took careful aim, and squeezed off a single shot. One of the sheq slammed back against a rock face then tumbled down through vegetation to land in the white water of a stream.

Some creatures seem to attain the status of myth even though proven to be little different from other apparently prosaic species. On Earth the lion contends with the unicorn, the wise old elephant never forgets, and gentle whales sing haunting ballads in the deep. It stems from anthropomorphism, is fed by both truth and lies, and over time firmly embeds itself in human culture. On Myral, where I had spent the last ten years, only a little of such status attached to the largest autochthon – not surprising for a creature whose name is a contraction of 'shit-eating quadruped'. But rumours of something else in the wilderness, something that had no right to be there, had really set the myth-engines of the human mind into motion, and brought hunters to this world.

There was no sign of any sheq on the way out over the narrow vegetation-cloaked mounts. They only put in an appearance after I finally moored my blimp to a peak, above a horizontal slab on which blister tents could be pitched. My passengers noticed straight away that the slab had been used many times before, and that my mooring was an iron ring long set into the rock, but then campsites were a rarity amid the steep slopes, cliffs and streams of this area. It wasn't a place that humans were built for. Sheq country.

Soon after he disembarked, Tholan went over to the edge to try out one of his disposable vidcams. The cam itself was about the size of his forefinger, and he was pointing it out over the terrain while inspecting a palm com he held in his other hand. He had unloaded a whole case of these cams, which he intended to position in likely locations, or dangle into mist pockets on a line – a hunter's additional eyes. He called me over. Tameera and Anders followed.

'There.' He nodded downwards.

A seven of sheq was making its way across the impossible terrain – finding handholds amid the lush vertical vegetation and travelling with the assurance of spiders on a wall. They were disconcertingly simian, about the size of a man, and quadruped – each limb jointed like a human arm but ending in hands bearing eight long prehensile fingers. Their heads, though, were anything but simian, being small, insectile, like the head of a mosquito but with two wide trumpet-like probosces.

'They won't be a problem will they?' Tholan's sister, Tameera, asked.

She was the most xenophobic, I'd decided, but then such phobia made little difference to their sport, the aliens they sought out usually being the 'I'm gonna chew off the top of your head and suck out your brains' variety.

'No – so long as we leave them alone,' said Tholan. Using his thumb on the side controls of his palm com, he increased the camera's magnification, switching it to infrared then ultrasound imaging.

'I didn't load anything,' said Anders, Tholan's PA. 'Are they herbivores?'

'Omnivores,' I told her. 'They eat some of that vegetation you see and supplement their diet with rock conch and octupal.'

'Rock conch and octupal indeed,' said Anders.

I pointed to the conch-like molluscs clinging to the wide leaves below the slab.

Anders nodded then said, 'Octupal?'

'Like it sounds: something like an octopus, lives in pools, but can drag itself overland when required.' I glanced at Tameera and added, 'None of them bigger than your hand.'

I hadn't fathomed this trio yet. Brother and sister hunted together, relied on each other, yet seemed to hate each other. Anders, who I at first thought Tholan was screwing, really did just organise things for him. Perhaps I should have figured them out before agreeing to being hired, then Tameera would never have taken the shot she then took.

The hot chemical smell from the rifle filled the unbreathable air. I guessed they used primitive projectile weapons of this kind to make their hunts more sporting. I didn't know how to react. Tholan stepped forwards and pushed down the barrel of her weapon before she could kill another of the creatures.

'That was stupid,' he said.

'Do they frighten you?' she asked coquettishly.

I reached up and checked my throat plug was still in place, for I felt breathless, but it was still bleeding oxygen into my bronchi. To say that I now had a bad feeling about all this would be an understatement.

'You know that as well as putting us all in danger, she just committed a crime,' I said conversationally, as Tholan stepped away from his sister.

'Crime?' he asked.

'She just killed a C-grade sentient. If the Warden AI finds out and can prove she knew before she pulled the trigger, then she's dead. But that's not the main problem now.' I eyed the sheq seven, now six. They seemed to be confused about the cause of their loss. 'Hopefully they won't attack, but it'll be an idea to keep watch.'

He stared at me, shoved his cam into his pocket. I turned away and headed back. Why had I agreed to bring these bored aristos out here to hunt for Myral's mythic gabbleduck? Money. Those who have enough to live comfortably greatly underestimate it as a source of motivation. My fee from Tholan wasn't enough for me to pay off all I owed on my blimp, and prevent a particular shark from dropping in for a visit to collect interest by way of involuntarily donated organs. It would also be enough for me to upgrade my apartment in the citadel, so I could rent it while I went out to look at this world. I'd had many of the available cerebral loads and knew much about Myral's environment, but that wasn't the same as experiencing it. Still there was much for me to learn, to know. Though I was certain that the chances of my finding a gabbleduck – a creature from a planet light-centuries away – anywhere on Myral were lower than the sole of my boot.

'She only did that to get attention,' said Anders at my shoulder.

'Well, let's hope she didn't succeed too well,' I replied. I looked up at my blimp, and considered the prospect of escaping this trio and bedding down for the night. Certainly we would be getting nothing more done today, what with the blue giant sun gnawing the edge of the world as it went down.

'You have to excuse her. She's overcompensating for a father who ignored her for the first twenty years of her life.'

Anders had been coming on to me right from the start and I wondered just what sort of rich-bitch game she was playing, though to find out I would have to let my guard down, and that I had no intention of doing. She was too much: too attractive, too intelligent, and just being in her presence set things jumping around in my stomach. She would destroy me.

'I don't have to excuse her,' I said. 'I just have to tolerate her.'

With that, I headed to the alloy ladder extending down from the blimp cabin.

'Why are they called shit-eaters?' she asked, falling into step beside me. Obviously she'd heard where the name sheq came from.

'As well as the rock conch and octupal, they eat each other's shit – running it through a second intestinal tract.'

She winced.

I added, 'But it's not something they should die for.'

'You're not going to report this are you?' she asked.

'How can I – he didn't want me carrying traceable com.'

I tried not to let my anxiety show. Tholan didn't want any of Myral's AIs finding out what he was up to, so as a result he provided all our com equipment, and it was encoded. I was beginning to wonder if that might be unhealthy for me.

'You're telling me you have no communicator up there?' She pointed up at the blimp.

'I won't report it,' I said, then climbed, wishing I could get away with pulling the ladder up behind me, wishing I had not stuck so rigidly to the wording of the contract.

Midark is that time when it's utterly black on Myral, when the sun is precisely on the opposite side of the world from you. It comes after five hours of blue, lasts about three hours prior to the next five hours of blue – the twilight that is neither day nor night and is caused by reflection of sunlight from the sub-orbital dust cloud. Anyway, it was at midark that the screaming and firing woke me. By the time I had reattached my oxygen bottle and was clambering down the ladder, some floods were lighting the area and it was all over.

'Yes, you warned me,' Tholan spat.

I walked over to Tameera's tent, which lay ripped open and empty. There was no blood, but then the sheq would not want to damage the replacement. I glanced at Anders, who was inspecting a palm com.

'She's alive.' She looked up. 'She must have been

using her own oxygen supply rather than the tent's. We have to go after her now.'

'Clawframes in midark?' I asked.

'We've got night specs.' She looked at me as if she hadn't realized until then how stupid I was.

'I don't care if you've got owl and cat genes – it's suicide.'

'Do explain,' said Tholan nastily.

'You got me out here as your guide. The plan was to set up a base and from it survey the area for any signs of the gabbleduck – by clawframe.'

'Yes . . .'

'Well, clawframes are only safe here during the day.'

'I thought you were going to explain.'

'I am.' I reached out, detached one of the floods from its narrow post, and walked with it to the edge of the slab. I shone it down revealing occasional squirming movement across the cliff of vegetation below.

'Octupals,' said Anders. 'What's the problem?'

I turned to her and Tholan. 'At night they move to new pools and, being slow-moving, they've developed a defence. Anything big gets too close, and they eject stinging barbs. They won't kill you, but you'll damned well know if you're hit, so unless you've brought armoured clothing . . .'

'But what about Tameera?' Anders asked.

'Oh the sheq will protect her for a while.'

'While?' Tholan queried.

'At first they'll treat her like an infant replacement for the one she killed,' I told him. 'So they'll guide her hands and catch her if she starts to fall. After a time they'll start to get bored, because sheq babies learn very quickly. If

we don't get to her before tomorrow night's first blue,
she'll probably have broken her neck.'

'When does this stop?' He nodded towards the octupal activity.

'Mid-blue.'

'We go then.'

The clawframe is sporting development from military
exoskeletons. The frame itself braces your body. A spine
column rests against your back like a metal flatworm.
Metal bones from this extend down your legs and along
your arms. The claws are four times the size of human
hands, and splayed out like big spiders from behind
them, and from behind the ankles. Each finger is a piton,
and programmed to seek out crevices on the rock-face
you are climbing. The whole thing is stronger, faster and
more sensitive than a human being. If you want, it can
do all the work for you. Alternatively, it can just be set in
neutral, the claws folded back, while you do all the climbing yourself – the frame only activating to save your life.
Both Anders and Tholan, I noted, set theirs to about a
third-assist, which is where I set mine. Blister tents and
equipment in their backpacks, and oxygen bottles and
catalysers at their waists, they went over the edge ahead
of me. Tameera's clawframe scrambled after them – a
glittery skeleton, slaved to them. I glanced back at my
blimp and wondered if I should just turn round and go
back to it. I went over the edge.

With the light intensity increasing and the octupals
bubbling down in their pools we made good time. Later,
though, when we had to go lower to keep on course after
the sheq, things got harder. Despite the three of us being
on third-assist we were panting within a few hours, as

lower down there was less climbing and more pushing through tangled vegetation. I noted that my catalyser pack was having trouble keeping up – cracking the $CO_2$ atmosphere and topping up the two flat bodyform bottles at my waist.

'She's eight kilometres away,' Anders suddenly said. 'We'll not reach her at this rate.'

'Go two-thirds assist,' said Tholan.

We all did that, and soon our clawframes were moving faster through the vegetation and across the rock-faces than was humanly possible. It made me feel lazy – like I was just a sack of flesh hanging on the hard-working clawframe. But we covered those eight kilometres quickly and as the sun breached the horizon, glimpsed the sheq far ahead of us, scrambling up from the sudden shadows in the valleys. They were a seven again now, I saw: Tameera being assisted along by creatures that had snatched the killer of one of their own, mistaking her for sheq herself.

'Why do they do it?' Anders asked as we scrambled along a vertical face.

'Do what?'

'Snatch people to make up their sevens.'

'Three reasons I've heard: optimum number for survival, or seven sheq required for successful mating, or the start of a primitive religion.'

'Which do you believe it is?'

'Probably a bit of them all.'

As we drew closer, I could hear Tameera sobbing in terror, pure fatigue, and self-pity. The six sheq were close around her, nudging her along, catching her feet when they slipped, grabbing her hands and placing them in firmer holds. I could also see that her dark green slicksuit was spattered with a glutinous yellow substance, and felt my gorge rising at what else she had suffered. They had tried to feed her.

We halted about twenty metres behind on a seventy-degree slope and watched as Tameera was badgered towards where it tilted upright then past the vertical.

'How do we play this?' Tholan asked.

'We have to get to her before they start negotiating that.' I pointed at the lethal terrain beyond the sheq. 'One mistake there and . . .' I gestured below to tilted slabs jutting from undergrowth, half hidden under fog generated by a nearby waterfall. I didn't add that we probably wouldn't even be able to find the body; despite the tracker Tameera evidently wore. 'We'll have to run a line to her. Anders can act as the anchor. She'll have to make her way above, and probably best if she takes Tameera's clawframe with her. You'll go downslope to grab Tameera if anything goes wrong and she falls. I'll go in with the line and the harness.'

'You've done this before?' Anders asked.

'Have you?' I countered.

'Seems you know how to go about it,' Tholan added.

'Just uploads from the planetary Almanac.'

'Okay, we'll do it like you said,' he agreed.

I'd noticed all three of them carried fancy monofilament climbing winders on their belts. Anders set hers unwinding its line, which looked thick as rope with cladding applied to the monofilament on its way out. I took up the ring end of the line and attached the webbing harness Tholan produced from one of his pack's many pockets.

'Set?' I asked.

They both nodded, Tholan heading downslope and

Anders up above. Now all I had to do was get to Tameera through the sheq and strap her into the harness.

As I drew closer, the creatures began to notice me and those insectile heads swung towards me, probosces pulsating as if they were sniffing.

'Tameera . . . Tameera!'

She jerked her head up, yellow gunk all around her mouth and spattered across her face. 'Help me!'

'I've got a line here and a harness,' I told her, but I wasn't sure if she understood.

I was about three metres away when the sheq that had been placing her foot on a thick root growing across the face of stone abruptly spun and scrambled towards me. Tholan's Optek crashed and I saw the explosive exit wound open in the creature's jade-green torso – a flower of yellow and pink. It sighed, sagged, but did not fall – its eight-fingered hands tangled in verdancy. The other sheq dived for safer holds and pulled close to the rock-face.

'What the fuck!'

'Just get the harness on her!' Tholan bellowed.

I moved in fast, not so much because he ordered it but because I didn't want him blowing away more of the creatures. Tameera was lethargic at first, but then she began to get the idea. Harness on, I moved aside.

'Anders!'

Anders had obviously seen, because she drew the line taut through greenery and began hauling Tameera upwards, away from sheq now beginning to nose in confusion towards their second dead member. Stripped-off line cladding fell like orange snow. I reached out, shoved the dead sheq, once, twice, and it tumbled down the slope, the rest quickly scrambling after it. Tholan was moving aside, looking up at me. I gestured to a nearby mount with a flat top on which we could all gather.

'Got her!' Anders called.

Glancing up I saw Anders installing Tameera in the other clawframe. 'Over there!' I gestured to the mount. Within a few minutes we were all on the small area of level stone, gazing down towards where the five remaining sheq had caught their companion, realized it was dead and released it again, and were now zipping about like wasps disturbed from a nest.

'We should head back to the blimp, fast as you like.'

No one replied because Tameera chose that moment to vomit noisily. The stench was worse even than that from the glutinous yellow stuff all over her.

'What?' said Anders.

'They fed her,' I explained.

That made Anders look just as sick.

Finally sitting up, then detaching her arms from her clawframe, Tameera stared at her brother and held out her hand. He unhitched his pack, drew out her Optek rifle and handed it over. She fired from that sitting position, bowling one of the sheq down the distant slope and the subsequent vertical drop.

'Look you can't—'

The barrel of Tholan's Optek was pointing straight at my forehead.

'We can,' he said.

I kept my mouth shut as, one by one, Tameera picked off the remaining sheq and sent them tumbling down into the mist-shrouded river canyon. It was only then that we returned to the slab campsite.

*

Blue again, but I was certainly ready for sleep and felt a surge of resentment when the blimp cabin began shaking. Someone was coming up the ladder, then walking round the catwalk. Shortly, Anders opened the airtight door and hauled herself inside. I saw her noting with some surprise how the passenger cabin converted into living quarters. I was ensconced in the cockpit chair, sipping a glass of whisky, feet up on the console. She turned off her oxygen supply, tried the air in the cabin, then sat down on the corner of the fold-down bed, facing me.

'Does it disgust you?' she asked.

I shrugged. Tried to stay nonchalant. What was happening below didn't bother me, her presence in my cabin did.

She continued, 'There's no reason to be disgusted. Incest no longer has the consequences it once had. All genetic faults can be corrected in the womb . . .'

'Did I say I was disgusted? Perhaps it's you, why else are you up here?'

She grimaced. 'Well they do get noisy.'

'I'm sure it won't last much longer,' I said. 'Then you can return to your tent.'

'You're not very warm are you?'

'Just wary – I know the kind of games you people play.'

'You people?'

'The bored and the wealthy.'

'I'm Tholan's PA. I'm an employee.'

I sat there feeling all resentful, my resentment increased because of course she was right. I should not have lumped her in the same category as Tholan and his sister. She was in fact in my category. She had also casually just knocked away one of my defences.

'Would you like a drink?' I eventually asked, my mouth dry.

Now I expected her righteous indignation and rejection. But Anders was more mature than that, more dangerous.

'Yes, I would.' As she said it, she undid the stick seams of her boots and kicked them off. Then she detached the air hose from her throat plug, coiled it back to the bottle, then unhooked that from her belt and put it on the floor. I hauled myself from my chair and poured her a whisky, adding ice from my recently installed little fridge.

'Very neat,' she said, accepting the drink. As I made to step past her and return to the cockpit chair, she caught hold of my forearm and pulled me down beside her.

'You know,' I said, 'that if we don't report what happened today that would make us accessories. That could mean readjustment, even mind-wipe.'

'Are you hetero?' she asked.

I nodded. She put her hand against my chest and pushed me back on to the bed. I let her do it – lay back. She stood up, looking down at me as she drained her whisky. Then she undid her trousers, dropped them and kicked them away, then climbed astride me still wearing her shirt and very small briefs. Still staring at me she undid my trousers, freed my erection, then pulling aside the crutch of her briefs, slowly slid down onto me. Then she began to grind back and forth.

'Just come,' she said, when she saw my expression. 'You've got all night to return the favour.' I managed to hold on for about another thirty seconds. It had been a while. Afterwards, we stripped naked, and I did return the favour. And then we spent most of the blue doing things to each other normally reserved for those for whom straight sex has become a source of ennui.

'You know, Tholan will pay a great deal for your silence, one way or another.'

I understood that Tholan might not pay *me* for my silence. I thought her telling me this worthy of the punishment I then administered, and which she noisily enjoyed, muffling her face in the pillow.

We slept a sleep of exhaustion through midark.

Tameera wanted trophies. She wanted a pair of sheq heads to cunningly preserve and mount on the gateposts either side of the drive to her and Tholan's property on Earth. Towards the end of morning blue, we ate recon rations and prepared to set out. I thought it pointless to tell them of the penalties for possessing trophies from class-C sentients. They'd already stepped so far over the line it was a comparatively minor crime.

'What we need to discuss is my fee,' I said.

'Seems to me he's already had some payment,' said Tameera, eyeing Anders.

Tholan shot her a look of annoyance and turned back to me. 'Ten times what I first offered. No one needs to know.'

'Any items you bring back you'll carry in your stuff,' I said.

I wondered at their arrogance. Maybe they'd get away with it – we'd know soon enough upon our return to the citadel – but most likely, a drone had tagged one of the sheq, and as the creature died, a satellite eye had recorded the event. The way I saw it, I could claim I had been scared they would kill me, and had only kept up the criminal façade until we reached safety. Of course, if they did get away with what they'd done, there was no reason why I shouldn't benefit.

While we prepared, I checked the map in my palm com, input our position and worked out an easier course than the one we had taken the day before. The device would keep us on course even though Tholan had allowed no satellite link-up. By the sun, by its own elevation, the time, and by reading the field strength of Myral's magnetosphere, the device kept itself accurately located on the map I'd loaded from the planetary Almanac.

We went over the edge as the octupals slurped and splashed in their pools and the sun flung arc-welder light across the land. This time we took it easy on third-assist, also stopping for meals and rest. During one of these breaks I demonstrated how to use a portable stove to broil a rock conch in its shell, but Tholan was the only one prepared to sample the meat. I guess it was a man thing. As we travelled I pointed out flowering spider vines, their electric red male flowers taking to the air in search of the blowsy yellow female flowers: these plants and their pollinating insects having moved beyond the symbiosis seen on Earth to become one. Then, the domed heads of octupals rising out of small rock pools to blink bulbous gelatinous eyes at the evening blue, we moored our blister tents on a forty-degree slope.

Anders connected my tent to hers, whilst a few metres away Tholan and Tameera connected theirs. No doubt they joined their sleeping bags in the same way we did. Sex, in a tent fixed to such a slope, with a sleeping bag also moored to the rock through the groundsheet, was a bit cramped. But it was enjoyable and helped to pass most of the long night. Sometime during midark I came half awake to the sound of a voice. 'Slabber gebble-crab' and 'speg bruglor nomp' were its nonsensical utterances. The yelling and groaning from Tholan, in morning blue, I thought due to he and his sister's lovemaking. But in full morning I had to pick octupal stings from the fabric of my tent, and I saw that Tholan wore a dressing on his cheek.

'What happened?' I asked.

'I just stuck my damned head out,' he replied.

'What treatment have you used?'

'Unibiotic and antallergens.'

'That should do it.'

Shame I didn't think to ask why he wanted to leave his tent and go creeping about in the night. That I attributed the strange voice in midark to dream influenced things neither one way nor the other.

It was only a few hours into the new day that we reached the flat-topped mount from which Tameera had slaughtered the remaining sheq. I studied the terrain through my monocular and realized how the excitement of our previous visit here had blinded me to just how dangerous this area was. There wasn't a slope below seventy degrees and many of the river valleys and canyons running between the jagged rocks below were full of rolling mist. Clawframes or not, this was about as bad as it could get.

'Well, that's where they should be,' said Tholan, lowering his own monocular and pointing to a wider canyon floored with mist out of which arose the grumble of a river.

'If they haven't been swept away,' I noted.

Ignoring me, he continued, 'We'll work down from

where they fell. Maybe some of them got caught in the foliage.'

From the mount, we travelled down, across a low ridge, then up onto the long slope from which we had rescued Tameera. I began to cut down diagonally, and Anders followed me while Tameera and Tholan kept moving up high to where the sheq had been, though why they were going there I had no idea, for we had seen every one fall. Anders was above me when I began to negotiate a whorled hump of stone at the shoulder of a cliff. I thought I could see a sheq caught in some foliage down there. As I was peering through the mist, Anders screamed above me. I had time only to glance up, and drive my frame's fingers into stone when she barrelled into me. We both went over. Half detached from her frame, she clung around my neck. I looked up to where two fingers of my frame held us suspended. I noted that her frame – the property of Tholan and Tameera – was dead weight. Then I looked higher and guessed why.

Brother and sister were scrambling down towards us, saying nothing, not urging us to hang on. I guessed that was precisely what they did not want us to do. It must have been frustrating for Tholan: the both of us in one tent that could have been cut from its moorings – two witnesses lost in the unfortunate accident – but sting-shooting molluscs preventing him from committing the dirty deed. I reached round with my free claw and tightly gripped Anders's belt, swung my foot claws in and gripped the rock-face with them.

'Get the frame off.'

She stared at me in confusion, then looked up the slope and I think all the facts clicked into the place. Quickly, while I supported her, she undid her frame's straps, leaving the chest straps until last. It dropped into the mist: a large chrome harvestman spider . . . a dead one.

'Okay, round onto my back and cling on tightly.'

She swung round quickly. Keeping to third-assist – any higher assistance and the frame might move too fast for her to hang on – I began climbing down the cliff to the mist. The first Optek bullet ricocheted off stone by my face. The second ricochet, by my hand, was immediately followed by an animal grunt from Anders. Something warm began trickling down my neck and her grip loosened.

Under the mist, a river thrashed its way between tilted slabs. I managed to reach one such half-seen slab just before Anders released her hold completely as she fainted. I laid her down and inspected her wound. The ricochet had hit her cheekbone and left a groove running up to her temple. It being a head wound, there was a lot of blood, but it didn't look fatal if I could get her medical attention. But doing anything now with the medical kits we both carried seemed suicidal. I could hear the mutter of Tameera and Tholan's voices from above – distorted by the mist. Then, closer, and lower down by the river, another voice:

'Shabra tabul. Nud lockock ocker,' something said.

It was like hiding in the closet from an intruder, only to have something growl right next to you. Stirred by the constant motion of the river, the mist slid through the air in banners, revealing and concealing. On the slab, we were five metres above the gravelled riverbank upon which the creature squatted. Its head was level with me. Anders chose that moment to groan and I slapped my hand over her mouth. The creature was pyramidal, all but one of its three pairs of arms folded complacently over the jut of its lower torso. In one huge black claw it held the remains of a sheq. With the fore-talon of another claw, it was levering a trapped bone from the white holly-thorn lining of its duck bill. The tiara of green eyes below its domed skull glittered.

'Brong da bulla,' it stated, having freed the bone and flung it away.

It was no consolation to realize that the sheq corpses had attracted the gabbleduck here. Almost without voli-tion, I crouched lower, hoping it did not see me, hoping that if it did, I could make myself appear less appetizing. My hands shaking, I reached down and began taking line off the winder at Anders's belt. The damned machine seemed so noisy and the line far too bright an orange. I got enough to tie around my waist as a precaution, then I undid the straps to her pack and eased her free of that encumbrance. Now I could slide her down towards the back of the slab, taking us out of the creature's line of sight, but that would put me in the foliage down there and it would be sure to hear me. I decided to heave her up, throw her over my shoulder, and just get out of there as fast as I could. But just then, a bullet smacked into the column of my clawframe and knocked me down flat, the breath driven out of me.

I rolled over, looking towards the gabbleduck as I did so. I felt my flesh creep. It was gone. Something that huge had no right to be able to move so quickly and stealthily. Once on my back I gazed up at Tholan and his sister as they came down the cliff. My clawframe was heavy and dead, and so too would I be, but whether by bullet or chewed up in that nightmare bill was debatable.

The two halted a few metres above and, with their clawframes gripping backwards against the rock, freed their arms so they could leisurely take aim with their Opteks. Then something sailed out of the mist and slammed into the cliff just above Tameera, and dropped down. She started screaming, intestines and bleeding flesh caught between her and the cliff – the half-chewed corpse of a sheq. The gabbleduck loomed out of the mist on the opposite side of the slab from where it had disappeared, stretched up and up and extended an arm that had to be three metres long. One scything claw knocked Tameera's Optek spinning away and made a sound like a knife across porcelain as it scraped stone. On full automatic Tholan fired his weapon into the body of the gabbleduck, the bullets thwacking away with seemingly no effect. I grabbed Anders and rolled with her to the side of the slab, not caring where we dropped. We fell through foliage and tangled growth, down into a crevice where we jammed until I undid my frame straps and shed my pack ahead of us.

'Shabber grubber shabber!' the gabbleduck bellowed accusingly.

'Oh god oh god oh god!' Tameera.

More firing from Tholan.

'Gurble,' tauntingly.

'I'll be back for you, fucker!'

I don't know if he was shouting at the gabbleduck or me.

There was water in the lower part of the crevice – more than enough to fill my purifying bottle and to clean the blood from Anders's wound before dressing it. I used a small medkit diagnosticer on her and injected the drugs it manufactured in response to her injuries. Immediately her breathing eased and her colour returned. But we were not in a good position. The gabbleduck was moving about above us, occasionally making introspective and nonsensical comments on the situation. A little later, when I was trying to find some way to set up the blister tent, a dark shape occluded the sky above.

'Urbock shabber goh?' the gabbleduck enquired, then not being satisfied with my lack of response, groped down into the crevice. It could reach only as far as the ridge where my clawframe was jammed. With a kind of thoughtful impatience, it tapped a fore-talon against the stone, then withdrew its arm.

'Gurble,' it decided, and moved away.

Apparently, linguists who have loaded a thousand languages into their minds despair trying to understand gabbleducks. What they say is nonsensical, but frustratingly close to meaning. There's no reason for them to have such complex voice boxes, especially to communicate with each other, as on the whole they are solitary creatures and speak to themselves. When they meet it is usually only to mate or fight, or both. There's also no reason for them to carry structures in their skulls capable of handling vastly complex languages. Two thirds of their large brains they seem to use hardly at all. Science, in their case, often supports myth.

Driving screw pitons into either side of the crevice, I was eventually able to moor the tent across. Like a hammock, the tough material of the groundsheet easily supported our weight, even with all the contortions I had to go through to get Anders into the sleeping bag. Once she was safely ensconced, I found that evening blue had arrived. Using a torch, I explored the crevice, finding how it rose to the surface at either end. Then the danger from octupals, stirring in the sump at the crevice bottom, forced me back to the tent. The following night was not good. A veritable swarm of octupal swamping the tent had me worrying that their extra weight would bring it down. It was also very very dark, down there under the mist. Morning took for ever to arrive, but when it eventually did, Anders regained consciousness.

'They tried to kill us,' she said, after lubricating her mouth with purified water.

'They certainly did.'

'Where are we now?'

'In a hole.' She stared at me and I went on to explain the situation.

'So how do we get out of this?' she eventually asked.

'We've both lost our clawframes, but at least we've retained our oxygen bottles and catalysers. I wish I'd told Tholan to screw his untraceable com bullshit.' I thought for a moment. 'What about your palm com? Could we use it to signal?'

'It's his, just like the clawframe I was using. He'll have shut it down by now. Should we be able to get to it.' She looked up. Her backpack was up there on the slab, up there with the gabbleduck.

'Ah.'

She peered at me. 'You're saying you really have no way of communicating with the citadel?'

'Not even on my blimp. You saw my contract with Tholan. I didn't risk carrying anything, as he seems the type to refuse payment for any infringements.'

'So what now?' she asked.

'That rather depends on Tholan and Tameera . . . and on you.'

'Me?'

'I'm supposing that, as a valued employee, you too have one of these implants?' Abruptly she got a sick expression. I went on, 'My guess is that those two shits have gone for my blimp to bring it back here. If we stay in one place, they'll zero in on your implant. If we move they'll still be able to track us. We'll have to stay down low under the mist and hope they don't get any lucky shots in. The trouble is that to our friend down here we would be little more than an entrée.'

'You could leave me – make your own way back. Once out of this area they'd have trouble finding you.'

'It had to be said,' I agreed. 'Now let's get back to how we're going to get out of here.'

After we had repacked the blister tent and sleeping bag, we moved to the end of the crevice which, though narrow, gave easier access to the surface. Slanting down one way, to the gravelled banks of the river, was another slab, bare and slippery. Above us was the edge of the slab we had rolled from, and behind that, disappearing into mist, rose the wall of stone I had earlier descended. Seeing this brought home to me just how deep was the shit trap we occupied. The citadel was just over two hundred kilometres away. I estimated our travel rate at not much more than a few kilometres a day. The journey was survivable. The Almanac loadings I'd had told me what we could eat, and there would never be any shortage of water. Just so long as our catalysers held out and neither of us fell . . .

'We'll run that line of yours between us, about four metres to give us room to manoeuvre. I'll take point.'

'You think it's safe to come out?' Anders asked.

'Not really, but it's not safe to stay here either.'

Anders ran the line out from her winder and locked it, and I attached its end ring to a loop on the back of my belt before working my way up to the edge of the slab. Once I hauled myself up I was glad to see her pack still where I had abandoned it. I was also glad that Anders did not require my help to climb up – if I had to help her all the way the prospective journey time would double. Anders shrugged on her pack, cinched the stomach strap. We then made our way to where vegetation grew like a vertical forest up the face of the cliff. Before we attempted to enter this I took out my palm com and worked out the best route – one taking us back towards the citadel but keeping us under the mist, but for the occasional ridge. Then, climbing through the tangled vegetation, I couldn't shake the feeling that something was watching us, something huge and dangerous, and that now it was following us.

The first day was bad. It wasn't just the sheer physical exertion, it was the constant gloom underneath the mist sapping will and blackening mood. I knew Tameera and Tholan would not reach us that day, but I also knew that they could be back overhead in the blimp by the following morning blue if they travelled all night. But they would stop to rest. Certainly they knew they had all the time they wanted to take, to find and kill us.

As the sun went down, Anders erected one blister tent on a forty-degree slab – there was no room for the other tent. I set about gathering some of the many rock conches surrounding us. We still had rations, but I thought we should use such abundance, as the opportunity might not present later on. I also collected female spider vine flowers, and the sticky buds in the crotch branches of walker trees. I half expected Anders to object when I began broiling the molluscs, but she did not. The conches were like chewy fish, the flowers were limp and slightly sweet lettuce. The buds have no comparison in Earthly food because none is so awful. Apparently it was a balanced diet. I packed away the stove and followed Anders into the blister tent just as it seemed the branches surrounding us were beginning to move. Numerous large warty octupals were dragging themselves through the foliage. They were a kind unknown to me, therefore not commonly encountered, else I would have received something on them in the Almanac's general load.

In the morning, I was chafed from the straps in our conjoined sleeping bags (they stopped us ending up in the bottom of the bag on that slope) and irritable. Anders was not exactly a bright light either. Maybe certain sugars were lacking in the food we had eaten, because after munching down ration bars while we packed away our equipment we quickly started to feel a lot better. Or maybe it was some mist-born equivalent of SAD.

An hour after we set out, travel became a lot easier and a lot more dangerous. Before, the masses of vegetation on the steep slopes, though greatly slowing our progress, had offered a safety net if either of us fell. Now we were quickly negotiating slopes not much steeper than the slab on which Anders had moored the tent the previous night, and sparse of vegetation. If we fell here, we would just accelerate down to a steeper slope or sheer drop, and a final impact in some dank rocky sump.

We were higher, I think, than the day before – the mist thinner. The voice of the gabbleduck was mournful and distant there.

'Urecoblank . . . scudder,' it called, perhaps trying to lure its next meal.

'Shit, shit,' I said as I instinctively tried to increase my pace and slipped over, luckily catching hold before I slid down.

'Easy,' said Anders.

I just hoped the terrain would put the damned thing off, but somehow I doubted that. There seemed to me something almost supernatural about the creature. Until actually seeing the damned thing, I had never believed there was one out here. I'd thought Myral's gabbleduck as mythical as mermaids and centaurs on Earth.

'What the hell is that thing doing here anyway?' I asked.

'Probably escaped from a private collection,' Anders replied. 'Perhaps someone bought it as a pet and got rid of it when it stopped being cute.'

'Like that thing was ever cute?' I asked.

Midday. The first Optek shots began wanging off the stone around us, and the shadow of my blimp drew above. A kind of lightness infected me then. I knew, one way or another, we were going to die, and that know-ledge just freed me of all responsibility to myself and to the future.

'You fucking missed!' I bellowed.

'That'll soon change!' came Tholan's distant shout.

'There's no need to aggravate him,' Anders hissed.

'Why? Might he try to kill us?' I spat back.

Even so, I now led us a course that angled lower down into the mist. The firing tracked us, but I reckoned the

chances of being hit were remote. Tholan must have
thought the same because the firing soon ceased. When
we stopped to rest under cover of thicker vegetation, I
checked my palm com and nearly sobbed on seeing that
in one and half days we had covered less than three kilometres. It was about right, but still disheartening. Then,
even worse, I saw that ahead, between two mounts,
there was a ridge we must climb over to stay on course.
To take another route involved a detour of tens of kilometres. Undoubtedly the ridge rose out of the mist.
Undoubtedly Tholan had detected it on his palm com
too.

'What do we do?' Anders asked.

'We have to look. Maybe there'll be some sort of
cover.'

'Seeble grubber,' muttered the gabbleduck in the
deeper mist below us.

'It's fucking following us,' I whispered.

Anders just nodded.

Then even more bad news came out of the mist.

I couldn't figure quite what I was seeing out there in the
canyon beside us, momentarily visible through the mist.
Then all of a sudden the shape, on the end of its thin but
hugely tough line, became recognizable. I was looking at
a four-pronged blimp anchor, with disposable cams
taped to each of the prongs. We got moving again, heading for that ridge. I equated getting to the other side with
safety. Ridiculous, really.

'He's got . . . infrared . . . on them,' I said, between
gasps.

A fusillade sounding like the full fifty-round clip of an
Optek slammed into the slope just ahead of us.

'Of course . . . he's no way . . . of knowing which camera . . . is pointing . . . where,' I added.

Then a flare dropped, bouncing from limb to limb down through the vertical jungle, and the firing came again, strangely in the same area. I glimpsed the anchor again, further out and higher. Tholan and his sister had no real experience of piloting a blimp – it wasn't some gravcar they could set on autopilot. Soon we saw the remains of what they had been targeting: an old sheq too decrepit to keep up with its seven, probably replaced by a new hatching. It was hanging over the curved fibrous bough of a walker tree, great holes ripped through its body by Optek bullets.

We climbed higher as the slope became steeper, came to the abrupt top edge of this forest of walker trees, made quick progress stepping from horizontal trunk to trunk with the wall of stone beside us. After a hundred metres of this, we had to do some real climbing up through a crack to a slope we could more easily negotiate. My feet were sore and my legs ached horribly. Constantly walking along slopes like this put pressure on feet and ankles they were certainly not accustomed to. I wondered just how long my boots and gloves would last in this terrain. They were tough – made with monofibre materials used by the military – but nothing is proof against constant abrasion on stone. Maybe a hundred days of this? Who was I kidding?

By midday, we were on the slope that curved round below one of the mounts then blended in to the slope leading up to the ridge. Checking the map on my palm com, I saw that there was likely a gutter between the ridge and the mount. I showed this to Anders

'There may be cover there,' I said.

She stared at me, dark rings under her eyes – too exhausted to care. We both turned then, and peered down into the mist and canted forests. There came the sound of huge movement, the cracking of walker trunks, broken vegetation showering down through the trees below us.

'Come on.' I had no devil-may-care left in me. I was just as weary as Anders. We reached the gutter, which was abundant with hand- and footholds, but slippery with rock-slime. We climbed slowly and carefully up through thinning mist. Then the blimp anchor dropped into sight on its rope.

'Surprise!' Tameera called down to us.

The mist was now breaking, and I glimpsed the lumpy peak of the mount looming to our left. Higher up, its propellers turning lazily to hold it against a breeze up from the ridge, floated my blimp. Tholan and Tameera stood out on the catwalk, both of them armed, and I was sure I could see them grinning even from that distance. I swore and rested my forehead against slimy stone. We had about ten metres of clear air to the top of the ridge, then probably the same over the other side. No way could we move fast enough – not faster than a speeding bullet. I looked up again. Fuck them. I wasn't going to beg, I wasn't going to try to make any last-minute deals. I turned to Anders.

'We'll just keep climbing,' I said.

She nodded woodenly, and I led the way. A shot slammed into the rock just above me, then went whining down the gutter. They were playing for the moment. I glanced up, saw that the blimp was drifting sideways towards the mount. Then I saw it.

The arm folded out and out. The wrongness I felt

about it, I guess, stemmed from the fact that it possessed too many joints. A three-fingered hand, with claws like black scythes, closed on the blimp anchor and pulled. Seated on the peak, the gabbleduck looked like some monstrous child holding the string of a toy balloon.

'Brong da lockock,' it said.

Leaning over the catwalk rail, Tholan tried pumping shots into the monster. Tameera shrank back against the cabin's outer wall, making a high keening sound. The gabbleduck gave the blimp anchor a sharp tug and Tholan went over the edge. One long scream as he fell turned to an oomph as the monster caught him in one of its many hands. It took his rifle and tossed it away like the stick from a cocktail sausage, then it stuffed him into its bill.

'Keep going!' Anders shoved me in the back.

'It used us as bait to get them,' I said.

'And now it doesn't need us.'

I continued to climb, mindful of my handholds, aware that the gabbleduck was now coming down off its mount. We reached the ridge. I glanced down the other side into more mist, more slopes. I looked aside as the gabbleduck slid down into mist, towing the blimp behind it, Tameera still keening. It had its head tilted back and with one hand was shoving Tholan deeper into its bill. After a moment, it seemed to get irritated, and tore his kicking legs away while it swallowed the rest of him. Then the mist engulfed the monster, the blimp shortly afterwards. Tameera's keening abruptly turned to a long agonized scream, then came a crunching sound.

'It'll come for us next,' said Anders, eyeing the stirring mist then shoving me again.

We didn't stand a chance out here – I knew that.

'What the hell are you doing?'

I passed back the ring of the line that joined us together. 'Wind it in.'

She set the little motor running, orange line-cladding falling around her feet. I glanced at her and saw dull acceptance that I was abandoning her at last. The large shape came up out of the mist, shuddering. I began to run along the ridge. It was a guess, a hope, a chance – on such things might your life depend.

The anchor was snagging in the outer foliage of walker trees as the blimp, now free of two man weights and released by the gabbleduck, was rising again. I was going for the line first, though I'm damned if I know how I would have climbed the four-millimetre-thick cable. At the last moment I accelerated, and leapt: three metres out and dropping about the same distance down. My right leg snapped underneath me on the roof of the cabin, but I gave it no time to hurt. I dragged myself to the edge, swung down on the blimp cables, and was quickly in through the airtight door. First, I hit the controls to fold the anchor and reel in the cable, then I was in the pilot's seat, making the blimp vent gas and turning it towards where Anders waited. Within minutes, she was on the catwalk and inside and I was pumping gas back into the blimp again. But we weren't going anywhere.

'Oh no . . . no!' Anders's feeling of the unfairness of it all was in that protest. I stared out at the array of green eyes, and at the long single claw it had hooked over the catwalk rail. I guessed it would winkle us out of the cabin like the meat of a rock conch from its shell. I didn't suppose the bubble metal alloys would be much hindrance to it.

'Gurble,' said the gabbleduck, then suddenly its claw was away from the rail and we were rising again. Was it playing with us? We moved closer to the windows and looked down, said nothing until we were certainly out of its reach, said nothing for some time after that. At the last, and I don't care how certain the scientists are that they are just animals, I'm damned sure the gabbleduck waved to us, before it returned to its misty realm.

# 2

# PUTREFACTORS

Three moons chased each other across the umber sky and ferris flies spun in swarms above the goss thorns. On the white sand of the shore, where weed had collected in decaying banks like spills of tar, footprints were clearly visible. Prints from deck boots, Ansel reckoned. He squatted by one of them and stirred the sand with the barrel of his thin-gun, then stood and shrugged his rucksack more evenly on his shoulders. Glancing back at the shuttle resting on neutral grav out at sea, its lights reflecting off the foamy water, he saw that the pilot was now in the cargo bay, securing the AG sled with which he had brought Ansel ashore. The same sled the man had used to bring Kelly to this beach seven Fores days ago. The pilot said he would return here in another fifty days to pick Ansel up. Kelly would only be leaving this place in a body bag.

Ansel watched the shuttle rise silently from the sea. When it was a hundred metres up its thrusters spat twin blue flames and it fled into the sky. Afterwards he studied the moons.

In the Almanac the three moons were only numbered, though it was probable the colonists had named them.

He felt certain one of them had to be called cheese or some such, so closely did it resemble a wedge of Cheddar. As another moon, shaped like a lemon, and the smallest of the three, tumbled down behind the horizon, he moved off. The larger moon moved slowly across the sky and it was in the ruby light of this that Ansel followed the trail. He reckoned on gaining a good three hours on Kelly before sunrise. What he hadn't reckoned on was the sudden weakness and sickness that hit him almost as soon as he set out.

At Terran Holdings Company headquarters they'd said this might happen. It was his body's reaction to the symbiont – the creature inside him that enabled him to survive on the food here. But he had not expected it to be so bad. Fifty metres down the beach and he fell shuddering to his knees. Abruptly he vomited, and when he saw what he had brought up, he vomited again. On the sand before him was a slimy grey sheet of matter that moved slightly as he watched it. He pulled the bottle of aldetox provided for just this circumstance and swilled down a mouthful. In a minute, his symbiont quietened and he was able to stagger to his feet, then into the shade of a goss thorn sprouting from the shell debris farther up the beach. There he took off his rucksack and pulled out his thermal sleeping bag. It took him all his effort to climb inside and there he lay shivering till dawn.

Before the sun rose, the sky changed from umber to a delicate flesh-pink, then broke up into bars that were every pastel shade between that pink and a dark orange. When it finally breached the horizon, the sun itself was an intense topaz that spilled shadows before it like blue oil on the ground. Wearily Ansel pulled himself from his thermal bag then staggered down to the sea. With a small glassite saucepan he scooped clear water and gulped it down. It tasted vaguely of a fizzy stomach remedy, but of nothing else. He had been told it was safe. When he had drunk his fill, he washed his face and returned to his belongings. Now he felt hungry, and must forage for his food. There was supposed to be no problem with this. He looked up at the branches of the goss thorn where ferris flies hung like strange Christmas decorations. The long fruits that grew parallel to the inner branches of the tree were haired with fly spines. The direct download from the Almanac had provided him with more than enough knowledge to easily survive here. He knew it was inadvisable to eat fruits like this and so, packing away his bag and hoisting his rucksack, he moved off. Only a few minutes later he found his first cornul bush.

The cornul bush possessed a star-sectioned green stem and ferny leaves. In its branches were hundreds of fruits small enough to fit in the palm of a hand. They were yellow and red, green and white, and in as many different shapes as there were fruits on the bush. The Almanac had provided him with no explanation for this. He just knew that all of the fruits were edible for someone with the symbiont. Ansel plucked a white fruit, shaped like a banana, and studied it. This innocuous object would have killed him five days ago, after protracted painful convulsions, just as similar fruit had killed the Director and ten members of the board two months ago. He bit down and relished the taste explosion in his mouth. Even to people without the symbiont the fruits tasted like this, hence the way they had been so well received at the banquet in the Strine Station. No one had suspected a thing. No one would have believed that someone could smuggle highly toxic fruits aboard the station, then into a high-level Company banquet. After he had eaten his fill, Ansel moved on. He decided he should ask Kelly, before he killed him, just how he had managed that. Certainly, Kelly must have contacts on the station, and a shuttle secreted somewhere.

The footprints in the sand turned inland and soon became difficult to follow, but Ansel did not worry too much about this. The village of Troos lay a couple of kilometres from here. Kelly's family lived there, and that was where Ansel would doubtless find him.

Inland the fauna and flora changed markedly. The goss thorns were more dispersed now and here grew into solid trees with trunks like barrels, short and viciously thorned limbs, and blue-green spines hazing their bark. Occasionally things that looked vaguely like butterflies went winging past. Ansel knew these to be flying flowers – the ultimate pollen-carriers. Botanists and entomologists had concluded, after many years of discussion, that these flowers had once been nectar-feeding insects, and that this mutualism had been carried to its ultimate extreme. It was after he watched one of these objects fall on the still-attached flower of another plant, for mating, that the wind changed, and Ansel got his first hint of putrefactor.

The putrefactor was not the most pleasant of creatures. Ansel had heard descriptions of them and of the smell that often surrounded them, and thought nothing of it. The Almanac justly pointed out that the creature had its place in the environment of Fores, just as the maggot has its place in the environment of Earth. The putrefactor was the mortician of this world.

The 'factor was stretched out over the upper branches

of a huge goss thorn. It looked like a great spread of drying grey-green mucus deposited there. Ansel guessed that this one had not fed in quite a while, as it was possible to walk close to it without gagging. He knew the creature would have a territory covering about a square kilometre, and that anything that died in that territory would immediately become its property. Only death would motivate it. The 'factor had a store of patience to make a vulture look frenetic, often staying unmoving for periods of ten years or more.

Ansel closed his eyes for a moment to more clearly see the images and text scrolling down his visual cortex from the Almanac download:

*With a death in its territory the putrefactor will immediately tense, cracking away its hard outer covering, then ooze from its perch or hide. Its rate of travel is not much faster than a slug's, a creature it does resemble. On its arrival at the corpse, the factor spreads out and engulfs it completely, even should the corpse be ten times its size. Digestion is quick: the corpse broken down into simple organic compounds. Very little is wasted.*

Ansel opened his eyes and grinned to himself. He felt that the colonists' name for it was the most appropriate. It was called a 'shroudbeast' here.

Between the goss thorns, cornul bushes and areas overgrown with purple-stemmed briars, dark-green mosses blanketed the ground, and from this seed-stems with bulbous red heads sprouted like grass. The covering was soft but firm underfoot and made walking a pleasant experience even though he was heading uphill. Soon Ansel came upon tracks where the seed-stems were crushed down and he knew he was getting closer to the village. Farther in, these tracks were worn down to bare sandy ground that eventually brought him to a wider track, which in turn led to a gate in a goss-thorn fence. The thorns had not been removed from the posts and rails, and acted as a barrier to the wildlife. Beyond the fence the track wound between strip fields, some ploughed and some containing crops of tall plants with trumpet flowers. Passing between these fields, Ansel came quickly to the brow of a hill and looked down on Troos.

He crouched next to a field ditch and, through his image-intensifier, surveyed the village. Like many villages on many worlds where there was a surrounding wilderness, this was built at the edge of the river – the low wooden houses huddled together as if for comfort. To one side, large barns clustered, and beyond these projected a jetty to which several skiffs were moored. There seemed to be some activity around the barns, a couple of women at a well, but little else going on. Ansel clipped the intensifier at his belt then drew his thin-gun. He studied the display on the side of the weapon, grunted his satisfaction, holstered it, then stood and headed on down.

First, he must be polite, he decided. He would ask very considerately after the whereabouts of Kelly. He would find Kelly's daughter and two sons and ask them if they had seen their father. If it transpired that he was getting no cooperation, he would have to use stronger tactics. This he expected, as the colonists were a cantankerous and ungrateful bunch. When THC staff had returned here after the hundred years of the Corporate Wars they had discovered the descendants of the original miners lapsed into primitivism. For these people they brought in technology, education, contractual employment with its prospect of wealth and the chance to travel offworld. Their repayment had been a refusal of all contracts, obstinate mulishness, damage claims for the abandonment of their ancestors, and steading claims on land the Company had bought mineral rights to a hundred and eighty years ago. Ansel suspected he might have to get a little rough.

Ansel strolled into the village and down what he supposed must be the main street, to where the two women were standing at the well. As he approached, they took one look at him, hoisted up their skirts and headed towards the barns.

'Wait,' Ansel called, but they ignored him.

He calmly walked after them, round a two-storey building with a wide arched doorway through which he could see a scattering of tables and a bar with bottles racked behind. On the other side of this place, he came face to face with the two women, now accompanied by two men. None of these people looked happy to see him.

'What do you want, Company man?' asked the elder of the two men.

Ansel studied the bearded face and saw there the obstinacy he had expected.

'I want Kelly Segre Janssen,' he said.

'And why do you want him?' asked the younger man.

Ansel studied the two men. They both looked to be in their thirties, and as this place was without antiagathic technology that probably was their age. They were infants to him. He appeared to be the same as them, but was twice their age.

'I would prefer to speak to someone in charge,' he said.

'I am the elder here,' said the bearded one.

Ansel doubted that, but thought he would let it ride for the moment.

'Okay, it's a simple enough matter. The Company owes Kelly a substantial sum for information he provided for the Almanac. I'm here to make sure he gets it.'

The two men looked at each other.

'He's here to be my father's good friend,' said one of the women.

Ansel looked at her. 'You're Annette Segre Janssen?'

'I am.'

'You're right – I want to be your father's good friend.'

She said, 'You're here to kill my father because he smuggled cornul fruit aboard the Strine Station and used it to poison the Director and some Company officials.'

Obviously 'good friend' meant something different here, Ansel thought, and he stood no chance with subterfuge. He reached for his thin-gun then paused when he heard deliberate movement behind him. Whoever it was, was good. He had heard nothing until then. For a moment he hesitated, then in one motion he drew his gun, squatted and turned. A bright light flung him into darkness.

Ansel woke with his head throbbing and a foul taste in his mouth.

*Stunner.*

He reached to his belt and found his holster empty. His pack was gone as well. Carefully opening gritty eyes, he stared up at a plasmel ceiling. Underneath him he felt the cold pattern of metal decking.

'You won't find your gun, nor will you find any of those other lethal little devices you had concealed about your person, assassin,' someone said.

Ansel rolled and sat upright. He was in the cargo hold of a small shuttle. Sat on a plasmel crate was a grey-haired man of indeterminate age. He held a stubby pulse-gun pointed casually at Ansel's face. Ansel felt a sinking sensation in his gut when he recognized the grey uniform the man wore. He was Security – a monitor from Earth Central.

*Shit.*

'We've been expecting you for some time now. We knew the Company wouldn't let Kelly's actions go unpunished. Their sending you here was ill-considered though. They did it before Kelly's deposition was regis-tered at ECS and before they realized their need to cover up. I would guess that about now, other agents are on their way here to deal with you.'

*What the hell is he talking about?*

The monitor went on, 'You're our evidence. They can claim the symbionts here mutated over the last century, but they can't claim that of yours.'

While Ansel tried to make sense of that, the back door to the hold slid open and a woman walked in. She had black skin and blue eyes and wore an orange and grey suit. Ansel was struck at once by her assurance and the level calm of her gaze. Like himself she seemed to be about thirty years old. By her air he guessed her to be many times that. In one hand she carried a notescreen and in the other a short-range surgical laser. People of her age took precautions.

'Have you got it?' the monitor asked the woman.

'I have it,' said the woman. 'It's exactly the same so there has definitely been no mutation. It's a deliberate alteration to the 'factor's genome.'

'The time-scale the same?'

'Yes: thirty-seven years after implantation. Here, of course, that means thirty-seven years after conception. They've got a right to be angry,' she said.

'What the hell are you talking about?' asked Ansel.

The woman and the monitor looked at each other.

'He doesn't know?' asked the woman.

'You think he'd have agreed to implantation if he had?' asked the monitor.

They both looked at Ansel.

The monitor said, 'It's enough for you now to know that THC will want you dead.'

The woman glanced at the monitor then shrugged. *Yeah, right.*

Ansel had been with the Company for many years and done a lot for them. He was not the kind they had killed – he was the kind who did the killing.

'Okay, get up,' said the monitor.

He sounded angry. Ansel stood up and, as he stretched his legs and arms, the snout of the pulse-gun did not waver from his face.

The monitor nodded towards the door. 'Out of here.'

The shuttle had been manoeuvred into one of the large barns, which was why Ansel had not seen it from the hill. He followed the woman and the monitor out into orange sunset where the bearded villager and Kelly's daughter waited. The two of them glanced questioningly at the monitor.

'He'll give evidence. He is evidence,' said the monitor, prodding Ansel in the back with his pulse-gun.

As he walked ahead, Ansel noted that the bearded villager carried his pack. Perhaps his thin-gun was in

there, along with those other lethal devices to which the
monitor had referred.

When they reached one of the houses the monitor
leant close in behind him. 'Remember this, assassin:
you're just as much evidence dead as alive.'

Ansel nodded. Whatever this bullshit was he knew he
would never testify in an EC court. The Company had
too much pull and he would be bailed and gone in an
instant. But he had no intention of it coming to that. The
pistol snout nudged him in the back again and he entered
the house.

'Where's Kelly now?' Ansel abruptly asked.

Before the monitor could stop her Annette answered,
'My father is upriver getting the Book of Statements.'

Ansel noted the reverence in her voice. He smiled to
himself as the monitor shoved him forward.

'Secure him,' said the monitor tightly.

They tied him in a back bedroom, rough ropes securing his wrists and feet to the bedposts. He guessed the
monitor did not want him aboard the shuttle where he
might get free and have access to whatever weapons
might be there. As soon as the door closed he tested the
tension of the ropes. Steady flexing did not loosen them,
it only drew them tighter on his wrists and ankles, but
the frame of the bed moved. Its creaking brought the
bearded one to the door. Ansel closed his eyes and
decided to rest. Later.

When he woke he checked the timepiece set in the nail
of his right forefinger. Two hours had passed and he
hoped everyone in the house was asleep. He steadily
pulled on the ropes securing his wrists and managed
to slide himself far enough down the bed to hook his
feet under the bottom rail. There was one weapon the

monitor had been unable to remove, and perhaps had been unaware of: Ansel's home planet had a gravity of one and a half gees, and though he looked just like an Earthman, he was much stronger. He gripped the ropes around his wrists and pulled hard with his feet. There was a loud crack and he lay still, listening. No movement. He pulled again, steadily, until the tenon holding the bottom rail to the bottom bedpost broke through and the rail pulled away. With the toe of his boot he levered the rope that secured that leg up and over the post. Lying still, he listened again. Nothing. He levered the rail back and forth with his foot until the other tenon began to work free, finally pulling the rail all the way back onto the bed so that when it came out of its mortise hole it did not drop to the floor. With both legs free it was then a simple task to snap the top rail and get his hands free. He was removing the rope from his wrist when an explosion rattled the windows and fire seared the darkness.

Ansel was off his bed in an instant. The door was locked, but he turned the handle until something broke with a dull thud. Easing the door open, he peered through, just in time to see the bearded man rushing outside. On the table in that room rested his rucksack, which he stepped in and grabbed, before retreating to the bedroom. From outside came another explosion, and he could hear yelling. He did not speculate about the cause since he would find out once outside. In his rucksack he found his thin-gun, which he holstered, before opening the bedroom window and stepping through.

'It's the shuttle,' said the woman.

He spun to see her squatting in the darkness a few paces behind him. Automatically he drew his thin-gun

and aimed it at her. Then he looked ahead and saw that
the barn was burning.

*What the hell?*

'Where's the monitor?' he asked.

'In the shuttle,' she replied.

Ansel made no comment about that.

There were villagers running out of the houses, hastily
clothed, yelling questions to each other. Ansel stayed
where he was. The woman moved closer and he saw that
she wore a pack on her back and held her cutting laser.

'You can drop that,' he said.

After she did as he instructed, he snatched the device
up and put it in his belt. He then gestured with his gun
for her to move where he could see her more clearly,
before turning most of his attention to the fire and the
villagers. Silhouetted against flame came a striding
figure.

'Jesus,' said Ansel.

'Who is it?' the woman asked.

'Not a who, a what.'

Ansel suddenly had a very bad feeling about all this.

Two villagers ran towards the dark individual. One of
them went in close as if to grab him, but was grabbed in
turn by his throat and hoisted into the air. Whilst holding him there, the figure drew a weapon and fired it at
the other villager. The second one flew backwards with
smoke and flame trailing from where his head had been.
The first villager the figure dropped to the ground. He
did not get up again.

'What is that?' the woman hissed.

'Cybercorp Golem. Series Nineteen.'

'But Golem don't kill.'

'They do when the Company gets hold of them. They

crack the moral governors by giving them a full sensorium download from the mind of a psychopath. This
one's probably a Serban Kline.'

'It's probably here for you,' she said.

Ansel chewed that over. He could not understand why
the Company might want him dead. It seemed more
likely to him that the Golem was here after her and the
monitor. But he had an inkling of doubt – the kind of
doubt that had saved his life more than once. He could
of course go and ask the Golem, but knew that if its
answer was yes, it would be brief and non-verbal. He
needed time, and he needed to know what this woman
and the monitor had been on about earlier. He gestured
for her to move into the darkness behind the house ahead
of him.

'What's your name and what are you?' he asked her.

'Erlin. I'm an xenobiologist, mostly,' she replied.

'Do you have another shuttle, or a way of calling one
in?' asked Ansel.

'Hendricks had a comlink.'

Hendricks. So that was his name.

'Hendricks is toast. Keep moving. Head for the jetty.'

As Erlin led the way down to the river, Ansel gazed
back towards the village. The Golem was calmly entering each house. Each time it came out, that house would
burst into flame. It quite dispassionately shot anyone
who came within a few hundred metres of it. The villagers
were beginning to get the idea, and they too were running for their lives.

'Move it!' Ansel yelled at Erlin.

They reached the jetty ahead of some of the villagers.
Ansel quickly untied a skiff powered by a hydrodyn outboard of Company manufacture. He saw that only two

other skiffs bore outboards. He drew his gun, adjusted a setting on the side, and fired at each of the motors. The gun itself made not a sound, but the casing of the first outboard cracked open and leaked smoke, and the second motor blew in half, then fell off its boat and sank.

'What are you doing?' Erlin asked.

'It's after you or me, not your precious colonists. I'm slowing it a little,' he replied.

They scrambled into the boat. Ansel started the motor, turned the boat out into the river and headed upstream. As he wound the throttle round he looked back towards the village. All the houses were now burning and the villagers streaming down to the jetty. Behind them, silhouetted against the fire as it stepped over corpses, came the Golem.

'We won't get away. It won't stop,' said Erlin.

Ansel ignored that.

'Where exactly did Kelly go?' he asked.

'Why do you want to know? Do you think completing your mission will put you into favour?'

'Two reasons: first to complete my mission and second to get out of here. Maybe you're right, maybe the Company wants me dead for some reason. I'll find out. I'll get off this shit hole and find out. Kelly must have had access to a shuttle to get to the Strine Station.'

Erlin sat up straight.

'You don't want to kill him,' she said.

'I'll be the judge of that. Now, will you tell me where exactly Kelly went or do I have to pose my questions a little less pleasantly?'

Erlin stared at him for a long moment then shrugged. 'You'll change your mind when you get the full story. When you find out what's been done to you.'

Ansel stared at her.

*Been done to me?*

'You still haven't answered my question,' he said.

Erlin shrugged. 'For what it's worth, he's gone to the mountains. They're a day away. There's a waterfall with a trail going up beside it, which leads eventually to the place where their Book of Statements is kept. The place has religious significance to them, which was why Kelly wouldn't let Hendricks take him there in the shuttle.' Erlin paused then went on. 'Serban Kline . . . he's the one who went to the frame for multiple murder wasn't he?'

He replied, 'In total Serban Kline killed a hundred and eight women. He was clever and it took ECS years to track him down. They found him with his hundred and ninth victim. He'd had her for two weeks. They managed to give her back her face and body, but they never managed with her mind. In one of her more coherent moments she chose euthanasia.'

They motored on through the darkness.

When the morning sun broke the sky into its striated patterns, they had reached an area where the river widened and low trees with leaves big as bedspreads grew on the banks. Erlin woke from where she had made herself as comfortable as possible in the bottom of the boat, stretched, and gazed around. Ansel peered at her gritty-eyed and said nothing. She returned his look for a moment then opened her pack. Ansel had his gun pointed at her in a second. She ignored him and took out a food bar which she munched on contemplatively.

'What does ECS want with you?' Ansel asked eventually.

'I specialize in parasites. After they got Kelly's

deposition they wanted it checked in a hurry. I suppose I was the best they could get hold of at short notice.'

*Deposition?*

Ansel felt too tired to work it out. What possible evidence did Kelly possess, and of what?

'Take the tiller,' he told Erlin.

While she obeyed, Ansel lay down in the bottom of the boat and, clutching his thin-gun, closed his eyes and cued himself for light naps. No way would she get the drop on him. Anything untoward and he would be instantly awake. The engine was off and the sun high in the sky when Erlin shook him awake.

'We're at the waterfall,' she told him.

Ansel lay there with his head aching and that foul taste in his mouth. The last time this had happened he'd put it down to being hit by Hendricks's stunner. Now he wondered if it was a result of the symbiont in his stomach. He sat up carefully and blinked until his vision cleared. He looked at the waterfall, then turned to study Erlin. His gun was still in his hand.

'Why didn't you take it?' he asked her.

'There is no need. Will you listen to what I have to say now?'

'I'll listen, but not just yet,' said Ansel. He holstered his weapon and studied the waterfall.

It descended from the mountains down a giant's staircase, each step no more than five or ten metres. It bore the appearance of something constructed, but a glance at the surrounding mountains showed they bore the same shape, being naturally terraced. Pointing at a small jetty projecting into the deep pool below it, he said, 'Take us over there.'

Erlin switched the motor back on and took them

slowly towards the jetty. It soon became evident that there was another boat moored there.

'Kelly's,' said Erlin as she finally brought their boat athwart the jetty.

The boat was the twin of theirs. As they moored next to it Ansel peered inside, noting stains on the boards and the distinctive smell of putrefactor. Taking up his rucksack, he followed Erlin across the jetty. The path from there was easy enough to follow: there was only the one and it led straight up into the mountains.

As Ansel now led the way up the first slope he said, 'Okay, tell me.'

'A hundred and eighty years ago THC bought the mineral rights here,' she explained.

'Oh really,' said Ansel.

Erlin ignored his comment and continued. 'The life here is incompatible with human life, highly toxic in fact. When THC established a mining colony they miscalculated. Removing the toxins from the soil so food could be grown in it turned out to be unfeasible and they were soon incurring huge costs from shipping food in. Company biologists got round that one by adapting a Fores life form into a symbiont for the miners. It lived in their stomachs just as it now lives in yours, and in the stomachs of the miners' descendants – it's passed on in the womb. It breaks down Fores's proteins, sugars and carbohydrates into forms the human gut can digest.'

'Look, I know all this. I've got one. You mentioned a deposition earlier. What was that all about?' asked Ansel.

'The symbiont is an adapted putrefactor,' Erlin told him.

Ansel halted and turned to her. The Company medic

had neglected to mention this. The knowledge made him feel slightly sick.

Watching him steadily, Erlin went on, 'Unfortunately, after a period of approximately thirty-seven years, it was found that the symbiont changed and began to digest its host.'

'What?' said Ansel. What she'd just told him did not seem to gel. He was sixty years old, and with anti-agathics had an expected lifespan that had not yet been measured. Now this madwoman was telling him he would be digested in thirty-seven years. It made no sense. He had only been sent here for a brief search-and-destroy mission. The symbiont was merely a convenience to help him digest the local food.

'That makes no sense – the Company would have known.'

'Yes, of course they would have.'

And then it did make sense to him. He was suddenly angry as he gazed past her to the river below. After a moment he realized what he was seeing down there. Just coming into sight was a rowing boat being rowed along so fast it was leaving a foaming wake. He pointed.

'Oh hell,' said Erlin.

'Let's move it,' said Ansel, and they set out at a faster pace.

'Can you stop it?' Erlin gasped as they climbed.

'Yeah, funny,' said Ansel. Thirty-seven years. What did that matter when he was likely to be killed within the next few hours? He now understood that first conversation he had overheard between Erlin and Hendricks, and he knew the Golem was here for him as much as for them. The Company had done something nasty here, and they had done it again to him, but why had they done it? He glanced upslope, then back again. The Golem had reached the pool. He picked up the pace and shortly they reached a stairway cut into the rock.

'Look!' Erlin shouted.

Ansel glanced at her, then to where she was pointing. A shuttle was limping through the sky above them.

'It's Hendricks. He's alive. He's going for Kelly!'

'Climb,' said Ansel. The Golem was on the jetty now and it was gazing up at them. There was a chance now. If they could get to the shuttle . . . He noted that Erlin was flagging. She was an Earther and her legs could not match his. He considered leaving her behind, but decided not to. Fuck the Company. He halted.

'You keep going,' he said. 'I'll slow it.'

She watched him unshoulder his pack and open it.

'Go!' he shouted.

Erlin went.

Ansel ran through his mind all he knew about Golem Nineteens. They possessed a ceramal chassis wrapped round their more delicate components, so with the munitions he carried he could not hope to destroy it. Raking through his rucksack he pulled out a short cylindrical carton, out of which he tipped four flat discs each bearing digital displays. Studying the Golem's progress, he set the display on the first disc and left it on a step. After climbing for a minute, he set another disc, then the third higher up. He was setting the last disc when the first blew with an actinic white explosion, showering stone across the mountainside. He glanced down.

It had missed, but an area of the stairway had been converted to rubble. This slowed the Golem, but only a little. Ansel ran up after Erlin, reaching her as she reached the head of the stairway. Cut into the face of the mountain was an area of level stone.

'Drop the weapon, assassin!'

Hendricks leant against the back of the shuttle, between the two thrusters. The man's face was twisted with pain, for his left arm was gone at the elbow and through the charred holes in his clothing burnt skin showed. He had placed an emergency dressing over the stump and some sort of cream on the burns, but Ansel supposed the man had not wanted to dull his senses with painkillers. Erlin stood to the right of him, and another figure stood nearby with his face turned away from Ansel.

'We don't have time for this,' said Ansel.

Hendricks fired once between Ansel's feet, erupting splinters of stone that smacked against Ansel's legs. Ansel went down on one knee, then very carefully he removed his thin-gun from its holster and tossed it down.

'I've told him,' Erlin told Hendricks. 'I think he's with us.'

Ansel did not know if the monitor had heard her. Despite avoiding painkillers the man seemed out of it, his attention wandering. An explosion from below brought that attention back to Ansel.

'The Golem is coming up here,' said Ansel.

'It's true,' said Erlin.

Hendricks glanced at the third figure. That figure turned towards Ansel and exposed the horror of his face. One side of it was eaten down to the bone; the man's eye on that side a lidless ball in its socket. Kelly. There came a third explosion from below.

'We have to get out of here,' said Ansel.

'No can do, assassin,' said Hendricks. 'AG burnt out

when I landed.' Hendricks closed his eyes for a moment and his head dipped. Ansel stood and took a step towards his gun. He had to resolve this, and fast. The fourth explosive disc blew. He wondered if the Golem had been near any of them. Even if it had been right on top of one, the blast would only have stripped its covering.

'Am thirty-seven,' slurred Kelly. He held a thick book pressed to his chest.

'Where's your shuttle?' Ansel asked him.

Hendricks's head came up and he stared at Kelly. Kelly returned the look then pointed up the mountain. Just then Ansel heard a scrambling on the stair behind him. He dived and rolled, snatching up his thin-gun as he went past, turned and fired. The Golem was up on the edge. It seemed a fairly normal man with a shaven head, and carried a weapon similar to the one Hendricks held. Ansel's first shot hit it in the chest as it stepped forward. The explosion ripped a hole to expose gleaming ribs underneath. It tried to aim at him, but he hit it again and again. Abruptly pulsed-energy fire hit it from Hendricks's weapon. The Golem staggered then leant into the fusillade. Its face became a blackened pit and synthe-flesh fell burning from its arm. Its weapon was trashed and it threw it aside, but it continued to advance. All Ansel could do was keep firing, even though he knew his and the monitor's combined fire would not be enough.

'Get down, assassin!' Hendricks yelled.

What the hell for?

Instinct took over before Ansel could think of an answer to that question. All fire ceased and the Golem was running towards them. Suddenly there came a roar and blue fire speared above Ansel. The heat of it seared his back and he saw the Golem take that fire full on. It was stripped down to its metal chassis in an instant. It leant into flame then started to bend and distort. Abruptly it was coming apart and the blast picked it up and flung it over the edge. When the thruster motor cut out Ansel stood and glanced round at Hendricks.

'AG was out,' said the monitor. 'Not the thrusters.' He dropped the remote control he held, but managed to holster his pulse-gun before he fainted.

Ansel walked over and gazed down at the monitor. He owed the man. He turned and looked at Kelly. So easy now to complete his mission. Feeling an unaccustomed discomfort he became aware that Erlin was studying him.

'Come to kill me?' Kelly managed.

'Not now,' said Ansel, holstering his thin-gun.

'Hendricks wouldn't. Too . . . moral.'

Ansel understood in an instant.

Kelly limped forward and held out the book to him. Ansel could not understand how the man was not screaming. His clothes were stained horribly and he must be losing the flesh of his body just as he was losing the flesh on his face.

'Take it,' Kelly said.

Ansel took the book and tucked it under his arm.

'Are you a . . . good friend?' Kelly asked, and turned his back on him.

'I am,' said Ansel, and he drew his thin-gun and brought it up. Erlin's protest came half a second after the dull concussion that took the top off Kelly's head.


'Of course,' said Hendricks, a sneer in his voice, 'in those first thirty-seven years THC offered more than generous wages and free symbiont implantation so the colonists could partake of Fores's bounty. When the first colonists died in ways too horrible to imagine THC came storming to the rescue: "Look," they said, "we have this drug that seems, if taken in regular doses, to prevent the symbiont attacking its host. Admittedly it is expensive." Work it out for yourself, assassin.'

As he engaged AG and lifted it out of the valley, Ansel stared out of the screen of Kelly's shuttle. He knew how the Company operated, since he had spearheaded some nasty operations himself. But he had never expected to be on the receiving end. Forty years of loyal service and they had done this to him.

Hendricks said, 'The original colonist miners here were virtual slaves to the Company. In the end they were working the mines for one drug patch a month. Kelly's great-grandfather wrote all this down, and took signed statements from over five hundred miners. Kelly's deposition told us this, but we'd yet to see those statements.' Hendricks, who sat in the navigator's chair, rested his hand on the thick book on his lap.

'Bastards,' said Ansel, his voice flat.

'I'd imagine that for your service, in thirty-seven years the Company would have paid you in drug patches. After Kelly's deposition you became inconvenient, what with you possessing a new symbiont the precise twin of those here – proof that no mutation had taken place, that producing a killer symbiont had been precisely the Company's intention.'

Erlin leant forwards. She had been silent for a long while after he had killed Kelly, but that silence had ended when they reached Kelly's shuttle.

'He called you a good friend,' she had said.

'I know what he meant,' Ansel had replied.

'Not entirely I think.'

'Then explain it to me.'

'They live with certainties here, Ansel. They know their lives will be short and will end in horrifying agony unless they kill themselves. They have a celebration here called The Leaving. When a colonist feels his or her symbiont changing – usually signalled by stomach cramps – they throw a wild party. When the individual concerned is so drunk on cornul liquor he loses consciousness a good friend will cut his throat.'

Ansel swallowed drily as he engaged the thrusters. What of his prospects now? The Company would be unlikely to provide him with the drug the miners had used. All they would supply was a quick death.

'You are evidence. You'll come with us to Earth Central, and after this book is presented you'll stand in court and give your statement. THC will pay and they'll pay heavily,' said Hendricks.

'I'll come,' said Ansel.

# 3

# GARP AND GERONAMID

The grey-bearded park labourer reminded Salind of Earth and autumn, though the man was not raking up leaves. It was treefall on Banjer – a season with no real Terran equivalent – and the snakish creatures squirming from the pox of holes in the banoaks were dying. Having raked the fallen into slightly shifting drifts, the man began forking the spaghetti tangle into his wheelbarrow.

'I'll be damned,' said Salind, initiating the 'save' facility in Argus.

He watched the man for a while longer, then hoisted his rucksack more securely onto his shoulders before moving on. Shortly he came to where a black and twisted banoak had spilled from its hollow branches a thick crop of treels across the path. The banoak itself reminded him of a baobab, though he vaguely recollected it was not in fact a tree, being more akin to a tube worm. The parasitic treels were black and grey, and on average half a metre long. With their narrow heads and disc-shaped feeding mouths, they appeared more like lampreys than the eels after which they were named. Salind subvocalized a question and Argus, his internal augmentation, replied in its lecturing tone:

*Because its life cycle is utterly confined to the soft tissues and hollow branches of the banoak, it will attempt to feed on any soft tissue with which it comes into contact. Avoidance is recommended.*

Salind looked askance at the writhing mass as he stepped off the path and onto the spherule grass to bypass it.

'Why do they die?' he asked.

There came a pause from Argus as it accessed the relevant files.

*A poison from the aforementioned soft tissues accumulates in the creatures and kills them off in their fifth year. Shall I continue?*

'Might as well,' said Salind. 'I don't suppose Garp's there yet.'

*As I mentioned, the treel's entire life cycle is confined to the interior of the banoak. There it feeds on the soft tissues of the polychaete body, mates and lays its eggs. By their fifth year the treels die from a cumulative poison in the polychaete's flesh. It was first thought the poison served no other purpose than to rid the banoak creature of this parasite. It is now known that the treel's relationship with its host is mutualistic rather than parasitic. The treels, as well as feeding on the banoak, protect it from predation. Creatures that feed on the banoak inevitably ingest treels and can sicken and die from the poison concentrated inside them.*

'They harvest them, don't they?' said Salind, his attention drawn to the large tanker parked under some distant banoaks. He could hear the cavitating roar of a vacuum pump and see another park labourer sucking up the creatures with a wide-ribbed hose.

*The poison accumulates in their skin. For humans that substance works as a narcotic and mild hallucinogen. The treels are mulched, pressed and dried and what remains is mostly skin. They make a tea from it here.*

'I guess I'll have to give that a try then,' said Salind, though he did not particularly relish the prospect.

*The tea is as addictive as nicotine. Most people here drink it.*

'Then I'll take a detoxicant course afterwards. My audience will want to know what it's like.'

At the centre of the park stood a monolithic quartz crystal into whose lattices had been recorded the names and personal histories of the thousands who had died during the civil war here a century earlier. The deeply translucent crystal ran in its depths holograms taken randomly from those personal histories. Positioned all around it were seats for spectators, though they were unoccupied today and, studying the figure standing with his back to the crystal, Salind could understand why.

This man's clothing resembled an antique acceleration suit with its webwork of veins sandwiched in metallic fabric. Pipes were also visible at his joints and curved up from the neck ring, and fluid vessels were affixed here and there on the suit's surface. This clothing was not of great note though. Others dressed more exotically and few would so much as blink an eye at them. However, this man seemed ill: his face greyish and his eyes containing a sickly yellow tint. When he turned to gaze up at the crystal, it became evident that the tubes from the neck ring entered the base of his skull. As Salind drew closer he noted fingertips frayed down to the bone, eye irrigators at the man's temples, skull exposed through holes in shaven scalp. Closer still and he caught the first whiff of putrefaction. For what Garp suffered there was no cure – him being dead.

As soon as the Tarjen Network picked up on the story, Salind knew that it had to be his. It was a perfect footnote to the big story on Banjer at the moment: the imminent arrival of the Arbiter of Transition, the awesome AI Geronamid, and subsumption of this world into the Polity.

Since the civil war, during which a theocracy had been bloodily usurped then replaced by more conventional government, there had been plenty of murders solved, or not, by the usual methods. However, there had not been a reification of a murder victim in a hundred years.

When the strange cult of Anubis Arisen governed Banjer, every viable murder victim had been reified and sent after his murderer. The victim's dead brain was decoded and the essential mind and memory downloaded into an augmentation. Cybermotors at the joints moved the body, which was partially preserved by chemicals. Obviously more complex than this, the system utilized, in some reifs, surviving brain tissue, and historians argued that such were still alive. Others argued that reifs possessed self-determination and even whilst running fully on the augmentation were AI. For a century the whole argument had been moot, that is, until Garp came on the scene.

Salind had scanned the files at stopovers while en route to Banjer. Garp had been an inspector in the Banjer police force. The last five years of his life had been spent trying to convict a woman by the name of Deleen Soper, who had allegedly made a fortune manufacturing a drug called praist, somewhere on this world. During those five years he had made enough headway to become an annoyance to the Tronad – a criminal organization reputed to be close to seizing power on Banjer and of which Soper was, again allegedly, the head. Several ensuing attempts on his life impelled him to make a will specifying that should he die within a certain period he wanted to be reified, and for this purpose transferred funds to what was left of the Church of Anubis Arisen. Shortly after doing so, he revealed himself to be a praist addict going into terminal psychosis, turned up at the Church's headquarters, and after presenting the relevant documentation, shot himself through the heart.

'Hello, I'm Salind. I'm glad you agreed to speak to me.' Salind held out his hand.

Garp stared at this member for a moment, but made no move to take it. After a clicking gulp deep in his throat he said, 'I won't shake your hand. I don't yet know the strength of the cybermotors in my finger joints, also I shouldn't think it very pleasant shaking hands with a corpse.'

Salind forced a grin and dropped his arm to his side.

'Are you recording now?' Garp asked.

'I am, and obviously I have a lot of questions to ask you . . .'

Garp held up one hideous palm. 'One moment.'

At his throat he made an adjustment to a recessed control plate. There came a faint hissing sound. When he spoke next his voice was smoother. 'That's better. My vocal chords are decaying despite the vascular balm. Airborne bacteria.'

'An unusual experience, I'd imagine,' said Salind, feeling foolish.

Garp said nothing for a moment. Salind wondered if

he was being given an annoyed look. Perhaps he was, only Garp's mummified features revealed nothing.

'I'm a reif,' was all he said. And with that he took a handgun from his belt and held it up for Salind to see.

'Ah.' Salind held off from putting a call for help through Argus. Banjer being out-Polity for the present, Polity monitors could do nothing, and it would take at least ten minutes for the Tarjen staffers to get to him. Anyway, episodes like this made a story. The weapon – an old station-developed rail-gun – was the sort of thing that carried a twenty-round box and had a range measured in metres rather than kilometres. Salind thought it better suited to a museum.

'What exactly is that for?' he asked, keeping his voice level.

'I'm attached to it. You know that a reif's only protection under Banjer law is as part of the estate of the deceased? Only property laws apply.'

'Yes, I knew that. Tell me, why did you choose to be reified?'

'Because I needed more time than what remained to me to get her.'

'Ah, I see. You refer to Deleen Soper. Why were you so determined to prosecute her?'

'Because I was a detective,' said Garp.

'I note you use the past tense. You no longer work for the Banjer police?'

'I do not. I no longer have to get a court order for searches and I no longer have to present cases to a corrupt judiciary. The interesting thing is that I cannot commit a crime either. You have to be a person to commit a crime.'

Salind watched as Garp hooked the rail-gun back on his utility belt.

'There've been rumours of corruption but none have yet been proven,' he said. The presence of the gun was making him nervous and undermining his usual smooth technique. Garp pointed towards one of the far entrances of the park and began to stroll in that direction. Salind fell in beside him.

'Soper has been indicted for drug trafficking four times and for murder three times. Every time the case was brought before the same judge and then thrown out. In any Polity court the evidence would have been sufficient to have her mind-wiped or executed. I checked. She has, to my knowledge, three of the five city judges and most of the Council in her pocket, and that's only in this city.'

'Those are serious accusations. What proof do you have?'

'I had full sensorium recordings of conversations and bribes, documentation, and eighteen witnesses. When I . . . died, my files were dumped. Of the witnesses, four went offworld, and seven suffered fatal accidents while I was alive. Two more made official withdrawals of their statements, and the remaining five were hit while I was being reified.'

'Is Soper implicated in all this?'

Garp looked at Salind. 'What do you think? There's no admissible evidence and the judiciary is refusing the investigators permission to investigate.'

'What then are your intentions?'

Garp remained silent for a moment. He halted at a spill of treels before speaking. 'I saw the look you gave this gun. It's not what you think. It's the only piece of

hard evidence I possess.' He turned and gazed directly at
Salind, his eye irrigators hazing the air around his face
with spray. 'You know, they wiped me out. All my files,
even my personal files, were dumped from the system. It
was an accident they said. I might well have not existed.'
Garp walked on, crunching treels underfoot.

'This hard evidence . . .?' Salind said, moving round
the treel spill.

'Useless now of course. This weapon had her fingerprints and DNA traces on the handle. It was found by
the body of Aaron Dane. She'd blown off both his legs at
the knee before beating him to death with the barrel. And
so confident was she in her control of the judiciary, and
certain police officials, she didn't bother to get rid of the
evidence. I had it all on record . . .'

'Well, it'll all change with the arrival of Geronamid.
Corruption tends to wither under AI governance.'

Garp made a rough hacking sound. It took a moment
for Salind to realize it was a laugh. Garp glanced side-
wise at him. 'I do not possess your faith in AI governance.
Either the vote will be fixed to keep us out of the Polity
or if we go in Soper will refocus her business interests.
She's wealthy enough now to play the upright citizen.'

'Wouldn't you say that what such people do is more
about power than wealth?'

As they reached the gateway to the park, Garp did not
immediately reply. They walked out onto the pavement
alongside a street crammed with hydrocars. The air was
humid with their exhausts.

'Maybe, but Soper is not stupid enough to go up
against the Polity. She'll be a good citizen and her past
will be dumped just as absolutely as mine. The amnesty
will see to that. Soper is sitting back in a no-lose posi-

tion. If the Tronad prevents the Polity takeover they're okay. If they don't, they get amnesty; the slate wiped clean, a new beginning.'

'I can see how that would upset you.'

'Masterly understatement.'

'Perhaps we should begin at the beginning.' Salind pointed to a roadside café. 'Present your case to me and through me to the citizens of the Polity.'

Garp stopped at a crossing and before stepping out said, 'We'll need a private booth. My presence tends to put people off their lunch.'

Two five-metre-tall nacreous bull's horns framed a shimmering meniscus eight metres across. The shimmer broke, and somersaulting through it onto the black glass dais came a young man clad in a white slicksuit. His hair was blue, face painted.

'Well, I'm sure we could call it something like: "He fought what he has become – corruption".' said Salind.

Geoff, the staffer from the Tarjen offices, nodded, then made adjustments on the fullsense recorder he was holding – a device that could record with greater clarity than the hardware inside Salind's skull. A tall woman with an external aug almost covering her head gave them both a dirty look from amid the crowd of reporters.

'A rather flip way of treating his story. Garp was and is a good man,' said Geoff.

Salind studied him for a moment. Tarjen employed its staffers from the local population. It might be worth doing a few interviews.

'I'm sure that's true,' said Salind. 'But, though a good story, it's a footnote to the main event. This.' Salind gestured to the runcible portal as two Golem androids,

without artificial skin, stepped through and aside as
guards. He wondered what that was about. Their metal
skeletons were grey, almost corroded in appearance – a
highly unusual occurrence.

'If this is what you're here for, then shaddup and
watch,' said the woman.

'Get your bloody great metal head out of the way,
Merril,' said the man behind her.

'Is it my problem you're a short-arse?' she snapped
back.

'It's certainly my problem that your pea-brain needs
such a large augmentation.'

The bickering continued as next through the portal
came four Earth monitors in full battledress. They were
armoured and carried gas-system pulse assault rifles.
They moved out on either side to stand by the Golem
androids.

'Bit OTT,' said the man trying to see past Merril's
aug-shrouded head.

'All show,' said Merril. 'The effective forces are
already here.'

'You what?' said the man.

'She means,' said Salind, 'that Geronamid's agents
have probably been arriving here and establishing themselves over the last few months if not years.'

Geoff gave him a look then returned his attention to
his recorder.

'I don't need some kidrep from that Tarjen rag to
explain my words,' said Merril, without looking round.
Salind ignored her and nodded to the waiting crowd of
dignitaries.

'Probably knows every one of their dirty little

secrets . . . Bloody hell, that's a bit extravagant even for Geronamid.'

Those who had been watching the dignitaries, or sub-vocalizing commentaries, paused. There came an intake of breath. Through the portal had come two voluptuous women clad as fantasy barbarians. This was not what drew the attention though. That they each held silver chain leashes connecting to the collar of a huge allosaur did cause a little consternation.

'Someone tell me that's an automaton and not from the fossil gene project,' said the man behind Merril.

'That's an automaton and not from the fossil gene project,' said Salind.

'Thanks for that.'

Next came jugglers and street musicians, followed by a crowd who seemed to have just come from a party. The arrival lounge rapidly filled with a cacophony of sound and movement.

'Well where the hell is Geronamid?' asked Geoff, as he swept the area with the sensor heads of his recorder. Salind pointed to the lone acrobat who had come through first and was now doing back-flips in front of the increasingly irritated-looking allosaur.

'Him usually,' he said. 'Though it's difficult to tell. On Tarus Five Geronamid came through dispersed – memory units implanted in each of twelve circus clowns.'

The group of dignitaries began to make their way across the lounge, heading towards the acrobat.

'Looks like I was right,' said Salind. 'They'll have been told who to greet.'

The dignitaries had nearly reached the acrobat, who ceased his display and stood with his arms held out in greeting. There came a stuttering thud as of the sound of a lump of meat being thrown into a fan. The smile on the acrobat's face disappeared along with his head. Brains and pieces of bone sprayed over the allosaur.

After a shocked pause someone started screaming.

'Rail-gun,' commented Merril and chaos broke loose. Police and security agents were running around shouting into personal com units. Salind saw one of these men lose his leg then fall to the ground, his expression puzzled. Salind was still watching and recording when Geoff grabbed him and dragged him to the floor.

'Let me up! Let me the fuck up!' Salind yelled. Eventually Geoff rolled away and Salind scrambled to his feet. He scanned quickly and saw where Merril and the rest of the vultures were heading. The two skinless androids had pinned someone to the floor. The Earth monitors kept the crowd from gathering around this individual, and the Banjer police encircled the acrobat's remains.

'Let me through! Let me through!' yelled Salind, using his trusted elbows-and-knees technique to get to the forefront of the first crowd. When arrived there he recognized a slightly putrid smell, and seeing the pinned figure he felt a moment's horrible glee.

'Shit we've got a story,' he said, then paused. He felt the crowd clearing from behind him. A hot breath raised the hairs on the back of his neck. Turning, he looked straight into the tooth-filled mouth of the blood-spattered allosaur. It glanced aside at the dead acrobat then down at the prisoner. Salind quickly stepped aside.

'Murderer,' came the guttural accusation of the allosaur.

Garp glared up from the floor, his eye-irrigators work-

ing overtime. His eyes were blank white spheres overlaid
with narrow gridlines.

The room was clean, aseptic and not a very nice place to
be. Formchairs positioned against white tile were all in
perfect condition, no graffiti marred the walls, and not a
speck of dust or rubbish littered the banoak coral floor.
Yet the room smelt of vomit and fear. Salind tried to
ignore that, since it didn't apply to him, a Polity citizen.

'The AI Geronamid arrived on Banjer in the skull of
a living allosaur, reputedly resurrected by the fossil gene
project at the University of Earth on Midlantis Island. In
this "acting of parable" he demonstrated the coexistence
of the old and the new. The attempted assassination of
Geronamid by another resurrectee, one Abel Garp, a
reified officer of the Banjer police force, has undermined
the . . . Yes?' asked Salind.

The Banjer cop said nothing, but gestured to the door
with his thumb. Salind considered walking out right
then, since he didn't *have* to help them. But then, there'd
be more here for his story. Even though he was way
ahead of all the other agencies, he went.

The cop led him down a perfectly clean corridor and
opened another door for him. Salind entered and felt
suddenly as if he had stepped back five hundred years.

'An interrogation cell. How quaint,' he commented.

'Sit down,' instructed the man behind the desk.

Salind glanced up at the camera set up in the corner
of the room. A meaty hand on his back propelled him
gently but firmly to the stool on the other side of the
desk. He sat, and just to show his confidence he crossed
his legs and casually scanned his surroundings.

'You are Mr Gem Salind?'

'Just call me Salind, everyone does.'

The man opposite did not look up. 'I am Superintendent Callus – by name and nature some say. You are aware that when you came to Banjer you stepped out of Polity jurisdiction?'

Callus looked up and, placing his elbows on the desk, interlaced his fingers before his mouth.

'I was aware. I am also aware that I have broken no laws, be they of the Polity or Banjer,' Salind replied.

Callus nodded. 'Having knowledge of a serious crime and not reporting it to the authorities is a crime in itself.'

'So I understand, and if I'd knowledge of such I would, of course, report it to you immediately.'

'You knew what Garp intended.'

'No, if you'd listened to my statement at the time . . .'

'You saw the rail-gun.'

'Oh get real. It's all a matter of public record. If he threatened anyone it was Deleen Soper, and that's debatable.'

A hard hand clouted him on the back of his head.

'What the fuck!'

He half turned, but the thug behind him grabbed his hair and yanked his head back. He was forced to continue looking forwards.

'Around here we respect the law.' As Callus said this, the thug behind drove a fist into Salind's kidneys.

'You fucking—'

Another blow curtailed speech, and more blows followed.

*I'm being assaulted in the Siroc police headquarters!*

Message relayed.

Finally released, Salind fell from the chair onto his hands and knees and retched up his breakfast.

'Are you in pain? Would you like me to get a doctor?' Callus enquired.

Salind could not reply, so leaning over to peer down at him, Callus continued, 'I understand that you can record everything you see, hear and smell. Perhaps you'd like to edit that mess out.' He nodded towards the pool of vomit. 'Perhaps it would also be well for you to remember that you cannot see everything and not everything is said. In future I suggest you report to us before you release unsubstantiated stories about our citizens.'

*Message reply: Geoff is on his way over and the Tarjen legal department has been informed. Geoff also sends a personal message: They will only rough you up a little. If anything more was intended you would not have been taken to the police station. You would have been taken to the Groves.*

Finally managing to get his breath, Salind struggled to his feet and turned towards his attacker. The cop had stepped back and now stood with his hands behind his back – the perfect image of the disinterested observer. It had all been done very well.

'You won't get away . . . with this,' Salind managed, then could have kicked himself for such naïveté.

'Get away with what, exactly?' said Callus. 'Now, Mr Salind, if you could bear my words in mind we would be grateful for your cooperation.'

Callus stood up and reached across the desk to shake Salind's hand.

'Fuck off.' Salind moved to the door, keeping the both of them in view. No one followed him out. He staggered to the waiting room, then to the security barrier leading out onto the street. Fifty metres down the pavement, his breathing had become little easier when a hydrocar pulled up and its door popped open. He clambered in.

'You okay?' asked Geoff.

'I think they were acting as Deleen Soper's message delivery service.' Salind probed his bruised kidneys.

'Quite likely. What now?'

'Pull the legals off. I don't want anything getting in the way. Then I want to find out what's happening with Garp. Geronamid's people grabbed him didn't they?'

'Yes, then what?'

'Then I interview Deleen Soper.'

Geoff looked askance at him then pulled the hydrocar out into the traffic.

'Already been done,' he said.

'What, Merril's hack-and-slash job?'

'Yes, and Merril better keep her head down or she'll get a hack-and-slash job in return.'

'Really?'

'Really.'

The new Polity Embassy sprawled across twenty hectares of reclaimed marshland on the south side of Siroc, which was the capital city of the planet's main continent. At the centre of the complex rested a replica of the Millennium Dome of old London on Earth – an ironical architectural statement if ever there was one. The monitor driving one of the first antigravity cars to be used here remained reticent on the subjects of Garp and Geronamid. Salind became insistent.

'You know that criminal actions here are out of your jurisdiction for the moment. I had a nice police officer explaining that sort of thing to me only a few hours ago. So why did you people grab him?' he asked.

'As I have already told you, Mr Salind, I do not possess that information,' she replied.

Salind sat back as the car began to spiral down into the complex. 'Perhaps you can tell me who Garp killed?'

'An acrobat, I believe.' As she said this she touched her finger just below her ear – an unconscious action of someone listening to a comlink. She continued, 'Geronamid will see you. Perhaps he will explain.'

Salind grinned. There were thousands of reporters on Banjer who would have killed for this opportunity.

The monitor landed the car on a plascrete parking area and, after they disembarked, led the way toward a nearby building bearing the appearance of a Turkish mosque. One of the grey metal Golem came out to meet them.

'This Golem will take you to the Arbiter.' The monitor hurried off with her finger pressed below her ear. Salind studied the Golem. It had not been referred to by name, which probably meant it was a blank Golem being run by one of Geronamid's sub-programs. And close to it now, he realized it did appear corroded. Ceramal did not oxidize in air, so this must have been caused by a powerful acid or some kind of energy burst. He wondered it this was just for the look or the result of some ambassadorial cock-up. Salind queried Argus and received an immediate reply, but he put that on hold.

'This way,' said the Golem.

'Why the appearance?' Salind asked, as they entered the building.

'All part of Geronamid's implicit message,' it said.

'Which part?'

The Golem paused before replying. 'Membership of the Polity comes with all its advantages and drawbacks. All its AIs in every form. He would not want people to protest that the Polity had been mis-sold.'

'Wouldn't a less threatening appearance have been better?'

'Exactly the point,' said the Golem.

Salind listened to the message from Argus:

*The two Golem androids that accompany Geronamid when the AI is on Arbitration duty owe their appearance to a Separatist attack on the world Cheyne III. An assassin attempted to kill Geronamid who, at that time, travelled inside an Egyptian sarcophagus. When the attack failed the assassin keyed her weapon to self-destruct. The two Golem were caught in the backflash.*

After entering the mosque through an open arch, they traversed a marble hall to reach a wooden door the Golem opened by hand. In the antechamber beyond, an armoured ship droid hovered a couple of metres above the floor. Salind felt a tingling sensation run from the top of his head to his feet. There came a discordant buzzing from Argus.

'Clear,' spat the droid, and moved aside.

*What was that?*

*Weapons scan.*

'You will note,' said the Golem, 'very in-your-face.'

A second door admitted them to the repro interior of a mosque. Garp was sitting on a wooden chair with his arms crossed, a cable trailing across the floor from the sockets in his head. His eyes were the same as they had appeared in the arrivals lounge, but Salind had no idea what that meant. Geronamid stood off to one side finishing his lunch, which looked like half a wildebeest. Salind started to sweat as the Golem closed the door behind him, not because of the crunching gobbling sounds, but because he had just discovered his aug's external link was being blocked.

'Why aren't you allowing me a direct link to Tarjen?' he asked.

Geronamid gulped down a large dripping lump of flesh. A disembodied voice replied, 'You may record, and you will be allowed to transmit that recording once you leave here, should that be what you wish to do.'

Salind tried to locate the source of the voice then quickly gave up. Geronamid was speaking and he needed to know no more than that.

'Okay . . .' He nodded towards Garp. 'What are you doing to him?'

'Downloading information to my evidential submind,' Geronamid replied.

'Inadmissible evidence in a Banjer court and irrelevant after the Polity amnesty comes into effect, so why are you doing it?'

'Curiosity. In my position wouldn't you want to know?'

'Yes . . . What do you intend to do to Garp? Your seizure of him was illegal you know.'

'I will do nothing to him, and my seizure was not illegal.'

'He committed a crime here. He killed that acrobat. Surely he's the province of the Banjer police.'

The allosaur jerked its head up from the remains of its meal and abruptly paced toward Salind. He had to suppress the urge to turn and run. Now, the voice issued from its bloody mouth. 'The acrobat was called Houdini Friend. My friend.'

'Okay,' said Salind, swallowing drily. 'But that still doesn't change—'

Geronamid interrupted. 'The reif committed no crime as it is just an artefact which, since the recent seizure of Garp's remaining estate, has become the property of the Banjer government. The reif is under a destruction order and will duly be handed over for incineration.'

'I note you refer only to "the reif" and not to Garp. What about him? You accused him of murder yourself.'

'The murderer is whoever loaded the subversion program into him. He had no knowledge of what he was doing,' Geronamid replied.

'Surely that is evidence you could pass on to the police?'

'Why?'

'So the real murderer can be caught,' Salind suggested.

'You have been here for two weeks, and have learned nothing in that time?'

'I have not unlearned the necessity of due process, of . . .' Salind trailed off as the allosaur turned away, apparently losing interest in him. It looked at Garp.

'Ah, praist,' said the AI.

'Why am I here?' Salind asked, feeling at once foolish and angry.

'Worlds must join the Polity of their own free will. There must be no hint of coercion. Eighty per cent of the population must vote for entry. That's eighty per cent of the *entire* population.'

'Yes, I am aware of the charter.' Salind struggled to keep his face straight.

'Voting on most worlds is through net encryption – absolute anonymity, your vote registered by the click of a button.'

'Polling stations,' said Salind, getting some hint of where Geronamid was leading.

'Yes: polling stations. The government of Banjer managed to foist polling stations on us. Their argument being that five per cent of the population is without net access. We estimate that probably forty per cent of the population will be too frightened to vote.'

'So there'll be a void result. Why then are you here?'

'In some cases Polity intervention is allowed: humanitarian disaster, cases when widespread corruption in the governing authorities can be proven, and when widespread coercion is being used.'

Salind felt his scalp crawling. 'Are you saying that the Polity intends to intervene here?'

'That can be hugely damaging unless sufficiently justified. Such tactics can lead to rebellion against the "AI Autocrat of Earth" and not necessarily on the world on which we have intervened.'

Salind stared at the allosaur for a long moment as he chewed over that euphemistic word 'intervention', then shook his head in annoyance – he'd been trying to read the creature's expression.

'What do you intend, then?'

'My overall intentions I will make available to the free press when I am ready.'

'Then why the hell am I here?'

'You are here because you were first onto the story of Garp and because he wants you to know the rest of it.' The allosaur swung towards the reif. 'You see, there is no evidence that Soper was responsible for loading the subversion program into his aug, but there is plenty of proof available of her other crimes. Should you choose not to broadcast this conversation and so alert her, you can go with him to obtain this proof. Conveniently, Soper will be visiting one of her praist factories in a few days' time – one of eight hundred such places run by the Tronad.'

There it was: *justification*. Geronamid had not admitted the Polity intended intervention here, but the hint stood as wide as a barn door.

The allosaur swung back to Salind. 'It is well to remember that if not Soper, then certainly someone in the Tronad ordered the assassination attempt on me. Not because they thought it might succeed, but because the attempt in itself would bring home to the ruling council here on Banjer just how vulnerable they are and so stiffen their resolve to keep the Polity out.'

The Tronad was the main power here, not the Council?

Salind said, 'But you are sending Garp for destruction.'

Geronamid paced away and swung round with his snout poised over the reif. 'Garp is not there,' he said, then swung his snout towards the blank Golem. 'Garp is there.'

Salind turned to study the Golem. While behind him it had plugged a thick optic cable into a socket in the side of its chest. Now its stance was different. It held out its skeletal grey hands to stare at them, then it gazed across at Geronamid.

'Garp was running fully in his augmentation because viable brain tissue was being destroyed by his praist addiction. He is now a hundred per cent uploaded to this Golem,' said Geronamid.

Salind could feel his stomach turning over and over. His fortune was made. What a story! He had enough already to get his contract picked up by one of the Earth networks. Hell, he could even get investment for his own network. He watched as Geronamid swung its head back towards the reif.

'The reif will go for incineration as per the Council's request,' the AI said.

'About time,' said Garp the Golem.

'Thank you for agreeing to see me. Obviously I was wrong about this Garp character and his relationship to you. I'm not afraid of admitting to error. You'll have heard that my story has been withdrawn from the net?' Salind kept smiling as he studied the apartment. Soper was obviously a woman of baroque tastes. The place was full of preruncible furnishings and frankly strange decorations. He brought his attention finally back to the woman herself.

Deleen Soper bore the appearance of a sixteen-year-old girl – a sure sign she'd been using some of the less sophisticated rejuvenation treatments. She sported short-cropped blonde hair over elfin features and wore jeans and a check shirt. Her whole persona seemed that of a pretty farmgirl from some half-forgotten age. Salind knew her to be a hundred and forty-three years old, and responsible for the deaths of hundreds directly, and tens of thousands indirectly through the drug praist. He kept on smiling.

'Leave us, Turk,' she said, and gave an airy wave of her hand.

The butler character who had accompanied Salind from the front door all the way up the spiralling stairs of the building gave a wooden nod and departed. Salind guessed that the man's duties probably included more than butlering – he looked as if he could crush rocks in his armpits.

'Please, take a seat Mr Salind,' she said.

'My pleasure.'

Salind sat and watched her walk to an antique drinks cabinet and fill two small cups from a silver teapot.

'Tea?'

He nodded. Now was as good a time as any to try the stuff. She placed the drinks on an occasional table and sat in the armchair opposite.

'Please, conduct your interview,' she said.

Salind picked up the warm cup and sipped the drink. It tasted bitter and salty, then left an aftertaste of avocados. Like most of the preferred drinks of humankind it was an acquired taste.

'What was your relationship with Inspector Garp?' he asked as he placed his cup back down on the table. 'I'd like to hear your side of things.'

'It is a shame you did not think of that before you released your first story.'

Her expression, for a moment, had gone flat and characterless.

'Again, I apologize . . .'

Soper switched on a smile and began to talk. 'We had, for a brief time, a liaison. I finished it because it became evident he expected more from the relationship than I was prepared to give.'

'Like what exactly?'

Soper waved her hand at her surroundings. 'I am a wealthy woman. My family has made a fortune from our bangroves. Garp wanted some of that and I was not prepared to give. I do not like fortune hunters. When he realized my position he then started to make accusations.'

'He accused you of dealing in praist and being connected to the Tronad.'

Soper leant forward. 'Ridiculous of course. Why should I deal in praist? I have no need of the money.'

'His contention was that your family has always dealt in praist, that you made a fortune from it which you are now investing in legitimate businesses.'

'I thought you were here to listen to my side?'

That flat and dead look again.

'I'm sorry. Do go on.'

'My family have owned bangroves for centuries and our fortune grew from them.' She gestured to the drink before Salind, who took up the cup and drank again. This time the mouthful he took seemed more satisfying.

Soper continued, 'Praist is a drug dealt in by a small minority of the criminal element of Banjer. We have always been leaders here and the holders of moral . . .'

As she went on Salind accessed Argus.

*Praist statistics please.*

*Fifteen per cent of the population are praist users. That is approximately eighty million people. It is at the root of seventy-three per cent of all crimes committed here and ninety-two per cent of all suicides. It is speculated that terminal praist users will be the first to vote for Polity subsumption because of advanced Polity medical technologies. There is no cure for praist addiction here, and most users – those who do not commit suicide – are killed before the drug kills them. In the last year of addiction – addiction lasts eight solstan years – the user becomes psychotic.*

More than tens of thousands, then.

As the interview drew to a close Salind felt it less and less difficult to keep smiling. He found himself starting to see that maybe Garp had not told him all of the truth. Deleen Soper did not seem quite so monstrous face-to-face.

'I understand,' he said to Soper's latest contention. 'A cop in his position could manipulate anything. Coming from the Polity we tend to forget how much power such a police force can wield.'

'There, you see?'

Soper sat back and sipped her drink. Salind sipped his own. It had been topped up twice. Perhaps it was going to his head.

'What do you think of my collection?' Soper asked him.

'I think it's wonderful, Deleen.'

Soper stood. 'But you haven't seen it all.'

As he also stood, Salind felt a dizziness wash through him. He blinked and seemed to see rainbow haloes around various objects in the room. Soper conducted him around the apartment. She told him about the grandfather clock replicated about an original pendulum, and showed him carvings from banoak coral that would not have looked out of place in a Pharaoh's tomb. She showed him lurid paintings and boasted their value. Then she finally came to her most prized possession.

The drowning jar had been the favoured punishment for criminals in the early years of the Theocracy. Criminals were sealed inside to drown in the preservative the jar contained. This one was a fat urn-shape standing four feet high. The man still inside the jar, she told him, was the predecessor of the Banjer reifs, but from the wrong side of the law. She giggled and he laughed with her – surprised at how easily the laughter came. The man, with his bulbous eyes and protruding tongue, shifted and scratched at the inside of the jar. He looked like the reporter who had stood behind Merril in the arrivals lounge. Next, the butler was opening the street door for

Salind, and he then walked under a sky that was a sheet of skin flayed from the back of a giant. He stood on a bridge and gripped the rail, his mouth dry and bitter and terror rising up inside him. The drowned man was coming to drag him back to the jar and there to pull him down into a clammy embrace. And now Geronamid stood over him with treels oozing out of holes in its allosaur body. Salind started screaming, and didn't stop until a hydrocar pulled up and Geoff leapt out to press a pressure hypodermic against his neck. Then he blacked out. It took him a day to recover from the praist-based hallucinogen. And of course there was no proof that Deleen Soper had administered the drug.

Salind woke instantly and with crawling horror suffusing him. It was the middle of the night so Argus must have woken him with a betawave stim. He still wanted coffee though. He still had a hangover from the drug and still occasionally heard fingernails scratching against glass.

'What is it? You know I've had a tiring day,' he said, sitting upright on the futon.

*Geoff is on his way round to pick you up. His message is: 'Remember the hack-and-slash job?' There is also an untraced message: 'Cremation complete, will join you shortly.'*

'Yes,' Salind hissed, standing and heading for the hotel minibar. He took out an Instacup, pulled the tab on it, and by the time he had dressed the beverage was hot. Taking it with him he quickly left his hotel. Standing on the pavement under a leaden sky backlit by green moonlight, he sipped coffee until the hydrocar pulled up.

'Give me bad news or good news, but give me news,' he said as he got in beside Geoff.

'It's news, whether it's bad or good is something for

you to decide,' said the staffer. 'Oh, here, I have something for you.'

Salind took the small container Geoff handed him,
clicked out a pill and swallowed it with a mouthful of
coffee. He tossed the empty cup out of the window.

'Tell me.'

'We're going to the Groves. Our trusty police force
have found Merril Torson.'

'How? . . .'

'Oh the usual way when the Tronad wants to make a
point.'

They had nailed her to a banoak. The treels were in
her clothing, peeking from holes in her arms and stomach. A knot of intestines hung from one such hole.
Floodlights, and the red and green flashing lights on the
squad cars, cast the scene in a lurid glow. The uniformed
cops stood by their cars drinking tea from small flasks
while awaiting senior officers.

'She was a hack,' said Salind. 'But this is excessive
punishment.'

'The Tronad don't know the meaning of the word
excess,' said Geoff, as they both stepped out onto the
gravel.

'So this is how they hit people?' Salind gazed slowly
from side to side, making sure Argus was getting everything here and transmitting it.

'This was how traitors were killed by the underground
before the civil war, and it's now how the Tronad kill
people when they want to make a point. The holes were
made by whoever nailed her there. The treels have to be
pushed inside before they try to feed. They just keep
grinding away and pushing through in search of banoak

flesh. She probably died when one of them hit an artery. It can take anything from ten minutes to an hour.'

'You're very well informed.'

'We all are here. This is what happens to you if you go piss-off the Tronad. This is why very few people will turn out to vote next Moonday.'

They moved away from the car and closer to the crucified reporter. Salind felt sorry for Merril and a little sad, but nothing more than that. She wouldn't have suffered. Were they so primitive here they didn't realize she could have shut off the pain with her aug?

'Alright there. Keep back,' said one of the uniformed cops as he strolled over.

Salind turned to him. 'What's happened here, officer?'

'You got eyes ain't you?'

'A murder I take it. I think you should be aware that I know the victim.'

'Who don't? We know whose toes she stepped on,' said the cop, turning to inspect the corpse.

'So we can be expecting an arrest soon then?' said Salind.

The cop snorted then glanced over as another car pulled up. 'Yeah, there'll be an arrest. Some other toe-stepper'll get shat on. And here comes the biggest shitter of 'em all.'

Salind also watched as Callus and two of his thugs climbed from the car. Behind the car a van pulled up. He supposed that this must be Banjer's equivalent of a medical examiner or some such. He started to move in their direction, but Geoff caught hold of his shoulder.

'Not a good idea. Best to just watch,' he said.

'I only want to ask a reasonable question or two,' said Salind.

'Don't,' said Geoff. 'Callus is never in his best mood when he's clearing up after Soper. It won't just be a slap next time. It'll be a stiletto in your back followed by polite enquiries after your health for the benefit of your aug recording.'

Salind desisted. He turned to the uniformed cop. 'You realize her augmentation will have recorded everything she saw?'

The cop glanced at him and shook his head. 'That won't be much then.'

The man walked back to join his companions. On closer inspection Salind saw Merril's eyes had been gouged out. A treel worked its way out of one socket. Salind took out his pill container, clicked out a pill, and swallowed it dry.

From the van, two overalled figures bearing a stretcher approached the banoak. They conducted no forensic examination of the area, no careful search for evidence. After they deposited the stretcher on the ground, one of them took a crowbar from his belt and levered out the nails pinning the corpse to the tree. When it slid to the ground the two rolled it in a plastic sheet then passed a heating unit over this wrapping to shrink and seal it. As they carried the neat parcel back to the van Salind could still see treels moving about inside. While they loaded into the van he noted Callus spot him and start walking over with his thugs and two uniformed policemen in tow.

'We better be leaving,' said Geoff.

'I don't think so,' said Salind.

'I've warned you. That's all I can do.'

'Fine,' said Salind, but he did step back to put himself up against the car.

Callus came up before him and his two thugs moved round to either side of the inspector. They stood with their hands clasped before them. Salind had seen that pose before from other people who served the same purpose on other worlds – immediate testicle protection.

'Well, well, Mr Salind, what do you have to say for yourself?'

Salind was momentarily distracted from replying, for another car had pulled up. The third plain-clothes cop who stepped out seemed familiar. Someone in the Tronad probably – someone about whom Salind had read a file. Was this one of Soper's associates? He looked the part – a shaven-headed thug with slightly more muscle than necessary.

'Sorry . . . what?'

Callus went on, 'I suppose it was professional jealousy that made you do it.'

'Oh shit,' said Geoff.

Callus glanced at him. 'I imagine your accomplice will be able to tell us.'

'You have got to be kidding,' said Salind.

'I'll need your aug for evidence of course.'

Now the two thugs moved up on either side of Salind.

'My aug is internal and backs up to the Tarjen AI every four minutes. It doesn't retain a recording itself, but that backed-up information will prove I was nothing to do with this.'

*Shit, get me some help out here. This fucker is going to kill me.*

*Message received: the legal department is onto it right now.*

*I don't need the legal department! I need Polity monitors!*

*Polity monitors do not have jurisdiction here.*

Callus smiled. 'Here on Banjer we are aware how it is possible to interfere with computer-stored information.'

'Argus is encryption-sealed! Nothing less than a major AI could interfere with it! And it's internal – you haven't got the facilities here to remove it!'

Callus gave the nod to his two thugs. 'Mr Gem Salind, in the name of the Banjer Council I arrest you for the murder of Merril Torson, and with the powers vested in me by said Council, seize all evidential material. Please do not resist arrest.'

A fist like the bony end of a ham crashed into the side of Salind's head. He slid along the car and the second thug hook-punched him twice in the gut.

'I said "Please do not resist arrest" Mr Salind.'

Hazily he realized just what they intended. He would either die whilst resisting arrest or when they attempted to remove Argus. Case closed.

For a little fat guy Geoff could move very fast. He had jumped up on the bonnet of the car and slammed his recorder down on the second attacker's head before Salind thought to react. Salind punched the one on his right then fervently wished he'd used his boot. That hamfist came down again and the next thing he knew he was lying dazedly on the floor watching Geoff, his face covered with blood, being held by the scruff of the neck and having his head repeatedly pounded against the car's wing.

'That's enough!' someone bellowed.

Salind tried to stand as his attacker loomed over him. He saw the shaven-headed one moving up behind. Shavehead took hold of the thug by the shoulder and just threw him. The man hit the car then the ground, bounced and lay still. The second thug released Geoff in time to walk into a backhander that lifted him clean over the car. Salind staggered groggily to his feet. He glanced back and saw the two uniformed officers standing dumbfounded. Callus was on his knees holding his wrist. He looked up as Shavehead came up beside Salind, and real fear twisted his features. Scrabbling inside his coat he produced a nasty-looking pulse-gun.

'You gonna do it to me, Mikey?' asked Shavehead.

Callus did. The pulse-gun flashed. There came a thud and burst of smoke from Shavehead's chest.

'I just love this body.' Shavehead strode forward and drove his fist down into Callus's face.

Salind felt that familiar churning in his stomach: one hell of a story and now he knew the punchline, so to speak. One of the uniformed officers drew his own weapon – a similar pulse-gun to Callus's.

'Drake, put that away will you,' said Shavehead.

The cop looked at his weapon in bewilderment, then he holstered it.

'Inspector Garp,' he said.

With Argus now set to record only, Salind observed, 'So that's how you looked.'

The uniformed police had been in disarray, and let them leave without protest, though Salind wondered what they could have done to stop them with their ex-boss, firmly uploaded to a Golem chassis, there to facilitate matters.

'Yeah,' said Garp, 'ten years ago. Geronamid managed to piece together enough information to have this made.' Garp touched his face and chest.

They sat in Garp's car, Geoff in the back holding a medpatch to his head and groaning sporadically.

'When I looked like this I was the big man who was a royal pain to the Tronad. Callus was my partner until Soper bought him off. I think he slipped praist into my tea.'

'He won't be doing that again,' said Salind.

Garp gave him a slightly indifferent glance. Salind wondered if he was fully aware of the capabilities of the body he now occupied. He'd checked on Callus and the two others while Garp spoke to the uniformed officers. Callus and the one behind the car were dead. The third thug was not far from it.

They dropped Geoff at the Tarjen offices.

'I'm gonna keep my head down now. Soper is not going to sit on her hands after this. She'll want us all nailed to banoaks,' Geoff said, and with that disappeared inside.

'What now?' Salind asked. Without thinking he took out his pill container and clicked out a pill. Garp's hand clamped on his wrist and the pill fell to the floor. Salind fought the grip, suddenly unreasonably angry.

'What the hell do you think you're doing?' Garp asked.

Salind stared at him. He felt the hairs on the back of his neck rising. He was sure someone was scratching on the glass behind him.

'I . . . they're to stop me . . .'

'I know what they are. How long have you been a user?'

'Soper dosed me when I interviewed her. Didn't you see that on the net?'

'So a few days. She used pure derivative?'

'I don't know.'

'Nightmares during the day?'

'Yes.'

'I thought so. You're on fifteen strength. You're already at the level of a seven-year addict. You're losing it already.'

'I'll get a detoxicant treatment when this is over.'

'Be sure you do or I'll off you myself.'

Garp released his hand. Salind picked up the pill from the floor and quickly swallowed it. The feeling, like a looming wave of black chaos ready to fall on him, slowly receded. Not taking the next needed dose was unthinkable, as briefly he had seen how thin was the veneer over reality for him. Garp started the car and pulled away.

The ceramal mesh fence stood three metres high, carried a killing current and sported beam-break alarms set along the top. Beyond it, banoaks stretched up the hill in neat rows. Between the rows the ground seemed in constant motion, and in the distance a disc-shaped vacuum harvester, towing a collection tanker, worked its way down.

'They must have to empty those tankers quite often,' said Salind.

'Not as often as you might think. That's a Massey Vacpress. It sucks up the treels, presses out the juice and shoots the pressings into the tanker – almost pure treel-skin.'

As it drew closer Salind observed the waste juice pouring from pipes in the side of the harvester. The machine left the ground behind it completely clear of treels, but there were plenty yet to be sucked up. This had to be the first run of the morning. A driver sat in a bucket seat on the main harvester disc steering it with two levers. He wore blue armoralls and a sphere helmet.

'Why that gear?' he asked.

'The helmet's to prevent narcosis from the vapour, and it's their uniform.'

'Whose?'

'Soper's people.'

Salind nodded and wondered what the hell they were going to do now. No way were they going to get through that fence without setting off a mass of alarms, even if they managed not to fry themselves.

'Boring job,' he said, nodding at the driver. 'That'll be one to go with the Polity running things. They'll stick a submind in the harvester and that'll be that.'

'Okay, let's go,' said Garp.

They stepped out of the car and Garp popped the boot. From it he removed his rail-gun and walked over to the fence. The red sun breaking over the horizon cast his shadow behind him. He held the weapon out of view and waved. The driver raised a hand in return and continued down the row. Some minutes later the harvester neared the fence. Salind couldn't figure what Garp intended. Was he going to hold up the harvester? Garp showed him. As the machine reached the point where it had to turn to go down the next row Garp raised his weapon and fired a short burst. The driver disappeared in a cloud of red.

'Jesu! What the hell are you doing!'

Garp glanced at him. 'Well you said he'd be redundant.'

'You just killed him!'

'Yeah, I did didn't I. Come here.'

He took hold of Salind's shoulder and walked him to one side. Salind felt himself shaking. He'd seen some horrible things, but he'd never seen someone killed in such cold blood. The harvester kept going, from where it should have turned, and crashed into the fence. Electricity shorted through its body as it tore out a hundred-metre length of fencing and dragged it into the highway. Hitting the bank on the other side of the road it ground to a halt, its vacuum still roaring. Salind saw that the driver was still sitting in the bucket seat, though only from the waist down.

'You killed him,' he repeated.

'They all know what's going on in here. You've seen nothing yet. Come on, we've got to move fast now. The guards'll be here soon.'

Garp led him back to the car and started it up. He carefully drove it off-road and through the gap made by the harvester. Then he floored the accelerator and the turbine soon had them up to a hundred kloms up the cleared lane between the banoaks.

'They always come at a breach from the outside. We'll be too far in by then for them to do anything about us,' said Garp.

'What about getting out?' asked Salind.

'I shouldn't worry unduly about that.'

In a few minutes they reached the end of the grove and Garp dumped the car in an irrigation ditch. He gave it one shove to get it there, leaving a dent in the metal.

'You still recording?' he asked as he checked his rail-gun.

'Yes,' said Salind, wondering if that was the right thing to say.

'Good. Let's go take a look at the factory.' He hung the gun at his belt and turned his back to Salind. Looking over his shoulder he said, 'Hop on.'

This being his first piggy-back ride on the back of a psychotic Golem android, Salind did not know what to expect. He swore, after they covered four or five kilometres, it would be his last. In minutes they reached rocky terrain cut through by gravel roads. Banoaks grew in wild profusion here, with a low scrub of adapted thyme and spherule grass below them. On the higher ground the banoaks were bigger and older than in the grove. Perhaps they had been growing since before humans arrived on Banjer.

*How long do they live?*

*Oaks on the north continent have been dated at over five thousand years in age.*

Garp peered at him, and he wondered if the ex-policeman could listen in on these aug conversations. Garp pointed to a ring of pots strapped round one of the nearby oaks.

'Sap drains. You'll see how they use the sap in a bit. Still recording?'

'Yes,' Salind replied, prepared to give no more than that. He dry-swallowed another praist pill before following where Garp led. Soon they came to a rise overlooking a sprawl of warehouses. Garp pointed to the four trucks parked before the largest building.

'See, they're unloading cropsters,' he explained.

Salind's vision did not extend so far, for he did not have a Golem's eyes. He could just about see some activity.

*Argus, give me a visual feedback, magnification x10.*

*Processing.*

After a moment his vision flickered and suddenly he could view the scene up close. Trussed in straitjackets and with bags over their heads, people were being led from the trucks. One of them tried to run and soon fell flat on his face. The men doing the unloading, men dressed in armoralls like those worn by the one Garp had killed, stood laughing. One of them walked over to the fallen man and proceeded to beat him with a length of wood, only desisting when one of his companions called to him. He then dragged his victim to his feet and with more blows drove him back to the rest.

*Cut feedback.*

Salind's vision returned to normal.

'What the hell is going on down there?' he asked.

'They're all people who've done something to piss off Soper or one of her lieutenants. Or they're other disposable members of society. It's noticeable how few occupants our asylums and gaols have,' replied Garp.

'What are they going to do to them?'

'That's what you're here to see. Come on.'

Using banoak copses, scattered boulders and the occasional natural gully as cover, they worked their way closer to the buildings. Salind worried about the footprints they were leaving in the spherule grass as its little glassy bubbles burst under their feet, until he looked back and saw how quickly the footprints faded. When they were within a hundred metres of the main building Garp stopped in a low gully.

'Wait here. I'll be back in a few minutes.'

True to his word Garp soon returned. He carried two pairs of armoralls and two helmets. The helmet with a crack in it dripped blood. Salind selected the other one.

Garp told him, 'Just follow me and keep your mouth shut. You're going to see some pretty horrible things in there. Don't react. These people see it every day.'

'Can I start transmitting now?'

Garp glanced over to where a long and expensive-looking hydrocar was parked. 'Yeah, I reckon so. She's only got access to the Polity networks back in the city, and by the time she finds out it'll be too late.'

With some relief Salind turned his aug's transmitter back on.

They pulled on the armoralls, Salind trying not to notice his were still warm. Climbing from the gully to one side of the main building, they headed towards the doors. Those unloading the cropsters did not notice them for a moment. When they did, Garp raised his hand and continued walking. A hand was raised in return, but they were otherwise ignored. Salind just kept his head down and his teeth gritted. He'd just seen the previous possessors of the armoralls lying in a drainage ditch. Passing the trucks, they entered the building. Salind tried to ignore the crying from inside one truck.

*Message from Jennifer Tarjen: Great job, Salind. You're live on Earthnet right now!*

Somehow Salind couldn't get excited about that. He wondered how the Polity citizens were reacting to what he was seeing right now. Inside the building a group of three men were strapping cropsters to frames. They had it down to a fine art: no one escaped. After the victims were in place, two women went down the rows pulling bags from heads and pushing metal devices into the cropsters' mouths. Salind supposed those devices were to stop them biting through the tubes that were then forced down into their stomachs.

'Sap from the banoaks,' said Garp. 'It takes an hour or so to reach sufficient concentration in the bloodstream.'

Salind jumped when he heard an agonized scream from deeper in the building.

'That was a cropster whose sap levels just reached sufficient concentration,' said Garp.

'What the hell are they doing here?'

Garp explained, 'It was some lunatic ancestor of Soper's who first drank tea made from the treels that had fed on an enemy he had nailed to a banoak. He discovered that tea to be powerful indeed. He had discovered the human-specific narcotic, praist. In his subsequent gruesome experiments he also discovered that treels live longer in victims who like their tea too much, and that in those cases the yield of praist increases.'

Deeper in the building Garp abruptly halted and gestured ahead. Here an old grey-bearded man, who Salind thought resembled the park labourer he had observed before meeting Garp the reif, was doing something to one of those strapped to a frame. It took a moment for Salind to absorb this further horror. The woman on the frame was unconscious. The old man cut slits in her body and opened them with sprung clamps. Into the holes, through a wide funnel, he fed finger-length treels.

'During the later years of the cult of Anubis Arisen it was discovered that if you fed someone on pure banoak sap to get a sufficient concentration in the bloodstream, and if the treels are inserted just so, they will attach quickly without causing too much internal damage – without hitting an artery. Allowed to grow in a sap-fed human body for as much as five days, the yield of praist is fifty times more than when it was done the old way. The victim dies eventually, as you can see.' Garp gestured down the row of frames to where corpses hung, larger treels writhing in and out of holes in their bodies.

'This is a nightmare,' said Salind, and for once he

wasn't thinking about the story. He thought about what Geronamid had said: *eight hundred* of these places.

Garp nodded, then unhooked his rail-gun and handed it across. 'Protect yourself.'

'What?'

'I intend to use my hands,' said Garp, and walked over to the old man. The man looked up, grinning, for he obviously enjoyed his work. Garp reached out and pressed his hands to either side of the man's face, then twisted. Salind could hear the bones breaking from where he stood. Now Garp turned and headed back, passing Salind without looking at him as he headed for the building's entrance. Salind turned and followed. Reaching the first of the women, Garp chopped once and she went down. The next woman went down the same way. The first two of the three men strapping people to the frames, Garp grabbed and slammed together. They dropped soggily. The third man tried to run.

*Message from Jennifer Tarjen: Polity monitors coming in through the runcible and two gamma-class dreadnoughts in orbit. Geronamid has ordered immediate intervention on Banjer! This has to be because of your transmission!*

*Like hell*, thought Salind. Geronamid had intended intervention here from the start. Salind's transmission was just part of the justification.

*What's Geronamid doing now?*

*Message: Geronamid cannot be traced at present.*

Garp caught the third man by his collar, dragged him back and broke his neck. He was going to do them all. He just wasn't going to stop . . . Then there came a turquoise flash that left afterimages on Salind's retina. He saw Garp fly back, his clothing and skin burning. He hit the ground hard then immediately sat up. Deleen

Soper walked in from outside, three men in armoralls walking in behind her.

'It was obvious you'd been uploaded to a Golem,' she said. 'And typically arrogant of you to consider yourself invulnerable.' She held up her weapon and went on. 'This is Polity hardware. It will stop a Golem, as you've just found out.'

Garp began to chuckle, then to laugh.

'It amuses you that you are finally going to die?' she asked.

From where he was hiding behind a row of frames Salind shakily raised the rail-gun. He had to do something; had to commit. He couldn't just observe.

'I've already done that. It's not something that scares me,' Garp replied.

'It's a shame you can't be put on a frame,' said Soper.

'Nothing you can do but destroy me. You can't even use me for some idiot assassination attempt this time. You might have got your hands on a fancy gun, but no way you've got the tech to access Golem hardware.'

Soper leant the weapon across her shoulder and gazed down at Garp. 'No point in that now. The fact that I could get an assassin through all the Council's defences brought most of them back into line. I also gained the unexpected bonus of making Mr straight and true officer Garp kill an innocent Polity citizen.'

Salind could feel sweat running down his back. This was it: he could delay no longer.

*Message: Salind, put the gun down before you shoot your own foot off.*

*Who the hell?*

Just then he felt Argus go offline, but it wasn't him that had made it do so.

Garp now began to rise.

'Stay on the fucking ground!'

'Polity hardware,' said Garp, continuing to stand. 'Had you the opportunity I know that you would have some strong words for your supplier.'

Soper aimed her weapon at him and pulled the trigger, again and again. Nothing happened. Salind could see first confusion then terror growing in her expression. Her three accompanying thugs were backing off, ready to run. He tried the record facility in Argus – that didn't work either. On his feet now, Garp held his hands apart before him.

'Don't worry about me, Deleen. I'm not going to kill you.' For a moment she found hope, then Garp gestured to the doorway behind, which now filled with a huge shape. 'He's going to do that.'

Soper and her three thugs turned. Salind stepped out to see more clearly as Geronamid, still in the form of an allosaur, stepped delicately into the building.

For a moment, stillness, then Soper laughed with relief and tossed her weapon on the floor. 'You can't do that. You're an AI. It's against all Polity law.'

'Whatever gave you that idea?' asked Geronamid, pacing forward.

'You can't interfere in places where that law doesn't apply, and if it ever does apply here there'll be a general amnesty.'

'Who said anything about law?' Geronamid asked. 'But since you mention it, amnesty doesn't apply in cases of intervention.'

'What?'

Geronamid stepped in closer. Salind thought Soper must smell the last meal on the allosaur's breath. What happened next was nightmarish. Geronamid's head snapped to one side and one of Soper's men fell over. His head was gone. Geronamid spat the head at Soper's feet.

'I think I would like you to run now.'

Soper stared at the head for one interminable moment, then turned and fled, her men following fast. Salind understood now why Argus was totally offline. The AI had remotely shut it down: no recordings, no transmission. He watched the allosaur take off after the three and disbelievingly watched what happened in the shadowy interior of the building. No one would believe this: Polity AIs were just so measured and moral.

Breathing ash out of his burnt mouth, Garp stepped up beside Salind. 'Even AIs can get pissed off when a friend gets killed.'

'I guess so,' Salind replied, remembering the acrobat.

Soper's scream, the last one, seemed more protracted than that of her two fellows, probably because Geronamid took his time about eating her.

# 4

# THE SEA OF DEATH

*So lay they garmented in torpid light,*
*Under the pall of a transparent night,*
*Like solemn apparitions lull'd sublime,*
*To everlasting rest, – and with them Time*
*Slept, as he sleeps upon the silent face*
*Of a dark dial in a sunless place.*

—Hood

To say it is cold is to seriously understate the matter. The inside of the shuttle is at minus fifty centigrade because of what Jap calls 'material tolerances'.

'These coldsuits we're wearing – take 'em above zero and they'll fuck up next time you use 'em outside,' he told me.

'Yeah,' I said. 'Two centuries ago I'd have believed you, but things have moved on since then.'

'Economics ain't,' was his reply.

I am careful not to respond to his sarcasm.

The landing is without mishap, but I am surprised when the side of the shuttle opens straight down onto the surface of the planet Orbus.

'No point maintaining an entrance tunnel,' says Jap over the com.

I don't mind. It is for moments like this that I travel, and it is moments like this that fund my travel. I walk out with $CO_2$ snow crunching underfoot and the clarity of starlit sky above that you normally only get in interstellar space. I gaze across land like arctic tundra with its frozen lakes and hoared boulders. In the frozen lakes trapped faerie lights flicker rainbow colours.

'What's that?' I ask.

'Water ice. Below one-fifty it turns to complex ice and when it heats up and changes back it fluoresces. Talk to Duren if you want the chemistry of it.'

I don't need to. I remember reading that this is what comets do. It had taken a little while for people to figure that the light of comets was not all reflected sunlight – that comets emit light before they should.

'What's heating it up?' I ask, turning to gaze at the distant green orb of the dying sun.

'The shuttle, our landing. There's nothing else here to do it,' he replies.

We walk the hundred or so metres to the base and go in through a coldlock. In the lock we remove our coldsuits and hang them up. Jap points to the white imprint of a hand on the grey surface of the inner door.

'Keep your undersuit and gloves on until we're inside,' he tells me. I stare at the imprint in puzzlement. Is it some kind of safety sign? Jap obviously notes my confusion. He explains.

'Fella took his gloves off before going through the door,' he says.

The imprint is the skin of that fella's hand, and some of the flesh too. Later I speak to Linser, the base commander, and ask why they take such risks here. We stand in his room gazing out of a panoramic window across the frozen wastes.

'Thermostable and thermo-inert materials are expensive, Mr Gregory. A thermoceramic cutting head for a rock-bore costs the best part of fifty thousand New Carth shillings and has to be shipped in. Doped water-ice cutting heads can be made here. Coldsuits that can function from plus thirty to minus two hundred cost fifty times as much as the ones we use. That's a big saving for a small inconvenience,' he says.

'I never thought this operation short of funds,' I say.

'Energy is money and there's none of the former here. It costs fifteen hundred shillings a minute to keep one human alive and comfortable. We have over two thousand personnel.'

I walk up beside him and focus on what has now caught his attention. Machines for moving rock and ice are busily gnawing at the frozen crust out there. Floodlights bathe something that appears a little like a building site.

'Found an entrance right under our noses,' he tells me.

'Lucky,' say I.

He turns to me with an expression tired and perhaps a little irrational.

'Lucky? . . . Oh yes, you've been in transit. You haven't seen the latest survey results. You see, we were having a bit of a Schrödinger problem with the deep scanners. The energy of the scan was enough to cause fluorescence of the water ices down there, full-spectrum fluorescence. It was like shining a torch into a cave and having the beam of that torch turn on a floodlight. We saw only a fraction of it until we started using those low-energy scanners.'

'A fraction?' I say. 'Last I heard you'd mapped twenty thousand kilometres of tunnels.'

'That's nothing. Nothing at all. They're everywhere you see. Yesterday Duren told me that they even go under the frozen seas. We're looking at millions of kilometres of tunnels, more than a hundred million burial chambers with one or more sarcophagi in each.'

I absorb this information in silence, slot it in with a hundred other details I've been picking up right from Farstation Base to here.

'Obviously I want to see one of the sarcophagi,' I eventually tell him.

He glances at me.

'See and touch it I would have thought. Unfortunately you don't get to smell anything. Too cold for decay here,' he says.

'Seeing and hearing are the most important,' I reply. 'Most people don't go for full immersion for a documentary. There are much more enjoyable FI entertainments.'

'Okay, get yourself settled in and we'll run you down in an hour or so. Will you be needing any of your equipment off the shuttle?'

'No, I have my eyes and ears,' I reply.

He studies me, his inspection straying to the aug nestled behind my right ear. He seems too tired to display the usual discomfort of those confronted by a human recorder like myself.

The tunnels resemble very closely the Victorian sewers of Old London on Earth. The bricks are made of water ice and are, on the whole, over three quarters of a million years old. A strange juxtaposition of age and impermanence. Just raise the temperature and all the tunnels will be gone. Of course, the temperature will not rise here for many thousands of years. Duren, who walks with me to the first chamber, is distracted and gloomy. I have to really push to get anything out of him. Finally he comes out with a terse and snappy summation.

He tells me, 'It will keep on getting colder and colder, but not constantly so. Every eight hundred years we get the Corlis conjunction and the resultant volcanic activity. In about a hundred thousand years Corlis will fall in orbit round here and all hell will break loose for a time. The volcanic activity will destroy all these tunnels, melt all the ice. That'll last for a few hundred years then things will settle down and freeze again.'

'So future archaeologists will have to dig the sarcophagi out of the ice?' I ask.

He waves his hand towards a side chamber and we duck into there. The lights inside are of a lower luminescence than those outside. They don't want the light damaging things, apparently.

'Doubt that. Hundred thousand years and we'll know all we need to know about this place. We'll let them sleep in peace then.'

I study him and try to figure the tone of his voice. It is too difficult to read his expression through his coldsuit mask, though.

The sarcophagi are metallic chrysalids averaging three metres in length. I say metallic because they appear to be made of brass. I am told that they were made of something very complex that does have as its basis some copper compounds. I ask if it is organic. I am told no, it is manufactured – it isn't complex enough to be organic.

There are two sarcophagi in the chamber. One off alone, untouched and easily viewed, the other so

shrouded in scanning equipment, I don't know it is there
until Duren tells me I can look inside.

No one has yet opened a sarcophagus, simply because
there is not a lot more to be learned that has not already
been learned by scanning. Inside each sarcophagus, suspended in water ice that is thick with organic chemicals,
is an alien. These aliens are frightening. What is most
frightening about them is how closely they resemble us.
They have arms and legs much in proportion to our own.
Their bodies are longer and wasp-waisted, their feet
strange hooked two-toed things, and their hands equally
strange, with six fingers protruding from all sorts of odd
points, and no palms. Their heads . . . how best to
describe their heads? Take an almond and rest it on its
side, expand it only where the neck joins it, hang two
sharp barbs at the nose end and back from that punch a
hole straight through for eyes . . . It is theorized that they
had used some kind of sonar sense. This is one of the
theories.

When the first sarcophagus was found people started
to bandy about phrases like 'parallel evolution' while
others claimed credence for their own pet theories.
Those of a religious bent called the discovery proof of
the existence of God, though the selfsame people had
heretofore claimed that the discovery of no humanlike
races had also been proof of the existence of God.
Some claimed the discovery evidenced ancient alien
visitations of Earth, whilst still others talked of interstellar seeding. How so very personal, human and petty
is each theory. Coming to make my documentary about
the catacombs of Orbus and the passing destruction of
the moonlet Corlis I have not thought which of them to
give credence.

'Do you think it's parallel evolution?' I ask Duren as I peer through the scanner.

'Does a scorpion look like a human? It evolved under the same conditions and even on the same planet,' he says, and totally destroys the parallel evolution argument.

'What about interstellar seeding?'

'Same arguments apply,' he replies, and of course they do.

'God?' I ask.

He laughs in my face then says, 'I try to understand it. I don't try to cram it in to fit my understanding.'

He definitely has the essence of it there.

I hesitate to call this my first night here as there is little to mark the change from day to night. You could go outside and spot the sun in the sky, but as Orbus revolves about it once every three solstan centuries that wouldn't be much help. The personnel at the base work a shift system. My waking period concurs with that of Duren, Jap, and about five hundred others who I have yet to meet. After a night of mares in which I am chased down Victorian sewers by subzero rats I wake to a day of subterfuge and obfuscation. Something has happened and people either don't know or don't want to tell the nosy bastard from the Netpress. I use the most powerful weapon in my armoury to get to the bottom of it. Jap takes my bribe.

We don coldsuits in the ball-shrinking coldlock and step on out. Jap leads me to one of the tracked surface cars they call a crawler and we motor over to the nearby excavation. I still find it difficult to take in that the treads of the vehicle we ride in are made of doped water ice.

The whole idea of using such a substance makes me see our civilization as so delicate, so temporary. I guess my objection is that this is the truth.

The excavation is a tunnel that cuts at thirty degrees through rock and ice into the side of one of the Victorian sewers. This is the way I had come yesterday with Duren to view the body, so to speak. We climb out of the crawler and Jap approaches a suited figure who is walking up from the slope.

'What's happening, Jerry?' Jap asks over the com. He'd told me to keep my mouth shut and my ears open for the present.

The woman who replies sounds tired and irritated. 'Duren flipped. He cut open the sarc in B27 and started to thaw out the chicken. Security got on to him and he took his crawler into the system.'

Jap says, 'Always thought he was a bit too close to 'em. He was on it from the start wasn't he?'

'You know he was,' says the woman, her irritation increasing. I wince: Jap isn't very good at subterfuge.

'What's happening now?' he quickly asks.

'They still haven't found him and the computer quite competently tells us that for every hour that passes our chances of finding him halve. Ain't technology wonderful?'

'What about the sarcophagus and the corpse?'

'Linser says waste not want not or some such ancient bullshit. He's having them moved inside for intensive study . . . Here they come now.'

I stare down the slope and see one of the crawlers towing something up the slope. I glance round at Jap and make the hand signal he had only recently taught me. We both switch our com units to private mode.

'The Corlis intersection is in two solstan days. Would this Duren survive that?' I ask.

Jap replies, 'Depends where he is, but yeah, most likely, though not much beyond it. His suit would have to go onto $CO_2$ conversion after a day and that drains the power pack.'

'So he'd freeze and join the rest of them here.'

'That about sums it up, yeah.'

Corlis is hammering towards us at fifty thousand kilometres per hour; pretty slow in cosmological terms. It is the size of Earth's moon and not much different in appearance. Its major differences are its huge elliptical orbit and the smattering of ices on its surface. It will pass close enough to Orbus to perturb both their orbits. Orbus's orbit by only a fraction, Corlis's orbit will wind in a completely different spirograph shape round the sun. This has been happening for about three quarters of a million years and is set to change in a hundred thousand years, when Corlis will finally be captured by Orbus. It's funny, but I find most of the scientific staff rather reluctant to discuss the coincidence of dates: the aliens have been frozen for the same length of time that Corlis has been on its erratic orbit. Only Linser has anything useful to offer.

'These tunnels, chambers and sarcophagi are all that survived the disaster that sent Corlis on its way, or maybe they are all that survived Corlis's arrival in this system. The tunnels survived because they are so deep. There was probably a surface civilization but it's all gone now.'

It doesn't ring true.

'When Corlis passes here tomorrow, will we be safe?' I ask.

'Oh yes. The nearest disturbance will be five hundred kilometres away at a fault line,' Linser replies. I get him to show me exactly where on a map, then thank him for his help before going off to see if I can steal a crawler. It is a surprisingly easy task to accomplish.

Just kilometre after kilometre of brick-lined tunnels. To begin with I stop at a few side chambers but find them all depressingly the same. A map screen inside the crawler shows my current position and just how far I have to go. A quick inspection of the mapping index gives me files filled with thousands of such pages, and directories filled with thousands of such files. Linser told me they had mapped but a fraction of the system. I have to wonder if there is any point in continuing – it obviously covers the entire planet and is much the same everywhere. While I am studying this screen a message flicks up in the corner and is also repeated over my coldsuit com.

'Alright everybody, we're not going to find him before conjunction. I want you all back at base by twelve hundred, Linser out.'

I look at the message in the corner of the map screen and realize that the only reason I have not been caught is that a lot of crawlers are out being used in the search for Duren. It only occurs to me now that all the crawlers must have some sort of beacon on them, some way they can be traced, and that Duren must have disabled it on his own. I immediately try to use the crawler's computer to find out more about the beacon. On the menu I get beacon diagnostics and a hundred and one things I can do with said beacon. I cannot find where the damned thing is though.

'Number 107, didn't you get my message?'

Linser sounds a bit peeved. I ignore him while I continue to try to locate the beacon.

'Ah, I see,' says Linser. 'That crawler is not your property, Mr Gregory.'

I decide it is time for me to respond. 'I'll return it to you in one piece,' I say.

'How very civil of you. You do realize you're heading directly for the nearest fault line; an area that is going to become very dangerous in only a few hours from now?'

'Yes, I do know,' I reply. 'I'm sure that's where Duren is.'

There is a pause, then when Linser speaks again it is with a deal of irritation.

'So you think we have not already searched Duren's most obvious destination?' he asks.

I feel a sinking in the pit of my stomach, but stubbornness prevents me from turning the crawler round.

'You may have missed him,' I say.

'Well,' Linser replies. 'If you are intent on getting yourself killed then that is your problem. We will bill Netpress for any damage to the crawler and for the recovery of your body. Good day to you Mr Gregory.'

He manages to make me feel like a complete idiot and I nearly turn back, but the stubbornness remains. It has been pointed out to me that stubbornness is not strength. It is in fact a weakness. I keep driving. Two hours pass and the first tremor hits. As the tunnel vibrates and little flecks of ice fall onto the crawler's screen, I replay the conversation I'd had with Duren as we walked back to his crawler after viewing the dead alien.

'Most people would wonder if they are in cryostasis,' I had said.

'They're not,' Duren replied. 'They are decayed, even though they were pickled in brine before that brine froze.'

'Were they all preserved at the same time?' I asked.

'Oh yes.'

'How do you account for that then: a hundred million of them going into their sarcophagi at the same time?'

Duren was silent for a while. I didn't push him.

'I did say that they are not in cryostasis,' he said. 'I did not say that some attempt may not have been made to put them in such.'

'Is that what you think?'

'It's one possibility. Other possibilities include mass murder and mass suicide. It's weird, it's an anomaly, and it just is.'

A lump of ice falls from the ceiling and bounces off the screen of the crawler. I nearly fill my pants.

'You've got a lot of seismic activity out there,' says Linser over the com.

'No shit,' I reply.

Just at that moment a big one hits and the crawler slides a couple of yards to one side. I steer back central and note a huge crack dividing the icy ceiling and expos-ing rock a couple of metres above. Something occurs to me then, and I wonder if I will get a reply that will again make me feel stupid.

'Hey, Linser.'

'Yes.'

'They've been here for three quarters of a million years, I make that about a thousand conjunctions. How come I haven't seen any old damage in these tunnels? That's a thousand earthquakes.'

Again there is that long pause and I await Linser's slapdown. It does not come.

'That is an interesting question, Mr Gregory. There is no damage in the area where you are and that area is an unstable one. You must remember though that we only recently acquired the low-energy scanners and that area is the only unstable area we have mapped so far.'

'Yeah. Wouldn't it have been an idea to have mapped some of the other unstable areas before the conjunction?'

'For what purpose?' he asks.

'To find out if there's any old damage there.'

'I'm sure such information would be of interest to a planetary geologist, but we are here for the archaeology,' he says.

He either doesn't get it or is trying to give me the brush-off.

'If there's no damage there that will be because the damage has been repaired. Oh, by the way, you got any other crawlers in this area?'

'To answer your question: no we do not have any other crawlers in that area.'

'Then it looks like I've found Duren . . . Tell me, Linser, have you found any evidence, other than the tunnels and the sarcophagi, of their technology?'

'No, we have not.'

'Funny that,' I say, and get out of the crawler.

Duren is inside a large chamber that contains three sarcophagi. He has strung up lights all around and as I walk in through the round door he has his back to me. He is using a cutter to slice open a sarcophagus. There seems nothing scientific about what he is doing. It looks like vandalism. I speak to him over private com.

'Duren,' I say.

He turns and holds the business end of the cutting unit in my direction. The disruption field only has a range of a couple of centimetres. I have no intention of getting within that range.

'You . . . what are you doing out here?' he asks.

It strikes me that he does not sound particularly irrational.

'I've come to see what you are trying to prove,' I say.

Duren stares at me for a long moment then abruptly turns back to cutting open the sarcophagus. I move round to a position where I can better see what he is doing.

'You know, it was this place being frozen that led us astray,' he says. 'First you think of cryostasis and expect the bodies to be perfect. We found decayed bodies in thick frozen brine and thought it was cryostasis gone wrong. When we found no sign of their technology we then assumed this was some kind of burial.'

'What is the truth?' I ask.

He throws back the piece of sarcophagus he has cut away and it crashes to the floor.

'The truth? The truth is that—'

Oh isn't melodrama crap. When he is just about to fill me in on 'the truth' the biggest fucking earthquake hits. I am on a floor split by a crack a half a metre wide. A haze of broken ice fills the air and huge chunks fall from the ceiling. I hear Duren yelling over the com but cannot make out what he was saying. Something heavy bounces off the helmet of my suit and I realize that I might not actually get out of this alive. I bury my head under my arms and wish I had enough belief in something to pray to it. When the quake is over, some eight minutes later, Duren grabs my arm and hauls me to my feet.

'We'll do better in the crawlers,' he says.

We are in the crawlers when the next quake hits, and the one after that. My crawler ends up on its side with one tread smashed and the ice all around. I don't get out of it until Duren comes and raps on the screen.

'Is that it?' I ask, as I climb out the only door I can get through.

Duren shrugs. 'Might be a few more aftershocks, but that's the worst of it I think,' he says.

I study my surroundings. The tunnel is wrecked: the floor is a metre deep in shattered ice, and rock is exposed in many places. I follow Duren into the chamber.

'I didn't need to do it,' he says, and points.

The sarcophagus next to the one he had cut open has a huge dent in it where a boulder has fallen from the ceiling. There is also a split where the dent is deepest.

'They're not particularly strong and yet we've never found a broken one, just as we've never found a tunnel as badly damaged as that one,' he says, gesturing towards the tunnel.

'And what does that mean?' I ask, not sure I want to know the answer.

'This is a cold world and here we make things out of frozen water. It never occurred to us that those who lived here would do the same. Frozen, salty water filled with all kinds of impurities. We should have looked closer at those impurities,' he says.

'You're not exactly making yourself clear,' I say.

He gestures all around us at the shattered ice.

'Here is their technology. Here is the world in which they lived and will live when they have the energy.'

'What energy?' I ask.

'Geothermal,' he replies, as if it is obvious.

I only start to get it when the ice melts.

In some way the energy is distributed through the ice very evenly. One minute we are surrounded by shattered ice, the next minute we are up to our waists in water that has an almost glutinous consistency.

'Here they come,' says Duren while I wonder if I am going to drown on this insane world. It takes me a moment to digest what he has said. I turn to the door and see one of the aliens standing there up to its crotch in the water. Standing, it looks like an insectile man with a horse's skull for a head. I have never been this scared.

'What . . . what's happening?' I ask.

'The repair teams are about their work,' he says.

'I thought you said they were dead,' I say, and though wondering why I am whispering, am unable to stop myself.

'I never said such a thing. I may have misled you, but I never said they were dead.'

I feel like hitting him, but I don't dare move. A second alien comes in through the entrance. Both almond-shaped heads turn towards us. I know that if they come at us I will almost certainly shit my pants.

'But they were decayed,' I say.

'It takes energy to prevent decay. Decay is one form of entropy. With little energy to spare you don't squander it. If you have the technology you reverse entropy when you do have the energy . . . You know, it's easier to store information than to store bodies.'

The two aliens finish studying us then abruptly wade to the sarcophagi. One of them picks up the piece of metal that Duren had cut away and pushes it back into place.

'You're still not making yourself clear,' I say.

Duren turns his head towards me and I can see his expression. He looks as frightened as I feel, though it doesn't come over in his oh so correct voice.

'If I wanted to preserve you over a long period of time I would record your thought patterns to crystal and keep a spit of your genetic material to regrow your body. That's all I'd need.'

The aliens step back and trail their strange append-ages in the glutinous water. That water rises up in a glistening wave over the sarcophagi. Through it I can see the damage spontaneously repairing.

Duren goes on, 'I don't know how they did it. Their technology is in the water, mostly. I think there is some-thing here of both burial and preservation. They don't need entire bodies for resurrection. Maybe they've kept them so they can repair them from the DNA template, maybe that would use less energy.'

'If it's in the water, what are the sarcophagi for?' I ask.

'The technology is in the water; self-repairing, regen-erating. What they are, their minds and perhaps the DNA templates, are in the sarcophagi. We spent too much time studying the contents of the containers when we should have been studying everything but the contents of the containers.'

The water recedes from the sarcophagi and they are both whole and undamaged. It then proceeds to crawl up the walls and across the ceiling. The two aliens turn and observe us, or so it seems. They have no eyes.

'What now?' I ask Duren.

'I have no idea,' the scientist replies.

I see that the water on the floor, on the walls, and on the ceiling is dividing into liquid bricks – reforming to

how it was before the earthquake. I point this out to
Duren.

'Just enough geothermal energy from the quakes to
repair the damage they made. Neat,' he says.

One of the aliens squats and places its appendage in
the water again. A snake of water, like a rivulet in reverse,
traverses Duren's body. It seems to be probing all round
his coldsuit. When it tries to get into his mask he slaps
at it and it drops away, suddenly only water again. The
aliens tilt their heads then abruptly stride to the entrance
through ankle-deep water holding the shape of bricks.
We follow. We follow them out into the tunnel and there
see that the treads have melted away on both of the
crawlers. We follow them through the water to a point
where the water is suddenly ice again – a neat line
round the circumference of the tunnel. We watch them
climb back into their own sarcophagi – the water still
liquid inside – and seal themselves in.

'They didn't do anything,' I say.

'They wanted to,' said Duren, 'but they probably
didn't have the energy to spare.'

As we walk back to the crawlers I ask him what will
happen now that this is known.

'The project won't be shut down by accountants. We'll
get funding from Earth Central itself. Maybe, sometime,
we'll resurrect them all,' he says.

'It would be nice to see,' I say, after we have made a
call for help from the transmitter of my crawler. And I
wonder if we will see it, because, of course, the warming
of our coldsuits has damaged them, and they are already
starting to malfunction. Perhaps you, who are experiencing this documentary, will see.

# 5

# ALIEN ARCHAEOLOGY

The sifting machine had been working nonstop for twenty years. The technique, first introduced by the xeno-archaeologist Alexion Smith and frowned on by others in his profession as being too blunt an instrument, was being used here by a private concern. An Atheter artefact had been discovered on this desert planetoid: a species of plant that used a deep extended root system to mop up platinum grains from the green sands, which it accumulated in its seeds to drop on the surface. Comparative analysis of the plant's genome – a short trihelical strand – proved it was a product of Atheter technology. The planet had been deep-scanned for other artefacts, then the whole project abandoned when nothing else major was found. The owners of the machine came here afterwards in the hope of picking up something the previous searchers had missed. They managed to scrape up a few minor finds, but reading between the lines of their most recent public reports, Jael knew they were concealing something and, breaking into the private reports from the man on the ground here, learned of a second big find.

Perched on a boulder, she stepped down the magnification of her eyes to human normal so that now all she could see was the machine's dust plume from the flat green plain. The *Kobashi* rested in the boulder's shade behind her. The planetary base was some ten kilometres away and occupied by a sandapt called Rho. He had detected the U-space signature of her ship's arrival and sent a terse query as to her reason for being here. She expressed her curiosity about what he was doing, to which he had replied that this was no tourist spot before shutting down communication. Obviously he was the kind who relished solitude, which was why he suited this assignment and was perfect for Jael's purposes. She could have taken her ship directly to his base, but had brought it in low below the base's horizon to land it. She was going to surprise the sandapt, and rather suspected he wouldn't consider it a pleasant surprise.

This planet was hot enough to kill an unadapted human and the air too thin and noxious for her to breathe, but she wore a hotsuit with its own air supply, and in the one-half gravity could cover the intervening distance very quickly. She leapt down the five metres to the ground, bounced in a cloud of dust, and set out in a long lope, her every stride covering three metres.

Glimmering beads of metal caught Jael's attention before she reached the base. She halted and turned to study something like a morel fungus – its wrinkled head an open skin of cubic holes. Small seeds glimmered in those holes, and as she drew closer some of them were ejected. Tracking their path she saw that when they struck the loose dusty ground they sank out of sight. She pushed her hand into the ground and scooped up dust in which small objects glittered. She increased the sensitivity of her optic nerves and ramped up the

magnification of her eyes. Each seed consisted of a
teardrop of organic matter attached at its widest end to
a dodecahedral crystal of platinum. Jael supposed the
Atheter had used something like the sifting machine far
to her left to collect the precious metal; separating it from
the seeds and leaving them behind to germinate into
more of these useful little plants. She pocketed the seeds
– she knew people who would pay good money for them
– though her aim here was to make a bigger killing than
that.

She had expected Rho's base to be the usual inflated
dome with resin-bonded sand layered over it, but some
other building technique had been employed here.
Nestled below an escarpment that marked the edge of
the dust bowl and the start of a deeply cracked plain of
sun-baked clay, the building was a white-painted cone
with a peaked roof. It looked something like an ancient
windmill without vanes, but then there were three wind
generators positioned along the top of the escarpment –
their vanes wide to capture the thin air down here. Low
structures spread out from either side of the building like
wings, glimmering in the harsh white sun glare. Jael
guessed these were greenhouses to protect growing food
plants. A figure was making its way along the edge of
these towing a gravsled. She squatted down and focused
in.

Rho's adaptation had given him skin of a deep reddish
gold, a ridged bald head and a nose that melded into his
top lip. She glimpsed his eyes, which were sky blue and
without pupils. He wore no mask, his only clothing being
boots, shorts and a sun visor. Jael leapt upright and broke
into a run for the nearest end of the escarpment, where
it was little more than a mound. Glancing back she

noticed the dust trail she left and hoped he wouldn't see it. Eventually she arrived at the foot of one of the wind generators and from her belt pouch removed a skinjector and loaded it with a selection of drugs. The escarpment here dropped ten metres in a curve from which projected rough reddish slates. She used these as stepping stones to bring her down to the level of the base then sprinted in towards the back wall. She could hear him now – he was whistling some ancient melody. A brief comparison search in the music library in her left-hand aug revealed the name: Greensleeves. She walked around the building as he approached.

'Who the hell are you?' he exclaimed.

She strode up to him. 'I've seen your sifting machine; have you had any luck?'

He paused for a moment, then in a tired voice said, 'Bugger off.'

But by then she was on him. Before he could react she swung the skinjector round from behind her back and pressed it against his chest, triggered it.

'What the . . .!' His hand swung out and he caught her hard across the side of the face. She spun, her feet coming up off the ground, and fell in ridiculous slow motion in the low gravity. Error messages flashed up in her visual cortex – broken nanoconnections – but they faded quickly. Then she received a message from her body monitor telling her he had cracked her cheekbone – this before it actually began to hurt. Scrambling to her feet again she watched him rubbing his chest. Foam appeared around his lips, then slowly, like a tree, he toppled. Jael walked over to him thinking, *You're so going to regret that, sandapt.* Though maybe most of that anger was at herself – for she had been warned about him.

Getting him onto the gravsled in the low gravity was surprisingly difficult. He must have weighed twice as much as a normal human. Luckily the door to the base was open and designed wide enough to allow the sled inside. After dumping him inside she explored, finding the laboratory sited on the lower floor, living quarters on the second, the U-space communicator and computer systems on the top. With a thought, she summoned the *Kobashi* to her present location, then returned her attention to the computer system. It was sub-AI and the usual optic interfaces were available. Finding a suitable network cable, she plugged one end into the computer and the other into the socket in her right-hand aug, then began mentally checking through Rho's files. He was not due to send a report for another two weeks, and the next supply drop was not for three months. However, there was nothing about his most recent find, and recordings of the exchanges she had listened to had been erased. Obviously, assessing his find, he had belatedly increased security.

Jael headed back downstairs to study Rho, who was breathing raggedly on the sled. She hoped not to have overdone it with the narcotic. Outside, the whoosh of thrusters announced the arrival of the *Kobashi*, so she headed out.

The ship, bearing some resemblance to the thirty-yard-long abdomen and thorax of a praying mantis, settled in a cloud of hot sand in which platinum seeds glinted. Via her twinned augs she sent a signal to it and it folded down a wing section of its hull into a ramp onto which she stepped while it was still settling. At the head of the ramp the outer airlock door irised open and she ducked inside to grab up the pack she had deposited there earlier, then stepped back out and down, and returned to the base.

Rho's breathing had eased, so it was with care that she secured his hands and feet in manacles connected by four braided cables to a winder positioned behind him. His eyelids fluttering he muttered something obscure, but did not wake. Jael now took from the pack a bag bearing the appearance of a nineteenth-century doctor's bag, and four paces from Rho, placed it on the floor. An instruction from her augs caused the bag to open and evert, converting itself into a tiered display of diagnostic and surgical equipment, a small drugs manufactory and various vials and chainglass tubes containing an esoteric selection of some quite alien oddities. Jael squatted beside the display, took up a diagnosticer and pressed it against her cheekbone, let it make its diagnosis, then plugged it into the drug manufactory. Information downloaded, the manufactory stuck out a drug patch like a thin tongue. She took this up, peeled off the backing and stuck it over her injury, which rapidly numbed. While doing this she sensed Rho surfacing into consciousness, and awaited the expected.

Rho flung himself from the sled at her, very fast. She noted he didn't even waste energy on a bellow, but was spinning straight into a kick that would have taken her head off if it had connected. He never got a chance to straighten his leg as the winder rapidly drew in the braided cables bringing the four manacles together. He crashed to the floor in front of her, a little closer than she had expected, his wrists and ankles locked behind him – twenty years of digging in the dirt had not entirely slowed him down

'Bitch,' he said.

Jael removed a scalpel from the display, held it before his face for a moment, then cut his sun visor strap, before trailing it gently down his body to start cutting through the material of his shorts. He tried to drag himself away from her.

'Careful,' she warned, 'this is chainglass and very very sharp, and life is a very fragile thing.'

'Fuck you,' he said without heat, but ceased to struggle. She noted that he had yet to ask what she wanted. Obviously he knew. Next she cut away his boots, before replacing the scalpel in the display and standing.

'Now, Rho, you've been sifting sand here for two decades and discovered what, a handful of fragmentary Atheter artefacts? So, after all that time, finding something new was quite exciting. You made the mistake of toning down your public report to a level somewhere below dry boredom, which was a giveaway to me. Consequently I listened in to your private communications with Charles Cymbeline.' She leaned down, her face close to his. 'Now I want you to tell me where you've hidden the Atheter artefact you found two weeks ago.'

He just stared up at her with those bland blue eyes, so she shrugged, stood up and began kicking him. He struggled to protect himself, but she took her time, walking round him and driving her boot in repeatedly. He grunted and sweated and started to bleed on the floor.

'All right,' he eventually managed. 'Arcosect sent a ship a week ago – it's gone.'

Panting, Jael stepped back. 'There've been no ships here since your discovery.' Walking back around to the instrument display she began to make her selection. While she employed her glittering instruments his grunts soon turned to screams, but he bluntly refused to tell her anything even when she peeled strips of skin from his stomach and crushed his testicles in a set of forceps. But all that was really only repayment for her broken cheek-bone. He told her everything when she began using her esoteric selection of drugs, could not do otherwise.

She left him on the floor and crossed the room to where a table lay strewn with rock samples and from there picked up a geological hammer. Back on the top floor she located the U-space coms – the unit was inset into one wall. Her first blow shattered the console, which she tore away. She then began smashing the control components surrounding the sealed flask-sized vessels ostensibly containing small singularity generators and Calabri-yau frames. After a moment she rapped her knuckles against each flask to detect which was the false one, and pulled it out. The top unscrewed and from inside she withdrew a small brushed-aluminium box with a keypad inset in the lid. The code he had given her popped the box open to reveal – resting in shaped foam – a chunk of green metal with short thorny outgrowths from one end.

Movement behind . . .

Jael whirled. Rho, catching his breath against the door jamb, preparing to rush her. Her gaze strayed down to one of the manacles, a frayed stub of wire protruding from it. In his right hand he held what he had used to escape: a chainglass scalpel.

*Careless.*

Now she had seen him he hurled himself forward.

She could not afford to let him come to grips with her. He was obviously many times stronger than her. As he groped towards her she brought the hammer round in a tight arc against the side of his face, where it connected with a sickening crack. He staggered sideways, clutching his face, his mouth hanging open. She stepped in closer and brought the hammer down as hard as she could on the top of his head. He dropped, dragging her arm down. She released the hammer and saw it had punched a neat square hole straight into his skull and lodged there, then the hole brimmed with blood, and overflowed.

Gazing down at him, Jael said, 'Oops.' She pushed him with her foot but he was leaden, unmoving. 'Oh well.' She pocketed the box containing the Atheter memstore. 'One dies and another is destined for resurrection after half a million years. Call it serendipity.' She relished the words for a moment, then headed away.

I woke, flat on my back, my face cold and my body one big ache from the sharpest pain at the crown of my skull, to my aching face and on down to the throbbing from the bones in my right foot. I was breathing shallowly – the air in the room obviously thick to my lungs. Opening bleary eyes I lifted my head slightly and peered down at myself. I wore a quilted warming suit, which obviously accounted for why only my face felt cold. I realized I was in my own bedroom, and that my house had been sealed and the environment controls set to Earth-normal.

'You look like shit, Rho.'

The whiff of cigarette smoke told me who was speaking before I identified the voice.

'I guess I do,' I said, 'though who are you to talk?' I carefully heaved myself upright, then back so I was resting against the bed's headboard, then looked aside at Charles Cymbeline, my boss and the director of Arcosect – a company with a total of about fifty employees. He too looked like shit, always did. He was blond, thin, wore expensive suits that required a great deal of meticulous cleaning, smoked unfiltered cigarettes, though what pleasure he derived from them I couldn't fathom, and was very very dead. He was a reification – a corpse with chemical preservative running in his veins, skin like old leather, with bone and the metal of some of the cyber mechanisms that moved him showing through at his finger joints. His mind was stored to a crystal inside the mulch that had been his brain. Why he retained his old dead body when he could easily afford a Golem chassis or a tank-grown living vessel, I wasn't entirely sure about either. He said it stopped people bothering him. It did.

'So we lost the memstore,' he ventured, then took another pull on his cigarette. Smoke coiled out from the gaps in his shirt, obviously making its way out of holes eaten through his chest. He sat in my favourite chair. I would probably have had to clean it, if I'd any intention of staying here.

'I reckon,' I replied.

'So she tortured you and you gave it to her,' he said. 'I thought you were tougher than that.'

'She tortured me for fun, and I thought maybe I could draw it out until you arrived, then she used the kind of drugs you normally don't find anywhere outside a Batian interrogation facility. And anyway, it would have come to a choice between me dying or giving up the memstore, and you just don't pay me enough to take the first option.'

'Ah,' he nodded, his neck creaking, and flicked ash on my carpet.

I carefully swung my legs to one side and sat on the edge of the bed. In one corner a pedestal-mounted autodoc stood like a chrome insectile monk. Charles had obviously used it to repair much of the torture damage.

'You said "she",' I noted.

'Jael Feogril – my crew here obtained identification from DNA from the handle of that rock hammer we found embedded in your head. You're lucky to be alive. Had we arrived a day later you wouldn't have been.'

'She's on record?' I enquired, as if I'd never heard of her.

'Yes – Earth Central Security supplied the details: born on Masada when it was an out-Polity world and made a fortune smuggling weapons to the Separatists. Well connected, augmented with twinned augs as you no doubt saw, and, it would appear, lately branching out into stealing alien artefacts. She's under a death sentence for an impressive list of crimes. I've got it all on crystal if you want it.'

'I want it.' It would give me detail.

He stared at me expressionlessly, wasn't really capable of doing otherwise.

'What have you got here?' I asked.

'My ship and five of the guys,' he said, which accounted for the setting of the environmental control, since he certainly didn't need 'Earth-normal'. 'What are your plans?'

'I intend to get that memstore back.'

'How, precisely? You don't know where she's gone.'

'I have contacts, Charles.'

'Who I'm presuming you haven't contacted in twenty years.'

'They'll remember me.'

He tilted his head slightly. 'You never really told me what you used to do before you joined my little outfit.

And I have never been able to find out, despite some quite intensive inquiries.'

I shrugged, then said, 'I'll require a little assistance in other departments.'

He didn't answer for a while. His cigarette had burned right down to his fingers and now there was a slight bacony smell in the air. Then he asked, 'What do you require?'

'A company ship – the *Ulriss Fire* since it's fast – some other items I'll list, and enough credit for the required bribes.'

'Agreed, Rho,' he said. 'I'll also pay you a substantial bounty for that memstore.'

'Good,' I replied, thinking the real bounty for me would be getting my hands around Jael Feogril's neck.


From what we can tell, the Polity occupies an area of the galaxy once occupied by three other races. They're called, by us, the Jain, Csorians and the Atheter. We thought, until only a few years ago, that they were all extinct – wiped out by an aggressive organic technology created by the Jain, which destroyed them and then burgeoned twice more to destroy the other two races – Jain technology. I think we encountered it too, but information about that is heavily restricted. I think the events surrounding that encounter have something to do with certain Line worlds being under quarantine. I don't know the details. I won't know the details until the AIs lift the restrictions, but I do know something I perhaps shouldn't have been told.

I found the first five years of my new profession as a xeno-archaeologist something of a trial, so Jonas Clyde's arrival on the dust ball I called home came as a welcome relief. He was there direct from Masada – one of those quarantine worlds. He'd come to do some research on the platinum-producing plants, though I rather think he was taking a bit of a rest cure. He shared my home and on plenty of occasions he shared my whisky. The guy was nonstop – physically and mentally adapted to go without sleep. I reckon the alcohol gave him something he was missing.

One evening I was speculating about what the Atheter might have looked like when I think something snapped in his head and he started laughing hysterically. He auged into my entertainment unit and showed me some recordings. The first was obviously the view from a grav-car taking off from the roof port of a runcible complex. I recognized the planet Masada at once, for beyond the complex stretched a chequerboard of dikes and ponds that reflected a gas giant hanging low in the aubergine sky.

'Here the Masadans raised squirms and other unpleasant life-forms for their religious masters,' Jonas told me. 'The people on the surface needed an oxy-genating parasite attached to their chests to keep them alive. The parasite also shortened their lifespan.'

I guessed it was understandable that they rebelled and shouted for help from the Polity. On the recordings I saw people down below, but they wore envirosuits and few of them were working the ponds. Here and there I saw aquatic agrobots standing in the water like stilt-legged steel beetles.

The recording took us beyond the ponds to a wilderness of flute grasses and quagmires. Big fences separated the two. 'The best discouragement to some of the nasties out there is that humans aren't very nutritious for them,'

Jonas told me. 'Hooders, heroynes and gabbleducks prefer their fatter natural prey out in the grasses or up in the mountains.' He glanced at me, a little crazily I thought. 'Now those monsters have been planted with transponders so everyone knows if something nasty is getting close, and which direction to run to avoid it.'

The landscape in view shaded from white to a dark brown with black earth gullies cutting between islands of this vegetation. It wasn't long before I saw something galumphing through the grasses with the gait of a bear, though on Earth you don't get bears weighing in at about a thousand kilos. Of course I recognized it, who hasn't seen recordings of these things and the other weird and wonderful creatures of that world? The gravcar view drew lower and kept circling above the creature. Eventually it seemed to get bored with running, halted, then slumped back on its rump to sit like some immense pyramidal Buddha. It opened its composite forelimbs into their two sets of three 'sub-limbs' for the sum purpose of scratching its stomach. It yawned, opening its big duck bill to expose thorny teeth inside. It gazed up at the gravcar with seeming disinterest, some of the tiara of green eyes arcing across its domed head blinking as if it was so bored it just wanted to sleep.

'A gabbleduck,' I said to Jonas.

He shook his head and I saw that there were tears in his eyes. 'No,' he told me, 'that's one of the Atheter.'

Lubricated on its way by a pint of whisky the story came out piece by piece thereafter. During his research on Masada he had discovered something amazing and quite horrible. That research had later been confirmed by an artefact recovered from a world called Shayden's Find. Jain technology had destroyed the Jain and the

Csorians. It apparently destroyed technical civilizations
– that was its very purpose. The Atheter had ducked the
blow, forgoing civilization, intelligence, reducing themselves to animals, to gabbleducks. Tricone molluscs in
the soil of Masada crunched up anything that remained
of their technology, monstrous creatures like giant milli-
pedes ate every last scrap of each gabbleduck when it
died. It was an appalling and utterly alien nihilism.

The information inside the Atheter memstore Jael had
stolen was worth millions. But who was prepared to pay
those millions? Polity AIs would, but her chances of selling it to them without ECS coming down on her like a
hammer were remote. Also, from what Jonas told me, the
Polity had obtained something substantially more useful
than a mere memstore, for the artefact from Shayden's
Find held an Atheter AI. So who else? Well, I knew about
her, though until she stuck a narcotic needle in my chest
had never met her, and I knew that she had dealings with
the Prador, that she sold them stuff, sometimes living
stuff, sometimes human captives, for there was a black
market for such in the Prador Third Kingdom. It was
why the Polity AIs were so ticked off about her.

Another thing about Jael was that she was the kind of
person who found things out, secret things. She was a
Masadan by birth so probably had a lot of contacts on
her home world. I wasn't so arrogant as to assume that
what Jonas Clyde had blabbed to me had not been
blabbed elsewhere. I felt certain she knew about the
gabbleducks. And I felt certain she was out for the big
killing. The Prador would pay *billions* to someone who
delivered into their claws a living, breathing, *thinking*
Atheter.

A tenuous logic chain? No, not really. After she

embedded that rock hammer in my skull and as my consciousness faded I heard her say, *'One dies and another is
destined for resurrection, after half a million years. Call it
serendipity.'*

The place stank like a sea cave in which dead fish were
decaying. Jael brought her foot down hard, but the ship
louse tried to crawl out from under it. She put all her
weight down on it and twisted, and her foot sank down
with a satisfying crunch, spattering glutinous ichor
across the crusted filthy floor. Almost as if this were some
kind of signal, the wide made-for-something-other-than-
human door split diagonally, the two halves revolving up
into the wall with a grinding shriek.

The tunnel beyond was dank and dark, weedy growths
sprouting like dead man's fingers from the uneven walls.
With a chitinous clattering a flattened-pear carapace
scuttling on too many legs appeared and came charging
out. It headed straight towards her but she didn't allow
herself to react. At the last moment it skidded to a halt
then clattered sideways. Prador second-child, one eye-
palp missing and a crack healing in its carapace, a
rail-gun clutched in one of its underhands, with power
cables and a projectile belt-feed trailing back to a box
mounted underneath it. While she eyed it, it fed some
scrap of flesh held in one of its foreclaws into its
mandibles and champed away enthusiastically.

Next a bigger shape loomed in the tunnel and
advanced at a more leisurely pace, its sharp feet hitting
the floor with a sound like hydraulic chisels. The first-
child was big – the size of a small gravcar – its carapace
wider and flatter and looking as hard as iron. The upper
turret of its carapace sported a collection of ruby eyes

and sprouting above them it retained both of its palp-eyes, all of which gave it superb vision – the eyesight of a carnivore, a predator. Underneath its grating mandibles and the nightmare mouth they exposed, mechanisms had been shell-welded to its carapace. Jael hoped one of these was a translator.

'I didn't want to speak to you at a distance, since even using your codes an AI might have been listening in,' she said.

After a brief pause to grate its mandibles together, one of the hexagonal boxes attached underneath it spoke, for some reason, in a thick Marsman accent. 'Our codes are unbreakable.'

Jael sighed to herself. Despite having fought the Polity for forty years, some Prador were no closer to under-standing that to AIs no code was unbreakable. Of course all Prador weren't so dumb – the clever ones now ruled the Third Kingdom. This first-child was just aping its father, who was a Prador down at the bottom of the hier-archy and scrabbling to find some advantage to climb higher. However, that father had acquired enough wealth to be able to send its first-child off in a cruiser like this, and would probably be able to acquire more by cutting deals with its competitors – all Prador were competitors. It would need to make those deals, for what Jael hoped to sell, the father of this first-child might not be able to afford by itself.

'I will soon be acquiring something that could be of great value to you,' she said. Mentioning the Atheter memstore aboard *Kobashi* would have been suicide – Prador only made deals for things they could not take by force.

'Continue,' said the first-child.

'I can, for the sum of ten billion New Carth shillings or the equivalent in any stable currency, including Prador diamond slate, provide you with a living breathing Atheter.'

The Prador dipped its carapace – perhaps the equivalent of someone tilting their head to listen to a private aug communication. Its father must be talking to it. Finally it straightened up again and replied, 'The Atheter are without mind.'

Jael instinctively concealed her surprise, though that was a pointless exercise, since this Prador could no more read her expression than she could read its. How had it acquired that knowledge? She only picked it up by running some very complicated search programs through all the reports coming from the taxonomic and genetic research station on Masada. Whatever – she would have to deal with it.

'True, they are, but I have a mind to give to one of them,' she replied. 'I have acquired an Atheter memstore.'

The first-child advanced a little. 'That is very interesting,' said the Marsman voice – utterly without inflection.

'Which I of course have not been so foolish as to bring here – it is securely stored in a Polity bank vault.'

'That is also interesting.' The first-child stepped back again and Jael rather suspected something had been lost in translation. It tilted its carapace forward again and just froze in place, even its mandibles ceasing their constant motion.

Jael considered returning to her ship for the duration. The first-child's father would now be making its negotiations, striking deals, planning betrayals – the whole complex and vicious rigmarole of Prador politics and economics. She began a slow pacing, spotted another ship louse making its way towards her boots and went over to step on that. She could return to *Kobashi*, but would only pace there. She played some games in her twinned augs, sketching out fight scenarios in this very room between her and the two Prador, and solving them. She stepped on four more ship lice, then accessed a downloaded catalogue and studied the numerous items she would like to buy. Eventually the first-child heaved itself back upright.

'We will provide payment in the form of one half diamond slate, one quarter a cargo of armour scales and the remainder in Polity currencies,' it said.

Jael balked a little at the armour scales. Prador exotic metal armour was a valuable commodity, but bulky. She decided to accept, reckoning she could cache the scales somewhere in the Graveyard and make a remote sale by giving the coordinates to the buyer.

'That's acceptable,' she said.

'Now we must discuss the details of the sale.'

Jael nodded to herself. This was where it got rather difficult. Organizing a sale of something to the Prador was like working out how to hand-feed white sharks while in the water with them.

I gazed out through the screen at a world swathed in cloud, encircled by a glittering ring shepherded by a sulphurous moon, which itself trailed a cometary tail resulting from impacts on its surface a hundred and twenty years old – less than an eyeblink in interstellar terms. The first settlers, leaving just before the Quiet War in the Solar System, had called the world Paris –

probably because of a strong French contingent amidst them and probably because 'Paradise' had been overused. Their civilization was hardly out of the cradle when the Polity arrived in a big way and subsumed them. After a further hundred years the population of this place surpassed a billion. It thrived, great satellite space stations were built, and huge high-tech industries sprang up in them and in the arid equatorial deserts down below. This place was rich in every resource – surrounding space also swarming with asteroids that were heavy in rare metals. Then, a hundred and twenty years ago, the Prador came. It took them less than a day to depopulate the planet and turn it into the hell I saw before me, and to turn the stations into that glittering ring.

'Ship on approach,' said a voice over com. 'Follow the vector I give you and do not deviate. At the pick-up point shut down to minimal life-support and a grabship will bring you in. Do otherwise and you're smeared. Understood?'

'I understand perfectly,' I replied.

Holofiction producers called this borderland between Prador and Human space the Badlands. The people who haunted this region hunting for salvage called it the Graveyard and knew themselves to be grave-robbers. Polity AIs had not tried to civilize the area. All the habitable worlds were still smoking, and why populate a space that acted as a buffer zone between them and a bunch of nasty clawed fuckers who might decide at any moment on a further attempt to exterminate the human race?

'You got the vector, Ulriss?' I asked.

'Yeah,' replied my ship's AI. It wasn't being very talkative since I'd refused its suggestion that we approach using the chameleonware recently installed aboard. I eyed the new instruments to my left on the console, remembering that Earth Central Security did not look kindly on anyone but them using their stealth technology. Despite ECS being thin on the ground out here, I had no intention of putting this ship into 'stealth mode' unless really necessary. Way back, when I wasn't a xeno-archaeologist, I'd heard rumours about those using inadequate chameleonware ending up on the bad end of an ECS rail-gun test firing. 'Sorry, we just didn't see you,' was the usual epitaph.

My destination rose over Paris's horizon, cast into silhouette by the bile-yellow sun beyond it. Adjusting the main screen display to give me the best view I soon discerned the massive conglomeration of station bubble units and docked ships that made up the 'Free Republic of Montmartre' – the kind of place that in Earth's past would have been described as a banana republic, though perhaps not so nice. Soon we reached the place designated and main power shut down, the emergency lights flickered on. The main screen powered down too, going fully transparent with a photo-reactive smear of blackness blotting out the sun's glare and most of the space station. I briefly glimpsed the grabship approaching – basically a one-man vessel with a massive engine to the rear and a hydraulically operated triclaw extending from the nose – before it disappeared back into the smear. They used such ships here since a large enough proportion of their visitors weren't to be trusted to get simple docking manoeuvres right, and wrong moves in that respect could demolish the relatively fragile bubble units and kill those inside.

A clanging against the hull followed by a lurch told me the grabship now had hold of *Ulriss Fire* and was taking us in. It would have been nice to check all this with exterior cameras – throwing up images on the row of sub-screens below the main one – but I had to be very careful about power usage on approach. The Free Republic had been fired on before now, and any ship that showed energy usage above the level enabling weapons, usually ended up on the mincing end of a rail-gun.

Experience told me that in about twenty minutes the ship would be docked, so I unstrapped and propelled myself into the rear cabin where, in zero-g, I began pulling on my gear. Like many visitors here I took the precaution of putting on a light spacesuit of the kind that didn't constrict movement, but would keep me alive if there was a blow-out. I'd scanned through their rules file, but found nothing much different from when I'd last read it: basically you brought nothing aboard that could cause a breach – this mainly concerned weaponry – nor any dangerous biologicals. You paid a docking tax and a departure tax. And anything you did in the intervening time was your own business so long as it didn't harm station personnel or the station itself. I strapped a heavy carbide knife to my boot, and at my waist holstered a pepperpot stun-gun. It could get rough in there some-times.

Back in the cockpit I saw *Ulriss Fire* was now drawing into the station shadow. Structural members jutted out all around and ahead I could see an old-style carrier shell, like a huge hexagonal nut, trailing umbilicals and docking tunnel connected to the curve of one bubble unit. Unseen, the grabship inserted my vessel into place and various clangs and crashes ensued.

'Okay, you can power up your airlock now – nothing else, mind.'

I did as instructed, watching the display as the airlock connected up to an exterior universal lock, then I headed back to scramble out through the *Ulriss Fire*'s airlock. The cramped interior of the carrier shell smelt of mould. I waited there holding onto the knurled rods of something that looked like a piece of zero-g exercise equipment, eyeing brownish splashes on the walls while a saucer-shaped scanning drone dropped down on a column and gave me the once-over, then I proceeded to the docking tunnel, which smelt of urine. Beside the final lock into the bubble unit was a payment console, into which I inserted the required amount in New Carth shillings. The lock opened to admit me and now I was of no further interest to station personnel. Others had come in like this. Some of their ships still remained docked, while others had been seized by those who owned the station to be broken for parts or sold on.

Clad in a coldsuit Jael trudged through a thin layer of $CO_2$ snow towards the gates of the Arena. Glancing to either side she eyed the numerous ships down on the granite plain. Other figures were trudging in from them too and a lucky few were flying towards the place in grav-cars. She'd considered pulling her trike out of storage, but it would have taken time to assemble and she didn't intend staying here any longer than necessary.

The entry arches – constructed of blocks of water ice as hard as iron at this temperature – were filled with the glimmering menisci of shimmer-shields, probably scavenged from the wreckage of ships floating about in the Graveyard, or maybe from the surface of one of the depopulated worlds. Reaching one of the arches, she pushed through a shield into a long anteroom into which all the arches debouched. The floor was flat granite cut with square spiral patterns for grip, and a line of airlock doors punctuated the inner wall. This whole set-up was provided for large crowds, which this place had never seen. Beside the airlock she approached was a teller machine of modern manufacture. She accessed it through her right-hand aug and made her payment electronically. The thick insulated lock door thumped open, belching vapour into the frigid air, that froze about her and fell as ice dust. Inside the lock the temperature rose rapidly. $CO_2$ ice ablated from her boots and clothing, and after checking the atmosphere reading down in the corner of her visor she retracted visor and hood back down into the collar of her suit.

Beyond the next door was a pillared hall containing a market. Strolling between the stalls she observed the usual tourist tat sold in such places in the Polity, and much else besides. There, under a plasmel dome, someone was selling weapons, and beyond his stall she could hear the hiss and crack of his wares being tested in a thick-walled shooting gallery. There a row of food vendors were serving everything from burgers to alien arthropods you ate while they were still alive and which apparently gave some kind of high. The smell of coffee wafted across, along with tobacco, cannabis and other more esoteric smokes.

All around the walls of the hall stairs wound up to other levels, some connecting above to the tunnels leading to the arena itself, others to the pens and others to private concerns. She knew where to go, but had some other business to conduct first with a dealer in biologicals. Anyway, she didn't want the man she had specifically come here to see to think she was in a hurry, or anxious to buy the item he had on offer.

The dealer's emporium was built between four pillars, three floors tall and reaching the ceiling. The lower floor was a display area with four entrances around the perimeter. She entered and looked around. Aisles cut to a central spiral stair between tanks, terrariums, cages, display cases and stock-search screens. She spotted a tank full of Spatterjay leeches, 'Immortality in a bite! Guaranteed!', a cage in which big scorpion-like insects were tearing into a mass of purple and green bones and meat, and a display containing little tubes of seeds below pictures of the plants they would produce. Mounting the stair she climbed to the next floor where two catadapts were studying something displayed on the screens of a nanoscope. They looked like customers, as did the thin woman who was peering into a cylindrical tank containing living Dracocorp augs. On the top floor Jael found who she was looking for.

The office was small, the rest of the floor obviously used for living accommodation. The woman with a severe skin complaint, baggy layered clothing and a tricorn hat sat back with heavy snow boots up on her desk, crusted fingers up against her aug while she peered at screens showing views of those on the floors below. She was nodding – obviously conducting some transaction or conversation by aug. Jael stepped into the room, plumped herself down in one of the form chairs opposite and waited. The woman glanced at her, smiled to expose a carnivore's teeth and held up one finger. Wait one moment.

Her business done, the woman took her feet off the desk and turned her chair so she was facing Jael.

'Well, what can I do for *you*?' she asked, utterly focused. 'Anything under any sun is our motto. We're also an agent for Dracocorp and are now also branching out into cosmetics.'

'Forgive me,' said Jael, 'if I note that you're not the best advert for the cosmetics.'

The woman leant an elbow on the table, reached up and peeled a thick dry flake of skin from her cheek. 'That's because you don't know what you're seeing. Once the change is complete my skin will be resistant to numerous acids and even to vacuum.'

'I'm here to sell,' said Jael.

The woman sat back, not quite so focused now. 'I see. Well, we're always prepared to take a look at what . . . people have to offer.'

Jael removed a small sample tube from her belt cache, placed it on the desk edge and rolled it across. The woman took it up, peered inside, a powerful lens clicking down from her hat to cover her eye.

'Interesting. What are they?'

Jael tapped a finger against her right-hand aug. 'This would be quicker.'

A message flashed across to her giving her a secure loading eddress. She transmitted the file she had compiled about the seeds gathered on that dusty little planet where she had obtained her real prize. The woman went blank for a few minutes while she ran through the data. Jael scanned around the room, wondering what security there was here.

'I think we can do business – once I've confirmed all this.'

'Please confirm away.'

The woman took the tube over to a combined

nanoscope and multispectrum scanner and inserted it inside.

Jael continued, 'But I don't want money, Desorla.'

Desorla froze, staring at the scope's display. After a moment she said, 'This all seems in order.' She paused, head bowed. 'I haven't heard that name in a long while.'

'I find things out,' said Jael.

Desorla turned and eyed the gun Jael now held. 'What do you want?'

'I want you to tell me where Penny Royal is hiding.'

Desorla chuckled unconvincingly. 'Looking for legends? You can't seriously—'

Jael aimed and fired three times. Two explosions blew cavities in the walls, a third explosion flung paper fragments from a shelf of books and a metallic tongue bleeding smoke slumped out from behind. Two cameras and the security drone – Jael had detected nothing else.

'I'm very serious,' said Jael. 'Please don't make me go get my doctor's bag.'

Broeven took one look at me and turned white – well, as pale as a Krodorman can get. He must have sent some sort of signal, because suddenly two heavies appeared out of the fug from behind him – one a boosted woman with the face of an angel and a large grey military aug affixed behind her ear, the other an ophidapt man who was making a point of extruding the carbide claws from his fingertips. The thin guy sitting opposite Broeven glanced round, then quickly drained his schooner of beer, took up a wallet from the table, nodded to Broeven and departed. I sauntered over, turned the abandoned chair round and sat astride it.

'You've moved up in the world,' I said, nodding to Broeven's protection.

'So what do I call you now?' he asked, the whorls in the thick skin of his face flushing red.

'Rho, which is actually my real name.'

'That's nice – we didn't get properly acquainted last time we met.' He held up a finger. 'Gene, get Rho a drink. Malt whisky do you?'

I nodded. The woman frowned in annoyance and departed. Perhaps she thought the chore beneath her.

'So what can I do for you, Rho?' he enquired.

'Information.'

'Which costs.'

'Of course.' I peered down at the object the guy here before me had left on the table. It was a small chainglass case containing a strip of chameleoncloth with three crab-shaped and, if they were real, gold buttons pinned to it. 'Are those real?'

'They are. People know better than to try cheating me now.'

I looked up. 'I never cheated you.'

'No, you promised not to open the outer airlock door if I told you what you wanted to know. My life in exchange for information and you stuck to your side of the deal. I can't say that makes me feel any better about it.'

'But you're a businessman,' I supplied.

'But I'm a businessman.'

The boosted woman returned carrying a bottle of ersatz malt and a tumbler which she slammed down on the table before me, before stepping back. I can't say I liked having her behind me. I reached down and carefully opened a belt pouch, feeling the tension notch up a bit. The ophidapt partially unfolded his arms and fully extended his claws. I took out a single blue stone and placed it next to the glass case. Broeven eyed the stone for a moment then picked it up between gnarled forefinger and thumb. He then produced a reader and placed the etched sapphire inside.

'Ten thousand,' he said. 'For what?'

'That's for services rendered – twenty-three years ago – and if you don't want to do further business with me, you keep it and I leave.'

He slipped the sapphire, and the glass case, into the inner pocket of his heavy coat, then sat upright, contemplating me. I thought for a moment he was going to get up and leave. Trying to remain casual I scanned around the interior of the bar and noticed it wasn't so full as I remembered it being and everyone seemed a bit subdued, conversations whispered and more furtive, no one getting shit-faced.

'Very well,' he said. 'What information do you require?'

'Two things: first I want everything you can track down about gabbleducks possibly in or near the Graveyard.' That got me a quizzical expression. 'And second I want everything you can give me about Jael Feogril's dealings over the last year or so.'

'A further ten thousand,' he said, and I read something spooked in his expression. I took out another sapphire and slid it across to him. He checked it with his reader and pocketed it before uttering another word.

'I'll give you two things.' He made a circular gesture with one finger. 'Jael Feogril might be dealing out of her league.'

'Go on.'

'*Them* . . . a light destroyer . . . Jael's ship docked with it briefly only a month ago, before departing. They're still out there.'

I realized then why it seemed so quiet in the bar and elsewhere in the station. The people here were those who hadn't run for cover, and were perhaps wishing they had. It was never the healthy option to remain in the vicinity of the Prador.

'And the second thing?'

'The location of the only gabbleduck in the Grave-yard, which I can give you without even doing any checking, since I've already given it to Jael Feogril.'

After he'd provided the information I headed away – I had enough to be going on with and, maybe, if I moved fast . . . I paused on my way back to my ship, seeing that Broeven's female heavy was walking along behind me, and turned to face her. She walked straight past me, saying, 'I'm not a fucking waitress.'

She seemed in an awful hurry.

On the stone floor two opponents faced off. Both were men, both were boosted. Jael wondered if people like them ever considered treatment for excessive testoster-one production. The bald-headed thug was unarmed and resting his hands on his knees as he caught his breath, twin-pupil eyes fixed on his opponent. The guy with the long queue of hair was also unarmed, though the plate-like lumps all over his overly muscled body were evidence of subcutaneous armour. After a moment they closed and began hammering at each other again, fists impact-ing with meaty snaps against flesh, blows blocked and diverted, the occasional kick slamming home, though neither man was really built for that kind of athleticism.

Inevitably, one of them was called 'Tank' – the one with the queue – and the other was called 'Norris'. These two had been hammering away at each other for twenty minutes to the growing racket from the audience, but whether that noise arose from the spectators' enjoyment of the show or because they wanted to get to the next event was debatable.

Eventually, after many scrappy encounters, Tank managed to deliver an axe kick to the side of Norris's head and laid him out. Tank, though the winner, needed to be helped from the arena too, obviously having over-extended himself with that last kick. Once the area was clear, the next event was announced and a gate opened somewhere below Jael. She observed a great furry muscular back and wide head as a giant mongoose shot out. The creature came to an abrupt stop in the middle of the arena and stood up to the height of a man on its hind quarters. Jael discarded her beer tube and stood, heading over towards the pens. The crowd were now shouting for one of the giant cobras the mongoose dispatched with utterly unamazing regularity. She wasn't really all that interested.

The doors down into the pens were guarded by a thug little different to those who had been in the ring below. He was there because previous security systems had often been breached and some of the fighters, animal, human or machine, had been nobbled.

'I'm here to see Koober,' said Jael.

The man eyed her for a moment. 'Jael Feogril,' he said, reaching back to open the door. 'Of course you are.'

Jael stepped warily past then descended the darkened stair.

Koober was operating a small electric forklift on the

tines of which rested the corpse of a seal. He raised a hand to her then motored forward to drop the load down into one of the pens. Jael stepped over and peered down at the ratty-looking polar bear that took hold of the corpse and dragged it back across ice to one corner, leaving a gory trail.

Koober, a thin hermaphrodite in much-repaired mesh-inlaid overalls, leapt down from the forklift and gestured. 'This way.' He led her down a stair into moist rancid corridors then finally to an armoured door he opened with a press of his hand against a palm lock. At the back of the circular chamber within, squatting in its own excrement, was the animal she had come to see – thick chains leading from a steel collar to secure it to the back wall.

A poor-looking specimen, about the size of a Terran black bear, its head was bowed low, the tip of its bill resting against the ground. Lying on the filthy stone beside it were the dismembered remains of something obviously grown hastily in a vat – weak splintered bones and watery flesh, tumours exposed like bunches of grapes. While Jael watched, the gabbleduck abruptly hissed and heaved its head upright. Its green eyes ran in an arc across its domed head, there were twelve or so of them: two large egg-shaped ones towards the centre, two narrow ones below these like underscores, two rows of small round ones arcing out to terminate against two triangular ones. They all had lids – the outer two blinking open and closed alternately. Its conjoined forelimbs were folded mummy-like across the raised cross-hatch ribbing of its chest, its gut was baggy and veined, and purple sores seeped in its brown-green skin.

'And precisely how much did you want for this?' enquired Jael disbelievingly.

'It's very rare,' said Koober. 'There's a restriction on export now and that's pushed prices up. You won't find any others inside the Graveyard, and those running wild on Polity worlds have mostly been tagged and are watched.'

'Why then are you selling it?'

Koober looked shifty – something he seemed better at doing than looking after the animals he provided for the arena. 'It's not suitable.'

'You mean it won't fight,' said Jael.

'Shunder-club froob,' said the gabbleduck, but its heart did not seem to be in it.

'All it does is sit there and do that. We put it up against the lion' – he pointed at some healing claw marks in its lower stomach – 'and it just sat there and started muttering to itself. The lion tried to jump out of the arena.'

Jael nodded to herself, then turned away. 'Not interested.'

'Wait!' Koober grabbed her arm. She caught his hand, turned it into a wrist lock forcing him down to his knees.

'Don't touch me.' She released him.

'If it's a matter of the price . . .'

'It's a matter of whether it will even survive long enough for you to get it aboard my ship, and even then I wonder how long it will survive for afterwards.'

'Look, I'll be taking a loss, but I'm sure we can work something out . . .'

Inside, Jael smiled. When the deal was finally struck she allowed that smile out, for even if the creature died she might well net a profit just selling its corpse. She had no intention of letting it die. The medical equipment and related gabbleduck physiology files aboard *Kobashi* should see to that, along with her small cargo of frozen Masadan grazers – the gabbleduck's favoured food.

I was feeling slightly pissed off when, after the interminable departure from Paris station, the grabship finally released *Ulriss Fire*. On the way out I'd seen another ship departing the station under its own power. It seemed that there were those for whom the rules did not apply, or those who knew who to bribe.

'Run system checks,' I instructed.

'Ooh, I never thought of that,' replied Ulriss.

'And there was I thinking AIs were beyond sarcasm.'

'It's a necessary tool used for communicating with a lower species,' replied the ship's AI. I still think it was annoyed that I wouldn't let it use the chameleonware.

'Take us under,' I said, ignoring the jibe.

Sudden acceleration pushed me back into my chair, and I felt, at some point deep inside my skull, the U-space engine come online. My perception distorted, the stars in the cockpit screen faded and the screen greyed out. It lasted maybe a few seconds, then *Ulriss Fire* shuddered like a ground car rolling over a mass of deep potholes, and a starry view flicked back into place.

'What the fuck happened?'

'Checking,' said Ulriss.

I began checking as well, noting that we'd travelled only about eighty million miles and had surfaced in the real in deep space. However, I was getting mass readings out there.

'We hit USER output,' Ulriss informed me.

I just sat there for a moment, racking my brains to try

and figure out what a 'user' was. I finally admitted defeat. 'I've no idea what you're talking about.'

'I see,' said Ulriss, in an irritatingly superior manner. 'The USER acronym stands for Underspace Inference Emitter—'

'Shouldn't that be UIE, then?'

'Do you want to know what a USER is, or would you rather I began using my sarcasm tool again?'

'Sorry, do carry on.'

'A USER is a device that shifts a singularity in and out of U-space via a runcible gate, thus creating a disturbance that knocks any ships that are within range out of that continuum. The USER here is a small one aboard the Polity dreadnought currently three thousand miles away from us. I don't think we were the target. I think that was the cruiser now coming up to port.'

With the skin crawling on my back, I took up the joystick and asserted positional control, nudging the ship round with a spurt of air from its attitude jets. Stars swung across the screen, then a large and ugly-looking vessel swung into view. It also looked like a flattened pear, but one stretched from a point on its circumference. It looked battered, its brassy exotic armour showing dents and burns that its memform and s-con grids had been unable to deal with, and which hadn't been repaired since. Missile ports and the mouths of railguns and beam weapons dotted that hull, but they looked perfectly serviceable. Ulriss had neglected to mention the word 'Prador' before the word 'cruiser'. This is what had everyone checking their online wills and talking in whispers back in Paris.

'Stealth mode?' suggested Ulriss, with a degree of smugness.

'Fucking right,' I replied.

The additional instruments came alight and a luminescent ribbing began to track across the screen before me. I wondered how good the chameleonware was, since maybe bad chameleonware would put us in even greater danger – the Prador suspecting some sort of attack if they detected us.

'And now if you could ease us away from that thing?'

The fusion drive stuttered randomly – a low-power note and firing format that wouldn't put out too-regular ionization. We fell away, the Prador cruiser thankfully receding, but now, coming into view, a Polity dreadnought. At one time the Prador vessel would have outclassed a larger Polity ship. It was an advantage the nasty aliens maintained throughout their initial attack during the war: exotic metal armour that could take a ridiculously intense pounding. Now Polity ships were armoured in a similar manner, and carried weapons and EM warfare techniques that could pierce to the core of Prador ships.

'What the hell is happening here?' I wondered.

'There is some communication occurring, but I cannot penetrate it.'

'Best guess?'

'Well, ECS does venture into the Graveyard, and it is still considered Polity territory. Maybe the Prador have been getting a little bit too pushy.'

I nodded to myself. Confrontations like these weren't that uncommon in the Graveyard, but this one was bloody inconvenient. While I waited something briefly blanked the screen. When it came back on again I observed a ball of light a few hundred miles out from the cruiser, shrinking rather than expanding, then winking out.

'CTD imploder,' Ulriss informed me.

I was obviously behind the times. I knew a CTD was an antimatter bomb, but an 'imploder'? I didn't ask.

After a little while the Prador ship's steering thrusters stabbed out into vacuum and ponderously turned it over, then its fusion engines flared to life and began taking it away.

'Is that USER still on?' I asked.

'It is.'

'Why? I don't see the point.'

'Maybe ECS is just trying to *make* a point.'

The USER continued functioning for a further five hours while the Prador ship departed. I almost got the feeling that those in the Polity dreadnought knew I was there and were deliberately delaying me. When it finally stopped, it took another hour before U-space had settled down enough for us to enter it without being flung out again. It had all been very frustrating.

People knew that if a ship was capable of travelling through U-space it required an AI to control its engines. Mawkishly they equated artificial intelligence with the godlike creations that controlled the Polity, somehow forgetting that colony ships with U-space engines were leaving the Solar System before the Quiet War, and before anyone saw anything like the silicon intelligences that were about now. The supposedly primitive Prador, who had nearly smashed the Polity, failed because they did not have AI, apparently. How then did they run the U-space engines in their ships? It came down, in the end, to the definition of AI – something that had been undergoing constant revision for centuries. The thing that controlled the engines in the *Kobashi*, Jael did not call an AI. She called it a 'control system', or sometimes a 'Prador control system'.

*Kobashi* surfaced from U-space on the edge of the Graveyard far from any sun. The coordinates Desorla had reluctantly supplied were constantly changing in relation to nearby stellar bodies, but checking her scanners Jael saw that they were correct, if this black planetoid – a wanderer between stars – was truly the location of Penny Royal. The planetoid was not much bigger than Earth's moon, was frigid, without atmosphere, and had not seen any volcanic activity quite possibly for billions of years. However, her scans did reveal a cannibalized ship resting on the surface and bonded-regolith tunnels winding away from it like worm casts to eventually disappear into the ground. She also measured EM output – energy usage – for signs of life. Positioning *Kobashi* geostationary above the other ship, she began sending signals.

'Penny Royal, I am Jael Feogril and I have come to buy your services. I know that the things you value are not the same as those valued by . . . others. If you assist me, you will gain access to an Atheter memstore, from which you may retain a recording.'

She did not repeat the message. Penny Royal would have seen her approach and been monitoring her constantly ever since. The thing called Penny Royal missed very little.

Eventually she got something back: landing coordinates – nothing else. She took *Kobashi* down, settling between two of those tunnels with the nose of her ship only fifty yards from the other ship's hull. Studying the other vessel she recognized a Polity destroyer, its sleek lines distorted, parts of it missing as if it had slowly been draining into the surrounding tunnels. After a moment she saw an irised airlock open. No message – the invitation was in front of her. Heading back into her quarters she donned an armoured spacesuit, took up her heavy pulse-rifle with its underslung mini-launcher, her sidearm and a selection of grenades. Likely the weapons would not be sufficient if Penny Royal launched some determined attack, but they might and that was enough of a reason. She resisted the impulse to go and check on the gabbleduck, but it was fine, its sores healed and flesh building up on its bones, its nonsensical statements much more emphatic.

Beyond *Kobashi* her boots crunched on a scree surface. Her suit's visor set to maximum light amplification, she peered down at a surface that seemed to consist entirely of loose flat hexagonal crystals like coins. They were a natural formation and nothing to do with this planetoid's resident. However, the thing that stabbed up through this layer nearby – like an eyeball impaled on a thin curved thorn of metal – certainly belonged to Penny Royal.

Jael finally stepped into the airlock, and noticed that the inner door was open too, so she would not be shedding her spacesuit. For no apparent reason other than to unnerve her, the first lock door swiftly closed once she was through. Within the ship she necessarily turned on her suit lights to complement the light amplification. The interior had been stripped right down to the hull members. All that Penny Royal had found no use for elsewhere lay in a heap to one side of the lock, perhaps ready to be thrown outside. The twenty or so crew members had been desiccated, hard vacuum freeze-drying and preserving them. They rested in a tangled pile like some nightmare monument. Jael noticed the pile consisted only of woody flesh and frangible bone. No clothing there, no augs, no jewellery. It occurred to her that Penny Royal had not thrown these corpses outside because the entity might yet find a use for them.

She scanned about herself, not quite sure where to go now. Across the body of the ship from her was the mouth of one of those tunnels, curving down into darkness. *There?* No, to her right the mouth of another tunnel emitted heat a little above the ambient. Stepping over hull beams she began to make her way towards it, then silvery tentacular fingers eased out around the lip of the tunnel and heaved out an object two yards across and seemingly formed by computer junk from the ship compressed into a sphere. Lights glimmered inside the tangle and it extruded antennae, and eyes like the one she had seen outside. Settling down it seemed to unravel slightly, whereupon a fleshless Golem unpeeled from its surface, stood upright and advanced a couple of paces, a thick-ribbed umbilicus still keeping it connected.

During the Prador–Human war it had been necessary to quickly manufacture the artificial intelligences occupying stations, ships and drones, for casualties were high. Quality control suffered and these intelligences, which in peacetime would have needed substantial adjustments, were sent to the front. As a matter of expediency, flawed crystal got used rather than discarded. Personality fragments were copied, sometimes not very well, successful fighters or tacticians recopied. The traits constructed or duplicated were not necessarily those evincing morality.

Some of these entities went rogue and became what were described as black AIs.

Like Penny Royal.

Standing at his shoulder the boosted woman, Gene, gave Koober the confidence to defy me. I'd already told him that I knew Jael had bought the gabbleduck from him, I just wanted to know if he knew anything else: who else she might have seen here, where she was going . . . anything really. I was equally curious to know how Broeven's ex-employee had ended up here. It struck me that this went beyond the bounds of coincidence.

'I don't have to tell you nothing, Sandman,' he said, using my old name with its double meaning.

'True, you don't,' I replied. I really hated how the scum I'd known twenty years ago all seemed to have floated to the top. 'Which is why I'm prepared to pay for what you can tell me.'

He glanced back at his protection, then crossed his arms. 'You were the big man once, but that ain't so now. I got my place here at the Arena and I got a good income. I don't even have to speak to you.' He unfolded his arms and waved a finger imperiously. 'Now piss off.'

Not only was he defiant, but stupid. The woman, no matter how vigilant, could not protect him from a seeker bullet or a pin coated with bone-eating nanite glued to a door handle. But I didn't do that sort of stuff now. I was retired. I carefully reached into my belt pouch and took out one of my remaining etched sapphires. I would throw it, and while the gem arced through the air towards Koober and the woman I reckoned on getting the drop on them. My pepperpot stun-gun was lodged in the back of my belt. Of course I'd take her down first. I tossed the gem and began to reach.

She moved. Koober went over her foot and was heading for the ground. The sapphire glimmered in the air still as the barrel of a pulse-gun centred on my forehead. I guess I was rusty, because I didn't even consider throwing myself aside. For a moment I just thought, *that's it,* but no field-accelerated pulse of aluminium dust blew my head apart. She caught the gem in her other hand and flipped it straight back at me. With my free hand I caught it, my other hand relaxing its grip on my gun and carefully easing out to one side, fingers spread.

'I believe my boss just told you to leave,' she said.

Koober was lying on the floor swearing, then he looked up and paused – only now realizing what had happened.

I nodded an acknowledgement to Gene, turned and quickly headed for the stair leading up from the pens, briefly glimpsed an oversized mongoose chewing on the remains of a huge snake on the arena floor, then set out towards the market where I might pick up more information. What the hell was a woman like her doing with a lowlife like Koober? It made no sense, and the coincidence of her being here just stretched things too far. I wondered if Broeven had sent her to try and cash in – guessing I was probably after something valuable. Such thoughts concerned me – that's my excuse. She came at me from a narrow side-tunnel. I only managed to turn a little before she grabbed me, spun me round and slammed me against the wall of the exit tunnel. I turned, and again found myself looking down the barrel of that pulse-gun. People around us quickly made themselves scarce.

'Koober had second thoughts about letting you go,' she said.

'Really?' I managed.

'He is a little slow, sometimes,' she opined. 'It occurred to him, once you were out of sight, that you might resent his treatment of you and come back to slip cyanide in his next soy-burger.'

'He's a vegetarian?'

'It's working with the animals – put him off meat.'

I watched her carefully, wondering why I was still alive. 'Are you going to kill me?'

'I haven't decided yet.'

'Have you ever killed anyone?'

'Many people, but in most cases the choice was theirs.'

'That's very moral of you.'

'So it would seem,' she agreed. 'Koober is shit-scared of you. Apparently you're a multiple murderer?'

'Hit man.'

'Murderer.'

*Ah*, I thought I knew what she was now.

'I think you know precisely who I am and what I was,' I said. 'Now I'm a xeno-archaeologist trying to track down stolen goods.'

'I stayed here too long,' she said distractedly, shaking her head. 'It was going to be my pleasure to shut Koober down.' She paused for a moment, considering. 'You should stay out of this, Rho. This has gone beyond you.'

'If you say so,' I said. 'You've got the gun.'

She lowered her weapon, then abruptly holstered it. 'If you don't believe me, then I suggest you go and see a dealer in biologicals called Desorla. Apparently Jael visited her before coming to see Koober, and their dealings involved Jael shooting out the cameras and security drones in Desorla's office.'

'Just biologicals?'

'Desorla has . . . connections.'

She moved away, and right then I felt no inclination to go after her. Maybe she was feeding me a line of bull-shit or maybe she was giving me the lead I needed. If not, I'd come back to the pen well prepared.

In the market one of the stallholders quickly directed me towards Desorla's emporium. I entered through one of the floor-level doors and found no activity inside. A spiral staircase led up, but a gate had been drawn across it and locked. I recognized the kind of lock immediately and set to work on it with the tools about my person. Like I said, I was rusty, it took me nearly thirty seconds to break the programs. I climbed up, scanned the next floor, then climbed higher still to the top floor.

The office was clean and empty, so I kicked in the flimsy door into the living accommodation. Nothing par-ticularly unusual here . . . then I saw the blood on the floor and the big glass bottle on her coffee table. Step-ping round the spatters I peered into the bottle, and in the crumpled and somewhat scabby pink mass inside a nightmare eyeless face peered out at me. Then something dripped on top of my head. I looked up . . .

Over by the window I caught my breath, but no one was giving me time for that. Arena security thugs were running towards the emporium and beyond them I could see Gene striding off towards the exit. I opened the window just as the thugs entered the building below me, did a combination of scramble and fall down the outside of the building and hit the stone flat on my back. I had to catch my breath then. After a moment I heaved myself upright and headed for the exit, closing up the visor and hood of my envirosuit and keeping Gene just in sight. I went fast through an airlock far to the left of her, and some paces ahead of her, and was soon running down counting arches. I drew my carbide knife and dropped down beside one arch, hoping I'd counted correctly.

She stepped out to my left. I knew I could not give her the slightest chance or she would take me down yet again. I drove the knife in to the side, cut down, grabbed and pulled. In a gout of icy fog her visor skittered across the stone. Choking, she staggered away from me, even then drawing her pulse-gun, which must have been cold-adapted. I drove a foot into her sternum, knocked the last of her air out. Pulse-gun shots tracked along the frigid stone past me and I brought the edge of my hand down on her wrist, cracking bone and knocking the weapon away. Her fist slammed into my ribs and her foot came up to nearly take my head off. Blind and suffocating she was the hardest opponent I'd faced hand-to-hand . . . or maybe it was that rustiness again. But she went down, eventually, and I dragged her to *Ulriss Fire* before anoxia killed her.

'Okay,' I said as she regained consciousness. 'What the fuck killed her?'

After a moment of peering at the webbing straps binding her into the chair, she said, 'You broke my wrist.'

'Talk to me and I'll let my autodoc work on it. You set me up, Gene. Is that your real name?'

She nodded absently, though whether that was in answer to my question I couldn't tell. 'I noticed you said "what" rather than "who".'

'A human who takes the trouble to skin someone alive and nail them to the ceiling without making a great deal more mess than that shouldn't be classified as a who. It's a thing.' I watched her carefully, – trying to read her. 'So maybe it was a thing . . . rogue Golem?'

'Rho Var Olssen, employed by ECS for wet ops outside the Line, a sort of one-man vengeance machine for the Polity who maybe started to like his job just a little too much. Who are you to righteously talk about classifications?'

'So you know about me. I had you typed when you insisted on calling me a murderer. Nothing quite so moralistic as an ECS agent working outside of her remit – helps to justify it all.'

'Fuck you.'

'Hit a nerve did I?' I paused, thinking that perhaps I was being a little naïve. She was baiting me to lead me away from the point. 'So it was a Golem that killed Desorla?'

'In a sense,' she admitted grudgingly. 'She was watched and she said too much – to Jael, specifically.'

'Tell me more about Jael.'

Staring at me woodenly she said, 'What's to tell? We knew her interest in ancient technology and we knew she kept a careful eye on people like you. We put something in the way of your sifter and made sure she found out about it.'

I felt hollow. 'The memstore . . . it's a fake?'

'No, it's the real thing, Rho. It had to be.'

I thought about me lying on the floor of my home with a rock hammer embedded in my skull. 'I could have died.'

'An acceptable level of collateral damage in an operation like this,' she said flatly.

I thought about that for one brief horrible moment.

Really, there were many people on many worlds trying to find Atheter artefacts, but how many of them were like me? How many of them were so *inconvenient*? I imagined this was why some AI had reckoned my life an 'acceptable level of collateral damage'.

'And what is this operation?' I finally asked. 'Are you out to nail Prador?'

She laughed.

'I guess not,' I said.

'You worked out what Jael was doing yourself. I don't know how . . .' She gazed at me for a moment but I wasn't going to help her out. She continued, 'If she can restore the mind to a gabbleduck she has an item to sell to the Prador that will net her more wealth than even she would know how to spend. But there's a problem: you don't just feed the memstore to the gabbleduck, you're not even going to be able to jury-rig some kind of link-up using aug technology. That memstore is complex alien tech loaded in a language few can understand.'

'She needs an AI . . . or something close . . .'

'On the button, but though some AIs might venture outside Polity law as we see it, there are certain lines even they won't cross. Handing over a living Atheter to the Prador is well over those lines.'

'A Prador AI, then.'

'The only ones they have are in their ships – their purpose utterly fixed, and hard-worked. They don't have the flexibility.'

'So what the fuck—'

'Ever heard of Penny Royal?' she interrupted.

I felt a surge of almost superstitious dread. 'You have got to be shitting me.'

'No shit, Rho. You can see this is out of your league. We're done here.'

'You put some kind of tracer in the memstore.'

She gave me a patronizing smile. 'Too small. We needed U-tech.'

Suddenly I got the idea. 'You put it in the gabbleduck.'

'We did.' She stared at me for a long moment, then continued resignedly, 'The signal remains constant, giving a Polity ship in the Graveyard the creature's location from moment to moment. The moment the gabbleduck is connected to the memstore, the signal shuts down, then we'll know that Penny Royal has control of both creature and store, and then the big guns move in. This is over, Rho. Can't you see that? You've played your part and now the game has moved as far beyond you as it has moved beyond me. It's time for us both to go home.'

'No,' I said. I guessed she didn't understand how being tortured, then nearly killed, had really ticked me off. 'It's time for you to tell me how to find Jael. I've still got a score to settle with her.'

Jael did not like being this close to Golem. Either they were highly moral creatures who served the Polity and would not look kindly on her actions, and who were thoroughly capable of doing something about them, or they were the rare amoral/immoral kind, and capable of doing something really nasty. No question here – the thing crammed in beside her in the airlock was a killer, or rather, it was a remote probe, a submind that was part of a killer. As she understood it, Penny Royal had these submind Golem scattered throughout the Graveyard, often contributing to the title of the place.

After the lock pressurized, the inner door opened to admit them into the *Kobashi*. While Jael removed her spacesuit the Golem just stood to one side – a static silver skeleton with hardware in its ribcage, cybermotors at its joints and interlinked down its spine, and blue-irised eyeballs in the sockets of its skull. She wondered if it had willingly subjected itself to Penny Royal's will or been taken over. Probably the latter.

'This way,' she said to it once she was ready, and led the way back towards the ship's hold. Behind her the Golem followed with a clatter of metallic feet. Why did it no longer wear syntheflesh and skin? Just to make it more menacing? She wasn't sure Penny Royal was that interested in interacting with people. Maybe the usual Golem coverings just didn't last in this environment.

At her aug command a bulkhead door thumped open and she paused beside it to don a breather mask before stepping through into an area caged off from the rest of the hold. The air within was low in oxygen and would slowly suffocate a human, but having it mix with the rest of the air in the ship while this door was open wasn't a problem, as the pressure differential pushed the ship air into here. The briefly higher oxygen levels would not harm the hold's occupant, since its body was rugged enough to survive a range of environments – probably its kind was engineered that way long ago. Beyond the caged area in which they stood, the floor was layered a foot deep with flute-grass rhizomes – as soggy underfoot as sphagnum. The walls displayed Masadan scenery overlaid with bars so the occupant didn't make the mistake of trying to run off through them. Masadan wildlife sounds filled the air and there were even empty tricone shells on the rhizome mat for further authenticity.

The gabbleduck looked a great deal more alert and a lot healthier than when Koober owned it. As always when she entered the cage, it was squatting in one corner. Other than via the cameras in here she had seen it do nothing else. It was as if, every time she approached, it heard her and moved to that corner, which should not have been possible since the bulkhead door was thoroughly insulated.

'Subject appears adequate,' said the Golem. 'It will be necessary to move it into the complex for installation.'

'Gruvver fleeg purnok,' said the gabbleduck dismissively.

'The phonetic similarity of the gabble to human language has always been puzzling,' said the Golem.

'Right,' said Jael. 'The memstore?' She gestured to the door and the Golem obligingly moved out ahead of her.

She overtook the Golem in the annex to the main airlock, opened another bulkhead door and led the way into her living area. Here she paused. 'Before I show you this next item, there are one or two things we need to agree.' She turned and faced the Golem. 'The gabbleduck and the memstore must go no deeper into your complex than half a mile.'

The Golem just stared at her, waiting, not asking the question a human would have asked. It annoyed Jael that Penny Royal probably understood her reasoning and it annoyed her further that she still felt the need to explain. 'That keeps it within the effective blast radius of my ship. If I die, or if you try to take from me the gabbleduck or the memstore, I can aug a signal back here to start up the U-space engine, the field inverted and ten degrees out of phase. The detonation would excise a fair chunk of this planetoid.'

The Golem just said, 'The AI here is of Prador manufacture.'

'It is.'

'My payment will be a recording of the Atheter memstore, and a recording of the Prador AI.'

'That seems . . . reasonable, though you'll receive the recording of the Prador AI just before I leave.' She didn't want Penny Royal to have time to work out how to crack her ship's security.

At that moment, the same Prador AI – without speaking – alerted her to activity outside the ship. Using her augs she inspected an external view from the ship's cameras. One of the tunnel tubes, its mouth filled with some grublike machine, was advancing towards *Kobashi*.

'What's going on outside?' she asked politely.

'I presume you have no spacesuit for the gabbleduck?'

'Ah.'

Despite her threat, Jael knew she wasn't fully in control here. She stepped up to one wall, via her aug commanding a safe to open. A steel bung a foot across eased out then hinged to one side. She reached in, picked up the memstore, then held it out to the Golem. The test would come, she felt certain, when Penny Royal authenticated that small item.

The Golem took the memstore between its finger and thumb, and she noticed it had retained the syntheflesh pads of its fingers. It paused, frozen in place, then abruptly its ribcage split down the centre and one half of it hinged aside. Within lay optics, the grey lump of a power supply and various interconnected units like steel organs. There were also dark masses spread like multi-armed starfish that Jael suspected had not been there when this Golem was originally constructed. It pressed the memstore into the centre of one of these masses, which writhed as if in pain and closed over it.

'Unrecognized programming format,' said the Golem.

*No shit,* thought Jael.

The Golem continued, 'Estimate at one hundred and twenty gigabytes, synaptic mapping and chronology of implantation . . .'

Jael felt a sudden foreboding. Though measuring a human mind in bytes wasn't particularly accurate, the best guesstimate actually lay in the range of a few hundred megabytes, so this memstore was an order of magnitude larger. But then, her assumption and that of those who had found it was that the memstore encompassed the life of one Atheter. This was not necessarily the case. Maybe the memories and mind maps of a thousand Atheter were stored in that little chunk of technology.

Finally the Golem straightened up, reached inside its chest and removed the memplant, passing it back to Jael. 'We will begin when the tunnel connects,' it said. 'How will you move the gabbleduck?'

'Easy enough,' said Jael, and went to find her tranquillizer gun.


Ulriss woke me with a 'Rise and shine, the game's afoot . . . well, in a couple of hours – the signal is no longer dopplering so Jael's ship is back in the real.'

I lay there blinking at the ceiling as the lights gradually came up, then pushed back the heat sheet, heaved myself over the edge of the bunk and dropped to the floor. I staggered, feeling slightly dizzy, my limbs leaden. It always takes me a little while to get functional after sleep, hence the two-hour warning from Ulriss. After a moment, I turned to peer at Gene, who lay slumbering in the lower bunk.

'Integrity of the collar?' I enquired.

'She hasn't touched it,' the ship AI replied, 'though she did try to persuade me to release her by appealing to my sense of loyalty to the organization that brought me into being.'

'And your reply?'

'Whilst no right-thinking AI wants the Prador to get their hands on a living Atheter or one of their memstores, your intent to retrieve that store and by proxy carry out a sentence already passed on Jael Feogril should prevent rather than facilitate that. Polity plans will be hampered should you succeed, but beside moral obligations I am a free agent and Penny Royal's survival or otherwise is a matter of indifference to me. Should you fail, however, your death will not hamper Polity plans.'

'Hey thanks – it's nice to know you care.'

Sleepily, from the lower bunk, Gene said, 'You're rather sensitive for someone who was once described as a walking abattoir.'

'Ah,' I said, 'so you're frightened of me. That's why you gave me the coding of that U-space signal?'

She pushed back her blanket and sat up. She'd stripped down to a thin singlet and I found the sight rather distracting, as I suspect was the intention. Reaching up she fingered the metal collar around her neck. 'Of course I'm frightened – you've got control of this collar.'

'Which will inject you with a short-duration paralytic, not blow your head off as I earlier suggested,' I replied.

She nodded. 'You also suggested that if I didn't tell you what you wanted to know you would demonstrate on me the kind of things Jael did to you.'

'I've never tortured anyone,' I said, before remembering that she'd read my ECS record. 'Well . . . not anyone
that didn't deserve it.'

'You would have used drugs, and the other techniques
Jael used on you.'

'True,' I nodded, 'but I didn't need to.' I gazed at her.
'I think you've been involved in this operation for a while
and rather resent not being in at the kill. I was your
opportunity to change that. I understand – in the past I
ended up in similar situations myself.'

'Yes, you liked to be in at the kill,' she said, and
stooped down to pick up her clothing from where she
had abandoned it on the floor – she'd sacked out after
me, which had been okay as soon as I put the collar on
her since Ulriss had been watching her constantly.

I grunted and went off to find a triple espresso.

After a breakfast of bacon, eggs, mushroom steak and
beans (the first two having no connection with pigs or
chickens), a litre of grapenut juice and more coffee, I
reached the stage of being able to walk through doors
without bouncing off the doorjamb. Gene ate a mega-
prawn steak, drank a similar quantity of the same juice,
and copious quantities of white tea. I thought I might try
her breakfast next time I used stores or the synthesizer.
Supposing there would be a next time – only a few minutes
remained before we surfaced from U-space. Genc followed
me into the cockpit and sat in the co-pilot's chair, which
was about as redundant as the pilot's chair I sat in, with
the AI Ulriss running the ship.

We surfaced. The screen briefly showed stars, then
banding began to travel across it. I glanced at the additional controls for chameleonware and saw that they had
been activated.

'Ulriss—'

'Jael's ship is down on the surface of a free-roaming planetoid next to an old vessel that seems to have been stripped and from which bonded-regolith tunnels have spread.'

'So Penny Royal is there and might see us,' I supplied.

'True,' Ulriss replied, but that was not my first concern. The view on the screen swung across, magnified and switched to light amplification, bringing to the fore the planetoid itself and the Prador cruiser in orbit around it.

'Oh shit,' I opined.

We watched the cruiser as, using that stuttering burn of the fusion engine, Ulriss took us closer to the planetoid. Luckily there had been no reaction from the Prador ship to our arrival, and as we drew closer I saw a shuttle detach and begin heading down.

'I wonder if this is part of Jael's plan,' I said. 'I would have thought she'd get the memstore loaded then meet the Prador in some less vulnerable situation.'

'Agreed,' said Gene through gritted teeth. She glanced across at me. 'What do you intend to do?'

'I intend to land.' I adjusted to screen controls to give me a view of Jael's ship, the one next to it, and the surrounding spread of pipe-like tunnels. 'She's probably in there somewhere with the memstore and the gabble-duck. Shouldn't be a problem getting inside.'

We watched the shuttle continue its descent and the subsequent flare of its thrusters as it decelerated over the network of tunnels.

'It could get . . . somewhat fraught down there. Do you have weapons?' Gene asked.

'I have weapons.'

The Prador shuttle was now landing next to Jael's vessel.

'Let me come in with you,' said Gene.

I didn't answer for a while. I just watched. Five Prador clad in armoured spacesuits and obviously armed to the mandibles departed the shuttle. They went over to one of the tunnels and gathered there. I focused in closer in time to see them move back to get clear of an explosion. It seemed apparent that they weren't there at either Jael's or Penny Royal's invitation.

'Of course you can come,' I said, eventually.

Jael frowned at the distant sound of the explosion and the roar of atmosphere being sucked out – the latter sound abruptly truncated as some emergency door closed. There seemed only one explanation: the Prador had placed a tracker on the *Kobashi* when she had gone to meet them.

'Can you deal with them?' she asked.

'I can deal with them,' Penny Royal replied through its submind Golem.

The AI itself continued working. Before Jael the gabbleduck was stretched upright, steel bands around its body and a framework clamping its head immovably. It kept reaching up with one of its foreclaws to probe and tug at the framework, but being heavily tranquillized it soon lost interest, lowered its limb and began muttering to itself.

From this point, equipment – control systems, an atmosphere plant and heaters, stacked processing racks, transformers and other items obviously taken from the ship above – spread in every direction and seemed chaotic-ally connected by optics and heavy-duty superconducting cables. Some of these snaked into one of the surrounding tunnels where she guessed the ship's fusion reactor lay. Lighting squares inset in the ceiling illuminated the whole scene. She wondered if Penny Royal had put this all together after her arrival. It seemed possible, for the AI, working amidst all this like an iron squid, moved at a speed almost difficult to follow. Finally the AI moved closer to the gabbleduck, fitting into one side of the clamping framework a silver beetle of a ship's autodoc, which trailed optics to the surrounding equipment.

'The memstore,' said Penny Royal, a ribbed tentacle with a spatulate end snapping out to hover just before Jael's chest.

'What about the Prador?' she asked. 'Shouldn't we deal with them first?'

Two of the numerous eyes protruding on stalks from the AI's body flicked towards the Golem, which abruptly stepped forward, grabbed a hold in that main body, then merged. In that moment Jael saw that it was one of many clinging there.

'They have entered my tunnels and approach,' the AI replied.

It occurred to her then that Penny Royal's previous answer of 'I can deal with them' was open to numerous interpretations.

'Are you going to stop them coming here?' she asked.

'No.'

'They will try to take the memstore and the gabbleduck.'

'That is not proven.'

'They'll attack you.'

'That is not proven.'

Jael's frustration grew. 'Very well.' She unslung her

combined pulse-rifle and launcher. 'You are not unintelligent, but you seem to have forgotten about the instructions I left for the *Kobashi* on departing. Those Prador will try to take what is mine without paying for it, and I will try to stop them. If I die, the *Kobashi* detonates and we all die.'

'Your ship will not detonate.'

'What?'

'I broke your codes two point five seconds after you began using them upon departing your ship. Your ship AI is of Prador construction, its basis the frozen brain tissue of a Prador first-child. The Prador have never understood that no code is unbreakable and your ship AI is no different. It would appear that you are no different.'

Another boom and the thunderous roar of atmosphere departing reached them. Penny Royal quivered, a number of its eyes turning towards one tunnel mouth.

'However,' it said with a heavy resignation, 'these Prador are showing a marked lack of concern for my property, and I do not want them interrupting this interesting commission.' Abruptly the Golem began to peel themselves from Penny Royal's core, five of them in all, until what was left was a spiny skeletal thing. Dropping to the floor they detached their umbilici and scuttled away. Jael shuddered – they moved without any emulation of humanity, sometimes on all fours, but fast, horribly fast. They also carried devices she could not clearly identify. She did not suppose their purpose to be anything pleasant.

'Now,' said Penny Royal, snapping the spatulate end of its tentacle open and closed, 'the memstore.'

Jael reached into her belt cache, took out the store and handed it over. The tentacle retracted and she lost it in a blur of movement. Items of equipment shifted and a transformer began humming. The autodoc pressed its underside against the gabbleduck's domed head and closed its gleaming metallic limbs around it. She heard a snickering, swiftly followed by the sound of a bone drill. The gabbleduck jerked and reached up. Tentacles sped in and snaked around its limbs, clamping them in place.

'Wharfle klummer,' said the gabbleduck, with an almost frightening clarity.

Jael scanned around the chamber. Over to her right, across the chamber from the tunnel mouth Penny Royal had earlier glanced at – the one it seemed likely the Prador would be coming from if they made it this far – was a stack of internal walling and structural members from the cannibalized ship. She headed over, ready to duck for cover, and from there watched the AI carry out its commission.

How long would it take? She had no idea but it seemed likely to not take long. Now the autodoc would be making nanotube synaptic connections in line with a program the AI had constructed from the cerebral schematic in the memstore, it would be firing off electrical impulses and feeding in precise mixes of neuro-chemicals – all the stuff of memory, thought, mind. Already the gabbleduck seemed straighter, its pose more serious, its eyes taking on a cold metallic glitter. Or was she just seeing what she hoped for?

'Klummer wharfle,' it said. Wasn't that one of those frustrating things for the linguists who studied the gabble, that no single gabbleduck had ever repeated its meaningless words? 'Klummer klummer,' it continued. 'Wharfle.'

'Base synaptic network established,' said Penny Royal.
'Loading at one quarter – layered format.'

Jael wasn't sure what that meant, but it sounded like
the AI was succeeding. Then, abruptly, the gabbleduck
made a chittering, whistling clicking sound, some of the
whistles so intense they seemed to stab straight in behind
Jael's eyes. Something else happened: a couple of optic
cables started smoking, then abruptly shrivelled, a processing rack slumped, something like molten glass
poured out and hissed on the cold stone. After a moment
Penny Royal released its grip upon the creature's claws.

'Loading complete.'

After a two-tone buzzing Jael recognized as the sound
of bone and cell welders working together, the autodoc
retracted. The gabbleduck reached up and scratched its
head. It made that sound again, and after a moment
Penny Royal replied in kind. The creature shrugged and
all its bonds folded away. It dropped to the floor and
squatted like some evil Buddha. It did not look in the
least bit foolish.

'They chose insentience,' said Penny Royal, 'and put
in place the means of retaining that state, in U-space,
constructed there before they sacrificed their minds.'

'And what does that mean?' Jael asked.

Three stalked eyes swivelled towards her. 'It means,
human, that in resurrecting me you fucked up big time
– now, go away.'

She wondered how it had happened: when Penny
Royal copied the memstore, or through some leakage
during the loading process. There must have been a
hidden virus or worm in the store.

Suddenly, both the gabbleduck and Penny Royal were
enclosed in some kind of bubble. It shifted slightly, and

where it intersected any of the surrounding equipment, sheared clean through. Within, something protruded out of nothingness like the peak of a mountain – hints of vastness beyond. Ripples, like those in sunlit water, travelled down to the tip, where they ignited a dull glow that grew brighter with each succeeding ripple.

Jael, always prepared to grab the main chance, also possessed a sharply honed instinct for survival. She turned and ran for the nearest tunnel mouth.

'Something serious happened in there,' I said, looking at the readings Ulriss had transmitted to me on my helmet display.

'Something?' Gene enquired.

'All sorts of energy surges and various U-space signatures.' I read the text Ulriss had also transmitted – text since a vocal message, either real-time or in a package, would have extended the transmission time and given Penny Royal more of a chance of intercepting it and breaking the code. 'It seems that just before those surges and signatures the U-signal from the gabbleduck changed. They've installed the contents of the mem-store . . . how long before the Polity dreadnought gets here?'

'It isn't far away – it should be able to jump here in a matter of minutes.'

'Then what happens?'

'They either bomb this place from orbit or send down an assault team.'

'You can't be more precise than that?'

'I would guess the latter. ECS will want to retrieve the gabbleduck.'

'Why? It's just an animal.'

I could see her shaking her head within her suit's helmet. 'Gabbleducks are Atheter even though they've forgone intelligence. Apparently, now Masada is part of the Polity, they are to receive the same protections as Polity citizens.'

'Right.' I began tramping through the curiously shaped shale towards the hole the Prador had blown in one of Penny Royal's pipes. The protections Polity citizens received were on the basis of the greatest good for the greatest number. If a citizen needed to die so ECS could take out a black AI, I suspected that citizen would die. A sensible course would have been to retreat to *Ulriss Fire* and then retreat from this planetoid, however, human Polity citizens numbered in the trillions and the gabbleduck population was just in the millions. Polity AIs would be quite prepared to expend a few human lives to retrieve the creature.

'Convert to text packet for ship AI,' I said. 'Ulriss, when that dreadnought gets here, tell it that we're down here and that Penny Royal doesn't look likely to be escaping so maybe it can hold off on the planet busters.'

After a moment, I received an acknowledgement from Ulriss, then I stepped into the gloom of the pipe and looked around. To my right the tunnel led back towards the cannibalized ship. According to the energy readings the party was to my left and down below. I upped light amplification then said, 'Weapons online' – a phrase shortly repeated by Gene.

My multigun suddenly became light as air as suit assister motors kicked in. Cross hairs appeared on my visor, shifted from side to side as I swung the gun across. A menu down one side gave me a selection of firing modes: laser, particle beam and a list of projectiles

ranging from inert to high explosive. 'Laser,' I told the
gun, because I thought we might have to cut our way in
at some point, and it obliged by showing me a bar graph
of energy available. I could alter numerous other settings
to the beam itself, but the preset had always been the
best. Then I added, 'Auto-response to attack.' Now, if
anyone started shooting at me, the gun would take control of my suit motors to aim and fire itself at the
aggressor. I imagined Gene was setting her weapon up
to operate in the same manner, though with whatever
other settings she happened to be accustomed to.

The tunnel curved round and then began to slope
down. In a little while we reached an area where debris
was scattered across the floor, this including an almost
intact hermetically sealing cargo door. Ahead were the
remains of the wall out of which it had been blown. I
guess the Prador had found the cargo door too small for
them, either that, or had started blowing things up to
attract attention. The Prador were never ones to tap
gently and ask if anyone was in. We stepped through the
rubble and moved on.

The pipe began to slope down even more steeply and
we both had to turn on the gecko function of our boot
soles. Obviously this was not a tunnel made for humans.
Noting the scars in the walls I wondered just precisely
what it had been made for. What did Penny Royal look
like anyway? Slowly, out of the darkness ahead resolved
another wall with a large airlock in it. No damage here.
Either the Prador felt they had made their point or this
lock had simply been big enough to admit them. I went
over and gazed at the controls – they were dead, but there
was a manual handle available. I hauled on it, but got
nowhere until upping the power of my suit motors. I

crunched the handle over and pulled the door open.
Gene and I stepped inside. Vapour fogged around us
from a leak through the interior door. I pulled the outer
closed then opened the inner, and we stepped through
into the aftermath of a battle that seemed to have moved
on, because distantly I could hear explosions, the thunderous racket of rail-guns and the sawing sound of a
particle cannon.

The place beyond was expanded like a section of
intestine and curved off to our right. A web of support
beams laced all the way around, even across the floor.
Items of machinery were positioned here and there in
this network, connected by s-con cables and optics. I recognized two fusion reactors of the kind I knew did not
come from the stripped vessel above and wondered if it
was just one in a series so treated. In a gap in the web of
floor beams, an armoured Prador second-child seemed
to have been forced sideways halfway into the stone, its
legs and claw on the visible side sticking upwards. It was
only when I saw the glistening green spread around it
that I realized I was seeing half a Prador lying on the
stone on its point of division. Tracking a trail of green
ichor across I saw the other half jammed between the
wall beams.

'Interesting,' said Gene.

It certainly was. If something down here had a weapon
that could slice through Prador armour like that – there
was no sign of burning – then our armoured suits would
be no defence at all. We moved out, boots back to gecko
function as like tightrope walkers we balanced on beams.
With us in so precarious a position this was a perfect time
for another Prador second-child to come hurtling round
the corner ahead.

The moment I saw the creature, my multigun took command of my suit motors and tracked. I squatted to retain balance, said, 'Off auto, off gecko,' then jumped down to the floor. Gene was there before me. Yeah – rusty. The second-child was emitting a ululating squeal and moving fast, its multiple legs clattering down on the beams so it careened along like a gravcar flown by a maniac. I noticed that a few of its legs were missing, along with one claw, and that only a single palp-eye stood erect, directed back towards whatever pursued it. On its underside it gripped in its manipulator hands a nasty rail-gun. It slammed to a halt, gripping beams, then fired, the smashing clattering racket painful to hear as the gun sprayed out an almost solid line of projectiles. I looked beyond the creature and saw the sparks and flying metal tracking along the ceiling and down one wall, but never quite intersecting with the path of something silvery. That silvery thing closed in, its course weaving. It disappeared behind one of the reactors and I winced as rail-gun missiles spanged off the housing leaving a deep trail of dents. The thing shot out from under the reactor, zigged and zagged, was upon the Prador in a second, then past.

The firing ceased.

The Prador's eye swivelled round then dipped. The creature reached tentatively with its claw to its underside. It shuddered, then with a pulsing spray of green ichor, ponderously slid into two halves.

I began scanning round for whatever had done this.

'Over there,' said Gene quietly, over suit com. I looked where she was pointing and saw a skeletal Golem clinging to a beam with its legs. It was swaying back and forth, one hand rubbing over its bare ceramal skull, the other hanging down with some gourd-shaped metallic object enclosing it. Easing up my multigun I centred the cross hairs over it and told the gun, 'Acquire. Particle beam, continuous fire, full power,' and wondered if that would be enough.

The Golem heard me, or it detected us by some other means. Its head snapped round a full hundred and eighty degrees and it stared at us. After a moment its head revolved slowly back as if indifferent. It hauled itself up and set off back the way it had come. My heart continued hammering even as it moved out of sight.

'Penny Royal?' I wondered.

'Part of Penny Royal,' Gene supplied. 'It was probably one like that who nailed Desorla to her ceiling.'

'Charming.'

We began to move on, but suddenly *everything* shuddered. On some unstable worlds I'd experienced earthquakes, and this felt much the same. I'd also been on worlds that had undergone orbital bombardment.

'Convert to text packet for ship AI,' I said. 'Ulriss, what the fuck was that?'

Ulriss replied almost instantly, 'Some kind of gravity phenomena centred on the gabbleduck's location.'

At least the Polity hadn't arrived and started bombing us. We moved on towards the sound of battle, pausing for a moment before going round a tangled mass of beams in which lay the remains of another second-child and a scattering of silvery disconnected bones. I counted two Golem skulls and was glad this was a fight I'd missed. Puffs of dust began lifting from the structures around us, along with curls of a light metal swarf. I realized a breeze had started and was growing stronger, which likely meant that somewhere there was

an atmosphere breach. Now, ahead, arc light was flaring
in accompaniment to the sound of the particle cannon.
The wide tunnel ended against a huge space – some
chamber beyond. The brief glimpse of a second-child
firing upwards with its rail-gun, and the purple flash of
the particle weapon told us this was where it was all
happening.

*Bad choice*, thought Jael as she ducked down behind a
yard-wide pipe through which some sort of fluid was
gurgling. A wind was tugging at her cropped hair, blowing into the chamber ahead where the action seemed to
be centred. She unhooked her spacesuit helmet from her
belt and put it on, dogged it down, then ducked under
the pipe and crawled forward hugging the wall.

The first-child had backed into a recess in the chamber wall to her right, a second-child crouched before it.
The three Golem were playing hide-and-seek amidst the
scattered machinery and webworks of beams. Ceiling
beams had been severed, some still glowing and dripping
molten metal. There was a chainglass observatory dome
above, some kind of optical telescope hanging in gimbals
below it. An oxygen fire was burning behind an atmosphere plant – an eight-foot pillar wrapped in pipes and
topped with scrubber intakes and air-output funnels.
The smoke from this blaze rose up into a spiral swirl then
stabbed straight to a point in the ceiling just below the
observatory dome, where it was being sucked out.
Around this breach beetlebots scurried like spit bugs in
a growing mass of foamstone.

The other second-child, emitting a siren squeal as it
scurried here and there blasting away at the Golem, had
obviously been sent out as a decoy – a ploy that worked

when, sacrificing two of its legs and a chunk of its carapace, it lured out one of the Golem. The first-child's right
claw snapped out and Jael saw that the tip of one jaw of
it was missing. From this an instantly recognizable
turquoise beam stabbed across the chamber and nailed
the Golem centre on. Its body vaporized, arms, legs and
skull clattering down. One arm with the hand enclosed
by some sort of weapon fell quite close to Jael and near
its point of impact a beam parted on a diagonal slice.
Some kind of atomic shear, she supposed.

Watching this action, Jael was not entirely sure which
side she wanted to win. If the Prador took out the two
remaining Golem they would then go after the Atheter
in the chamber behind her. Maybe they would just ignore
her, maybe they would kill her out of hand. If the Golem
finished off the Prador they might then turn their attention on her. And she really did not know what to expect
from whatever now controlled them. Retreating and
finding some other way out was not an option – she had
already scanned Penny Royal's network of tunnels and
knew that any other route back to *Kobashi* would require
a diversion of some miles, and she rather suspected that
thing back there would not give her the time.

The decoy second-child lucked out with the next
Golem, or rather it lucked out with its elder kin. Firing
its rail-gun into the gap between a spherical electric
furnace and the wall, where one of the Golem was
crouching, the second-child advanced. The Golem shot
out underneath the furnace towards the Prador child. A
turquoise bar stabbed out, nailing the Golem, but it
passed through the second-child on the way. An oily
explosion centred on a mass of legs collapsed out of
sight. The first-child used its other claw to nudge out its

final sibling into play. The remaining Golem, however, which Jael had earlier seen on the far side of the room, dropped down from above to land between them.

It happened almost too fast to follow. The Golem spun, and in a spray of green the second-child slid in half along a diagonal cut straight through its body. The first-child's claw and half its armoured visual turret and enclosing visor fell away. Its fluids fountained out as it fell forward, swung its remaining claw and bore down. The Golem collapsed, pinned to the floor under the claw containing the particle weapon. A turquoise explosion followed underneath the collapsing Prador, then oily flames belched out.

Jael remained where she was, watching carefully. She scanned around the chamber, but there seemed no sign of any more of those horrible Golem. The Prador just lay there, its legs sprawled, its weaponized claw trapped underneath it, its now-exposed mandibles grinding, ichor still flowing from the huge excision from its visual turret. Jael realized she couldn't have hoped for a better outcome. After a moment she stepped out, her weapon trained on the Prador.

'Jael Feogril,' its translator intoned, and it began scrabbling to try and get some purchase on the slick floor.

'That's me,' said Jael, and fired two explosive rounds straight into its mouth. The two detonations weren't enough to break open the Prador's enclosing artificial armour, but their force escaped. Torn flesh, organs, ichor and shattered carapace gushed from the hole the Golem had cut. Jael stood there for a moment, hardly able to see through the green sludge on her visor. She peered down at something like a chunk of liver hanging over her arm, and pulled it away. Yes, a satisfactory outcome, apart from the mess.

'Jael Feogril,' said a different voice. 'Drop the gun, or I cut off your legs.'

I was telling myself at the time that I needed detail on the location of the memstore. Rubbish, of course. The energy readings had located it in the chamber beyond – somewhere close to the gabbleduck. I should have just fried her on the spot then gone on to search. Twenty years earlier I would have, but now I was less tuned in to the exigencies of surviving this sort of game. Okay, I was rusty. She froze, seemed about to turn, then thought better of it and dropped the weapon she'd just used to splash that Prador.

With Gene walking out to my left I moved forward, cross hairs centred on Jael's torso. What did I want? Some grandstanding, some satisfaction in seeing her shock at meeting someone she'd left for dead, a moment or two to gloat before I did to her what she had done to the first-child? Yeah, sure I did.

With her hands held out from her body she turned. It annoyed me that I couldn't see her face. Glancing up I saw that the beetlebots had about closed off the hole, because the earlier wind had now diminished to a breeze.

'Take off your helmet,' I ordered.

She reached up and undogged the manual outer clips, lifted the helmet carefully then lowered it to clip it to her belt. Pointless move – she wouldn't be needing it again. Glancing aside I saw that Gene had moved in closer to me. No need to cover me now, I guessed.

'Well hello, Rho,' said Jael, showing absolutely no surprise on seeing me at all. She smiled. It was that smile, the same smile I had seen from her while she had peeled strips of skin from my torso.

'Goodbye, Jael,' I said.

The flicker of a high-intensity laser punched smoke, something slapped my multigun and molten metal sprayed leaving white trails written across the air.

'Total malfunction. Safe mode – power down,' my helmet display informed me. I pulled the trigger anyway, then gazed down in bewilderment at the slagged hole through the weapon.

'Mine, I think,' said Jael. In one smooth movement she stooped, picked up her weapon and fired it. Same explosive shell she'd used against the Prador. It thumped into my chest, hurling me back, then detonated as it ricocheted away. The blast flung me up, trailing flame and smoke, then I crashed down feeling as if I'd been stepped on by some irate giant. My chainglass visor was gone and something was sizzling ominously inside my suit. Armoured plates were peeled up from my arm, which I could see stretched out ahead of me, and my gauntlet was missing.

'What the fuck are you doing here with him?' Jael enquired angrily.

'He turned up on Arena before I left,' Gene replied. 'Just to be on the safe side I was keeping to the Pens until Penny Royal's Golem left.'

'And you consider that an adequate explanation?'

'I put Arena Security onto him, but he somehow escaped them and ambushed me outside.' Gene sounded somewhat chagrined. 'I let him persuade me to give him the U-signal code from the gabbleduck.'

I turned my head slightly but only got a view of

tangled metal and a few silver Golem bones. 'Ulriss,' I whispered, but received only a slight buzzing in response.

'So much for your wonderful ECS training.'

'It was enough to convince him that I still worked for them.'

So, no ECS action here, no Polity dreadnought on the way. I thought about that encounter I'd seen between the Prador cruiser and the dreadnought. I'd told Gene about it and she'd used the information against me, convincing me that the Polity was involved. Of course, what I'd seen was the kind of sabre-rattling confrontation between Prador and Polity that had been going on in the Grave-yard for years.

'What's the situation here?' Gene asked.

'Fucked,' Jael replied. 'Something's intervened. We have to get out of here now.'

I heard the sounds of movement. They were going away, so I might survive this. Then the sounds ceased too abruptly.

'You used an explosive shell,' Gene noted from close by.

'What?'

'He's still alive.'

'Well,' said Jael, 'that's a problem soon solved.'

Her boots crunched on the floor as she approached, and gave me her location. I reached out with my bare hand and slid it into slick silvery metal. Finger controls there. I clamped down on them and saw something shimmering deep into twisted metal.

'Collar!' I said, more in hope than expectation, before heaving myself upright.

Jael stood over me, and beyond her I saw Gene reach up towards her neck then abruptly drop to the floor. I swung my arm across as Jael began to bring her multi-gun up to her shoulder. A slight tug – that was all. She stood there a moment longer, still aiming at me, then her head lifted and fell back, attached still at the back of her neck by skin only, and a red stream shot upwards. Air hissing from her severed trachea, she toppled.

I carefully lifted my fingers from the controls of the Golem weapon, then caught my breath, only now feeling as if someone had worked me over from head to foot with a baseball bat. Slowly climbing to my feet I expected to feel the pain of a broken bone somewhere, but there was nothing like that. No need to check on Jael's condition, so I walked over to Gene. She was unconscious and would be for some time. I stooped over her and unplugged the power cable and control optics of her weapon from her suit, then plugged them in to mine. No response and of course no visor read-out. I set the weapon to manual and turned away. I decided that once I'd retrieved the memstore – if that was possible – I would come back in here and take her suit, because mine certainly would not get me to *Ulriss Fire*.

The hum of power and the feeling of distorted perception associated with U-jumping greeted me. I don't know what that thing was poised over the gabbleduck, nor did I know what kind of force-field surrounded it and that other entity that seemed the bastard offspring of a sea urchin and an octopus. But the poised thing was fading, and as it finally disappeared, the field winked out and numerous objects crashed to the floor.

I moved forward, used the snout of my weapon to lift one tentacle, and then watched it flop back. *Penny Royal*, I guessed. It was slumped across the floor beams and other machinery here. The gabbleduck turned its head as if noticing me for the first time, but it showed no particular signs of hostility, nor did it seem to show any signs of it containing some formidable alien intelligence. I felt sure the experiment here had failed, or rather, had been curtailed in some way. *Something's intervened,* Jael had said. Nevertheless, I kept my attention focused on the creature as I searched for and finally found the memstore. It was fried but I pocketed it anyway, for it *was* my find, not something ECS had put in the path of my sifting machine.

Returning to the other chamber, I stripped Gene of her spacesuit and donned it myself. I wasn't concerned about whether she lived or died.

'Ulriss, we can talk now.'

'Ah, you *are* still alive,' the AI replied. 'I was already composing your obituary.'

'You're just a bundle of laughs, you know that?'

'I am bursting with curiosity and try to hide that in levity.'

I explained the situation, to which Ulriss replied, 'I have put out a call to the Polity dreadnought we sighted and given it this location.'

'Should we hang around?'

'There will be questions ECS will want to ask, but I don't see why we should put ourselves at their disposal. Let their agents find us.'

'Quite right,' I replied.

I bagged up a few items, like that Golem weapon, and was about to head back to my ship when I glanced back and saw the gabbleduck crouching in the tunnel behind.

'Sherber grodge,' it informed me.

Heading back the way I'd come into this hell-hole I kept checking back on the thing. Gabbleducks don't eat people, apparently – they just chew them up and spit them out. This one followed me like a lost puppy. Every time I stopped it stopped too and sat on its hindquarters, occasionally issuing some nonsensical statement. I got the real weird feeling, which went against all my training and experience, that this creature was harmless to me. I shook my head. Ridiculous. Anyway, I'd lose it at the airlock.

When I did finally reach the airlock and began closing that inner door, one big black claw closed around the edge and pulled it open again. I raised my gun, cross hairs targeting that array of eyes, but I could not pull the trigger. The gabbleduck entered the airlock and just sat there, close enough to touch and close enough for me to fry if it went for me. What now? If I opened the outer airlock door the creature would die. Before I could think what to do, a multi-jointed arm reached back and heaved the inner door closed, whilst the other arm hauled up the manual handle of the outer door, and the lock air pressure blew us staggering into the pipe beyond.

I discovered that gabbleducks can survive in vacuum . . . or at least this one could.

Later, when I ordered Ulriss to open the door to the small hold of my ship, the gabbleduck waddled meekly inside. I thought then that perhaps something from the memstore had stuck. I wasn't sure – certainly this gabbleduck was not behaving like its kind on Masada.

I also discovered that gabbleducks will eat raw recon bacon.

I hold the fried memstore and think about what it might have contained, and what the fact of its existence means. A memstore for an Atheter mind goes contrary to the supposed nihilism of that race. A race so nihilistic could never have created a space-faring civilization, so that darkness must have spread amidst them in their last days. The Atheter recorded in the memstore could not have been one of the kind that wanted to destroy itself, surely?

I'm taking the gabbleduck back to Masada – I feel utterly certain now that it wants me to do this. I also feel certain that to do otherwise might not be a good idea.

# 6

# ACEPHALOUS DREAMS

Having no head, or one reduced, indistinct, as certain insect larvae . . . Such things he considered as the pool spread to his foot and melded round the rubber sole of his boot. He would leave distinctive footprints: Devnon Macroboots, fifty-seven New Carth shillings a pair; they were only sold from one place and there was not much of a turnover in them. Carth was somewhat off the tourist route, religious fanaticism not being much of a draw in such enlightened times.

*No resistance at all.*

Daes stepped back from the pool and walked slowly round the corpse – the grub – his right boot leaving a bloody ribbed imprint and the incomplete DEV at each step. He was not a tall man, Daes, and his weightlifter's physique made him appear shorter. He was exceptionally physically strong, and this strength had been sufficient to drive the carbide-edged machete through the flesh, bone and gristle of Anton Velsten's neck. No resistance. The machete had not even slowed, and Daes had not even felt a tug. The head, Anton's head, had not tumbled away spouting blood as it would have in most holodramas. It had remained balanced on Anton's neck,

displaced by only a fraction, unmoved by the hydraulic
pressure of the blood that spurted out sideways until the
head became fully detached when Anton, unstrung
puppet fashion, collapsed to the floor in the shroud of
his priestly robes.

Daes smiled to himself when he reached a position
giving him clear sight of the severed neck. There was
always plenty of blood flowing in the holodramas, but
they did not often show this sort of thing: in the pool of
blood there was a second immiscible pool of well-chewed
Carthian prawns, special fried rice, that piquant sauce
they made at the Lotus Garden, and bile. Sniffing and
wrinkling his nose, Daes was also made aware that Anton
had emptied his bowels in his last moments.

'Are you with your god now, Anton?' Daes asked. The
bowl of night over the roof-port made his voice sound
flat and meaningless as it drank his words. Daes surveyed
the ranked gravcars for any sign of movement, any sign
that he had been observed, but there seemed to be none
of either. It was late and the faithful were always early to
bed and early to rise. Witnesses were not a requirement
though, and few people got away with murder. He
dropped the machete onto the corpse, turned, stooped,
and picked up Anton's head. It was surprisingly heavy.
Holding it by the dark blood-soaked hair Daes studied
Anton's face. Nothing there. In death terror had fled and
all that remained was the expression etched there by
Anton's vicious and debauched life. Daes dropped the
head into the bag he had stolen from a ten-pin bowling
alley – perfect for the task, waterproof too – then he
squatted down by the corpse.

'All done, but for one last sign,' he said.

Reaching out, he dipped his finger in blood and drew

on the ground a figure '8' turned on its side. It was the sign for infinity, but meant so much else to him. He then took up the bag and headed for his own gravcar, quickly stepped inside, and with the turbines at their quietest and slowest, lifted the car from the roof.

Eight hours maximum. The corpse was sure to be discovered in the next two hours. Fingerprints and DNA would be identified at the scene within the following hour, and access to runcible transport denied directly after. He reckoned the search would first be centred at the runcible facility. They would expect him to try to get off planet, to one of the Line worlds – expected it of any murderer. He smiled to himself as he directed his cleverly stolen Ford Nevada gravcar out of the city and away from the facility, to a glow on the horizon that was not where the sun rose.

It was a place where godless Carthians came with mylar glide wings to have fun in the thermals above the volcano. This activity was frowned on by the Theocracy and attempts had been made to ban the sport, but the Theocracy only had power over those who voluntarily subjugated themselves to it. Polity law ruled on Carth and the monitors of Earth Central were never far away. With the Ford set on hover, Daes opened the door and dropped the bowling bag and its grisly contents into the caldera. As a necessity he was very high up and only able to discern a pinprick, near subliminal in its brevity, as the head struck the lava and incinerated.

'Resurrect the fucker now,' said Daes, and wondered if he might be going insane. Perhaps a plea of insanity . . . no, he felt completely and utterly sane, as always. When they finally caught him he would be tried with all fairness and sympathy. His memories would be read by an

AI; his life rolled out, dissected, and completely understood by a mind quite capable of such. What made him
what he was would be discovered, recorded, and perhaps
be the subject of lengthy study. He would be gone by
the time that study reached any conclusions; taken to a
disintegrator and in less than a second converted into
a pool of organic sludge and flushed into the Carthian
ocean for the delectation of its plankton. There was a
kind of poetry to such an ending. Daes didn't like
poetry. He closed the door of the Ford, his eyes watering
from the sulphur fumes, then turned the vehicle back
towards the city.

'Do you want to live?'

The Golem Twenty-seven that had entered his cell
was only identifiable as an android by her deliberately
flawed perfection. The artificial skin and flesh of her right
arm was transparent and through it Daes could see her
gleaming ceramal bones, the cybermotors at her joints,
and the tangles of optic cables. Otherwise she was completely beautiful; a blonde-haired teenager with wide
amber eyes and a pertly nubile body clothed in a short
silk toga. Daes remained on his bunk and waited for her
to continue.

'Very well,' she said, and turned to go.

Daes sat up. 'Wait, wait a minute. Of course I want to
live.'

She turned. 'Then please be civil enough to reply
when I ask a question.'

'Okay. Okay.' Daes waved her to a seat.

She sat and smiled briefly at him before continuing.
'Your memcording has been analysed and those memories you attempted to conceal have been revealed and

intensively studied. We even know why you drew the sign for infinity beside his body.'

Daes stared at her – he had not expected this.

She continued. 'Yet, despite the years of abuse you suffered at the hands of Anton Velsten while in the theocratic college, you are still considered sane and culpable, simply because you could have later reported him and had him sent for readjustment.'

'I preferred how I readjusted him.'

'Apparently.'

'And so, nothing can stop me going to the disintegrator,' said Daes.

'The intervention of the AI Geronamid can.'

Daes shivered at the mention of the name. Geronamid was the sector AI. What the hell interest would it have in a minor criminal like himself?

'Why would Geronamid want to get involved?'

'AI Geronamid has need of a subject for a scientific trial. This trial may kill you, in which case it would be considered completion of sentence. Should you survive, all charges against you will be dropped.'

'And the nature of this trial?'

'Cephalic implantation of Csorian node.'

'Okay, I agree, though I have no idea what Csorian node is.'

The Golem stood and as she did so the door slid open. Daes glanced up at the security eye in the corner of the cell and stood also. She nodded to the door and he followed her out. In the corridor a couple of policemen glared at him with ill-concealed annoyance but showed no reaction beyond that. Outside the station she led him to a sleek gravcar styled after one of the twenty-second-century electric cars. He thought, briefly, about escape, but knew he stood no chance. His companion might look like a teenage girl but she was strong enough to rip him in half. Once they were seated in the gravcar it took off without her touching the controls and sped away at a speed well above the limit. He wondered if some minuscule part of Geronamid was controlling it.

'You didn't tell me. What's a Csorian node?'

'If we knew that with any certainty we would not be carrying out this trial,' replied the Golem.

'You know it's some sort of implant.'

'We do, but only because it was found in the body of a Csorian.'

'A Csorian has been found?'

'Oh yes, underneath the ruins on Wilder. The body is about a hundred thousand years old. The node was attached to its hindbrain.'

Daes turned that over in his mind. The Csorians were one of the three dead stellar races: the Jain and the Atheter being the other two. They supposedly died out a hundred thousand years before the human race had set out for the stars. All that remained of their civilizations were a few ruins of coraline buildings and the descendants of those plants and creatures to survive from their biotechnology.

'It was one of the last of them then,' he said.

'Yes.'

He considered for a moment before going on. 'Surely Geronamid should have been able to work out what this node is.'

'Perhaps he has. Who can tell?'

Daes noted that the gravcar was well above the traffic lanes and still rising. He heard the door seals lock down and wondered where the hell they were going. When he turned to the Golem to ask her, he saw that she had called up something on the screen. Here was a creature much like a praying mantis only without the long winged abdomen. From the back of its thorax extended a ribbed tail that branched into three. At the branch point was a pronounced thickening from which grew a second pair of insectile legs.

'It was about a metre long. We think the hindbrain had something to do with reproduction,' said the Golem.

'That's a Csorian?' asked Daes.

'It is. We are reasonably sure that their society was much like that of the social insects of Earth; wasps, ants, hornets and the like.'

'They had hive minds just the same?'

'This is what we suppose.'

Daes smiled to himself. It had come as one shock in many when arrogant humanity had discovered it wasn't the only sentient race on Earth, it was just the loudest and most destructive. Dolphins and whales had always been candidates because of their aesthetic appeal and stories of rescued swimmers. Research in that area had soon cleared things up: Dolphins couldn't tell the difference between a human swimmer and a sick fellow, and were substantially more stupid than the animal humans had been turning into pork on a regular basis. Whales had the intelligence of the average cow. When a hornet built its nest in a VR suit and lodged its protests on the Internet it had taken a long time for anyone to believe. They were stinging things, creepy crawlies, how could they possibly be intelligent? At ten thousand years of age the youngest hive mind showed them. People believed.

'So a hive mind got into space long before we did. I find that gratifying to hear,' said Daes.

The Golem gazed at him speculatively. 'Your misanthropy is well understood. You do realize that if you'd had it corrected you would not be in the situation you are now in.'

'I liked my dislike of humanity. It kept me sane.'

'Very amusing,' said the Golem, turning back to the screen. The picture she now called up was of a small ovoid with complex mottling on its surface. Daes noted it, then gazed through the windows and saw the sky becoming dark blue and stars beginning to show. The planet had now receded. He pushed his face to the window to try and get a look down at it and saw only a shuttle glinting like a discarded needle far below.

'This is the node. We know that it contains picotech and likely biofactured connections to its host's brain. We first thought it some kind of augmentation.'

'Well that seems the most likely,' said Daes, turning back.

'Yes, but this node is three centimetres long, two wide and has a density twice that of lead.'

'So?'

The Golem looked at him. 'Every cubic nanometre of it is packed with picotech. Under scan we have so far managed to identify two billion picomachines with the ability to self-replicate. They also all cross-reference. There is a complexity here that is beyond even Geronamid's ability.'

There was a sound, slightly like a groan, from within the workings of the gravcar. Daes felt the artificial gravity come on and when he gazed out the windows now saw nothing but starlit space. As he turned to fire another question at the Golem his seat slapped him lightly on his back and the gravcar surged towards a distant speck. He decided to be annoyed.

'Am I supposed to be impressed by all this?'

'No,' said the Golem. 'You are just supposed to be thankful that you are still alive.'

Daes grimaced and peered ahead at the speck as it drew closer. 'When can I speak to Geronamid?'

The Golem looked at him.

'Ah,' he said. 'You never told me your name.'

'It is my conceit to name this part of myself Hera,' said a very small part of the AI Geronamid.

The speck resolved into a flat disc of a ship whose size did not become evident until they drew very close. What Daes had first taken to be panoramic windows set in the side of the vessel soon resolved into bay doors the size of city blocks. The ship had to be at least two kilometres in diameter.

'This is where you are,' said Daes.

'Yes, the central mind is here,' replied Hera.

The bay doors drew aside and the gravcar sped in then landed on a wide expanse of gridded bay floor. The moment the doors closed behind there came a boom of wind as atmosphere was restored in the bay. The car's seals automatically disengaged and Geronamid's Golem opened her door. Daes quickly opened his door and followed.

'Is the node here?' he asked as they approached a dropshaft.

'It is, as are the remains of the Csorian, and much of their recovered technology.'

They stepped into the irised gravity field and it dropped them down into the ship. Ten floors down they stepped out into a wide chamber filled with old-style museum display cases. Hera led him past an aquarium containing corals in pastel shades of every colour, past a tank containing plants that bore translucent fruit like lumps of amber, a case containing pieces of coral with something like circuitry etched or grown on their inner faces. She brought him finally to the tank containing the remains of the Csorian – whole and almost lifelike.

'It wasn't in this condition surely?' he said.

'No, only four per cent of it was recoverable.'

'What about DNA?'

'Scraps only. Not enough to build up a large enough template.'

'AIs did it with dinosaurs.'

'In that case there was more material to work with. What is in this case is all we have of the Csorians . . . Here, this is what we have come to see.'

She led him past the Csorian to a small bell jar over a jade pedestal. Underneath the jar lay the node – in appearance a simple pebble. Daes stepped closer. As he did so he felt a slight displacement, a sense of dislocation, and from this he knew that the ship was on the move.

'Where are we going?'

'A living world without sentient life. You must be isolated while the node does whatever it does.'

'What?' Daes turned to her to protest. Her hand moved so fast he hardly registered it moving. Fingertips brushed his neck and from that point he felt his body turning to lead.

'Don't worry. I'll be with you,' said Hera, as he slipped into darkness.

*

Something huge was poised on the edge of his being, not inimical, but dangerous and vast and ready to drown him out of existence. Anton was a small and insignificant thing on the ground at his feet even though armies were marching out of his severed neck. Daes decided to laugh and leap into the sky, and this being his wish he did so, for he knew this was a dream. When he woke, though, that huge something was still there.

'How do you feel?' asked Hera.

Daes opened his eyes and stared at the domed ceiling. He turned his head aside and saw the Golem sitting in a form chair beside the sofa he lay upon. They were in a comfortably furnished house of some kind. Greenish light filtered in through the wide windows.

'Where are we?' he asked.

'The world only has a number.'

'I thought you said this was uninhabited,' said Daes, sitting up and studying their surroundings.

'Geronamid prepared this place for you some time ago,' said Hera.

'For me?'

'Well, for the next person under a death sentence when it decided to implant the node.'

'I was lucky that time occurred when it did.'

'Yes, five seconds later and someone else would have been chosen.'

Daes stood and stretched his neck. 'It's in me then?'

'Yes, you will not know it is there until the picotech starts to work.'

'And when will that be?'

'We do not know. It is not working at the moment, though.'

'How can you be sure of that?'

'I am taking readings from numerous detectors implanted in your body.'

'I didn't give permission for that,' said Daes.

Hera shrugged. 'To put in a suitable parlance,' she said, 'tough.'

Daes stared at her for a long moment. It was all perfectly clear to him: Geronamid could do with him what it liked now.

'What do I do while I wait for this node to . . . activate?'

'Explore, sleep, eat, all those things you would not be doing had your sentence been passed either five seconds later or earlier.'

'Do you need to continually remind me?'

'Yes, it would seem that I do.'

Without responding to that Daes turned and walked to the window. He gazed out at a wall of jungle twenty metres away. The intervening area had been scorched to grey ash, but even there the ground was scattered with reddish-green sprouts, and fungi like blue peas. A bewildering surge of feeling hit him: he wanted to be out there, to drive his fingers into the black earth, and to see and feel growing things.

'You say that picotech isn't working yet?' he said.

When Hera did not reply he turned to her.

'No, I *said* it wasn't working, now I *say* that something is happening,' she replied.

Daes swallowed a sudden surge of fear. What the hell was he doing here? He should have gone to the disintegrator. At least that would have been clean and quick, and right now he would know nothing, feel nothing.

'What's happening?'

'I do not know,' said Hera. 'The node is reduced in

size and picomachines are diffusing through your body. What they are doing will become evident in time.'

Daes pressed his hands against the thick glass of the window, and noted that the skin on the backs of them was peeling.

'I want to go outside,' he said.

The air was frigid in his mouth. He had expected it to be warm and humid.

'This equates to the Jurassic period on Earth,' said Hera.

'How do you work out that equation then?' Daes asked sarcastically.

'Quite simply really. The ecosystems have not evolved to the complexity of mutualism between species.'

'And that means?'

'No flowers and no pollinators. The equations are more complex than that, obviously, but my explanation stands.'

'You mean it will do for a stupid human like me,' said Daes. 'Why the hell is it so damned cold? This looked like jungle from in there.'

'It is jungle, and for this place it is unseasonably hot.'

'Couldn't you have chosen a warmer planet?'

'I don't know.'

'What the hell is that supposed to mean? You are Geronamid.'

'I am a part, and now a separate part.'

Daes turned to study her, then damned himself for a fool. If she gave anything away in her expression that would be because she wanted to. It was so easy to forget what she was.

'Why?' he asked.

'Because my direct link has been severed, it being possible to use such a link for direct informational attack on Geronamid itself. This planet is in quarantine for the duration of this trial. The only link we do have is a com-link to a second isolated submind of Geronamid's in orbit.'

'Is Geronamid that scared then?'

'Cautious, I think would be a better term.'

Daes turned away from her and regarded the cold jungle. There was a path of sorts, probably beaten by one of the AI's machines. He headed for it, ash caking his boots, and little fungi bursting all around where he stepped. The vegetation on either side of the path sprouted from thick cycad bodies and bore a hard and sharp look. On the slimy root-bound ground scuttled arthropods like skeletons' hands, which he watched hunting long black beetles that sobbed piteously when caught and eaten alive. He had gone only ten metres into the jungle when he suddenly felt sick and dizzy. He went down on his knees and before he knew what he was doing he was pushing his fingers into the black and sticky earth. Immediately his dizziness receded and he suddenly found himself gazing about himself with vast clarity of vision. On the bole of a scaled trunk nearby he observed an insect bearing the shape of a legged stiletto with a head in which eye-pits glinted like flecks of emerald. Then he found himself gazing up the bole of the tree; vegetation looming above him. Then he was feeling his way along the ground with a familiar heat shape ahead of him. He leapt on it before it could escape and bit down and sucked with relish, filling himself but never assuaging the constant hunger. Then . . . then he was back.

'What the hell is happening to me?' he said, blinking

to clear strange visions from his eyes as he stared into the jungle.

'You would be the best one to answer that question,' said Hera. 'Tell me what you are feeling.'

Daes stumbled to his feet and turned back towards the residence Geronamid had provided. He saw now that it was one of those instant fold-out homes used by ECS for refugees and the like. It seemed sanctuary indeed for him.

'I want to go back,' he said, walking quickly towards it.

'What happened?' Hera asked, quickly moving to his side.

Daes gestured to the creatures that swarmed on the jungle floor. 'I saw through their eyes, and when they didn't have eyes, I felt what they felt.' He stepped through the door that opened for him and moved to a sink unit before one of the panoramic windows. Resting his hands on the composite he saw that the skin on the back of them had ceased to peel, but when he lifted those hands up to inspect them more closely he saw that his palms left, along with the black mud, white smears on the edge of the sink. He was about to say something about this to Hera when he saw that the smears were fading. Also, something bulked behind his eyes and he felt himself almost stooping under its weight. Involuntarily he turned and surveyed the room. Centring on the Golem he strode towards her and grasped her transparent wrist, and of course she easily pulled away. Now she held up her arm and observed the white smear on her wrist as it faded.

'Picotech leeching from your body. Outside it—'

Hera froze and Daes found himself gazing out of her

eyes at himself. He lifted her arms and opened and closed her hand, sensing as he did so the surge of optic information packages and diffusing electrons in her solid-state core. And he understood it all.

'—was obviously sending out probes to sample and test its environment.'

He was back in himself as Hera paused. She tilted her head.

'By my internal clock I can only presume I went offline for fourteen seconds.' She looked at Daes queryingly. But he had no reply, for now he was closely studying and understanding the workings of his own mind – taking apart all his memories and all his motivations and sucking up every dreg of information it was possible to find. A flower he had seen as a child, named as an adolescent, and found dried and pressed in the pages of a book in the theocratic college library, was tracked in all its incarnations through his life as a straight line of information. And there were millions of these lines. He felt an analytical interest whenever he encountered anything in his mind that related to the Csorians, and anything related to the prehistory of Earth. At the last he experienced the bleed-over of alien memory, and its huge logic and utterly cold understanding terrified him. Then suddenly it was all over and he was standing in a room, on a planet, being watched by a Golem android.

'I know what the node is,' he said to Hera.


Anton Velsten never sneered. He left that to the others, just as, in the end, he left it to them to hold Daes across the table. That he used a gel on Daes's anus was not indicative of any concern for the boy. Velsten just found it more pleasurable that way, and less likely for him to hurt himself. When the others took their turns, Velsten stepped back and gave a running commentary – his voice devoid of emotion.

'And Pandel is at the gate. And he's in and getting up to speed. Oh dear, Pandel loses it in the first ten metres. What's this? What's this? Damar is leading with a head . . .'

So it went on, and when they were all done, Anton scrawled the sign of infinity on Daes's forehead, with Daes's own semen-diluted shit.

The others who watched, beyond this room and beyond this incarnation, dissected every increment of every moment and understood the event utterly. They saw that it was the culmination of Velsten's power game. Of course Velsten had to die at Daes's hand. The shame could not be admitted – the shame of being unable to fight. How could he expose those memories to AI inspection? Then there was vengeance, and that was oh so sweet.

'Hello, Anton,' said Daes, strolling from his gravcar out towards the man.

Velsten was tall, and with his mild 'I am listening to you' expression, and dressed as he was in his flowing robes, he was – it could not be avoided – priestly. He halted and regarded Daes estimatingly before moving his hands into a supplicating gesture, perhaps to apologize and explain about pressing business.

'You don't even recognize me, do you?' Daes asked.

Velsten now put on the pose of deep thoughtfulness as he watched Daes come to stand before him.

'I feel we have met,' said Anton, pressing his hands together as if in prayer. 'But I'm afraid I have a terrible memory for names and in my ministry I meet so many people. What was it? Amand? Damar?'

'I was one of the first to receive your ministry, Anton,' said Daes.

Velsten now started to become really concerned.

'I'm so sorry, but as pleasant as this meeting is I do have pressing business,' he said turning away.

'It's remiss of you not to remember someone you buggered, Anton.'

Velsten froze, and slowly turned back. The transformation in his expression surprised even Daes. Now Velsten gazed at Daes with superiority as he folded his arms. He nodded his head as he no doubt wondered what to do with this inconvenient little roach.

'Daes,' he said, and sighed.

Daes watched him for a moment then he unzipped the bag he had stolen from the bowling alley and took out the machete. Velsten's expression changed to one of contempt.

'Do you really think you would get away with using that?' he asked.

'Oh no, you wrong me. I don't expect to get away with this. I don't really care.'

Velsten's expression changed once again and his fear showed. He held out his hand as if to push Daes away. Daes swung the machete across and the hand thumped to the plascrete a couple of metres away. Velsten stared at his jetting wrist and made a strangled whining sound before capping his other hand over it.

'That probably doesn't even hurt yet, and it won't get a chance to,' said Daes, relishing the expression of horror on Velsten's face. He stepped in and pirouetted with the machete and for one strange instant thought he had

missed, that was until he once again faced Velsten. The
man was a statue for a moment, before blood jetted out
sideways from his neck, then he went over, his head
separating from his body as he fell.

*No resistance at all.*

Daes inspected his hands for the nth time and saw that
there was absolutely nothing wrong with them. Now,
when he touched objects, he left no white smear. He
reached out for his coffee cup, took it up, and sipped.

'Restful night?' Hera enquired.

'Not really. I had some very strange dreams when I
wasn't being woken by those weird noises. What the hell
was that?' said Daes.

'It doesn't have a name as yet. It's a large arthropod
that deposits its egg-sacs high in the trees. It is apparently a painful process,' Hera replied.

'Apparently.' Daes sipped some more coffee and wondered at the Golem's seeming impatience. All emulation,
but it did need to know.

'You said you knew what the node is,' said Hera.
'Then, having grabbed my attention, you claimed great
weariness and just had to go to bed.'

'That is very true.'

'Perhaps, now you are rested, you can tell me what
you know.'

Daes shook his head. 'Sorry, can't do that.'

'Why?'

'Because *I* cannot.' By stressing the personal pronoun
he hoped Hera would really get the picture. There were
things he simply could not do and things he could not
say. That his mind had been reformatted he had no
doubt, but he was not too upset by this. There were the

things he could do . . . Looking out of the window he surged up high and gazed out through a cluster of eyes at spiky treetops. Scanning round he found another example of the creature he had hunted, clinging to a flower spike like an upright bunch of giant blue grapes. This creature was a white spider with a dagger of a body and mouthparts that appeared complex enough to dismantle a computer . . . and put it back together again. It clung with those mouthparts as its body heaved and strained and dripped transparent sacs on the foliage. The creature he was in could not hear the sounds the one in view nor itself made, but through other ears he could hear the hootings and raspings. Fleeing on with his awareness he found it diffusing into an ice-crusted sea in which finned silver footballs fed on air-plant sprouts of weed.

'Will you ever be able to tell?' Hera asked.

An island chain revealed to him multilegged creatures like the skeletal spider-things, but these possessed bat wings and the superb vision of aerial predators. But they were no good – their simple light bodies would take millennia of adjustment to carry a greatly enlarged braincase. His awareness now snapped back to something on the other side of the continent he presently occupied. Here he observed a herd of grazing beasts: six-legged and reptilian. The braincase below the three eye-stalks possessed complexity in control of the creatures' complex digestive system – a chemical laboratory in itself. It would be necessary to push them into a predatory lifestyle, thus freeing up cerebral space – again a task taking millennia. However, near the house, he had observed a better option than this. And of course, inside the house was the best option of all. He would continue to search though – for the moment. The smallest fraction of his awareness studied the Golem.

'I want you to contact the second Geronamid submind.'

'I am in com—'

Daes wholly occupied all her systems in an instant. He found the open comlink to the submind in orbit and probed up to it, tried to widen that link. In seconds he had created computer subversion routines and used them to try and get a hold, to control. The comlink immediately shut down. Within him there was a calmness – this had been expected, and in the process he had learnt much. Next time he would not be so brutal. He withdrew from Hera.

'—munication with the . . . I see . . . I hope you understand now that your quarantine is total. You have no way of leaving this planet without Geronamid's intercession.'

'I understand,' said Daes, and everything else that he was. 'I want information.'

'You realize that if you do manage to take control of the submind above, it will be instantly obliterated?'

'I require information,' was all he said.

'What information?'

'Everything you have on the Csorians and all related research.'

'That is a lot of information.'

'I have the capacity.'

'Then link to me again, but do not drown me out this time,' she said.

Daes eased into her, carefully circumventing those areas from which her awareness evolved: her ego, self-image – what she was.

Through the comlink Hera spat the request into orbit,

and the response was immediate. Daes realized that this
had been expected as there was no delay whilst the information was trawled from the AI net. As he scanned and
sorted this information, calmly noting that all of the
Csorian civilization discovered was but archaeological
remains, he realized that whilst he could be just Daes, in
truth he was now some other entity. Daes was in fact now
a submind of *himself*, and his whole self was centred on
the node in which he felt a crammed multitude. However, through vast and spreading awareness he observed
picotech chains of superconductor spearing across the
surface of the planet, spreading their informational network through the ocean depths, and flailing in the air like
cobwebs as they connected with every life-form, insinu-
ated themselves into every niche of the biosphere. One
third of the planet now lay under this net, this awareness,
and within hours only this network would meet on the
other side and he would be able to observe all, and be
ready. That was it though. He felt a flush of fear that was
his own and the crying of that multitude. Upon completion of the network, dispersion and implantation became
a necessity, for thereafter the network would begin to
degrade as does all life – with the accumulation of copy-
ing errors, the degrading of the basic templates – only
faster, because of its complexity, and the delicacy of its
picoscopic strands. One time only: one chance.

'You don't know what wiped out my race,' said Daes.

'Your race?' enquired Hera.

'You, submind, do not know what I am . . . become.
Geronamid certainly does. I want to communicate with
the AI directly.'

'You can only communicate with the submind

directly. Who will communicate with Geronamid when you have withdrawn,' said Hera. 'But you know that.'

Daes felt the network gathering behind him like a looming shadow. Geronamid had chosen this location because of the spider creatures outside. He saw in an instant that their braincases possessed sufficient room for primitive intelligence, and that their mouthparts were sufficiently complex for the fast development of tool-using ability. Nothing would be lost, as the bulk of each of the thousands of Csorian intelligences he contained could be stored as a picotech construct in each insectile mind. But those intelligences would be unable to immediately bloom. Transferred down the generations whilst the creatures were subtly impelled towards development of more complex brains, it would be millennia before the Csorian race could be reborn. This option was unacceptable to the multitude whilst such viable intelligences as Daes himself and these AIs were available. He must take Geronamid, subsume that AI.

'Yes, I do know that,' he said.

The planetwide network had stalled, all his mentality now focused on this moment. He felt the link establish to the orbital submind, and replayed Hera's words: *Who will communicate with Geronamid when you have withdrawn.* This meant that the submind possessed some way of linking with the AI Geronamid in total. There had to be a way for himself to get through before the submind was destroyed.

The comlink to the orbital submind opened, and Daes slid into it like syrup into a sore throat. The safety controls and trips he had observed on his first attempt, he easily circumvented as his awareness flooded up into orbit, subversion programs uncoiling in the silicon logic

of the submind like tight-wound snakes. In a nanosecond he found the underspace link to Geronamid in
total and prepared himself to storm that bastion. Then
something flooded out of the link; vast and incompre-
hensible. His subversion programs began to consume
themselves. He felt a huge amused awareness bearing
down on him with crushing force. Then that force eased.

*I offer you only two choices.*

Through allowable awareness Daes saw the massive
geosat poised above the planet. There was no possibility
of mistaking its purpose. It was one long internally
polished barrel ringed by the toroid of a giant fusion
reactor. In some areas the weapon had acquired the
name 'sun gun', which seemed an inadequate descrip-
tion for something that could raise square kilometres of
its target to a million degrees Celsius in less time than it
took to blink – a blink that would see all the stored intelligences gone.

*Destruction?*

Geronamid replied: *Is one choice. I have known for long
enough that the Csorian node contains the zipped minds of
some members of that race, ready to be implanted and
unzipped in another race that has the capacity to take
them. That second race will not be the human race. I could
have destroyed the node, but that is not my wish. When you
reattain your full capability the human race will be on an
equal if not superior footing to you.*

*It will take thousands of years*, Daes replied.

*You have slept for longer than that.*

Almost with a subliminal nod Daes drew back down
the informational corridor of the comlink, flooded
through Hera, and back into his human body. For a
moment he gazed at Hera, then he turned to the door

of the house and stepped through and outside. She followed him as he walked into the jungle and stood observing the spider creatures in the trees.

'This then, is completion of my sentence,' said Daes . . . just him.

'More life than you would have enjoyed,' she replied.

He inspected his hand as the skin began to peel and the substance of his flesh began to sag. Quickly seating himself he pushed those hands into soft cold ground. Inside him the intelligences separated and began transmitting into the network established in the area. In the transference they took with them the substance of his body, widening channels through the ground to the nanoscopic then microscopic, up the trunks of the trees, penetrating the hanging spider creatures through clinging complex feet. His own awareness breaking apart, Daes felt the subliminal agony he would have felt at his execution, as he similarly disintegrated. Csorian minds occupied primitive braincases, and spider creatures crawled down from the trees with ill-formed ideas, hopes and ambitions.

Hera gazed up into the sky at the descending shuttle, then returned her attention to the creature crouching by the scaled bulb of a large cycad. It was gnawing away with the intricate cutlery of its mouthparts – behaviour that had never before been observed. But then there was a lot of that now. Some had begun to build spherical nests around their egg-clusters and to defend them from other predators whilst the eggs ripened and hatched, still others plucked hard thorns from the leaf tips of cycads and used them to spear their prey.

As the shuttle landed in the jungle behind her, she

watched the creature back off from what it was doing and turn towards her, waving its forelimbs in the air. The noise of the shuttle engines then sent it scuttling into the undergrowth. She walked over to the cycad and inspected the creature's work. Neatly incised into the scales of the cycad was an '8' turned on its side – the sign for infinity.

She did not know if that was a suitable remnant to bequeath.

'Goodbye, Daes,' she said, and turned away.

# 7

# SNOW IN THE DESERT

A sand shark broke through the top face of the dune only to be snatched by a crab-bird and shredded in mid-air. Hirald squatted down, turned on her chameleonwear and faded into the violet sand, only her Toshiba goggles and the blunt snout of her singun visible. The crab-bird was a small one, but she had quickly learnt never to underestimate them. If the prey was too large for one to take, it would take pieces instead. No motile source of protein was too large to attack. The shame was that all the life-forms on Vatch were based on left-helix proteins, so to a crab-bird human flesh was completely without nourishment. The birds did not know this and just became irritable as their hunger increased. The circle was vicious.

The bird stripped the shark of its blade-legs and armoured mandibles and flew off with the bleeding and writhing torso, probably to feed to its chick. Hirald stood up and faded back into existence; a tall woman in a tight-fitting body suit webbed with cooling veins and hung with insulated pockets. On her back she carried a desert survival pack, for the look of things. The singun went into a button-down holster that looked as if it might

hold only a simple projectile weapon, not the formidable
device it did hold. She removed her goggles, mask and
hat, and tucked them away in one of her many pockets
before moving on across the sand. Her thin features,
blue eyes and long blonde hair were exposed to oven
temperatures and skin-flaying ultraviolet. Such had been
the way of things for many weeks now. Occasionally she
drank some water; a matter of form, just in case anyone
was watching.

He was called, inevitably, Snow, but with his plastron
mask and dust robes it was not immediately evident he
was an albino. The mask, made from the shell of an
Earth-import terrapin, was what identified him to those
who knew of him – that, and his tendency to leave
corpses behind him. At last count the reward for his
stasis-preserved testicles was twenty thousand shillings,
or the equivalent value in precious metals like copper or
manganese. Many people had tried for the reward and
their epitaph was just that: they had tried. Three people
at the water station, on the edge of the Menilar flat, were
waiting to try. They had weapons, strength and skill,
balanced against the crippling honour code of the
Andronache. Snow had all the former and no honour
code. Born on Earth so long ago even he doubted his
memories of the time, he had long since dispensed with
anything that might get in the way of plain survival.
Morality, he often argued, is a purely human invention
only to be indulged in times of plenty. Another of his
little aphorisms ran something along the lines of: if
you're up shit creek without a paddle, don't expect the
coast guard. His contemporaries on Vatch never knew

what to make of that one, but then Vatchians had no use
for words like creek, coast or paddle.

The water station was an ovoid of metal mounted
ten metres above the ground on a forest of scaffolding.
Nailing it to the ground was the silvery tube of the geothermal energy tap that provided the power for the transmuter; the reason it was possible for humans to exist on
this practically waterless planet. The transmuter took
complex compounds, stripped them of their elementary
hydrogen, and combined that with the abundant oxygen
given off by the dryform algae that turned all the sands
of Vatch to violet. Water was the product, but there were
many interesting by-products; strange metals and silica
compounds were one of the planet's main exports.

As he topped the final dune Snow raised his image-
intensifier to his eyes and scanned ahead. The station was
in reality a small city, the centre of commerce, the centre
of life. Under his mask he frowned to himself. He did not
know about the three men specifically, but he knew their
type would be there. Unfortunately he needed water to
take him on the last stage of his journey and this was the
only place. A confrontation was inevitable.

Snow strode down the face of the dune and onto a
dusty track snaking towards the station. At the side of the
road a water thief lay dying at the bottom of a condensation jar. He scratched at the hot glass with blistered
fingers as Snow passed, but Snow ignored him. It was
harsh punishment, but how else to treat someone who
regarded his fellow human beings as no more than walking water barrels? As he drew nearer to the station the
cries of the hawkers and stallholders in the ground city
reached out to him, like the chorus from a rookery, and
he could see the buzz of activity in the scaffold maze.

Soon he entered the ground city and its noisy life, soon after, his presence was noted and reported. By the time he passed through the moisture lock of the Sand House – a ubiquitous name for hostelries – and was taking off his mask in the cool interior, the three killers were buckling on their weapons and offering prayers to their various family gods.

'My pardon, master. I must see your tag. The Androche herself has declared the law enforceable by a two-month branding. The word is that too many outlaws now survive on the fringe.' The waiter could not help staring at Snow's pink eyes and bloodless face.

'No problem, friend,' said Snow, and after fumbling through his robes produced his micro-etched identity tag and handed it over. The waiter glanced at the briefly revealed leather-clad stump that terminated Snow's left arm and pretended not to notice. He put the tag through his portable reader and was much relieved when no alarm sounded. Snow was well aware that not everyone was checked like this, only the more suspicious-looking customers, like himself.

'What would you like, master?'

'A litre of chilled lager,' said Snow.

The waiter looked at him doubtfully.

'Which I will pay for now,' said Snow, handing over a ten-shilling note. The waiter looked alarmed by such a large sum in cash money and hurried off with it as quickly as he could. When he came back with a litre of lager in a thermos stein with combination-locked top, many eyes followed his progress. Here was an indication of wealth. Snow would not have agreed with this. He had worked it out. A litre of water would only have cost two shillings less, and the water lost through sweat evaporation little different. Two shillings, plus a little, for imbibing fluid in a much more pleasant form. He had nearly finished his litre and was relishing the sheer cellular pleasure of rehydration when the three entered the Sand House. He recognized them for what they were almost immediately. Before paying the slightest attention to them he drained every last drop of lager from the frictionless vessel.

'You are Snow, the albino,' said the first, standing before his table. Snow observed her and felt a gnawing depression. Even after all these years he could not shake an aversion to killing women, or in this case girls. She could not have been more than twenty. She stood before him attired in monofilament coveralls and weapons harness. Her face was elfin under a head of cropped black hair spiked out with gold-fleck grease.

'No, I'm not,' he said, and turned his attention elsewhere.

'Don't fuck with me,' she said with a tiredness that was beyond her years. 'I know who you are. You are an albino and your left hand is missing.' He returned his attention to her.

'My name is Jelda Conley. People call me Whitey. I have often been confused with this Snow you refer to and it was on one such occasion that I lost my hand. Now please leave me alone.'

The girl stepped back, confused. The Andronache honour code did not allow for creative lying. Snow glanced past her and noted one of her companions speaking to the owner who had sent the nervous waiter over. The lies would not be enough. He watched while the owner called over the waiter and checked the screen of his tag reader. The companion approached the girl, whispered in her ear.

'You lied to me,' she said.

'No I didn't,' said Snow.

'Yes you did!'

This was getting ridiculous. Snow stared off into the distance and ignored her.

'I challenge you,' said the girl.

There, it was said. Snow pretended he had not heard her.

'I said I challenge you.'

By the code she could now kill him. It was against the law but accepted practice. Snow felt a sinking sensation as she stepped back.

'Stand and face me, coward.'

With a tiredness that was wholly genuine Snow rose to his feet. She snatched her slammer. Snow reacted. She hit the floor on her back with the front of her mono-filament coverall breaking down and a smoking hole between her pert little breasts. Snow stepped past the table, past her, strode to the moisture lock, vomit held back by clenched teeth. Hoping the whole thing had been too fast for anyone to be sure of the weapon he had used.

It rested on the violet sands at the edge of a spaceport, which was strewn with huge flying-wing shuttles, out-buildings and hangars. It stood between the spaceport and the sprawl of Vatchian buildings linked by moisture-sealed walkways and the glass domes that covered the incongruous green of the parks. And in no way did it resemble any of the constructs around it. It was stan-dard; to be found on a thousand planets of the human

Polity, and it was the reason the expansion of the human race beggared the imagination. The runcible facility was a mirrored sphere fifty metres across, seemingly prevented from rolling away by the two L-shaped constructs of the buffers on either side of it. All around it, the glass-roofed embarkation lounges; a puddle of light. Within, the Skaidon gate performed its miracle every few minutes; bringing in quince, mitter travellers, from all across the Polity, and sending them away again.

Beck stood back from the arrivals entrance and watched the twin horns of the runcible on its dais of black glass. He watched the shimmer of the cusp between and impatiently checked his watch, not that they would be late, or early. They would arrive on time to the nanosecond. The runcible AI saw to that. Precisely on time a man stepped through the shimmer, a woman, another man, another woman. They matched the descriptions he had been given, and his greeting was effusive as they came through into the lounge.

'Your transport awaits outside,' he told them, hurrying them to exit. The Merchant did not want them to stay in the city. He wanted them out, those were Beck's instructions, amongst others. Once they were in the hover transport the man Beck took to be the leader caught hold of his shoulder.

'The weapons,' he said.

'Not here, not here,' said Beck nervously, and took the transport out of the city.

Out on the sand Beck brought the transport down and as the four climbed out he pulled a large case from the back of the transport. He was sweating, and not just because of the heat.

'Here,' he said, and opened the case.

The man reached inside and took out a small shiny pistol, snub-nosed and deadly looking.

'The Merchant will meet at the prearranged place, if he manages to obtain the information he seeks,' he said. He did not know where that was, nor what the information was. The Merchant had not taken him that far into his trust. It surprised him that he had been allowed knowledge of this; hired killers here on Vatch.

The man nodded as he inspected the pistol, smiled sadly, then pointed the pistol at Beck.

'Sorry,' he said.

Beck tried to say something just as he became aware of the arm coming round his face from the man who had moved behind him. A grip like iron closed around his head, locked, wrenched and twisted. Beck hit the sand with his head at an angle it had never achieved in life. He made some choking sounds, shivered a little, died.

Snow halted as two proctors came in through the lock. They looked past him to the corpse on the floor. The eldest of the two, grey-bearded and running to fat, but with weapons that looked well used and well looked after, spoke to him.

'You are Snow,' he said.

'Yes,' Snow replied. This man was not Andronache.

'A challenge?'

'Yes.'

The man nodded, looked calculatingly at the two Andronache at the bar, then turned back to the moisture-lock. It was not his job to pick up the corpses. There was an organization for that. The girl would be in a condensation jar within the hour.

'The Androche would speak with you. Come with

me.' To his companion he said, 'Deal with it. Her two friends look like they ought to spend a little time in detention.'

Snow followed the man outside.

'Why does she want to see me?' he asked as they strode down the scaffolded street.

'I didn't ask.'

Any conversation ended there.

The Androche, like all in her position, had apartments up in the station she owned. The proctor led Snow to a caged spiral stair and unlocked the gate.

'She is above,' was all he said. As Snow climbed the stair the gate clanged shut behind him.

The stairway ended at a moisture-lock hatch next to which depended a monitor and screen unit. Snow pressed the call button and waited. After a few moments a woman with cropped grey hair and a face that was all hard angles looked out at him.

'Yes?'

'You sent for me,' said Snow.

The woman nodded and the lock on the hatch clunked open. He spun the handle and it rose on its hinge to allow him access. He climbed into a short metal-walled corridor that ended at a single panel door of imported wood. It looked like oak to Snow; very expensive. He pushed the door open and entered.

The room was filled with a fortune in antiques; a huge dining table surrounded by carved chairs. Plush eighteenth-century furniture, oil paintings on the walls, hand-woven rugs on the floor.

'Don't be too impressed. They're all copies.'

The Androche approached from a drinks cabinet. She carried two glasses half filled with an amber drink. Snow studied her; she was an attractive woman. He estimated her age as somewhere between thirty-five and a hundred and ninety. Three centuries earlier the second figure would have been forty-five, but rejuvenation treatments had come a long way. She wore a simple toga-type dress over an athletic figure. At her hip she carried an antique – or replica – revolver.

'You know my name,' said Snow meaningfully as he accepted the drink.

'I am Aleen,' she replied to his unspoken question.

Snow hardly heard her. He was relishing his first sip.

'My God, whisky,' he said, eventually.

'Yes,' said Aleen, taking a sip from her drink then gesturing to a nearby sofa. They moved there and sat facing each other.

'Well, I'm here. What do you want?'

'Why is there a reward of twenty-five thousand shillings for your testicles?'

'Best ask the Merchant Baris that question, but I see it was rhetorical. You already know the answer.'

Aleen nodded and Snow leant towards her.

'I would be glad to know the answer,' he said.

Aleen smiled, Snow leant back.

'There is a price,' he said.

'Isn't there always? . . . There is a man. He is the chief proctor here. His name is David Songrel.'

'You want me to kill him.'

'Of course. Isn't that what you are best at?'

Snow kept silent. Aleen lay back against the edge of the sofa then and regarded him over her drink.

'That is not all I want from you.'

He turned and looked at her and at that moment she lifted her feet up onto the sofa so that he could see that

she wore nothing underneath. He wondered if she
shaved or if she was naturally bald in that area. Still meeting him eye to eye she dropped one leg back to the floor,
reached between her legs, and began to masturbate,
gently, with two fingers. Snow wondered what it was that
turned her on; his white body and pink eyes? Other
women had said it was almost like being made love to by
an alien, or was it that he was a killer? Probably a bit of
both.

'Part of the price?'

She nodded and put her glass to one side, then she
slid closer to him on the sofa and hooked one leg over
the back of it.

'Now,' she said, reaching up and pulling apart her toga
to expose breasts just like those of the girl he had killed.
Snow searched himself for an adverse reaction to that,
and when he found there was none he stood up and
unclipped his dust robes.

'You're white as paper,' said Aleen in amazement as
he peeled off his under suit, and then her eyes strayed to
the covered stump terminating his left arm. She said
nothing about that.

'Yes,' said Snow as he knelt between her legs and
bowed down to run his tongue round her nipples. 'A
blank page,' he went on as he worked his way down. She
caught his head.

'Not that,' she said. 'I want you inside me, now.'

Snow obliged her, but was puzzled at something he
had heard in her voice. It had almost been as if that part
of the act was the most important. Perhaps she wanted
white-skinned children.

*

Hirald called out before approaching the fire. It had been her observation that the Andronache got rather twitchy if you walked into one of their camps unannounced. As she walked in she was surprised to see that these were not Andronache. There were two men and two women dressed in monofilament survival suits that looked to be of Mars manufacture. Hirald noted this but pretended not to notice the weapons laid out on a groundsheet that one of the men had hastily covered at her arrival. She walked to the fire and squatted down. One of the women tossed on another crab-bird carapace and watched her through the flames. The man who had covered the weapons, a tall Marsman with caste markings tattooed on his temples, was the first to speak.

'You've come a long way?' he asked.

'Not so far as you,' said Hirald. She looked from him to the woman across the flames, who also had caste marks on her face. The other couple: the man a Negro with incongruous blue eyes and the woman Hirald thought could have come from anywhere until she noted the caps over the neural plugs behind her ears. She was corporate then; from one of the families.

'Yes, we have come a way,' said the man, touching his caste mark.

'We search,' said the Negro intently. 'Perhaps you can help us. We search for one who is called Snow. He is an albino.'

They all looked at Hirald then, avidly.

'I have heard of him,' said Hirald, 'and I have heard that many people look for him. I do not know where he is though.'

The woman with the neural plugs looked suspicious.

Hirald continued to forestall anything more she might say.

'You are after the reward then?'

The four looked to each other, then the latter three looked to the Marsman. He smiled to himself and casually reached for the covered weapons next to him. Hirald glanced at the corporate woman, who was staring back at her.

'Jharit, no.'

Jharit stopped with his hand by the covering.

'What is it, Canard Meck?'

The woman, now identified as a member of the Jethro Manx Canard corporate family, slowly shook her head then looked to Hirald, who had not yet moved.

'We have no dispute with you, but we would prefer it if you left our camp, please.'

'But she knows. She might tell him,' said Jharit.

Canard Meck looked to him and said, 'She is product.'

Jharit snatched his hand from the weapons and suddenly looked very frightened. He flinched as Hirald rose to her feet. Hirald smiled.

'I mean no harm, unless harm is meant.'

She strode out into the darkness without checking behind. No one moved. No one reached for the weapons.

Snow removed the pistol from its holster in his dust robes and checked the charge reading. As was usual it was nearly at full charge. The bright sunlight of Vatch acting on the photovoltaic material of his robes kept the weapon constantly charged through the socket in the holster. The weapon was a matt black L, five millimetres thick with only a slight depression where a trigger would normally have been. It was keyed to Snow. No one else could fire it. The beam it fired was of antiphotons; a misnomer really, as what it consisted of was protons field-accelerated to the point where they became photonic matter. Misnomer or not, this beam could burn large holes in anyone Snow cared to point it at.

David Songrel was a family man. Snow had observed him lifting a child high in the air while a woman looked on from the background, just before the door to his apartments closed. Snow wondered why Aleen wanted him dead. As the owner of the water station she had much power here, but little over the proctors who enforced planetary law, not her law. Perhaps she had been involved in illegalities of which Songrel had become aware. No matter, for the present. He rapped on the door and when Songrel opened it he stuck the pistol in his face and walked him back into the apartment, closing the door behind him with his stump.

'Daddy!' the little girl yelled, but the mother caught hold of her before she rushed forward. Songrel had his hands in the air, his eyes not leaving the pistol. Shock there, knowledge.

'Why,' said Snow, 'does the Androche want you dead?'

'You're . . . the albino.'

'Answer the question please.'

Songrel glanced at his wife and daughter before he replied, 'She is a collector of antiquities.'

'Why the necessity for your death?'

'She has killed to get what she wants. I have evidence. We intend to arrest her soon.'

Snow nodded then holstered his pistol.

'I thought it would be something like that. She had two proctors come for me you know.'

Songrel lowered his hands, but kept them well away from the stun-gun hooked on his belt.

'As Androche she does have the right to some use of the proctors. It is our duty to guard her and her property. She does not have freedom to commit crime. Why didn't you kill me? They say you have killed many.'

Snow looked to Songrel's wife and child.

'My reputation precedes me,' he said, and stepped past Songrel to drop onto a comfortable-looking sofa. 'But the stories are in error. I have killed no one who has not first tried to kill me . . . well, mostly.'

Songrel looked to his wife.

'It's Tamtha's bedtime.'

His wife nodded and took the child from the room. Snow noted the little girl's fascinated stare. He was quite used to such. Songrel sat himself in an armchair opposite Snow.

'A nice family you have.'

'Yes . . . will you testify against the Androche?'

'You can have my testimony recorded under seal, but I cannot stay for a trial. If I was to stay this place would be crawling with Andronache killers in no time. I might not survive that.'

Songrel nodded.

'Why did you come here if it was not your intention to kill me?' he asked, a trifle anxiously.

'I want you to play dead while I go back and see the Androche.'

Songrel's expression hardened.

'You want to collect your reward.'

'Yes, but my reward is not money, it is information. The Androche knows why the Merchant Baris has a

reward out for my death. It is a subject I am under-
standably curious about.'

Songrel interlaced his fingers in his lap and stared
down at them for a moment. When he looked up he said,
'The reward is for your stasis-preserved testicles. Perhaps
like Aleen he is a collector, but that is beside the point.
I will play dead for you, but when you go to see Aleen I
want you to carry a virtual recorder.'

Snow nodded once. Songrel stood up and walked to
a wall cupboard. He returned with a holocorder that he
rested on the table and turned on.

'Now, your statement.'

'He is dead,' said Aleen, a smile on her face.

'Yes,' said Snow, dropping Songrel's identity tag on
the table. 'Yet I get the impression you knew before I
came here.'

Aleen went to the drinks cabinet and poured Snow a
whisky. She brought it over to him.

'I have friends amongst the proctors. As soon as his
wife called in the killing – she was hysterical apparently
– they informed me.'

'Why did you want him killed?'

'That is none of your concern. Drink your whisky and
I will get you the promised information.'

Aleen turned away from him and moved to a computer console elegantly concealed in a Louis XIV table.
Snow had the whisky to his lips just as his suspicious
nature took over. Why was it necessary to get the information from the computer? She could just tell him. Why
had she not poured a drink for herself? He placed the
drink down on a table, unsampled. Aleen looked up, a
dead smile on her face, and as her hand came up over

the console Snow dived to one side. On the wall behind him a picture blackened then flared into oily flames. He came up on one knee and fired once. She slammed back out of her chair onto the floor, her face burning like the picture.

Snow searched hurriedly. Any time now the proctors would arrive. In the bathroom he found a device like a chrome penis with two holes in the end. One hole spurted out some kind of fluid and the other hole sucked. Some kind of contraceptive device? He traced tubes back to the unit that contained the bottle of fluid and some very complicated straining and filtering devices. To his confusion he realized it was for removing the contents of a woman's womb, probably after sex. She collected men's semen? Shortly after, he found a single stasis bottle containing said substance. It had to be his own, and now he had an inkling of an idea; a possible explanation for his situation of the last five years. He opened the bottle and washed its contents down the sink just before the proctors broke into the apartment. Not that there was very much of value in it.

Hirald looked at the man in the condensation bottle, her expression revealing nothing. He was alive beyond his time; some sadist had dropped a bottle of water in with him to prolong his suffering. He stared at Hirald with drying eyes, the empty bottle by his head, his body shrunken and badly sunburnt, his black tongue protruding. Hirald looked around carefully, there were harsh penalties for what she was about to do, then held a small chrome cylinder against the glass near the man's head. There was a brief flash. The man convulsed and the bottle was misted with smoke and steam. He died. Hirald replaced the device in her pocket, stood and walked on. Her masters would not have been pleased at her risking herself like this, but then they did not have complete control over her actions.

Snow was glad to leave the station behind him and this was reflected in his pace. He walked away at a kilometre-eating stride and occasionally swore with obscene precision. After the death of Aleen, Songrel had not felt obliged to honour his promise and Snow had spent two days in protective custody while the wheels of justice ground out slow due process. Luckily the appointment of the new Androche, traditionally a time of holiday and peace, had given him a needed respite. He had a day before the killers came after him.

Passing the condensation jar he noted that the man was now dead, his body giving up the last of its water for the public good. He paused for a moment to observe the greasy film on the inside of the jar before moving on. Someone had finished the poor bastard off. Snow wondered if that same someone might be after him, for the same purpose.

Out of sight of the station Snow left the road and set out across a spill of desert to a distant rock field. There he would be able to lose himself, if a sand shark did not get him first. He drew his pistol as he walked and kept his eyes open. One sand shark twitched its motion-detecting palps above the sand but shortly subsided. It must have fed in the last solstan year. It would be quiescent for another year to come.

Without event Snow reached the rock field and was putting away his pistol when a flash of reflected light alerted him to possible danger. Andronache, he thought, and readied himself for another challenge, only this time there was no challenge.

Automatic fire flicked his dust robes and scored pain across his ribs. Splinters from a nearby rock impacted on his mask. Snow dropped and quickly pulled himself behind a rock.

'Idiot,' he said. It had been some time since anyone other than an Andronache killer had tried for him. He had forgotten that their honour code did not apply to all. He crouched down further as rock shattered above his head and rained splinters down on him.

'Hey, Snow!'

Snow did not reply.

'Hey, Snow, if you stick anything out make sure it's not worth money!'

There was laughter at this rapier wit. Two of them at least. Snow ground his teeth then pulled a couple of shiny spheroids from his belt. A volley of shots hit the rock so he supposed that at least one of them was changing position. Holding one of the spheroids to his mouth he twisted its top with his teeth then threw it hard in the general direction of the laughter. The explosion seemed completely out of proportion to the size of the object he had thrown, but then most explosives were merely matter, not field-compressed antimatter. Snow was up and running as shattered stone rained down and a great dust-cloud spread. He was behind another rock before the screams started.

'You bastard! I'll have your balls off with a blunt knife for that!'

The voice had come from that formation to the right. The screaming came from the one to the left of it. Snow fired at the first until he got a reply, two replies. There was someone else a lot closer. Three of them then, unless there were others who were more canny. He fired a few more times, rock disintegrating and fragmenting at each hit, then he checked the charge on his pistol, holstered it, and waited, listening intently. The screaming had become a steady groaning and swearing.

Sporadic firing splintered the rock between him and his antagonists. This did not disconcert Snow. He knew it was covering fire for the one who was creeping up on him. He heard the first betraying scrape of shock armour against stone shortly after one such burst of fire. It was out to his left. He drew his pistol and, pointing in that direction, waited. Then, a distraction, the groaning of the wounded man abruptly ceased.

'David! David! Answer me!'

No answer. Snow wondered if someone else had just joined the game. Thinking on this he almost missed the flicker of movement as the creeper stood up and sighted on him down the barrel of an Optek assault rifle. It was all the man had time to do. Snow fired once, his pistol on its highest setting. The man turned into an explosion of burning flesh, grisly remnants stuck to the rock and smoked.

'Oh my God! Oh you bastard!'

Snow wondered at the talker's sense of proportion. He hadn't started this. It was not his fault that they had underestimated his armament. He glanced in the direction of the rock formation the man was concealed behind and saw him come out and come running towards him. He was firing wildly, his Optek on automatic. Snow had no time to return fire. He dived for cover. Abruptly the firing stopped. Snow waited for a moment then slowly peered out from cover. The man was flat on his face, the top of his head lying about a metre in front of him. Walking towards him, an Optek resting across her shoulder, was the most beautiful woman Snow had ever seen, and he had seen a lot.

Three Optek rifles, a dilapidated laser only a fool or a desperate man would risk firing, food, aged desert survival packs and suits, a little cash money, and now useless identity tags; the sum remains of three lives. These had been poor men; staking all on one last gamble for wealth. They had tried. Snow removed what was of most value and easily transportable; the money, liquid rations, power packs and filters from the suits, and left the rest in plain sight for anyone who wanted to take it. The woman, Hirald, retained one Optek rifle and ammunition, she did not seem interested in the rest. On the other side of the rock field, away from the stink of opened bodies and the sudden interest of crab-birds and sickle flies, Snow made a fire from old carapaces and removed his mask in the light of evening. He was curious to note that the woman had not replaced her mask since the first moment he had seen her that morning, and her skin looked as clear and as perfect as it had looked then. She sank down next to him by the fire, with a grace that could only reflect superb physical condition.

'What brought you to the rock field?' he asked her.

'I made a shortcut across the Thira and was on my way back to the road and civilization, and I of course found one of the nastier aspects of this civilization.'

Snow was doubtful about this reply. He had crossed the Thira a couple of times and knew it to be rough going. Hirald looked as fresh as someone after a month's sojourn in a water station.

'I see,' he said.

'You are Snow,' she said, turning and fixing him with eyes that were violet in the fading light. He felt his stomach lurch at that look, then immediately felt a self-contempt, that after all these years he could still react this way to mere physical attractiveness, no, beauty.

'Yes, I am.'

'I would like to travel with you for a while.'

'You know who I am, then you will know at once why I am suspicious of your motives.'

She smiled at him and he felt that lurch again. He turned and spat in the fire.

'I'm crossing the Thira,' he said.

'I have no problem with that,' she told him.

Snow lay back and rested his head on one of the packs. He pulled a thermal sheet across his body and stared up at the sky. The red-tinted swathe of stars was being encroached on by asteroids of the night. A single sword of light cut the sunset.

'Why?' he asked.

'Because I'm lonely, and after the water station I would have travelled on alone. I felt like a change.'

Snow grunted in reply and closed his eyes. She was not out to kill him. He had given her ample opportunity as they crossed the rock field. But she did have motives as yet unrevealed to him. Whatever, she would never keep to the pace he set and would soon abandon him, and the unsettling things he was feeling would soon go away. He slept.

Sunlight on his face, bringing the familiar tingling prior to burning, had his hand up and closing his mask across before he was fully awake. He looked across the dead

ashes of the fire at Hirald and got the unsettling notion
that she had not changed position all night. He sat up,
then after a muttered good morning, went behind a rock
and urinated into his condenser pack. Following the
ritual of every morning for many years now he then
emptied the moisture collectors of his under suit into it
as well. The collector bottle he emptied into his drinking bottle before dipping his toothbrush and cleaning
his teeth. By the time he had finished his ablutions and
come out from behind the rock, Hirald had opened a
breakfast-soup ration pack and it was bubbling under its
lid. Snow reached for another pack, but she held up her
hand.

'This is for you. I have already eaten.'

'Did you sleep at all?'

'A little. Tell me, how is it you are in possession of pro-
scribed weaponry?'

'Took it off someone who tried to kill me,' he lied,
but he could hardly tell her he had brought it here before
the runcible proscription and modified it himself over
the so very many years since. He sat down and drank his
breakfast. When he had finished they set out across the
Thira. Hirald noted him looking at her after an hour's
walking and closed her mask. He thought no more of
it; lots of people did not like the masks and were prepared to pay the price of water-loss not to wear them so
much.

By midmorning the temperature had reached forty-
five degrees and was still rising. A sand shark broke out
of the surface of a dune and came scuttling after them
for a few metres, then halted, panting like a dog, either
too tired or too well fed to continue, that or it had
sampled human flesh before and found it without

nourishment. When the temperature reached fifty and the cooling units of Snow's under suit were labouring under the load, he noted that Hirald still easily matched his pace. When a crab-bird dropped clacking out of the sky at them she brought it down with one shot before Snow could even think of reaching for his weapon. She was a remarkable woman, yes, remarkable. Shortly after midday Snow called a halt.

'We'll rest until evening then continue through the night and tomorrow morning. The following night should bring us out the other side.'

Hirald nodded in agreement. Snow wondered why she had not suggested this earlier. Surely she had not travelled only by day across here? Surely not.

They slept under the reflective shelter of Snow's day tent, then moved on at sunset after he had checked their position by the satellite beacons. They walked all night and most of the following morning, and when they finally set up the tent again Snow was exhausted. With a hint of irritation he told Hirald he wanted privacy in the tent and suggested she set up her own. Once inside his tent he sealed up and stripped naked. He then cleaned himself and the inside of his under suit with a cycle sponge; a device that made it possible to stay clean with a quarter-litre of water and little spillage. After this he pulled on a pair of towelling shorts and lay back with his miniature air cooler humming away at full power. It was luxury of a kind. After half an hour's sleep he woke and opened the tent to look outside. Hirald was sitting in the sand with her mask open. She was watching the horizon intently, her stillness quite unnatural.

'Don't you have a day tent?' Snow asked.

She shook her head.

'Come and join me then,' he said, reversing back into his tent. Hirald stood and walked over, the effects of the baking sun seemingly negligible to her. She entered the tent and closed it behind her, then after a glance at Snow she began to remove her survival suit. Snow turned away for a moment then thought, what the hell, and turned back to watch. She had not asked him to turn his head. Under her suit she wore a single skin-hugging garment that ended above her knees and elbows and in an arc exposing perfectly formed collarbones. The material of the garment was like white silk, and almost translucent. Snow swallowed drily, then tried to distract himself by wondering about her sanitary arrangements. As she lifted her legs up to remove her trousers from her feet he saw then how the matter was arranged and wondered if a blush was evident on his white skin. The garment had a vent from the lower part of her pale pubic hair round to the top crease of her buttocks.

As she finally took off her trousers Hirald looked at him and noted the direction of his gaze. He raised his eyes and met her eye to eye. She smiled at him and while smiling stretched the sleeves of the garment down and off over her hands and rolled it down below her breasts. Snow cleared his throat and tried to think of something witty to say. She was a succubus, a lonely desert man's fantasy. Still smiling she came across the tent on her hands and knees, put her hand against his chest and pushed him back, sat astride him, and with her pale hair falling either side of his head, leant down and kissed him on the mouth. Her mouth was sweet and warm. Snow was thoroughly aware of her hard little nipples sliding from side to side against his chest. He touched the skin of her shoulders and found it dry and warm. She sat back then and looked down at him for a moment. There was something strange about that look; a kind of cold curiosity. She slid forward onto his stomach then turned and reached back to pull his shorts down and off his legs. He was amazed at just how far she could twist and bend back her body. Once his shorts were removed she slid back until his penis rested between her buttocks then, after raising herself a little, she continued to push back, bending it over until it almost caused him pain, then with a swift movement of her pelvis, took it inside her. Snow groaned, then gritted his teeth as she started to ride him, staring down at him with that strange expression on her face.

In the evening, when it was time to move on, Snow moved with a bone-deep lethargy. He had not slept much during the afternoon. Each time he had tried to relax after a session of sex Hirald would do something, whether that would be to take his penis in her mouth or assume some position he could not resist. This had been after her climax while she rode him. It had been so intense that she had cried out and shuddered uncontrollably, and after it she had looked down at herself in surprise and shock. Thereafter she had been eager to repeat the experience. Snow felt sore and drained.

As they walked across the darkened violet sands they had talked little, but there had been one conversation that had raised Snow's suspicions.

'Your hand, how did you lose it?'

'Andronache challenge. It was shredded by a flack shell.'

'How is it now?'

Snow had paused before replying. Did she know?

'What do you mean; how is it? It was amputated. It is no longer there.'

'Yes,' she had said, and no more.

The sun was breaking the horizon and the night asteroids fading out of the sky when they reached the rock field at the edge of the Thira. With little energy to spare for conversation, Snow set up his day tent and collapsed inside, instantly asleep. When he woke in the latter part of the day it was to discover himself undressed under a blanket with Hirald lying beside him. She was up on her elbow, her head propped on her hand, looking at his face. As soon as she saw that he was awake she handed him a carton of mixed juice. He sat up, the blanket sliding down. She was naked. He drank the juice.

'I'm glad you came along,' he said, and the rest of the day was spent in pleasant activity. That night they moved deep into the rock field. The following day passed much as the one before.

'I think it fair to tell you I have an implant,' Snow said as he rested after some particularly vigorous activity. 'You won't get pregnant by me, and my sperm is little more than water and a few free proteins.'

'Why do you feel it necessary to tell me this?' Hirald asked him.

'As you know, there is a reward out for my testicles, stasis-preserved. This is not because the Merchant Baris particularly wants me dead. I think it is because he is after my genetic tissue. It has value, of a kind. At the water station the Androche . . . seduced me.' Snow was uncomfortable with that. 'She did it so she could collect my sperm, probably to sell.'

'I know,' said Hirald. Snow looked at her and she went

on, 'He is after your testicles to provide him with an endless supply of your genetic material.'

Snow considered that. Of course there had to be more
to Hirald than he had supposed, but the Olympic screwing had clouded his thought-processes somewhat.

'He wouldn't get that . . . meiosis only leaves half the
chromosomes in each sperm,' he said.

'He would get there eventually. Your testicles could be
kept alive and producing spermatozoa for a very long
time. It is the next best thing to having your entire living
body to provide the genetic material. I suspect Baris
thought it unlikely he could get away with that. He'd
never get you off-planet without your consent. This way
he also corners the market.'

'You know an awful lot about what Baris wants.'

Hirald looked at him very directly.

'How is your hand?'

Snow looked down at the stump. He unclipped the
covering and pulled it off. What he exposed was recog-
nizably a hand, though deformed and almost useless. The
covering had been cleverly made to conceal it, to make
it look as if the hand was missing.

'It will be no different from its predecessor in about
six solstan months. I intended to walk out of one water
station without a hand, then into another station with a
hand and a new identity.'

'What about your albinism?'

'Skin dye and eye lenses.'

'Of course you cannot take transplants.'

'No . . . I think you should explain yourself.'

'The people I work for want the same as Baris; your
genome.'

'You've had opportunity . . .'

'No, they want the best option; you, willingly. I want you to gate back to Earth with me.'

'Why?'

'You are regenerative. It is the source of your immortality. We know this now. You have known it for more than a thousand years.'

'Still, why?'

'We have managed to keep your secret for the last three hundred years, ever since it was discovered. Ten years ago a mistake was made and the knowledge was leaked. Now many organizations know about you, and what you represent; whoever can decode your genome has access to immortality, and through that, access to wealth and power unprecedented. Baris is one who would like this. He was the first to track you down. There will be others.'

'You work for Earth Central.'

'Yes.'

'Wouldn't it be better just to kill me and destroy my body?'

'Earth Central does not suppress knowledge.' Hirald smiled at him. 'You should be old enough to understand the futility of this. It wants this knowledge disseminated so that it cannot cause damage, cannot put power into the hands of the wrong people. The good it would do is immense also. The projections are that in ten years a treatment could become available to make anyone regenerative, within limits.'

'Yet till now it kept a lid on things,' said Snow, an old hand at spotting discrepancies like this.

'It guarded your privacy. It did not suppress knowledge. Not suppressing knowledge is not equal to seeking it out.'

'Is Earth Central so moral now?' wondered Snow,

then could have kicked himself for the stupidity. Of course Earth Central was. Only human beings and other low-grade sentients could become corrupt, and Earth Central was the most powerful AI in the human polity. Hirald, noting his discomfiture, did not answer his question.

'Will you come?' she asked him.

Snow looked to the wall of the tent as if looking out across the rock field.

'This requires thought, not instant decisions. Two days should bring us to my home. I will . . . consider.'

Draped in chameleon cloth the hover transport was indistinguishable from the surrounding dunes. Inside the transport Jharit shuffled a pack of cards and played a game men like him had played in similar situations for many centuries. His wife, Jharilla, slept. Trock was cleaning an antique revolver he had picked up in an auction at the last water station. The bullets he had acquired with it stood in neat soldierly rows on the table before him. Canard Meck was plugged in, trying to pick up information from the net and the high-speed conversations the runcible AI had with its subminds. The call came as a relief to all of them but her; she resented dropping out of that world of perfect logic and pure clarity of thought back into the sweat-stink of the transport.

'I am Baris,' said the smiling face from the screen.

Coming straight to the point Jharit said, 'You have the information?'

'I have,' said Baris, his smile only slightly less, 'and I will be coming to join you for the final chase.'

Jharit and Trock exchanged a look.

'As you wish. You are paying.'

'Yes, I am.' The Merchant's smile was gone now. 'Turn on your beacon and I will join you within the hour.'

'How are you getting out here?' asked Canard Meck.

'By AGC of course,' said Baris, turning to look towards her.

'All AGCs are registered. The AI will know where you are.'

Baris flicked his fingers at this and his face assumed a look of contempt.

'No matter. We will continue from your position to . . . our destination, in the transport.'

'Very well,' said Canard Meck.

Baris waited for something more to be said, and when nothing was he gave a moue of disappointment. The screen blanked.

The Merchant arrived in a fancy repro Macrojet AGC. He climbed out dressed in sand fatigues and was followed by two women dressed much the same. One of them carried a hunting rifle and ammunition belts. The other carried various unidentifiable packages. Baris struck a pose before them. He was a handsome man. Not one of the four reacted to this foolish display. They knew that anyone who had reached the Merchant's position was no fool. Jharit and Jharilla looked at him glassy eyed. Trock looked at the rifle. Canard Meck looked briefly at one of the women, took in the imbecilic smile, then back to the Merchant.

'Shall we be on our way then?' she said.

Baris shook his head and still smiling he clicked his fingers and walked to the transport. The two women followed him as obediently as dogs. The four came after: hounds of a different breed.

★

Out of the rock field reared the first of the stone buttes, carved by wind-blown sand to resemble a statue of something manlike sunk up to its chest in the ground. In the cracks and divisions of its head, mica and quartz glittered like insectile eyes. Snow led the way to the base of the butte where slabs of the same stone lay tilted in the ground.

'Here,' he said, holding his hand out to a sandwich of slabs. With a grinding, the top slab pivoted to one side to expose a stair dropping a short distance to the floor of a tunnel. 'Welcome to my home.'

'You live in a hole in the ground?' said Hirald with a touch of irony.

'Come and find out.'

As they climbed down the slab swung back across above them and wall lights clicked on. Hirald noted that the tunnel led under the butte and had already worked things out by the time they reached the chimney with its rails pinned up the side and the elevator car. They climbed inside the car and sprawled in the seats ringing the inside, looked out of the windows as it hauled them up the chimney cut through the centre of the butte.

'This must have taken you some time,' said Hirald.

Snow said, 'The shaft was already here. About two hundred years ago I first found it. Others had lived here before me, but in rather primitive conditions. I've been improving the place ever since.'

The car arrived at its destination and they walked from it into a complex of moisture-locked rooms at the head of the butte. With a drink in her hand Hirald stood at a polarized panoramic window and looked out across the rock field for a moment, then returned her attention to the room and its contents. In a glass-fronted case along one wall was a display of weapons dating from the twenty-second century and at the centre of this a sword dating from some prespace age. Hirald had to wonder. She turned from the case as Snow returned to the room, dressed now in loose black trousers and a black open-necked shirt. The contrast with his white skin and hair and pink eyes gave him the appearance of someone who might have a taste for blood.

'There's some clothing there for you to use if you like, and the shower. No problem with it cycling. There's plenty of water here,' he told her. Hirald nodded, placed her drink down on a glass-topped table, and headed back into the rooms Snow had come from. Snow watched her go. She would shower and change and be little fresher than she already was. He had noted with some puzzlement how she never seemed to smell bad, never seemed dirty.

'Whose clothing is this?' Hirald asked from the room beyond.

'My last wife's,' said Snow.

Hirald came to the door with clothing folded over one arm. She looked at him questioningly.

'She killed herself about a century ago,' he said in a flat voice. 'Walked out into the desert and burnt a hole through her head. I found her before the crab-birds and sand sharks.'

'Why?'

'She grew old and I did not. She hated it.'

Hirald had no comment to make on this. She went to take her shower, and shortly returned wearing a skin-tight body suit of translucent blue material, which she did not expect to be wearing for long once Snow saw her in it. Snow was occupied though; sat in a swivel chair looking at a screen, he was back in his dust robes, his terrapin mask hanging open. She walked up behind him to see what he was looking at. She saw the hover trans-port on the sand and the two women pulling a sheet over it. The Merchant Baris she recognized, as she recognized the four hired killers.

'It would seem Baris has found me,' said Snow, his tone cold and flat.

'What defences does this place have?'

'None, I never felt the need for them.'

'Are you sure they are coming here?'

'It seems strange that he has chosen this particular rock field on the whole planet. I'll have to go and settle this.'

'I'll change,' said Hirald, and hurried back to get her suit. When she returned Snow was gone. When she tried to follow she found the elevator car locked at the bottom of the shaft.

'Damn you Snow!' she yelled, slamming her fist against a doorjamb, leaving a fist-shaped dent in the steel. She then walked back a few paces, turned, and ran and leapt into the shaft. The rails pinned to the edge were six metres away. She reached them easily, her hands lock-ing on the polished metal with a thump. Laboriously she began to climb down.

Jharit smiled at his wife and nodded to Trock, who stood beyond her strapping on body armour. This was the one. They would be rich after this. He looked at the narrow-beam laser he held. He would have preferred something with a little more power, but it was essential that the body not be too badly damaged. He turned to Baris as the Merchant sent his two women back to the transport.

'We'll go in spread out. He probably has scanning equipment in the rock field and if there's an ambush we don't want him to get too many of us at once.'

Baris smiled and thumbed bullets into his rifle, adjusted the scope. Jharit wondered about him, wondered how good he was. He gave the signal; they spread out and entered the rock field.

They were coming to kill him. There were no rules, no challenges offered. Snow braced the butt of his pistol against the rock and sighted along it.

'Anything?' asked Jharit over the com.

'Pin cameras,' Jharilla told him. 'I burnt a couple out, but there has to be more. He knows we're here.'

'Me too,' said Trock.

'Remember, narrow beam. We burn too much and there's no money. A clean kill. A head shot would be nice.'

There was a whooshing sound, a brief scream, static over the com. Jharit hit the ground and moved behind a rock.

'What the hell was that?'

'He's got a fucking APW! Fucking body armour's useless!'

Jharit felt a sinking sensation in his gut. They had expected projectile weapons, perhaps a laser.

'Who . . .?'

There was a pause.

'Trock?'

'Jharilla's dead.'

Jharit swallowed drily and edged on into the rock field.

'Position?'

'Don't know.'

'Meck?'

'Nothing here.'

'Baris?'

There was no reply from the Merchant.

Snow dropped down off the top of the boulder and pulled the remaining two spheroids from his belt. With his teeth he twisted their tops right round. The dark-skinned one was over to his left. The Marsman over to his right. The others were further over to the right somewhere. He threw the two spheroids right and left and moved back then flicked through multiple views on his wrist screen. A lot of the cameras were out, but he pulled up a view of the Marsman. Two detonations. As the Marsman hit the ground he realized he had thrown too far there. He was close. He flicked through the views again and caught the other stumbling through dust and wreckage, rock splinters embedded in his face. Ah, so. Snow moved to his left, checking his screen every few seconds. He halted behind a tilted slab and after checking his screen once more he squatted down and waited. With little regard for his surroundings Trock stumbled out of the falling dust. Snow smiled grimly under his mask and sighted on him. Red agony cut his shoulder. The smell of burning flesh. Snow rolled to one side, came up onto his feet, ran. Rock to one side of him smoked, pinged as it heated. He dived for cover, crawled amongst broken rock. The firing ceased. Now I'm dead, he thought. His pistol lay in the dust back there somewhere.

*

'He dropped the APW, Trock. He's over to your left. Take him down, I can't get a sighting at the moment.'

Trock spat a broken tooth from his mouth and walked in the direction indicated, his antique revolver in his left hand and his laser in his right. This was it. The bastard was dead, or perhaps not. I'll cut his arms and legs off, the beam should cauterize sufficiently. Trock did not get time to fire. The figure in dust robes came out of nowhere to drop-kick him in the chest. The body armour absorbed most of the blow, but Trock went over. Before he could rise the figure was above him. A split-hand blow drove through his visor and deep into his eyes, two fingers each, and burst them. It was a strike Snow had learnt over a thousand years before. By the time Trock started screaming and firing Snow was gone again.

Snow coughed as quietly as he could, opened his mask and spat out a mixture of bloody plasma and charred tissue. The burn had started at his shoulder and penetrated his left lung. A second more and he would have been dead. The pain was crippling. He knew he would not have the energy for another attack like that, nor would he be likely to take any of the others by surprise. The man had been stunned by the explosion, angered by the injuries to himself. Snow edged back through the rock field, his mobility rapidly decreasing. When a shadow fell across him he looked up into the inevitable.

'Why didn't you take his weapon?' asked Jharit, nodding back in the direction of Trock, who was no longer screaming. He was curled foetal by a rock, a field dressing across his eyes and his body pumped full of self-administered painkillers.

'No time, no strength . . . could only get him through his visor,' Snow managed.

Jharit nodded and spoke into his com.

'I have him. Home in on my signal.'

Snow waited for death, but Jharit squatted in the dust by him seemingly disinclined to kill him.

'Jharilla was a hell of a woman,' said Jharit, removing a stasis bottle from his belt and pushing it into the sand next to him. 'We were married in Viking City twenty solstan years ago.' Jharit pulled a wicked ceramal knife from his boot and held it up before his face. 'This is for her you understand. After I've taken your testicles and dressed that wound I'll see to your other injury. I don't want you to die yet. I have so much to tell you about her, and there is so much I want you to experience. You know she—'

Jharit turned at a sound, rose to his feet and drew his laser again. He stepped away from Snow and looked around. Snow looked beyond him but could see nothing.

'If you leave here now, Marsman, I will not kill you.'

The voice was Hirald's.

Jharit fired into the rocks and backed towards Snow.

'I have a singun and I am in chameleonwear. I can kill you any time I wish. Drop your weapon.'

Jharit paused for a moment as if indecisive, then he whirled, pointing his laser at Snow. The expression on his face told all. Before he could press the trigger he collapsed into himself; a central point the size of a pinhead, a plume of sand standing where he stood, then all blasted away in a thunderclap and an encore of miniature lightnings across the ground. Snow slowly shoved himself to his feet as he looked in awe at the spot Jharit had occupied. He had heard of such weapons and not believed. He looked across as Hirald flickered back into existence only a few metres away. She smiled at him, just before the first shot ripped the side of her face away.

Snow knew he yelled, he might have screamed. He looked on in impotent horror as the second shot smacked into her back and knocked her to the ground. Then there: Baris and the corporation woman, walking out of the rock field. Baris sighted again as he walked, hit Hirald with another shot that ripped half her side away. Snow felt his legs give way. He went down on his knees. Baris came before him, a self-satisfied smirk on his face. Snow looked up at him, trying to pull the energy together to throw it all in one attempt. He knew it was what Baris was waiting for. It was all he could do. He glanced aside at the woman, saw she had halted some way back. She was looking past Baris at Hirald, a look of horror on her face. Snow did not want to look. He did not want to know.

'Oh my God. It's her!'

Snow pulled himself to his feet, dizziness making him lurch. Baris grinned and pointed the rifle at his face, relished his moment for the half a second it lasted. The hand punched through his body, knocked the rifle aside, lifted him and hurled him against a rock with such force he stuck for a moment, then fell leaving a man-shaped corona of blood. Hirald stood there, revealed. Where the syntheflesh had been blown away glittering ceramal was exposed, her white enamel teeth, one blue eye complete in its socket, the ribbed column of her spine. She observed Snow for a moment then turned towards the woman. Snow fainted before the scream.

*

He was in his bed and memories slowly dragged themselves into his mind. He lay there, his throat dry, and
after a moment felt across to his numbed shoulder and
the dressing. It was a moment before he dared open his
eyes. Hirald sat at the side of the bed, and when she saw
he was awake she helped him up into a sitting position
against his pillows. Snow observed her face. She had
repaired the damage somehow, but the scars of that
repair work were still there. She looked just like a human
woman who had been disfigured in an accident. She
wore a loose shirt and trousers to hide the other repairs.
As he looked at her she reached up and self-consciously
touched her face, before reaching for a glass of water to
hand to him. Gratefully he drained the glass, that touch
of vanity confusing him for a moment.

'You're a Golem android,' he said, in the end, unsure.

Hirald smiled and it did not look so bad.

She said, 'Canard Meck thought that.' When she saw
his confusion she explained, 'The corporation woman.
She called me product, which is an understandable
mistake. I am nearly indistinguishable from the Golem
Twenty-two.'

'What are you then?' Snow asked as she poured him
another glass of water.

'Cyborg. Underneath this syntheflesh I am ceramal.
In the ceramal a human brain, spinal column, and other
nerve tissues.'

Snow sipped his drink as he considered that. He was
not sure what he was feeling, but it certainly was not the
horror he had first felt.

'Will you come to Earth with me?'

Snow turned and looked at her for a long time. He

remembered how it had been in the tents as she, he realized, discovered that she was still human.

'You know, I will never grow old and die,' she said.

'I know.'

She tilted her head questioningly and awaited his answer. A slow smile spread across his face.

'I'll come with you,' he told her. 'If you will stay with me.' He put his drink down and reached out to take hold of her hand. What defined humanity? There was blood still under her fingernails and the tear duct in her left eye was not working properly. It didn't matter.

# 8

# CHOUDAPT

A single biolight clung to a hull bone, its tick head thrust into a ship's artery. In the light's dim blue luminescence Simoz observed the generator palpitating like a sick heart as it drew in plankton-rich sea water. Canvas straps secured the generator to the inner hull and a heavy skein of cables issued from under the dripping rim of its bivalve shell and was stapled to hull beams that disappeared into the darkness where the motors hummed. Simoz subvocalized an acid observation.

*Very nice.*

The doctor mycelium, the symbiont which monitored and repaired his body and fought off those things beyond the compass of his immune system, was of course defensive.

Biotech is efficient, cheap, and self-propagating.

*Yeah, but what people fail to mention about it, is the smell.*

This is a crosstech ship.

*Mike, it stinks like a Billingsgate gutter.*

A nicely colourful historic reference only marred by the fact that you have never been to Earth.

*Picky.*

'The motors are ceramic nanofacture,' said Harbing.

Simoz supposed they must be – biotech ship motors made a sound he usually associated with wet sex.

'Where from?' he asked, not allowing the internal bickering to affect his outward demeanour.

'Nanofactured on the Outlink Station Ooerlikkon and transmitted via Circe,' Harbing replied.

Simoz studied the Mate with interest, consciously not focusing on the man's more obvious augmentations and adaptations, which was difficult. From his two-toed feet to the hairless white dome of his head the Mate was a full choudapt with numerous cyber implants. His mouth was the worst; with its feeding palps moving across his chin to emphasize his words. Simoz looked him in the eye and showed no evident reaction to the flickering of his nictitating membranes.

'You've had no rejection problems?' he asked.

This question puzzled Harbing. Simoz allowed his gaze to drop to the scanner link Harbing had grafted just above his hip. There were pustules around the disc of bright metal and a slight leakage of pus from behind it.

'I don't quite understand what you're getting at,' said Harbing.

Simoz nodded to himself.

*Sharp drop in IQ a couple of weeks after infection.*
Obviously . . . I am ready now.

Simoz concentrated his gaze on the link and Harbing glanced down. His puzzlement increased when he saw the signs of his own body rejecting its technology. Simoz let things go no further than that. He quickly reached out and put his right hand behind Harbing's head. His left hand he clamped across the Mate's mouth and he winced as the palps pinched at his palm. Harbing struggled, but to no avail, then his eyes grew wide in shock as Mike

extended its nano-mycelium body from the palm of
Simoz's hand down the man's throat.

*Are you in?*

I am in . . . cutting motor functions.

Harbing dropped as if someone had cut his strings.
Simoz knelt with him as he collapsed, his hands still in
position.

*Can you link?*

Parasitic fungus is primitive form. Aggression. Fungal
form, dead.

*What happened?*

No link established.

'Damn!'

You are vocalizing.

*I was aware of that. We'll try again in the Wrack. With-
draw from him and blank out the last minute or so.*

Withdrawn.

Simoz removed his hands and cradled Harbing's
head. After a moment Harbing opened his eyes.

'What . . . what happened?'

Simoz gestured to the generator.

'You were showing me the generator then you just
keeled over,' he said.

'I feel sick,' said Harbing.

Understandable. The fungus is breaking down in his lym-
phatic system.

*Will he be all right?*

He will not notice as soon as he is reinfected.

*How long till that happens?*

It has probably already happened. I have noted a high
degree of spore incursion on this ship.

*And that means?*

The spores are in the air of this ship. Forty per cent of my function at present is keeping them from infecting you. They are especially prevalent in here.

*I thought they wouldn't infect me.*

Not a primary infection, but they could make you ill.

*What about the retrovirus?*

I am keeping it in somnolent form until I have made suffi-cient alterations.

*What?*

The fungal form here shows extreme divergence and I am altering the retrovirus to suit.

*A mutation? Could that be it? Something the original virus missed?*

There is that possibility.

Simoz helped Harbing to his feet then pointed to the scanner link at Harbing's waist.

'It might have something to do with that,' he said.

Harbing gaped at the signs of rejection. 'Yeah . . . yeah, I gotta do something about that.'

'Perhaps you should see the ship's doctor.'

'Yeah, I'll do that.'

Somewhat bemusedly Harbing turned and tottered from the engine room. After casting a glare of suspicion at the generator, Simoz followed.

Here was a city enclosed in a translucent bubble, steady on a copper-coloured sea. It could have been mistaken for something built had it not been for the veins in the surface of the bubble. The crosstech ship, apparently the bastard offspring of a dredger and a manta ray, circled the bubble to where a split developed in the meniscus and it drew aside like stage curtains. On the deck of the ship Simoz noted the stench of decay wafted to him on the sea breeze, then glanced aside to where a cluster of smaller, house-sized bubbles surfaced and were drawn away by the tide. These bubbles were mostly opaque but with inset glass windows. Through some of these he saw human faces staring out – faces blank of human expression.

*They keep washing up at the mouth of the Thranx.*

It is where the currents take them.

*Some of the other Wrack cities have taken to burning any that get close.*

A perhaps understandable reaction.

The ship motored in through the opening and drew in to docks in the shape of lily pads clustered around the organic city. Ramps terminating in spiked hooks lowered from the crosstech ship and punctured the pads, securing the vessel in place. Simoz picked up his kitbag and quickly moved to one of them, but before he reached it, Harbing and another crew member moved in on him.

'Why are you here?' Harbing asked.

Simoz studied him. 'I told you: I have some biotech samples I hope to sell here. There some problem?'

'There's problem,' said the other crew member.

'I don't see it,' said Simoz, moving to go past the two men. As he did so he kept a wary eye on the other crewman. This man was shorter than Harbing, but heavily muscled. A computer link below his right ear was leaking pus and a suppurating hollow above his hip indicated where a scanner link had once been seated.

Late stages of infection.

*I know.*

The man reached out and caught hold of Simoz by the biceps, his expression alternately puzzled and blank.

'Problem,' he said leadenly.

Simoz caught hold of the man's wrist, pulled him in and thumped him hard under the sternum. The man went down coughing and wheezing.

Harbing stood back gazing at the scene in bewilderment. 'I don't . . . I don't understand.'

'You will,' said Simoz, and quickly headed for the ramp. Two other crewmen were watching him from the bows of the ship. They too were without expression.

*We'll have to move fast. There's a defensive reaction here. I guess I don't smell right.*

It was predicted.

Once on the queasy surface of the docks Simoz quickly headed for an entry portal, meanwhile passing a female choudapt walking a pet on a lead. This pet was a sea louse a metre long, its ribbed black shell painted with flowers and rococo patterns, its mandibles and saw-toothed mouth grinding and dripping foamy saliva.

*Choud.*

I see through your eyes.

Simoz felt there to be something quite perverse about these people keeping as pets the creatures whose genome they had spliced into their own bodies. He increased his pace as the choud turned to watch him with its glowing eyepits. He was through the entrance portal and moving quickly into the alleys and precincts when the creature started to fight its leash and show an inclination to come after him.

*This could get ever so slightly lethal. Can't you do anything?*

I can try to copy the pheromonal signature.

*Do so.*

You will not know right away if it is working.

Simoz found himself in a dank alley free of choudapts or chouds. The floor and walls of the alley were dead bio-facture and for a moment he felt safe enough to open his kitbag and quickly remove the tools of his trade. At his belt he holstered a thin-gun. Over his shoulder he slung the strap of a laser carbine. In his pockets he placed various smaller implements of destructive potential. Then he stood and kicked his bag to one side.

*Chouds. Jesus. Some idiot must have brought in a wild one. What other explanation is there? Probably full of fungal spores. I'd bet it was found in a freed bladder.*

People quickly forget. And there are other explanations.

*Yes, I know. I'd imagine you find the life-cycle interesting, there being certain similarities with yourself.*

I do find it interesting though I would dispute that it is similar to myself. The parasitic fungus here is without sentience; the subminds it develops are of the level of an ant or a bee. It is also worth noting that it is wholly natural and was here long before humans arrived and turned seaweed into living accommodation and spliced themselves with native life-forms.

*Do I detect disapproval?*

Only of incompetence. The original bioengineers should have detected the choud parasite and its method of transmission. Subsequent generations should have been given immunity to it by taking on a different adapted form.

*Should haves and should haves. We've a job to do. Will you try not to kill it this time? We need that location.*

I will try.

Simoz moved to the mouth of the alley and studied the crowds. On the other side of the flattened pipe of a street he saw the choudapt woman walking her choud. It showed no reaction to him, so his body must now be emitting the pheromone. As he stood there watching the people of the Wrack, and trying to decide who to go for and how, a young choudapt woman walked past him and turned into the mouth of the alley. He nodded to her, but she did not acknowledge his presence. He silently turned and followed her. Halfway into the alley she realized he was behind her and abruptly turned, opening her mouth, perhaps to say something, perhaps to scream. He slammed his hand over it, tripped her and forced her back against the ground. Mike went in.

Parasitic fungus primitive form again. I try to . . .

*Come on Mike – just do it gently.*

Fungal form, dead.

*Oh for chrissake.*

It would seem that the fungus is unable to achieve adult form in humans and in juvenile form cannot survive my . . . inspection. I would suggest that we take an actual choud next.

*Oh great idea.*

Simoz removed his hand and the woman abruptly opened her eyes.

'You all right?' he asked. 'You just keeled over.'

'It's dead. You killed it,' she said.

'You got me there,' said Simoz, reaching into his pocket for a shock stick.

'How did you do it?'

The woman sat upright. She was a choudapt without evident augmentations. Her hands and feet were two-toed and her skin a bluey green with the angular hard-ness of exoskeleton. She had retained her hair, which was long and anaemic blonde and spilled all the way

down the plastimail slip she wore. She had used irides-
cent paint on her mouth palps so that they looked like
some curious item of jewellery.

'I have a doctor mycelium inside me,' Simoz replied.

'Then you must be ECS.'

*She is showing surprising acuity in the circumstances.*

Not surprising.

Mike's reply had a hint of dry sarcasm behind it.

*I suggest you elaborate.*

She is Earth Central Security as well. She is a Monitor.
Her boosted immune system must have resisted infection
for a long time and it is helping her recover very quickly
now.

Simoz left the shock stick in his pocket and helped the
woman to her feet.

'Simoz,' he said.

'Haline,' the woman replied.

What a gas.

Simoz frowned. It was very unlike the mycelium to
make jokes. Perhaps it was feeling the strain.

'What's happening here?' Haline asked.

Nodding to the mouth of the alley and heading in that
direction, Simoz said, 'I'll tell you while you lead me
somewhere I can, without interference, get hold of a
choud.'

Haline stared at him then turned to the left as they
departed the alley.

'Something was controlling me,' she said.

'A parasitic fungus,' said Simoz. 'It was here when
only chouds lived in the bladders of the wracks. Fairly
simple vector: it lives in the choud's body and drives
the creature to climb into a bladder and cut it free.
That bladder drifts to another wrack where there are

uninfected chouds. There it makes the choud find a
secure place to encyst . . . cocoon itself. It then feeds on
the choud's body and produces spores which spread
through the wrack and infect other chouds. The set-up
in the wrack is then something like that of social insects
on Earth – the main fungus has a primitive mind and it
controls the others by means of pheromonal messages.
Those other chouds, once infected for a number of years,
then act like new queens leaving a bee's nest; they climb
into a bladder and cut it away to start the cycle all over
again. They start their own colonies. Only the fact that
infected and uninfected chouds can detect each other
has prevented a complete takeover by the fungus, but
then that's evolution for you.'

'But . . . us?' said Haline.

'Come on, you're a choudapt. Ninety per cent human
and ten per cent choud. It's why you like the horrible
things as pets.'

'Oh yes, of course, but . . . how is it I don't know about
this . . . this fungus?'

'It was supposedly wiped out two centuries ago by a
manufactured retrovirus.'

'Then how has this happened?'

'That's one of the things I'm here to find out,' said
Simoz as he gazed around, 'Where are we going?'

'To the centre. You can buy a choud there.'

'I see.'

'What else do you need to know?'

'I need to know where the encysted choud is hidden.
That's why I need to lay hands on another one. Mike can
winkle the location of the "mother" fungus from one of
its mature kin. We tried it with you but the fungal form

apparently doesn't mature in human hosts and is a bit delicate.'

*And while I'm thinking about it, Mike, how the hell am I going to put my hand over a choud's mouth.*

Unfortunately there is not enough seal in such mouth parts.

*What?*

You will not have to put your hand over its mouth, but in its mouth.

*Oh great.*

As they walked down the flattened artery of a causeway, beyond whose translucent walls bubble houses clustered like giant eyeballs, Simoz watched the folk around him. Many of them had obviously been having problems with their augmentations – the cyber implants and links that joined living human to his technology. None of the humans showed any reaction to him, but the few chouds he saw turned and fought their leashes, foam dripping from mouth parts like slime-coated cutlery sets.

*How long will she hold out?*

Her immune system is boosted but not as efficient as myself. She has been reinfected already, but the fungus will not be well established for an hour or so.

*Efficient as yourself?*

Mere fact.

*Okay, what about the pheromonal signature?*

She is giving it off.

*So she can go buy us a choud and bring it to a suitable location.*

Very practical of you.

*Improvisation my friend. Improvisation.*

The centre was the point from which branched all the main causeways of the Wrack. Those causeways ran down the sepals of the giant pseudo-flower of the plant, which was also the city. Here the bubble buildings were stacked in profusion like berries heaped over a spread hand. Myriad tubeways connected these separate bubbles, some of which were houses and some of them offices, shops, restaurants – all the usual paraphernalia of that entity called a city. By way of these tubes and through some of the bubbles, Haline led Simoz to her home. Then she went alone to make the required purchase. Simoz made himself comfortable in a chair fashioned from the scales of a giant fish and scanned his surroundings. He noted the veins in the ceiling at which a couple of biolights were feeding, and on the floor the slow traverse of a tile-cleaning slime mould. He saw that she had a food plant of old biofacture and one he recognized as producing a fruit that in its ancestry had both apples and pigs. He only gradually became aware of how dim it was in the place and how few biolights Haline seemed to have. The sudden simultaneous agony at his shoulder and calf told him abruptly where the other biolights had gone.

'Shit!'

Simoz jerked from the chair and felt the chitinous legs of the biolights dig into his calf and his back. He pulled his thin-gun from its holster and pointed at the biolight on his leg. The pain was incredible and it took him a moment to realize that with such a shot he would likely blow his foot off. Gritting his teeth he reholstered the gun and took the shock stick out of his pocket. He touched the end of the stick to the biolight on his back and pressed the button. The shock convulsed the light and he felt it rip from his back and heard it thud on the floor. A spill-over of energy paralysed his shoulder and sent him stumbling.

'Fucking hell!'

You are not thinking straight.

'Oh fucking brilliant!'

I am blocking this light's breathing holes. It is detaching.

The second biolight fell from his leg and scuttled across the room. Simoz drew his thin-gun and aimed at the one that had fallen behind him. The light emitted by its baggy body had taken on a reddish tinge from his blood. It was on its back, its six legs curled in tight, its tick mouth bubbling. The thin-gun coughed and the bio-light exploded, spraying glowing ichor and translucent organs in every direction. Simoz noted half its body stuck to the side of the chair, its legs quivering, before he turned to search out the other light. It scuttled from under a synthewood coffee table and he shot at it twice, leaving smoking holes in the floor. It ran up the wall then came across the ceiling at him. He hit it as it dropped towards him. Warm flesh and glowing ichor plastered his face and shoulders. He wiped the substance from his eyes and stepped out from under the other two lights on the ceiling. They showed no sign of moving.

*What the hell was that?*

There was a delay before Mike replied. Simoz felt the wounds in his shoulder and calf being sealed by the mycelium, the pain fading.

Choud DNA has been used in all biofacture here. These lights are fifty-three per cent choud.

*Enough for a mature fungal form?*

Yes.

*Did you read it?*

I did.

*You have the location of the mother fungus?*

I do.

Just then the door to the room opened and Haline entered with a small choud straining at the leash she held. Simoz studied her and she blankly returned his gaze before absently releasing the leash. The choud surged forward, its many legs rustling against the floor. Simoz shot it through the head and it stopped dead, then slowly curled into a perfect ball. Haline showed little reaction.

'Why have you done this to my home?' she asked, her words dull.

Simoz walked towards her, but as he drew close she suddenly stepped forward with her hands held out like blades. Simoz touched the shock stick to her forearm and she slammed back against the door then slid down it to the floor. He dragged her aside and stepped out of her home.

*I take it you stopped producing the pheromone?*

I did not have spare function. My repair of you and my continued alteration of the retrovirus used it all.

*Continued alteration?*

The divergence of this parasitic fungus is greater than I thought.

Simoz stooped down and parted the rip in his trouser leg to reveal a ragged circle of pink scar tissue.

*Quick work.*

You need to be completely functional. You have a bit of a journey and anything of more than forty per cent choud biofacture will be trying to kill you.

*Where to?*

The anchor root. The encysted choud is there.

*Perhaps it would be better to release the virus here.*

That would defeat the object of us coming here. I need to read the mother fungus. It will be the only way for us to find some clue as to how it got here.

*A dubious bet at best I think.*

Our only one. If there is even the slightest evidence that the fungal infection was deliberate then there must be an investigation, as that would likely mean Separatist activity. If there is some other cause, we need to know that, to prevent it happening again.

At the centre point of the Wrack lay an open well around whose edges were gathered leaf-shaped platforms. Simoz watched people walk on to these, whereupon they dropped gently into the well. Thick stalks from the platforms were rooted into the wall of the well and slid down as if following invisible grooves.

*There must be another way down.*

It is likely that this living elevator is based more on wrack DNA than choud DNA.

*I think we should find out before we try it.*

Walking across the wide plaza, Simoz was conscious of puzzled stares cast in his direction and of chouds straining at leashes. He noted a floor-cleaning creature, like a flattened choud, become aware of his presence then turn after him in painfully slow pursuit. He also noted a heavily choudapted human: a man wearing only a pouch belt, his body completely sheathed in plates of exoskeleton, turn in his direction and slowly come after him. Upon reaching the well Simoz reached down and pressed his hand to the rough surface of one leaf.

*Are you in?*
I am.
*Come on, things are getting fraught round here.*
This biotech is ninety per cent wrack-based.

Simoz glanced back and saw general movement in his direction as of a crowd attracted by a curiosity. He doubted he would be able to survive their attention.

*Out of choices.*

Simoz stepped onto the leaf and it immediately swung out over the well and slowly began to descend. He observed that the stalk penetrated the woody wall through a wet slot, a slot that opened before it and closed after it like a zipper. The leaf platform reached ten metres down when he glanced up and saw the heavy choudapt follow him over the edge on another. Another ten metres down and he saw something fall over the rim above to come hurtling down with a whistling squeal – the cleaning creature. It hit the edge of his platform to scrabble for a moment with inadequate legs, then fell out of sight. Returning his attention to the man above, Simoz saw him staring down, his saw-toothed palps clacking before his mouth.

He could jump.
*Thank you for that.*

Simoz drew his thin-gun and held it in his right hand, retaining his shock stick in his left. Standing close to the edge of his platform, the man did not jump, but withdrew something from one of his pouches and pointed it at Simoz. No time to react – Simoz had not expected personal armament here. Something slapped his leg and he peered down at the ugly dart buried in his thigh. It consisted of a glassy blade with feathery flights, with two testicular sacks pulsing between the two.

Neurotoxin.

Simoz's leg went completely dead and gave under him. He grabbed the dart and pulled it free, black poison dripping from its hollow point. He fired upwards blowing a lump out of the edge of the platform above, driving his attacker back out of sight. Two more shots blew holes straight through the upper platform, but his choudapt attacker abruptly jumped over the edge. Simoz fired at him again as he hurtled down. One shot took a lump from the man's shoulder and tore away a plate of exo-skeleton. Without apparently noticing his wound, the man landed solidly, his clawed toes driving into the material of the platform. Simoz snap-shot at him as the numbness spread to his other leg then edged up to his sternum. The shot missed.

'Earther!' the choudapt snarled and flung himself forward. Simoz shot again and had the satisfaction of seeing an arm cartwheel away as his attacker fell back off the platform, then his own arms went dead and his vision faded.

Simoz.

  . . .

  Simoz.

  *I hear you.*

  That is good.

  *Is it?*

  Yes. Had there been no immediate response from you . . .

  *What?*

  You would have been dead.

  *How damaged am I?*

The neurotoxin has caused extensive nerve damage. I am now controlling all your autonomous functions.

*What about my unautonomous ones?*

I am using myself to establish links across the damaged areas.

*My feet are hurting.*

. . .

*That's better.*

Re-establishing visual cortex.

Simoz blinked as his vision returned, but there seemed to be something wrong with it. Though everything was sharper it also seemed somehow false. He blinked again and tried to move his arms. They responded to him, but yet again there seemed to be something wrong – some feeling of disconnection. Levering himself upright, he attempted to stand, but only got halfway before falling flat on his face.

*Something not quite right here.*

There is a disparity of function. Try again.

Simoz finally managed to stand. As he stood there swaying, his hands suddenly seemed to catch on fire. He screamed and abruptly sat down.

I must use one hundred per cent of my function. Disconnecting from cerebrum.

*Mike, no, wait!*

The burning in his hands became a deep soreness, a tingling, numbness, then went away completely. Warily Simoz stood again and checked his surroundings. Everything seemed to be working perfectly now, only inside him there lay a terrible emptiness.

*Mike?*

. . .

*Mike?*

Simoz nodded to himself, then stooped and retrieved his weapons. He was alone in the anchor root, and especially aware that no corpse without an arm lay here on the floor where the platform had come to rest.

*I don't know if you can hear me, Mike, but this has to be Separatist terrorism. Why else would someone be wandering about with a neurotoxin weapon?*

Simoz stepped off the platform and walked to where an arm lay in a pool of watery blood. He circled until he found a smeared area of the same then followed the dripped trail into a side-branching tunnel of the anchor root, stepping warily on slippery floor under the blue luminescence. The biolights were restless on the ceiling and it was because he was keeping half an eye on them that he did not immediately see the choudapt. There came a low whickering sound and Simoz ducked before he knew why he was ducking and glanced behind him to see one of the neurotoxin darts bouncing across the floor. He fired reflexively at a half-seen shape, then pursued when that shape rose from the shadows at the side of the tunnel and fled.

*Damnit Mike, this is the only way. You didn't give a precise location for that encysted choud. I'd bet this bastard knows where it is.*

Before rounding a corner in the tunnel Simoz slowed to a walk, since he had no wish to run straight into one of those darts, and glancing back had the dubious pleasure of seeing biolights dropping from the ceiling and scuttling towards him. Not allowing himself panic, he reached into his pocket, removing a shock grenade the size and shape of an acorn. He then edged to the corner and carefully peeked round, guessing the dark shape squatting in the shadows to be the choudapt. Simoz flipped the cap on the grenade and tossed it round. A white flash followed by lots of electric sizzlings ensued. Glancing back at the biolights that were approaching he flipped a grenade in their direction too, closing his eyes against the flash. He opened his eyes to see biolights scattered across the floor of the tunnel, their legs in the air and the luminescence they emitted faltering, then he stepped round the corner.

The choudapt lay sprawled across the tunnel. Simoz advanced on the man and kicked away the tubular dart thrower lying next to his outstretched left hand. The stump of his right arm had some sort of bio field-dressing over it, as did the wound in his shoulder, and he was breathing raggedly. Simoz squatted down next to him and removed the shock stick from his pocket. He altered a setting on its thumb wheel and touched the end of it to the choudapt's neck. The low buzzing convulsed the man and he immediately opened his eyes and started to move, but froze as the barrel of Simoz's thin-gun pressed against his forehead.

'Separatist?' asked Simoz.

The man just sneered at him. Simoz altered the setting on his shock stick and touched what he assumed to me the man's most sensitive area. Judging by the screech that followed he guessed he had been right.

'Separatist?' he asked again.

'Yes,' said the man.

Simoz noted the slight distraction in the man's expression. Keeping the shock stick to his groin he turned and shot the biolight that had been creeping up behind. Before the man could react Simoz had his thin-gun back in his face.

'The parasitic fungus, where did you get it from?'

The man showed an inclination not to answer. Simoz made that inclination go away. When the man had stopped screaming he seemed more inclined to cooperate.

'We got it from a preserved choud exported before the retrovirus was used here.'

'Is it just you here? No, silly question. You'd only lie. I want you to stand very slowly and carefully, then very slowly and carefully I want you to walk to the encysted choud.'

The man looked at him blankly for a moment, then obeyed. Simoz tried to analyse that blank look, knowing that somehow he had made a mistake here.

'What was the plan? You knew someone would be here with the retrovirus at some point. Or is this just the usual terrorism?'

'Yes, terrorism. It works.'

*Now that, Mike, was a lie. I wonder what's really happening here.*

'Just show everyone what big guns you've got and they'll do what you want?'

'That's right,' said the choudapt.

'Okay, stop there. Turn round.'

The choudapt halted and turned. He was grinning.

Simoz continued, 'The fungal form has been altered to counter the retrovirus, but you knew that the virus would be altered to suit. You also knew that at some point it would be released here. So the question is: what result are you after?'

The choudapt's palps moved in what Simoz could only assume to be a rude gesture.

'You won't get out of here,' the choudapt said. He

nodded back down the tunnel. 'It won't just be the biolights. Every piece of biotech will be after you. Right now
the lifting platforms have ceased to function.'

'You know, I'm carrying the virus in my body. The
fungal parasites would die very quickly,' said Simoz.

'Then release it.'

'I see . . . turn and continue walking.'

*Mike, do not release the virus. Whatever happens, do not
release it.*

As they reached the end of the tunnel Simoz tossed a
shock grenade behind him to deter the pursuing biolights, which had now been joined by some armoured
multi-legged thing whose function he could not guess.
The choudapt led him through another tunnel, a narrow
tunnel that seemingly terminated at a wall, but then the
wall parted before him. In the place beyond the choudapt
turned to Simoz, who peered past him at the second
choudapt crucified by woody growths to the wrack wall.
This other one opened crusted eyes but did not speak.

'Tarin controls the Wrack city. He controls every
fungal parasite and therefore all the biotech here. Go
on, Earther, release your virus – kill them all,' the first
choudapt said.

'I see,' said Simoz. 'You've undermined all the
biotech. If I release the virus what happens?'

'You destroy the Wrack and kill a hundred thousand
people. We claim extreme incompetence on the part of
ECS and recruit a million to our cause.'

'Then I won't release the virus.'

As he said this he heard the wall opening behind him.
Without looking he shot behind himself and heard a
bubbling squeal.

'You'll die either here or on your way out and someone else will come and release the virus here. We win all ways.'

'*You* don't,' said Simoz.

The choudapt had time only to raise his remaining arm. The thin-gun coughed, the side of the man's head opened like a hinged lid and a haze of bone and brain splashed out behind him. He staggered back and fell at the feet of the encysted choudapt, Tarin. Simoz now turned and fired twice, splashing luminous blood up the walls. He tossed a shock grenade out into an encroaching wall of chitinous legs, glowing bodies, and hints of armour. The wall fell in chaos and he counted the last two grenades in his pocket. Then he turned, walked forward and stepped over the dead choudapt to look into Tarin's eyes. There was a ripping sound as Tarin opened his crusted lips.

'No win . . . Earther,' he said, spittle running from the side of his mouth.

*Knock once for yes and twice for no. Are you hearing this, Mike?*

Simoz's stomach muscles clenched twice and he grinned at his doctor mycelium's little joke.

*You have to go in, Mike, and take over. This was always a possibility: you have to leave me even if that means you leave me to die.*

There was a long pause then his stomach muscles clenched once.

'I always win,' said Simoz.

The choudapt Tarin opened his mouth to make some reply. Simoz didn't wait for it. He slammed his hand over that crusted mouth.

*Goodbye, Mike,* he managed before his legs went numb and the sight faded from his eyes. As he fell he could feel his hand bonded to the choudapt's mouth. The thin-gun fell from the numb fingers of his other hand before a pool of blackness filled his skull.

. . .

Simoz.

. . .

Simoz.

# 9

# ADAPTOGENIC

*Another murder-louse made its scuttling charge, its trilobite body holding level as a pointer on me as its multitude of legs found purchase on the weed-slippery rocks. I watched the creature with a crawling sensation in my guts as it reached the perimeter. There was always the horrible suspicion that this time one might make it, this time I'd end up as a paralysed egg-carrier or diced by those grinding mandibles. But no, with admirable and reassuring efficiency the Tenkian strobed from its tripod and the louse became a messy explosion of legs, carapace and pink ichor. This is, of course, adding to my problems. Every louse the autogun splatters means more food to attract more lice. They are coming with greater frequency now. Soon I'll have to move the crate to a cleaner area, try to find somewhere to hide it, where it won't be swept away. There's enough power left in the gun's batteries for it to follow on its impellers . . . A cleaner area . . . In a day or so all areas on this side of the planet will be swept clean. I face choices; the lice, drowning, or ceasing to be human. Why the hell am I worrying about the crate? I really wish I'd missed that auction.*

\*

'Good morning Mr Chel,' said the two-and-a-half-metre-tall two-hundred-kilo monster who worked as security guard for Darkander. I gave Jane a look of long-suffering and stood still while I was scanned for comlinks or any of the other equipment Darkander considered an unfair advantage.

'You are clean, Mr Chel.'

My chip card was next and the monster took it from me between a finger and thumb like the grab on a cometary mining ship. After a moment he returned it.

'Your credit is good, Mr Chel.'

After she too had been checked out Jane joined me. I smiled mild approval at her cool.

'Is it always like that?' she asked, tucking her card into one of the many pockets of her coverall.

'Always. No extra information access. No comlinks and no AIs. Darkander is very strict about it.'

'Isn't that a bit discriminating?'

'Some free AIs once took him to court on those grounds. They lost out on a protection of antiquities law about two centuries old. He then pointed out to them that should they bring another action and win he would be forced to close down. They left him alone. Anyway, what do you think?'

Darkander's is an anachronism. It is a huge scan-shielded warehouse where all manner of items are stacked haphazardly and sold by lot. There is no computer bidding, no microsecond business transactions. Starting from lot one everything comes under Darkander's wooden hammer. It is a place for human experts with a relish for competition, an eye for bargains and deals, and a dislike of paying taxes. People like Jason Chel. Me.

'Now, I'm not going to point anything out to you, as I'm often watched. Anything that takes your interest mark on the list, then come back to me when you've finished. I'll tell you how high to go.'

Jane smiled then swayed off amongst the chaos of goods. As I watched her go I felt a degree of discomfort. I'd promised her this visit some time ago, when I'd been drunk, and had since tried very hard to get out of it. Well, now she was here. Hopefully she wouldn't cause too much harm. I slowly followed her in and allowed my gaze to wander casually to the objects I was after. There was a box of what looked like pre-runcible tiles, probably from the belly of a shuttle, a Thrakework sculpture of Orbonnai skulls, something that looked like the shell of a mollusc – I hadn't a clue what it was, but was prepared to risk a few credits on it – and finally there was the Golem Six android, which after my cursory inspection the day before I felt sure had the mind of a Three or Four. This last item was the one I really wanted. Made before the twenty-third revision of the Turing Test, these Golem were much in demand. Of course, now the auction was starting I did not look too closely at it, I instead showed a great deal of interest in some chainglass blades which were quite obviously faked to look like Tenkians.

The bidding started off with the usual lack of alacrity as Jane rejoined me.

'Let me see,' I took the note screen from her and studied the items she had marked. To my annoyance I noted she had marked the tiles. 'I think we'll have a cup of coffee. These' – I tapped the stylus against the lot number of the tiles – 'won't be up for a while, and they are the first on your . . . list.'

I had decided to be generous.

We sat sipping our way through a cup of coffee each as the auction progressed. At the lot before the tiles we sauntered out, and as soon as this was sold we moved into Darkander's view. The short bald-headed man who was reputed to be a multibillionaire flicked a glance in my direction and tried to start the bidding at five hundred. I caught hold of Jane's arm before she could raise it. The figure Darkander suggested dropped in fifties until it was fifty, then started to rise again in twenty-fives. Jane began to bid, and as she did so I looked to see who she was bidding against. When the figure reached four twenty-five I nudged her.

'Drop it.'

'Why?'

'You're out of your league here and that's about all they're worth.'

The bidding continued to the figure of five seventy-five.

'See the fat little guy over there?' I directed Jane's attention to that individual. 'He's the agent for the Ganymede runcible AI. It probably wants to give its containment sphere that old-world look.'

The mollusc shell was next but no one made a bid. It went into the next lot, which appeared to be a collection of all sorts of junk, but I'd seen a really old digital watch lying in there and had not expected a chance at it. I swore to myself for not going for the shell straight away, but I just wasn't paying attention. On this next lot the bidding was tried at fifty then dropped to ten. No one went for it so I gave Darkander the nod. 'Going once,' he told me. 'Going twice.' I couldn't believe it. I saw the runcible agent glance at me suspiciously and begin to raise his hand. He was too late, for the hammer went down. 'Sold to Mr Chel.' I managed to keep a straight face.

'Good?' Jane asked.

'Yes, very good . . . I think.'

The Thrakework sculpture went to the woman in black. She'd always had a taste for the macabre. I bid against her a couple of times, but when I saw that wild look come into her eyes I gave up. I knew her of old.

There was half an hour before the Golem was to come up for auction, so with a nod to the lady – she didn't see, she was fumbling with her death's-head charm and staring at the sculpture with a horrible avidity – I went to authorize the credit transfer for my buy, and leaving Jane to her own devices, took the boxes out to my Ford gravcar.

The mollusc shell was interesting. I noted that the box it came in had the same shipment marks, stamps and tape as the packing strewn about the Golem. This told me no more than that they'd come from the same world. I wanted some hint as to value and did not relish the prospect of initiating a computer search to identify this shell. Life, in its unbelievable abundance in the fifth of the galaxy thus far explored, had often used this sensible method of self-preservation. There were probably more types of shell than excuses for taxation. I put the shell aside and opened the other box.

For most of the contents of this box I could justify the price paid with resale through my shop, but no more. The digital watch was a dog. The case and the strap, which I thought to be ceramal greyed with age, turned out to be one of the later matt ceramals. There was nothing inside the case. I swore and was about to sling the box to the

front of the van compartment when something caught
my eye.

It was a bracelet set with manufactured diamonds and
therefore of little value. It was cheap costume jewellery,
yet something gave me pause. Something wrong with
it . . . I glanced back into the auction room and saw that
it would soon be the Golem's turn. I'd have to find out
later. In a rather distracted mood I returned, after
another scanning, to Jane's side in the auction room, and
bid two hundred over the odds for the Golem. Only as
Jane and I were leaving did I notice the desperate gaze
of a late arrival.

Chaplin Grable is the kind of man you learn to avoid
at Darkander's, the kind of man who'll sidle up beside
you and start asking the kind of questions you really
don't want to answer if you're after anything in particular. Then he'll give you his jaundiced opinion on various
objects in the warehouse, and sidle away. After he's gone
you feel the immediate urge to check your pockets, your
credit rating, then go home for a shower. That day he
stuck to me like a piece of dogshit on an instep.

'Look, all I want is a copy, downloaded copy, it's easy
money.'

I glanced towards Jane, who was then involved in bidding for an arty-looking mobile made from genuine
fossil-fuel-based plastic, if the label was to be believed. I
felt a certain relief that she was not at my side then.

'How much?'

'Four hundred, that's fair. I'll use all my own stuff. It's
easy—'

I was curious. 'A thousand.'

'Oh come on, for that piece of junk? I only want it for
the Historical Society. Six hundred.'

'Funny, I thought I said a thousand.'

'Seven fifty. That's it, easy, final offer, no more, capiche capoot.'

'Not interested.'

Of course I was, very interested, but if there was good money to be made here I intended to make it, not to pass it on to this slime bag.

'Okay okay, a thousand, done, a thousand.'

'Go away,' I told him. Then I saw something in his expression I didn't like at all, something incongruous. I turned away and headed for my gravcar with the android walking along behind me.

'A thousand is a lot,' it said.

'It is.'

I inspected it contemplatively. But for the loss of the syntheflesh covering of one side of its face and one arm it might well have been human. Many of its kind had since been accepted as such. It was just an unfair quirk of the law that defined this one as a machine and later models as sentient creatures.

'What's your name?' I asked it.

'Paul G6B33.'

'Why do you think he's interested in your memory, Paul?'

'I do not know. I have no long-term memory other than Cybercorp contract and base program.'

Grable had obviously loused. There was nothing of value in this android's mind. I should have sold him a copy. Too late now.

'Get in the back of the car, Paul.'

My android obeyed me.

*

*The Tenkian autogun followed with its impeller humming like an AC transformer and its turret revolving with martinet vigilance. A couple of lice came out from the rocks behind, but it did not fire for they did not come into the shifting perimeter. They stayed to feed on the remains of their fellows, their mandibles clacking with relish.*

*I had a hell of a time with the crate. I slipped once and grazed my knee, then sat on a wet rock, swearing, with water soaking into the bum of my trousers. I could open the crate and maybe its contents would follow me as obediently as Paul G6B33, if its power pack wasn't down. Finally I abandoned it in a suitable crevice weighed down with crusted rocks, then I moved on. The world-tide is coming with the rise of Scylla's binary companion and I have to prepare myself. I don't like to think about how.*

After taking the precaution of dropping Jane off at her residence – I didn't want her with me where I was going next – I took Paul straight to a prospective buyer. There was the usual jam up at the atmosphere lock and it took two hours before we were out of the city dome and cruising into the outlands. Paul had remained silent until we were speeding towards the distinctly curved horizon over the landscape of yellow ice-cliffs and weirdly phosphorescent mists.

'What place is this?' he asked with idiot precision.

I pointed out of the screen. 'I suppose I could give you a total of twelve guesses, but no, you only get three.'

He gazed out of the screen at the massive loom of Jupiter filling half the sky, its red eye-storm gazing down at us speculatively.

'We are on one of Jupiter's moons,' he said. I decided he definitely had the mind of a Three, since a Five never felt the need to state the obvious. But as far as antique value went, a Five was half the value of a Three.

'Yes, but can you figure which moon?'

There was a long pause then the statement, 'Ganymede.' If he'd got it wrong I would have been most surprised. Threes are not capable of guessing. If they do not have enough data to come to a conclusion they say so.

'Correct,' I told him, superfluously, and slowly began to bring the gravcar down towards an expensive residence set in the face of a sulphur-crusted cliff. The lock of a garage opened for us and we were soon climbing out of the car to be greeted by the goddess. Why do I call Henara the goddess? Because that is precisely what she looks like; Aphrodite, Diana, some supernal woman. She is nearly two metres tall and has the kind of build that will leave a man with a hollow feeling in the region of his groin. She has long luxuriant hair and a face to leave sculptors and painters feeling inadequate.

'Jason, so glad to see you . . . and who is this?'

Her voice set bits of me vibrating I did not know existed. She was fantastic. The AI that designed her deserved some kind of award, if it hadn't already got one. She was a Golem Twenty-three, I think. Human beings are never that close to perfection, or apotheosis.

'This is Paul G6B33,' I said, making the introductions. 'Paul, this is Henara Indomial, who I hope will soon be your new owner.'

Paul greeted her politely, and she led us into her home. In a few minutes I was sunk in a sofa, which was ridiculously luxurious, with a large scotch in my hand. Henara and I had an agreement that went back for ten years. She paid me a retainer so I would buy up any

Golem that came up for auction at Darkander's and offer it to her on a percentage basis. She was a free Golem and very very rich. The work of her endless life now was to make other Golem free. She bought them, upgraded them, and put them through the revised Turing Test. Then she set them free.

'There was a great deal of interest in him,' I told her. 'I had to pay two hundred more than expected.'

The credit transfer was made and I relaxed.

'One strange thing. Chaplin Grable offered me a thousand for a download copy of Paul's memory. Yet Paul only has his short-term memory and his base Cybercorp contract and programming.'

'Interesting,' said Henara with a noblesse oblige nod, then she turned her attention to Paul. 'Who owned you prior to Jason here?'

'I was attached to the Planetary Survey Corps in 2433,' was his reply, and I knew that was all she'd get. Assignment was in the contract memory. His skills and personality were in his base memory. I didn't think there was much to be learnt, so after a while I took my leave.

Back at my apartment I spread my remaining purchases out on a repro twentieth-century glass-top coffee table (no one can afford the real thing) and inspected each of the items minutely. Eventually, reluctantly, I picked up the bracelet and studied it. The metal it was made from, like the watch, was ceramal. There were eight lozenge diamonds spaced evenly round it, one for each colour of the rainbow plus one clear one. What made me suspicious about the object was the centimetre-thickness of the ceramal. It was perhaps the thickness needed for a chain used to tow asteroids, but hardly required for costume jewellery. I popped it open and inspected the clasp and hinges. What I found there increased my suspicion, and stirred up a little of the excitement I always thought dead until each time it reappeared. Where the bracelet opened there were pins on one side and sockets on the other. Where it hinged there were flexible mini conduits. The pins, I realized on seeing their reddish lustre, were made of carbon sixty doped ceramal, a very hard room-temperature superconductor. What I was holding certainly wasn't cheap costume jewellery. What it was I hadn't a clue. It was about then that the phone let me know someone wanted to speak with me.

'Yes, who is it?'

'Ah . . .'

The hologram of Chaplin Grable's most unbecoming features flickered into life before me.

'Henara Indomial has it. Go bother her.'

'I'm authorized to offer you two thousand for . . . what?'

'Henara Indomial.'

I waved my hand in the general direction of the eye and the face flickered out of existence. I didn't like the man. The phone called for my attention again.

'Look, you piece of—'

Henara appeared before me, her legs chopped off at the knees by the coffee table.

'Sorry, I thought you might be Grable.'

She looked at me quizzically and I explained the previous call to her. She smiled. I asked her what she wanted.

'Paul has his basic personality, his Cybercorp programming and a few giga of short-term memory. His long-term memory has actually been removed.'

'I told you that,' I said, confused.

'No, you misunderstand me. Up until the Golem Fifteen, compartmentalization was used, not wholemind programming. The LTM unit has been physically removed. Probably at about the same time as the missing syntheflesh and skin.

'Oh,' I said brilliantly.

'I would of course like you to acquire this LTM should it become available . . .'

'I'll see what I can do,' I told her.

Of course she was far too polite to bring my integrity into doubt. As she flickered out of existence I felt decidedly uncomfortable. I studied the bracelet. Could this be it? Seemed unlikely but I decided to check.

My hand scanner revealed a complexity it could not analyse. I used my system scanner and paid for time on one of the runcible subminds. It took a few minutes, but I soon received the analysis, along with the bill. The bracelet went under the name of a four-seasons changer. It was a twenty-seventh-century adaptogen laboratory. Not particularly old, but quite valuable if you can find the right buyer, and the right buyer was almost always an adapted human to beyond the fifth generation. I wondered, as always with the kind of morbid fascination that comes with the discovery of such an artefact, if it still worked. I was not to know then that one day the answer to that question was something my survival might depend on.

Three solstan days later I had expert advice on the changer and the advice was, 'Use this at considerable risk, the construction is far too complex and old for any kind of study that would not involve deconstruction, and why the hell do you want to know?' I was of course hoping for documented proof of working order, as this would double the value of the bracelet. There are experts and there are experts.

On the same day as I received this piece of negative equity I picked up the mollusc shell and listened for the sound of the sea – I hadn't identified the shell yet. There was no sound, and feeling hard put upon I shook it in irritation as one would shake any other piece of malfunctioning hardware. A cuboid crystal, with silver circuitry etched in three faces like strange glyphs, fell out and cracked the top of my coffee table. Okay, it wasn't that valuable, but I was attached to it, which was probably why I was pissed off enough to download a copy of what turned out to be Paul's LTM to sell to Grable before passing the original on to Henara. As was to be my luck at that time I discovered I could not find Grable anywhere. I ended up studying the memory myself, determined to make a decent profit somehow that week.

It took me a couple of days to run through the last mission. Much of my time was spent fast-forwarding by hand or by computer instruction, i.e. stop when something interesting occurs. It seemed to me that these Golem spent most of their time standing about waiting to be given orders. The tale I eventually managed to piece together was one of incompetence and failure.

The PSC had tried to establish a base on a planet called Scylla before something called the world-tide occurred. This was to be done by a mixed crew of hired labourers and androids. The whole thing was severely disorganized. The androids weren't complex enough and the workers not clever enough to sort out the discrepancy. There were disputes about pay and an attempt, considering the time limit on the project, at what can

only be described as extortion. I saw the base half-
finished and a belated attempt at evacuation. Some of the
humans got away, others boxed the androids and
attempted to seal the base against the world-tide. Paul
was not boxed because he was almost as useful as the
humans. He was a very new design. The rest was like
some Atlantean disaster; explosions, water, sparks, floating bodies. When Paul's memory greyed into auto
shutdown – after a long period of time recording the
marine life feeding – I realized what Grable had been
after. The androids. They were Golem Twos, the first
workable androids to be sold by Cybercorp – there had
only been one Golem One – and if still there they were
worth disgustingly huge amounts of money. I wondered
then where he got his information from and why Paul's
LTM had ended up in that shell. But even as I wondered
I packed the equipment I would need and sought the
required permissions for its transportation. By the next
solstan day I had booked myself for transmission to
Scylla's runcible, for while running through Paul's
memory I had seen a map and a map reference. I knew
where the base was.

*The crate is hidden. The world-tide is coming. And there are
only two things that stand between me and death. My Tenkian
autogun keeps the lice away, but there is no sensible way it
can keep me from drowning. There is another way though.
Even as I record this I pull up my sleeve and look at the
bracelet clasped around my wrist. The jewels seem to have
taken on a sinister glitter.*

Jane was not happy about my sudden business trip, but
I managed to bring her round, as I normally do. After

spending one pleasant night with her I got up early and
made my way to the transmission station. The runcible
transmission, the longest and most unbelievable part of
any interstellar journey, took no time at all. I don't even
try to pretend to know anything about the technology
that can shove me through an underspace non-distance
and drag me out a hundred or more light years away, and
in that I am more honest than most. Skaidon technology;
brought about by the linking of a human mind and AI.
It's impossible to understand unless you are both a
genius, like Skaidon himself, and plugged in. In my life
I have been neither and am unlikely to be. One moment
I was there standing in the containment sphere as before
the altar to Minotaur; silver bull's horns on a dais of
black glass, horns holding the shimmering disc of the
cusp, then one step after I am one hundred and twenty-
three light years away on the other side of another cusp
in an identical sphere: standardization across the galaxy
– as awesome as it is depressing.

Beyond the standard one G gravity in the containment sphere the gravity was rather less, but being a fairly
seasoned traveller I soon adjusted. A wide concourse led
from the row of containment spheres to a huge embarkation lounge; this was because I had arrived on the
moonlet Carla; the closest companion to Scylla, which
was too unstable for siting a runcible. At the opposite
end of the lounge I could see a delta-wing shuttle waiting to heave itself into a violet sky and was surprised to
see how few people there were waiting for the flight. I
made my way to an information console and called up
one of the runcible subminds.

'Name?'

'Jason Chel.'

'What information do you require, Jason Chel?'

'There are certain packages under my code and I wish to pick them—'

'The packages have arrived at cargo runcible four. There are AG drays available at all cargo runcibles.'

I regarded the console with a degree of suspicion. It had been very quick for a submind. Perhaps it was Carla AI taking an interest itself. The contents of one of my packages were unusual.

'Er, could you also tell me when the next shuttle is leaving for Scylla.'

'There will not be another shuttle to Scylla for two hundred solstan days.'

'What?'

'There will not be another shuttle—'

'I heard what you said. Why will there not be another shuttle to Scylla for two hundred days?'

'Because it is summer.'

'I beg your pardon?'

There came a sound very like a sigh from the console, as if it was tired of repeating this information to people who hadn't checked.

'Scylla is closed to all traffic for a period of two hundred and seventy-three solstan days during its summer season. All ground bases are sealed. This is due to the accelerated activity of dangerous life-forms at this time of the year.'

I walked away from the console feeling like a complete idiot. Some of the equipment I had in my luggage was brought along to deal with the life-forms I had seen in Paul's memory, a precaution which had cost me a fair lump of credit for transportation under seal. Now I'd discovered that in my eagerness I'd made a complete bollix.

I'd have to go back to Ganymede and wait three quarters of a year before I could come back. In a daze I headed for one of the bars at the edge of the lounge with the vague idea of getting plastered.

I was into my third scotch when a vaguely familiar figure slipped into the seat on the other side of my table. It took me a moment to recognize him, even then I wasn't quite sure. He looked too clean, too suave, not the man I'd known.

'What a surprise to meet you here,' said Chaplin Grable, and he grinned as amiably as a shark. I sat upright and looked at him in surprise. His smile made a small transition into a sneer as he took out a chainglass blade and began cleaning his nails. They didn't need cleaning.

'My contact tells me there was a small foul-up. He didn't get time to put the LTM back so he concealed it in the hammer-whelk shell.'

He glanced up from cleaning his nails and I wondered why I had always considered him to be a faintly ridiculous, irritating, but harmless fool.

'Seems the shell went into the next lot, which was then purchased by a Mr Chel. That would be you wouldn't it?'

He slid around the table into the seat next to me, his arm along the back of my chair and the chainglass knife held between his fingertips with its point pressing against his leg. I considered hitting down on the knife and driving it into his leg, but decided that was a fool's move. I needed to know how much he knew, how much he had planned. I put on my best buying and selling face.

'Grable, I doubt very much you could get away with using that here, so put it away and let's talk a little business.'

He watched me coldly and the knife disappeared with practised neatness into a wrist sheath. I'd have to watch him.

'Correct on the first point, a little awry on the second.'

'Your speech is somewhat altered, Mr Grable.'

'It suits the situation,' he said with a nasty smile.

I needed to get a step ahead of him. I decided to take a little gamble.

'Of course, it is a shame you don't know the location. Didn't your contact have time?'

It was a hit. Grable turned a sickly white, then came back with, 'But I'll have two hundred and seventy-three days in which to scan this planet and find the base.'

His was a hit as well.

'An arrangement, perhaps,' I suggested.

'Yes, it seems the most sensible course.'

I'd never understood the expression 'eyes like gimlets' until that moment. Grable had shed his normal unpleasant exterior and what was revealed underneath wasn't much better.

*About an hour ago I reached this location. It will do. There is a hollow in the surface with a sheltering overhang on the eastern side. Here I will be protected from the first destructive surge of the flood. All that remains is for me to survive when this area is under forty metres of sea. When I arrived here I sat on a fairly dry rock and fingered the bracelet. Nearby the autogun settled down on its tripod legs: an improbable steel mosquito. After a moment I pushed my fingernail under the edge of the green diamond. With a faint hum the diamond hinged out to reveal a polished cavity. I knew what to do next but was again reluctant. I looked across at the nearby scorched carcass of a murder-louse then moved over to it. It smelt of boiled lobster and was steaming slightly. Using a piece of shell I scooped up some ichor and dribbled it into the hollow in the bracelet. The diamond has now clicked back into place. I sit upon my rock and wait.*

Grable's contact on Carla was a man who ran an exclusive minishuttle service to Scylla. It wasn't illegal, just a little grey. The console had informed me that the planet was closed to all traffic at this time of its year, which didn't mean it was against any law to go there. All the individual protection laws had been thrown out centuries ago. If a person wanted to risk his own life that was his privilege, just so long as no other unconsenting individuals were put at risk. The powers that be look upon it as evolution in action, an imminently sensible view in my opinion.

His name was Warrack Singh and he had the appearance of someone out of a flat-screen pirate film; a kind of new-millennium Errol Flynn, deliberately so, I think. His companion was one of the later Golem and was perhaps the reason Singh's launch equipment and shuttle were in such good order, but then, with the money he charged there should have been no reason for the situation to be otherwise.

'We agreed on a percentage basis,' said Grable. He showed no anger and could have been discussing something completely irrelevant by the tone of his voice. It had been some time since Singh had told us he wanted a straight credit payment for transportation. I watched while Singh grinned rakishly, then I turned to help the Golem with the loading of our supplies and equipment.

'You want to go down there to find something in the summer, friend Grable, then you pay me first.'

Which didn't say much for his confidence in our chances. I wondered just how bad it could get down there. Perhaps I should have left Grable to it and come back in the winter. Too late now.

'We had an agreement,' said Grable, his tone not so easy now.

'We had an agreement in the winter, and you're in no position to argue, Grable.'

I took no part in the exchange. All I knew was that if I was Singh I would be watching my back from then on.

Singh's craft was not the usual delta-wing but a glide-effect re-entry shuttle covered with a ceramic outer skin. As I had noted on first seeing it, it was beautifully maintained, but I still felt queasy when looking at it. It was old. The AG units were a new addition – about a century back – as were the bolt-on fusion boosters. I knew we were going to be in for a rough ride.

Once everything was loaded and we had clearance from the runcible AI we boarded and the craft was sealed. Grable and I had the only seats available. The rest of the row had been folded down into the floor to make room for our baggage. Singh took a seat in the pilot's chair while the Golem checked something at the back of the shuttle. I stared through the front screen and saw huge bay doors sliding aside. Beyond lay the tight curve of a not too distant horizon. The moonlet Carla was only a few tens of kilometres across.

'Please strap yourselves in.'

I glanced up at the Golem then did as instructed. I was too used to travelling on shuttles with shock fields in the passenger areas. Grable seemed to have some trouble with his straps.

'Let me help you,' said the Golem.

It reached down and buckled his straps for him.

'We would not want you to get hurt,' it said, in the flattest of voices. I think Grable got the message.

The hum of the AG units made my teeth ache, but the lift was smooth and the shuttle slid out of the bay doors without a perceptible waver. I glanced across at Grable and noted with satisfaction that he had gone white. I had thought I was the soft one. Soon we were gliding rapidly above a landscape of jagged rocks with the glitter of runcible installations between like spilt mercury, then there was a roar as the old shuttle motors flung us out of Carla's well. The acceleration shoved me back into my seat and I prepared myself for more. We weren't far enough from the moonlet for the fusion motors to be ignited. When we were far enough I certainly knew it; the world grew a little dim around the edges. It comes as a surprise when you find out how much internal AG shields you from reality on the commercial passenger shuttles. The journey took us two solstan days and I'll say no more about it than that it was strained. Entry into Scylla's atmosphere was frightening, but it came as a relief.

*There are fifth-generation adapted people who can survive in vacuum. They live in the Outlink stations which travel on the edge of human expansion into the galaxy. Their adaptations are somewhat different from the kind the bracelet would deliver. It used localized genetic material, whether DNA-based or not. It read the code, picked the high-level survival characteristics, transposed them. I once saw a Sundancer human at Darkander's; his skin silver as mercury. It has never been made clear whether they are adapted humans or Sundancers with human shape. Everyone has seen high G*

*adapted humans. In all cases it was done with nanotech and
biointegration. I am about to join the ranks . . .*

*A sharp pain in my wrist as my blood follows a new path,
round the bracelet where it is used as a source of raw materials, and from where it comes out much changed. They are
in: the nanobots and nanofactories; reforming legions of the
invisible. I feel dizzy . . .*

*Now my heart is thundering at double speed. The
Tenkian! . . .*

*Ah, better. I altered its programming, widened its recogni-
tion parameters. Don't want to be shot by my own weaponry.
Now I will lie down on the sandy mud and stare at the sky.
This is why I spend so much time at Darkander's and why I
have such a love for antiquities: technology like sorcery, it
scares the shit out of me.*

*Losing it . . .*

*Blacking—*


It was two hours until dawn and the sky was the colour
of old blood and had clouds across it as ambiguous as
Rorschach blots. We stepped down the ramp onto rocky
ground that had been incinerated in a half-kilometre
radius from where we stood. According to Singh this was
what was called taking adequate precautions.

'How far do you have to travel from here?' he asked
Grable.

'You don't have to know that. All you have to know is
that we'll be back here in two days solstan.'

Grable took precautions as well, but then he had no
choice, that was the only information I had given him.
He did not know the direction in which we would be
going just yet. I took my own precautions.

'We'll see you then.'

The ramp retracted with swift finality and the shuttle rose with an eerie lack of sound on its AG. A few minutes later we saw the accelerating flare of its engines. The sound reached us as we hurriedly unpacked our equipment. Out of the corner of my eye I saw Grable quickly get hold of some kind of handgun and glance at me speculatively. By then I had a control box in my hand and was stepping back from my luggage.

'This should keep us secure,' I said, and flicked a nail against a touch plate.

The Tenkian autogun rose out of the box like some terrible chrome insect. Red and green lights flickered on its various displays and its barrel glimmered in the starlight. Soon it was hovering above the box with its turret revolving, pausing, considering.

'I have it programmed for a twenty-metre circle from me,' I said. I watched as Grable carefully holstered his gun. He didn't know what else I had it programmed for.

The sun was a spherical emerald when it breached the horizon and gave even the ash around us the appearance of life. Scylla's binary companion was days away yet, on the other side of the planet, where it had dragged the planetary sea. As the sun cleared the horizon the tint became less garish, but by then the life of Scylla was coming to meet us. The first murder-louse approached with the dainty and deadly purpose of a spider. The autogun killed it at an invisible line.

'If one of those gets through it's a toss-up between whether you get eaten or injected full of eggs,' Grable told me after he had named the creature.

'I'd have thought you more prepared,' I said.

He smiled bleakly and pulled on gloves that keyed in

at the wrists to the body armour he was wearing under his normal clothing. I felt a little foolish.

'I've an autogun as well, but not as good as that Tenkian.'

It killed nine more lice before we had the portable gravcar assembled and the rest of our equipment loaded upon it. Only when we were twenty metres above the ground with the autogun perched at the back of the craft did we relax, though not for long – the Tenkian's purpose then was one of dealing with creatures like a cross between a moth and a crab which seemed to want to come and visit.

'Okay, which way?' Grable asked. I took out my palm computer and called up my satlink, direction-finder and map. After a moment I read off the coordinates to him. There was a pause. I expected him to make his move then, but it wasn't to be. He punched the coordinates into the autopilot and off we went, just as if we were part-ners. I thought it likely he wanted to be sure I was telling the truth.

The trip took five hours. Once we passed over the edge of the incinerated area we got a look at what the surface of Scylla was really like. I realized then why this planet had first been named Shore. (Like probably a hundred other planets. How many Edens, New Earths and Utopias would there be if the naming of planets had been left to humans?) The surface was a tideland. The plant life was seaweeds: kelps and wracks and huge rotting masses of something like sargassum. There were rocky areas, muddy areas, sandy areas, and pools dotted across the shorescape like silver coins. Through a set of image-intensifiers I observed a multitude of different kinds of molluscs. There were plenty of arthropods as well, the murder-lice being the most prevalent. Perhaps there were other dominant kinds, but I didn't like to keep the intensifiers to my eyes for too long, as it meant my eyes weren't on Grable.

As we drew close to our destination we began to see centuries-old wreckage. I passed the intensifiers to Grable and pointed at the blurred squares and lines in the mudflats below us.

'Looks like the remains of an earlier attempt,' I said.

He glanced over but didn't accept the intensifiers.

'Where shall I put us down?'

I pointed to where a rock field rose up out of the mudflats. The entrance to the base was in such an area, if this place had not changed too much since Paul had been here. As Grable brought the craft down between two huge boulders he gazed out at the mudflats dubiously.

'It's an underground installation?' he asked.

'Yes, and before you ask, I brought a pump.'

A wide-field metals resonator found us the entrance in a matter of minutes. A shot from Grable's handgun turned the door into a molten ruin. After that we had to leave my pump labouring away for hours to get rid of the water and liquid mud. Sitting in the AGC we ate a meal of recon steak, croquette potatoes and courgettes, and watched the Tenkian splattering murder-lice with metronomic regularity. Off to one side the roar of the outlet hose was like the warming up of a shuttle engine. It was a good pump; made of nano-built ceramics and powered by a couple of minipiles.

After we had eaten we checked on the pump and found that a couple of rooms were now accessible and that the inlet hose had attached itself to a wall like a leech. I turned the pump off, moved the hose down into an underwater stairwell, and turned it on again. The exposed rooms contained little of value or interest other than orgiastic clumps of those molluscs called hammer-whelks, one shell of which had got me into all this. The floor was half a metre deep in reddish slimy mud.

Two hours passed and the outlet hose of the pump shifted, as one of its ground staples came out, and created a geyser over the mudflats. For a while we had a blue-shifted rainbow, until I went out and drove another staple into the rock. In another hour the next floor was revealed and things became a lot more interesting.

I hadn't expected to find human remains and was most surprised when I did. The man, or woman, had climbed into an armoured diving suit and died there. What I found was a skeleton inside a thick crust of grey corrosion. I only knew the skeleton was there because the salts that had corroded the armour had kept the faceplate clear, inside and out.

'The Golem Twos might be the same. They didn't make very good ceramal then,' said Grable.

'They crated them. There's a good chance the crates were some kind of vacuum-sealed plastic. Let's just hope we're lucky,' I told him.

We found three crates and our scans showed us the contents were intact. I felt a surge of joy, excitement, justification. Grable showed unexpected friendliness. We attached AG units and loaded two of the crates with efficient cooperation. Grable was all smiles.

'You get that last one and I'll detach the pump,' he suggested. Grinning, I raised my hand and entered the base. Only when I reached the crate, turned on the AG unit and found it didn't work, did the nasty distrustful part of my mind come out from under its stone and say, 'You dumb fuck.'

I ran outside in time to see the gravcar ten metres up in the air and rising. Its units were struggling and I noticed that a cluster of hammerwhelks was clinging to the underside.

'Grable you bastard!'

'The world-tide should be along in a few days! Enjoy your swim!'

For a moment I considered programming the Tenkian to go after him. But it was still spattering murder-lice. I shuddered to think what would happen to me without its protection.

*I am using the keypad now to input this. I have no choice. I came out of the blackness with a leaden heaviness in my lungs and a strange numbness to my skin. I staggered to my feet and felt the skin of my arm. It is no longer skin. It is an exoskeleton. I reached up to my face with hands like complex pincers and screamed at what I found there. My face has deformed horrifically. I looked down and saw my teeth lying in the mud. I have no need of them now. I managed to click my mandibles a few times before I blacked out again. I thought that perhaps my mind was becoming as irrelevant as my teeth. When I woke next I was feeding on the remains of the murder-louse I was stealing my shape from, and I felt no inclination to stop. That wasn't what got to me. What got to me was that I wasn't breathing, not at all.*

*The nightmare lasted perhaps ten hours before either I began to accept or something in the structure of my brain was altered or excised. I was frighteningly hungry and the lice beyond the perimeter of the autogun looked good. I turned the gun off and waited. In moments the lice were on me,* mandibles grating on my shell and ovipositors thumping against my torso like bayonets. I tore them apart like hand-fuls of weeds, then turned the autogun back on while I fed, cracking open legs and carapaces with my mandibles. It sure beat the hell out of the nutcrackers they provide in restaurants.

A minute ago the autogun showed a red light and I shut it down. No more lice came though. A steady vibration is shaking the air and the ground under my feet is jerking spas-modically. The binary is rising; another sun, a small blue sun. The horizon it breaches is a line of white and silver. The world-tide. At the first signs I folded the autogun and, copy-ing the lice I could see, I found a crevice and jammed myself in it. Here I am. The initial wave I estimate to be about twenty metres high; a mountain of water swamping the world. Behind it the sea is mounded up like a leashed monster. The sight is terrifying, exhilarating, magnificent. Now I must hold on.

The tide has passed. How many days? I don't know. All I know is that there was a time when I watched the surface get closer, then a time when I stood up and swatted away a murder-louse like an irritating fly, before sliding the nictitat-ing membranes from my eyes. I thought Grable would be gone, as would my lift off-planet. Even so, when the water was round my feet I reached into the remains of my jacket, extracted my palm computer, called up a map to locate the pick-up point and headed that way.

In the first moments of the tide I had nearly been dislodged from my crevice. Then the surges passed and in the company of murder-lice I swam in the sea, and I breathed. I did not have gills, but somehow my lungs had been altered to extract oxygen from the water. The lice left me alone as they fed on the masses of flotsam caught in the flood. I was almost enjoy-

*ing myself when the first dark shape blotted out the blue and green light.*

*They were a kind of flatfish but the size of great whites, and there was nothing amusing about their sideways-opening jaws and offset eyes. I got into my crevice with all speed as they hit the murder-lice. The water clouded with ichor and legs and pieces of carapace drifted before being snapped up by smaller fish.*

*There was little pleasure from then on. Next came the giant rays that ate lice and flatfish alike. There was a particularly unpleasant squid that I only saved myself from by discharging the Tenkian's cell into it. The rest of the time was a waking nightmare. I wasn't even safe in my crevice. A hammerwhelk joined me and I ignored it until it attached itself to my leg and drilled a centimetre-diameter hole through my shell. I managed to pull it away and extract its siphon from my leg before it hit any arteries, but the pain was beyond belief, and I didn't know how to scream. I swore then that Chaplin Grable was going to really pay. I swore that if I got out of this I would use the form I now had before being adapted back to human normal. I was going to eat him feet-first.*

*I stand by what remains of the gravcar. It is jammed between two shellfish-crusted slabs of rock where the world-tide left it. My laughter sounds like coughing and the ratcheting of claves. I pulled the hammerwhelks from the metal they had been clinging to when Grable lifted the craft and saw the holes they had made through into the oh so delicate control circuits. Grable's hand, in his armoured glove, is gripping the control column. I don't know where the rest of him is. I shall move on now. The Golem Twos are in a nearby crevice. My fortune in the human world is assured. I am heading for one of the sealed bases that were finally established here. It is about five hundred kilometres away and there will*

*be more world-tides to be endured before I reach it. The
Tenkian follows, operating on batteries taken from the gravcar. I will survive.*

# 10

# THE GABBLE

The shimmer-shield visor was the most advanced Jonas had been able to acquire. It only occasionally caught the light as if to let him know it was still there, it allowed a breath of the native air through to his face as he guided this clunky aerofan over the landscape – the breather unit only adding the extra ten per cent oxygen he required – and he could actually experience the damp mephitic smell of the swampland below. This would be the closest he could get to this world, Masada, without some direct augmentation.

Jonas looked around. The sky was a light aubergine, the nebula a static explosion across it, fading now with the rise of the sun, ahead of which the gas giant Calypse was in ascent: an opalescent orb of red, gold and green. Below him a flat plain of flute grasses was broken by muddy gullies like a cracked pastry crust over some black pie. From up here the grasses looked little different from tall reeds reaching the end of their season. The reason for their name only became evident when Jonas spotted the monitor transport and brought his aerofan down to land beside it. The grasses tilted away from the blast of the fan, skirling an unearthly chorus. The hollow stems were holed down their length where their side branches had dropped away earlier in the season. Thus each one played its own tune.

Settling on a rhizome mat, the fan spattered mud all around as it wound down to a stop. Jonas waited for that to finish before opening the safety gate and stepping down. The mat was firm under his feet – this might as well have been solid ground. He looked across. Three individuals stood in a trampled clearing, whilst a third squatted beside something on the ground. Jonas walked over, raising a hand when he recognized Monitor Mary Cole turning to glance towards him. She spoke a few quiet words to her companions, then wandered over.

'Jonas.' She smiled. He rather liked her smile: there was no pretension in it, no authoritarian air behind it. She was an ECS monitor here to do a job, so she knew the extent and limitations of her power and felt no need to belittle others. 'This is not what I would call the most auspicious start to your studies here, but I knew you would be interested.'

'What's this all about, Mary? I just got a message via aug to come and meet you at these coordinates to see something of interest to me.'

She shrugged as they turned to walk towards the clearing. 'That was from B'Tana. He likes rubbing people's noses in the rougher side of our job whenever the opportunity presents.' She glanced at him. 'Are you squeamish?'

'I've been working for Taxonomy as a field biologist for fifty-three years. What have you got here?'

'A corpse, or rather, some remains.'

Jonas halted. 'Should I be here, then?'

'Don't worry. This is not murder and you won't be

bringing any contamination to a crime scene. We got everything that happened here on sateye shortly after he screamed for help over his aug.'

Entering the clearing, Jonas glanced around. No doubt about what that red stuff was staining the flattened grasses and spattering nearby upright stalks. Mary held back to talk to one of her companions while he walked forward to stand beside the man working with the remains. There were fragments of bone scattered all about, the shredded rags of an envirosuit, one boot. The skull lay neatly divided in half, stripped clean, sucked dry.

'May I?' Jonas asked, gesturing to the bone fragments.

The man looked up from the handheld scanner he was running over the rhizome mat. Beside him rested a tray containing a chrome aug, a wristcom and a QC hand laser – all still bloody.

'Certainly – he's past caring.'

Jonas immediately nailed the forensic investigator as a Golem android. That was the way it was sometimes: a disparity between speech, breathing, movement, maybe even a lack of certain pheromones in the air. It never took him long to see through human emulation programs. He turned his attention to the fragments, squatted down and picked one up. It was a piece of thigh bone: as if someone had marked out a small diamond on that bone, drilled closely along the markings with a three-millimetre bit, down to the marrow, then chiselled the piece free.

'Hooder,' he said.

'Medium-sized,' the Golem replied.

Jonas turned to him. 'Who was this?' He nodded towards the remains.

The Golem winced and glanced towards Mary Cole, then said, 'A xenologist who came here to study mud snakes. We lose between five and ten each year.'

Jonas called over to Mary, 'Is this what you would call an educational outing for me?'

Glancing over she said, 'Jonas, you would not have been sent here if you needed that.' She nodded to her companions and they headed back towards the transport, then she came over and gestured at the remains. 'We get them all the time. They upload skills then come here thinking they're going to brilliantly solve all the puzzles. You, as you say, have worked for Taxonomy for fifty-three years. The maximum experiential upload is less than a year – enough for a language or some small branch of one of the sciences.'

Jonas watched the Golem stand, extend the head of his scanner on a telescopic arm, and began to swing like a metal detector.

'I upload,' he observed.

'Yes, on top of your fifty-three years of experience.'

'Granted,' he said. 'So you get a lot like this?'

'Certainly – there's a great deal here to study.'

Jonas knew that. Prior to twenty years ago this world had been out-Polity and ruled by a vicious theocracy. With the help of undercover ECS agents rebels managed a ballot of the planetary population, the result of which was the Polity subsuming this world. But events had been complicated. During that time some biophysicist had come here in a stolen Polity dreadnought and caused all sorts of mayhem. Jonas did not know the details, all he did know was that it had taken ECS twenty years to clear up the mess, and that some areas of the planet were still under quarantine. Also, at about the same time one of the four spheres of a transgalactic alien bioconstruct called Dragon had arrived, suicided on the planet's surface, and in the process, out of its mass, created a new race: dracomen. These creatures alone were worthy of centuries of study. They used direct protein replication rather than some form of DNA transcription and could mentally control their body growth and substantially alter their offspring. Their initial shape was based on a human thought-experiment: What might dinosaurs have been like if there had been no extinction and they had followed the evolutionary path of humans? But beside these the planet boasted much weird fauna: the tricones forever churning the soil, a multitude of herbivores, mud snakes, siluroynes, heroynes, hooders and the decidedly strange gabbleducks. And those were only the larger wild creatures.

'Do you know if there are any instructions concerning his remains?' Jonas asked.

'We will know soon enough,' said the Golem. He was squatting down now, digging at the ground with a small trowel. After a moment he stood, holding up some item about the size of a little finger.

'Memplant?' Jonas suggested.

The Golem nodded.

Jonas turned back to Mary. 'I'd like to make some recordings and measurements, and take a few samples. That okay?'

'That's fine. And if he has no special requirements concerning his physical remains I'll have Gryge,' she gestured to the Golem, 'box them up for you.'

'And a copy of the sateye recording?'

'Certainly.'

'Thanks.'

Jonas headed back to the aerofan for his holocorder and sampling equipment. He did not suppose he would learn anything new here, or from the recording – it would just be more information to feed Rodol's appetite. The AI was already digesting everything the locals knew about hooders, plus twenty years of ECS data, but its hunger was never satisfied.

Shardelle noted that within the last hour another forty-three linguists had come online, but that hour had also seen off sixty-two. Their number, now standing at just over seven hundred thousand, was in steady decline in the network. Comparative analyses with just about every language on record had been made. New languages had been generated for comparison – still no joy. Syntactic programs ranging from the deeply esoteric to the plain silly had been employed, but they had not come close to cracking one word, or a hint of a morpheme, of what was now being called The Gabble.

What precisely did *Yaw-craggle flog nabble goop*, mean, or *Scrzzz-besumber fleeble*? Even the AIs seemed to be failing, and they were making comparative analyses across a huge range of data: an enormous list of environmental parameters including the creature's location, the ambient temperature, variations in air mix, what the creature was looking at, hearing, smelling or otherwise sensing; the time of the day or night, what objects were in the sky; variations in the speakers themselves including size, sex, number of limbs and what they happened to be doing with them at the time, what had happened to them earlier. Occasionally concurrence did occur. Two gabbleducks had said *yabber* while peering into the distance and gesturing with one clawed limb. There had been other concurrences too. But utterly bewildering was that statistically, if the five hundred creatures under scrutiny had been generating random noise, there should be more concurrences than this. It was a maddeningly negative result. Shardelle, however, felt this was a negative that must indicate *something*.

Shardelle disconnected her aug from the linguistic network and at once her sight and hearing returned. Plumped in a comfortable chair she glanced around inside her ATV, but inevitably her gaze centred on the screen that was presently showing the view from holocam 107. This one was her favourite gabbleduck – the biggest and weirdest of them all. The creature was sitting in a stand of flute grass and in this pose its body was pyramidal. Its three pairs of forelimbs were folded monkishly over the jut of its lower torso, one fore-talon of one huge black claw seemingly beating time to some unheard song. Its domed head was tilted down, its duck bill against its chest. Some of its tiara of emerald eyes were closed. Obviously it was taking time out to digest its latest meal whose bones lay neatly stacked beside it.

What was known about this creature? Its double-helical Masadan equivalent of DNA was enormously long and contained coding enough for every species on this planet. But the sheer quantity of coding material did not necessarily mean the creature was complex – most of this could be parasitic and junk DNA. The first researchers into human DNA had been surprised to discover that lizards, lungfish and ferns possessed substantially more DNA than themselves, and that they had no more than common grass. What it did mean, however, was that as a species the gabbleducks were very old.

They were omnivores; often supplementing their diet

with flute grass rhizomes, fungi and, oddly, anything shiny they could lay their claws on. They possessed complex voice boxes, and as was already demonstrable, there seemed no reason for this. On the whole they were solitary creatures and spoke only to themselves. When they met it was usually only to mate or fight, or both. There was also no reason for them to carry structures in their skulls capable of handling vastly complex languages. Two thirds of their large convoluted brains they seemed hardly to use at all. In short: they were a puzzle.

Shardelle stood, walked along the metal floor of the ATV and climbed up into the chainglass bubble of the cockpit. Checking the map screen she noted the transponder positions for the two hooders in the area, then chose a route to take her back to the Tagreb complex that avoided them completely. She had seen what had happened to an ATV and its four occupants when they ignored this simple rule and drove close to one of the creatures for a look, or rather, she had seen the torn and very small fragments that remained of both people and vehicle. Taking up the joystick she drove herself rather than be guided in by Rodol. As an afterthought she mentally sent the detach command to her aug and removed the chrome slug of sophisticated computer hardware from the side of her head. She had some thinking to do and found that easier while driving, barebrained.

Taxonomic and genetic research bases, Tagrebs, looked like giant iron tulip flowers when stored in the vast hold of the research vessel *Beagle Infinity*. Launched, a Tagreb maintained its shape during entry into a planetary atmosphere while its AI came online. The AI then slowed the Tagreb in lower atmosphere with fusion thrusters before finally descending on the chosen location using gravmotors. Upon landing the flower opened, folding four petals down to the ground. From this five plasmel domes inflated – one at the centre and one over each petal. Their internal structures – floors, ceilings, walls and stairs – were inflated at the same time. The AI then took a look around to decide how best to continue.

Rodol, aware of the problems Masada might present, first injected a thick layer of a resin matrix into the boggy ground below to protect the base from the depredations of tricones – molluscan creatures that given time could grind their way through just about anything – before injecting the same substance into the hollow walls and floors of the structure itself. Next the AI woke its telefactors, which immediately took the requisite materials outside the base to construct an electrified perimeter fence and four gun towers. Unusually, these towers were supplied in this case with proton cannons capable of punching holes through thick armour, for some of the natives were anything but friendly. After three days the base was ready for the next stage. Automated landers descended inside the fence and the telefactors began bringing in supplies: food, bedding, nanoscopes, full-immersion VR suites, soaps and gels, nano micro and submacro assembler rigs, an aspidistra in a pot, autodocs, autofactories, holocams, coffee makers . . . Every item was slotted into its place or plugged in.

On day five a hooder came to investigate, attacked the fence, then retreated leaving its rear segment behind – incinerated by one of the cannons. On day six Rodol brought the fusion reactor fully online, supplying power to the multitude of sockets throughout the base. Lights embedded in the ceilings were ready to come on. Sanitary facilities were ready to recycle waste. Rodol stabbed filter heads down into the ground to suck up water, which was first cracked for its oxygen to bring the internal atmosphere to requirements, and thereafter pumped into holding tanks. The humans, haimans and Golem arrived shortly afterwards; disembarking from shuttles with massive hover trunks gliding along behind them. Only a few days after was it discovered that the five grav-platforms were not nearly enough for those who wanted to do fieldwork. Grudgingly, Rodol cleared Polity funds to pay the local population for twenty aerofans and five fat-tyred all-terrain vehicles.

Jonas arrived on foot, having been on the planet for six months getting to know the locals and many of the ECS monitors still assigned here. Six months later he raised in celebration a glass of malt whisky to the scene beyond the panoramic window of his upper-dome apartment and laboratory. It was in a befuddled state that two hours later he received the message through his aug.

'Hi, Jonas,' said Mary Cole.

She was standing in the middle of his apartment – to his perception, for the augram was being played directly into his mind.

'Hello, Mary.' He toasted her with his glass.

'This is not real-time or interactive so don't bother asking questions. I just want you to know that one of our coastal survey drones picked up precisely what you want, here . . .' The location downloaded into his aug. 'That's only five hundred and thirty kilometres from you. Have a nice one.'

As the image blinked out Jonas was already groping

for his aldetox. 'Rodol, I need the field autopsy gear, the big stuff, and I need it now!' he bellowed.

'What you require is available, but unfortunately the transport situation has not improved. All the gravplatforms are out and aerofans will not suffice,' the AI replied.

Jonas gulped water to wash down the pills. He was already starting to feel sober even though the aldetox had yet to take effect. 'What about the ATVs?'

'There are three here. Two require new drive shafts, which one of the autofactories is currently manufacturing. The other is assigned to Shardelle Garadon. Perhaps you should speak with her.'

Jonas returned to his chair while the aldetox took effect. Any of the ATVs had room enough to carry all the equipment he would require, initially, then came the problem of bringing specimens back. Perhaps he could get some help there from ECS? Something for a later date, he thought – plenty of work to do before then. After a moment he made a search for Shardelle's aug address, found it, and tried to make contact. Annoyingly her aug was offline. Instead, he found her apartment address within the Tagreb, stood, and unsteadily headed for the door.

Fifteen hundred and thirty-two linguists remained: the hardcore. The rest dismissed The Gabble as having less meaning than the sounds lower animals made. At least those sounds had a reason, some logical syntax, some meaning related to alarm, pain, pleasure or the basic 'I'm over here, let's fuck'.

Unfortunately only a third of that hardcore consisted of linguists who Shardelle felt had anything meaningful

to contribute. Of those, one Kroval – a haiman based on
Earth who in the silicon part of his mind held nearly
every known language in existence – had the most to
contribute. His analysis fined down to, 'The phonemes
are 80 per cent the anglic of Masada, and their disconnection from coherent meaning seems almost deliberate.
I can say with certainty that they are not parroting the
language, and perhaps a degree of understandable
human paranoia engendered by the unknown, or possibly unknowable, leads me to feel they might be deriding
it.'

The latest offering from a small group of the others,
who Shardelle labelled the lunatic fringe, had been, 'It
must be what is not said: meaning can be attributed to
the synergetic whole of negatives. We just need to isolate
the network of disaffirmative monads in a . . .' and so it
had continued until the speaker in question seemed in
danger of disappearing up his own backside. It was this
last that had led Shardelle to disconnect her aug and cast
it aside.

They seemed to be getting nowhere. In fact, over the
last six months, more imponderables had entered the
equation. On the biological front little more was known
than had been obtained by close scanning and sampling,
and that had cost them fourteen mobile scanners and
seven beetle-sized sampling drones – gabbleducks swatted them like flies and then, if they were shiny, ate them.
What Shardelle had been waiting for, like so many others
in the Tagreb, was a death. Other researchers had
obtained their subjects' corpses: a siluroyne, a heroyne,
loads of mud snakes. But it seemed gabbleducks were in
no hurry to die and not one corpse or any remains had
been picked up by the vast number of ECS drones con-

stantly scanning the planet. Shardelle wondered about that: why so much scanning activity, why the quarantine areas still, what was it that ECS was keeping quiet? No matter, she had enough puzzles to concern her at present. Perhaps she should slip out one night with a pulse rifle and solve the corpse problem. The Gabble, and its source, frustrated her that much.

*Time to sleep*, she decided. Thinking like that was a sure way to get her expelled from the Tagreb and the planet. Nothing gets killed, unless in self-defence, until its sentience level has been properly assessed.

Just then, as she was about to head for her bed, there came a hammering at her door. Shardelle grimaced and considered ignoring it, but there was urgency in that hammering – maybe the corpse? She opened the door expecting to see one of the others on her team. Who was this?

He held out a hand. 'Jonas Clyde . . . hooders. May I come in?'

Shardelle stood aside and waved him into her apartment. He looked younger than she had expected, but that meant nothing. His blond hair was cropped and he moved with athletic confidence. His face was tanned and his eyes electric green. His hands looked . . . capable. He scanned around quickly, his gaze coming to rest on her screen. The big gabbleduck was lolloping through the flute grasses.

'Moves like a grizzly bear,' he observed.

She of course recognized his name. Jonas Clyde was something of a legend in Taxonomy and usually studied exactly what he wanted on any new world. It had come as a pleasant surprise to Shardelle, upon hearing he was on this mission, that he had not chosen the gabbleducks.

'Substantially larger, though,' she said, closing the door.

He obviously auged through to her screen control for figures appeared along the bottom. 'Eight tonnes – not something you'd want to be standing in the path of.' He turned to her. 'I hear they eat people.'

'Chew, certainly . . . coffee?' She walked over to her coffee maker – an antique almost three centuries old – and began making an espresso.

'Yes please – same for me. You say "chew"?'

'Humans obviously disagree with their digestion, but if someone annoys them sufficiently they chew them up and spit out the pieces. But of course, like everything else with them, their behaviour is puzzling. Gabbleducks have pursued human prey across hundreds of kilometres, for no particular reason, and killed them. There was one case of a hunter shooting a clip from an Optek into one creature and it ignoring him completely. A recent one we observed via holocam: a gabbleduck abandoned its territory, crossed five hundred kilometres, and drowned a pond worker in her squirm pond. We don't know why.' Bringing two cups of espresso over she nodded to her sofa. He sat down. Placing the cups on the table between she took the armchair opposite. 'I was surprised you didn't choose them as your subject for study.'

He grimaced. 'They were my initial choice, but I have experience with dangerous fauna so it was suggested, rather strongly, that I choose the hooders. Obviously gabbleducks are dangerous, but not so lethal that it was felt necessary to fit every one with a transponder to know its location.'

'I see,' Shardelle nodded, sipped her espresso. 'So what can I do for you?'

'I want your ATV,' he replied.

'Nothing if not direct. What for?'

'Hooders are long-lived and practically indestructible.' He paused. 'That's a puzzle too – we were told by
the locals that when hooders reach a certain age they
break into separate segments and each segment grows
into a new hooder. This planet should be overrun with
them . . . perhaps some mechanism based on predator
prey ratio . . .' He sat gazing off into space.

'You were saying,' Shardelle prompted.

'Yes . . . yes. They are practically indestructible but for
one big fault. As you know, the sea tides here are vicious
– the moons and Calypse all interact in that respect.
Hooders sometimes stray down onto the eastern banks
at low tide, get caught there, then washed into deep water
and eventually drown. It takes a while, but it's deep off
the banks and hooders are very heavy.'

'And?'

'Occasionally a hooder corpse will get dragged up by
the bank current and deposited ashore.'

'I see – you have your corpse.'

'And no way of getting a large field autopsy kit to it.'

Shardelle gazed up at the screen. 'Where is it?'

Jonas touched his aug for a moment, frowned, then
pointed. 'Five hundred and thirty kilometres thataway –
straight to the coast.'

Shardelle nodded at the screen. 'He is about three
hundred kilometres in the same direction.'

'Your point?'

'Of course you can use my ATV, but under one condition: I'm coming with you.' Shardelle knew there was
more to her decision than the gabbleduck's presence on
the route. There was the escape from the frustration of

her research, which in that moment seemed to have translated into sexual frustration.

From the chainglass bubble cockpit Jonas glanced into the back of the ATV. Apparently these had been used as troop transports during the rebellion against the theocracy. Now either side of it was stacked from floor to ceiling with aluminium and plasmel boxes, strapped back against the sides, with only a narrow gangway leading back and elbowing right to the side door. It had been necessary for them to remove much of Shardelle's equipment, including the chair, but she did not seem to mind. He realized she was glad of this excuse for a journey to take her away from the meticulously boring research into gabbleduck biology, and the seemingly endless and fruitless analysis of The Gabble.

'How long will it take us, do you think?' he asked, now looking ahead. They were leaving the Tagreb enclosure, rolling across an area of trammelled flute grass through which new red-green shoots were spearing.

'How long do you want it to take?'

'Your meaning?'

'Sixty hours if we go non-stop. Rodol can guide the ATV during the night . . . do you need sleep?'

'No – I'm asomnidapted.'

'Ah, well I'm not.' She glanced back. 'I guess I could bed down there overnight.'

Jonas shook his head. Now they were on their way his urgency to get to the dead hooder had decreased. 'No, let's stop during night time. I may not need to sleep, but I don't want to spend that long just sat here. There's camping equipment in the back so you can get your head down.'

Shardelle guided the ATV down one of the many paths crushed through the flute grass and leading away from the Tagreb.

'And what will you do meanwhile?'

He tapped his aug. 'Continue my research. Rodol is sequencing the hooder genome and transmitting the results to me. I'm running programs to isolate alleles and specific coding sequences. I intend to built a full virtual model of hooder growth.'

'But first you need to be rid of the parasitic and junk DNA to get to the basic genome.'

'Yeah, obviously – I've got programs working on that first.'

'It'll probably be a massive task. The assumption has always been that hooders are the most ancient creature on the planet's surface. The gabbleduck is probably younger, and its genome is immense.'

'Yes, quite probably,' Jonas replied, then after a moment, 'I don't really like the term junk DNA.'

Once, centuries ago, no one had known what all the extra coding was for. Now it was known that it was history: old defensive measures that no longer applied, viruses incorporated into the genome, patches much like additional pieces of computer code to cover weaknesses in a program. Some biologists likened much of it to the scar tissue of a species, but Jonas felt that not entirely true because it could on occasion provide survival strategies. Perhaps a better analogy would be to the scar tissue and consequent experience of an old warrior.

'You have a better one?' Shardelle asked.

'Reserve, complementary or supplementary.'

'Very good.'

By midmorning the sun was passing underneath

Calypse, throwing the gas giant into silhouette. Jonas spotted the snout spurs of mud snakes cleaving the rhizome layer ahead of them – attracted by the vibrations the vehicle set up – but they disappeared from sight, perhaps recognizing the inedibility of ATV tyres. Checking her map screen Shardelle turned the vehicle away from flattened track and nosed it into flute grasses standing three metres tall. The cockpit skimmed this, its lower half in the grass. A faint hissing sound impinged under the varying hum of the hydrogen motor and hydrostatic gearing. Eventually they broke from the flute grasses and began negotiating a compacted slope where the old grasses had been flattened by the wind. When they reached a low peak a vista opened to one side of them. A fence stretched out of sight in two directions. Over the other side the ground was black, hazed with occasional reddish patches where new grass was sprouting.

'Quarantine area,' Shardelle observed. 'You were here for six months before the Tagreb arrived. Do you know what they're so worried about?'

'No monitor will answer direct questions, but by the methods being employed I'd guess biogenetic weaponry was employed.' He gestured to the blackened terrain. 'What you see here is only the flash-over area – the perimeter of a firestorm. I'd guess that the hypocentre was the strike point of an orbital beam weapon. They burnt that inner area right down to the bedrock and now they're watching to make sure nothing survived.'

'Seems rather excessive.'

Jonas decided to tell her the whole story, and wondered if she would think the actions ECS had taken here so excessive then. 'You have to consider: how did one man "steal" a Polity dreadnought? Mary Cole, a monitor I know, let slip that the research vessel *Jerusalem* was here for a time. You know what that means.'

She glanced at him. 'Jain technology?'

He nodded. 'A few fragments sit in the Tranquillity Museum on the moon. That part of the museum can be instantly ejected and destroyed by CTD. It seems that fact is the biggest part of the attraction of the exhibit, because what sits there in a chainglass case just looks like a few bits of coral. It's the potential though: a complexity of dead nanomachinery that still, as far as I know, defies analysis.'

'Someone used active Jain technology?'

'It would seem so. First to steal the dreadnought, then use both dreadnought and technology to hit this place.'

'I'm surprised anyone has been allowed here at all.'

'I'd guess the AI view is that they can't be overprotective. Three distinct and extinct ancient races have been identified: the Jain, Atheter and Csorians. Remnants of their technologies exist, so it's no good us burying our heads in the sand in the hope they'll go away. We have to learn how to deal with them, hopefully before we run head-first into something that might destroy us.'

'And of course there are those that are not extinct, like whatever created Dragon.'

'Precisely.'

She looked at him, waiting for something more, then prompted: 'Do you think we'll ever get the full story of what happened here?'

'The bones will be fleshed out in time. We know the Theocracy was supplying Separatists on Cheyne III and used technology, bought from Dragon, to destroy an Outlink station. The Polity supported the rebellion here which finally overthrew the Theocracy. Dragon changed

sides, apparently because it did not like blame being
attributed to it for the destruction of the station, and
assisted that rebellion before suiciding on the surface.
The guy who stole the dreadnought? Some Separatist
coming here on the side of the Theocracy. He and his
ship were incinerated while pursuing Polity agents to the
Elysium smelting facilities.'

'I heard that Agent Ian Cormac was involved,' said
Shardelle.

Jonas snorted. It amazed him how scientists, whose
entire ethos was based on logic and empirical proof,
sometimes believed complete rubbish.

'There is no such person,' he stated, which killed the
conversation for some time.

Shardelle listened to the engine wind down, and to the
slow ticking of cooling metal. She had parked the ATV
on a hillock that she knew extended in a ring some kilometres in diameter. It was a good place to camp, the
ground too dry for mud snakes. She liked the view as well
and felt safer being able to see for kilometres in either
direction. Rodol was watching by satellite and would
warn if anything was getting too close, but this vantage
gave them the opportunity to eyeball any of the natives
and decide themselves whether it might be necessary to
run. She turned to Jonas.

His eyes were closed, but obviously, not needing to,
he was not sleeping. He was auging – probably deep in
some virtuality in which the hooder genome lay across
his entire horizon and godlike he peeled away clumps of
it for analysis and compiled the resultant data. She
studied his profile, the hard intensity of his features, the
natural tan that came from spending a lot of time out-

side. Eventually she unstrapped herself and left him to it, turning on her shimmer-shield visor and snagging up her field tent and related equipment on the way out of the ATV. The landscape was red gilded by the nebula when he joined her an hour later. She was sitting in her camp chair before her tent, her visor flicking off and on as she sipped coffee.

'My apologies,' he said. 'I tend to get annoyed when anything blurs my focus.'

'Me too,' she replied. 'But I've been focused on The Gabble for so long I need a break. Incidentally I've no belief in mythical superhumans and perfectly understand that they are an AI creation to make us feel better about ourselves.'

'So you don't see Horace Blegg's hand in all this?' he queried, raising an eyebrow.

She laughed. 'No . . . I see here some ECS action which for a while will be considered a net gain for the Polity until the dirt starts to surface.'

'Mmmm . . . and talking of dirt: Rodol has finished sequencing the hooder genome.'

'Dirt?'

'There is none, or rather, surprisingly little.'

'What do you mean?'

'Still a lot of analysis to do, but thus far we've found nothing that can be identified as parasitic in the genome. There are, however, a vast number of superfluities, accounting for immune-response identifiers.'

'That makes no sense. If it's old enough to acquire so high a level of immune response, it will have acquired parasitic DNA as well.'

'You'd think.'

There was something he was not telling her. She let it

rest. At present she felt the most relaxed she had been in some time – just thinking about nothing and watching the world. She did not need his frustrations right then.

'I'm going to lie down now.' She cast away the dregs from her cup and returned it to her pack. Standing, she faced him. 'Would you care to join me?'

'I don't sleep,' he said, looking distracted.

'Don't be obtuse.'

He turned to her, focused, grinned.

'I promise not to be too rough with you,' she added, and to save pride turned away and entered her tent. She felt slightly miffed that he took so long following, and came in after she had turned on the oxygenator and stripped naked. He bowed in, quickly closing and sealing the entrance behind him. Shedding his breather gear he said, 'You surprised me.'

'Are propositions so rare for you?'

'Not rare, but frequently problematical.' He paused thoughtfully, as if about to launch into further explanation.

Shardelle reached across, snagged the front of his envirosuit and pulled him into a kiss then down on top of her. He seemed reluctant for a moment, then softened into it. His hands began caressing her with almost forensic precision, as if he was checking the location of all her parts. Eventually he backed off and struggled out of his envirosuit. There was not much foreplay after that. She did not want any, and came violently and quickly. After cleaning herself with wipes from her toiletries she said, 'Perhaps we should continue this in the morning.'

'Perhaps we should,' he replied.

She lay back relaxed, her body heavy on the ground as if someone had stepped up the strength of a gravplate below her. Closed her eyes for a second . . . He was shaking her by the shoulder.

'Come see.'

Shardelle lay bleary and confused before realizing that she must have fallen asleep. Checking her wristcom she saw that five hours had passed. 'What is it?'

'Heroynes.'

She took up her breather gear only, clicking only mouth mask into place, and stepped out naked with that up against her mouth. Out there, striding through the flute grasses, were four heroynes. She studied one closely. It stood on two long thin legs that raised it high above the grass itself, much like its namesake. Its body was L-shaped and squat with a long curved neck extending up from it. To its fore, numerous sets of forearms were folded as if in prayer. It had no head as such; the neck just terminated in a long serrated spear of a beak. Each of these creatures stood a good ten metres high, and moved swiftly across the terrain in delicate arching steps carrying them many metres at a time.

'Always weird,' she said into her mask.

She turned to him. He was fully dressed and watching her.

'Are you still tired?' he asked.

Her answer was no, and he took her from behind bent over the tyre of the ATV, then again in the morning, long and slow in the tent, before they set out. Shardelle felt this trip out was most therapeutic for her.

Jonas smiled to himself as he considered the night past. He felt enlivened and humanized by the experience, and certainly it had been beneficial for Shardelle. She seemed relaxed and easy, sated. But Jonas compartmentalized it as she started the ATV on its way, and returned his thoughts to some things that had been bothering him throughout the long watches of the night.

Hooders. Damn them.

Perhaps the sex had blown the crap out of his system because certain biological peculiarities now seemed clear to him.

The superfluities in the hooder genome could explain the lack of virally implanted parasitic DNA. The creature might have quite simply, from the beginning, had a powerful and almost complete immune response to viral attack. Dubious, but explainable. What was not explainable was something so obvious, he cursed himself as an idiot for not seeing it. The hooder was the top predator here. Hooders did not fight each other. Their prey were on the whole soft-bodied grazers with little more defence than speed. Why then did hooders need armour capable of stopping an anti-tank round?

'You know how hooders are hard to kill?' he asked.

The ATV was rolling down the hill into what was known as Dragon's Fall. Shardelle glanced at him with that slight lustful twist to her mouth. 'I know. It's why the Tagreb perimeter is supplied with proton weapons.'

He nodded, tried to concentrate on the matter in hand. 'It's their armour, and their speed, but mostly the armour.' He paused for a moment. 'You know there are other creatures with thick armour capable of bouncing bullets, but that's usually because there's something in their environment with a fair chance of cracking through it. The laminated chitin on a hooder stops most projectile weapons. Even lasers have little effect. You want to damage one of those creatures and you need to upgrade to APWs and particle weapons, and even then you're talking about the kind of armament most people couldn't even carry.'

'Maybe some other predator now extinct?'

'But what the hell would that be?'

She gestured ahead into the crater. 'We'll probably never know. ECS apparently had teams excavating this place for ages trying to find draconic remains. They didn't find much.'

'Tricones.' Jonas nodded.

The molluscan soil-makers of this planet were a problem in that respect. There were some fossils to be found in the mountains, but only there. Out here the tricones crunched up nearly everything solid down to a huge depth, and mostly all that could be found below the deep soil layer was the chalk then limestone remains of the tricones themselves.

'Maybe there's a parasitic reason for the thick shell,' Shardelle suggested. 'I'm thinking in terms of the Earth parasite of snails that thickens their shells to protect itself.'

'But that results in the snail being unable to breed. There's always some balance to be upset. I'd also expect to see some hooder uninfected – thin-shelled.' He shrugged. 'Then again, a general infection of them all may account for their low population.'

'Perhaps you'll find the answers on that beach.'

'Perhaps.'

Abruptly Shardelle slowed the ATV. He glanced at her and saw she was peering intently at the further edge of the crater. There were figures over there, humanoid.

'Dracomen,' she whispered excitedly.

Jonas initiated a visual program in his aug, magnified what he was seeing and cleaned up the image. Six dracomen, two of them carrying some animal corpse strapped to a pole between them, the other four scattered around them. Two of the others were small – dracoman children. This was the first time Jonas had seen them and he studied them closely. Though humanoid their legs hinged the wrong way, like birds. Their scaling was green over most of their bodies but yellow from groin to throat. Their heads were toadish, jutting forward on long necks. They carried rifles of some kind.

Shardelle set the ATV moving again, altering course to intersect with theirs.

'What are you doing?' Jonas asked.

'I want to talk to them.'

'We're not here to study dracomen. There's a whole branch of ECS that does that – military, now dracomen are being recruited.'

'Not study. You've got your corpse, but I still want mine. Dracomen hunt, as we can see – I'd just like some information on what exactly they do hunt.'

The dracomen obviously spotted that the ATV was heading in their direction, for the two carrying the pole laid it down and then they all stood waiting. As they drew closer, and he could see them clearer, Jonas began to wonder if this was a good idea. These creatures looked dangerous. Then he dismissed the idea as unworthy. They may have looked like something out of a VR hack-and-slash fantasy, but from what he knew they might well be more sophisticated and technically advanced than most Polity citizens. Shardelle parked the ATV on the brow of the crater edge ahead of them. Turning on their masks the two of them left the ATV.

'Good morning!' said Shardelle, holding up a hand and advancing.

One of them moved forward, its head tilted as it eyed her, almost like a cockerel coming to inspect a grub.

'We greet you,' it said, halting.

Jonas eyed the rifle this one carried. It seemed to be made of translucent bone and something shifted inside it like visible organs. It seemed alive.

'If you don't mind,' said Shardelle, 'I have some questions I would like to ask.'

Jonas now saw that their catch was a mud snake: a fat grublike body terminating in a hard angular head that looked something like a horse's skull. Yellow ichor ran from something that was stuck in the body just behind that skull: a short glassy shaft to the rear of which were affixed two testicular objects. The dracoman tracked the direction of his attention, then abruptly stooped and pulled the object from the mud snake. He now saw that this thing possessed a barbed point. It looked like a greatly enlarged bee sting. The dracoman did something with its rifle and the side of the weapon split open. It shoved the barbed object inside and closed the weapon up. All the time it did not take its eyes off Jonas.

'Ask,' it said.

'You hunt many animals,' said Shardelle.

That was not a question so the dracoman did not dignify it with a reply.

'Do you hunt gabbleducks?' she asked.

The dracoman exposed its teeth in something that might have been a grin. It glanced around at its fellows, who grinned similarly.

'No,' it replied.

'Why not?'

'We only hunt prey.'

'Not predators?' She gestured to their catch. 'Surely mud snakes are predators.'

'All predators are prey.'

'I don't understand.'

'Yes.'

'Do you hunt hooders?' Jonas interjected.

By the amount of exposed ivory he guessed that was a hilarious question to ask.

Shardelle waved a hand as if to dismiss his question. 'Why don't you hunt gabbleducks?'

'They are protected.'

'Under Polity law, yes, but I thought your people had been allowed hunting rights to feed yourselves . . . within limits.'

Some unspoken signal passed between the dracomen, for the two bearers once again took up the pole.

'Wait! You have to give me something!' said Shardelle.

Jonas glanced at her, realizing by the tone of her voice how desperate she was to find answers about the gabbleducks. The dracomen began to move off.

'Please,' she said.

One of the dracoman children halted and gazed up at her.

'The meat is forbidden,' it lisped, licking out a black forked tongue. It glanced at Jonas. 'Except to hooders.' Then the child scampered off after the adults.

'Delphic, just like their creator,' said Jonas.

'There was probably a wealth of information there, if we could figure it out,' Shardelle replied. She peered down the slope to where a tricone about half a metre long had breached. This creature consisted of three long cones joined like Pan pipes, each revealing in its mouths gelatinous nodular heads which extented sluglike to lift the

creature up, then propel it narrow end first back down
into the ground.

'We will,' said Jonas, turning back towards the ATV,
'given time.'

They made love on the second night, slowly, leisurely,
and most of the time Jonas remained in the tent with her
while she slept. He did not have to do that, but she was
glad he did.

'In the morning we should come upon your big
friend,' he said at one point. 'What do you intend?'

Shardelle grinned at him, suddenly unreasonably
happy. 'Well I'd like to ask him what he and the rest of
his kind have been talking about. Do you think he'll tell
me?'

He smiled. 'You know there's a kids' interactive book
you can find here. The technology is Polity stuff but the
stories were created here – distortions of old Earth fairy
tales. When I said to you it moves like a bear, I was thinking of one particular fairy tale: Goldilocks and the Three
Bears, but in this case the three bears were gabbleducks.'

'Your point?' Shardelle asked.

'Well she crept into their house to try their food and
their beds . . .'

'Yes, I know . . . and baby gabbleduck's bed was just
right . . .'

'It was,' said Jonas, 'and baby gabbleduck thought
Goldilocks just right when he ate her.'

'Is there a moral to this?'

'Just be careful. I don't want to lose you now I'm getting to know you.'

Frustration awaited in the morning with Rodol telling
them to divert from their course. Two hooders lay in their

way. It would be too dangerous to approach the giant gabbleduck.

'They might attack it,' said Shardelle, half minded to ignore Rodol's warning.

Jonas reached out and put a hand on her arm. 'On the way back – I promise you.'

They travelled through an area where the shore wind had blown fragments of dead flute grass inland and mounded it in drifts, then into an area clear of everything but new shoots. Evening sunset revealed the sea and the beach. They spent the night inside the ATV, Shardelle bedding down on the floor. At sunrise they travelled the remaining kilometre to the edge of a cliff, and they soon located the dead hooder.

The dune across which the enormous creature was draped imparted a curve to its forward segments, emphasizing its resemblance to a spinal column. Shardelle was reminded of ancient saurian exhibits in museums on Earth, and models and diagrams from the early years of the science of osteopathy. Its head was spoon-shaped, concave-side-down to the sand, its armour plates spreading in a radial pattern from the neck. Judging by the grooves leading down from the creature to the water's edge, its first discoverers had dragged it up the beach. They must have used some aerial craft to do this, since there was no sign of any other track marks in the sand.

'Do you know how we can get down there?' she asked, tapping up an elevation overlay on her map screen. The ATV rested above the beach just back from a steep muddy cliff. All around them the ground was level and had been scoured by the wind of even dead flute grass.

After auging for a moment, Jonas replied, 'Go right.'

Shardelle tracked elevation lines with her finger. 'Yeah, I think I see it.'

They travelled along above the beach for a kilometre, but downhill with the cliff growing shorter as they travelled and eventually petering out. A steep slope brought them down onto the sand and from there they travelled back below the cliff. Lower down it was jagged limestone. Shardelle looked up and saw burrows in the compacted soil above that, and many falls. Tricone shells were embedded up there, and many more shattered on the limestone. Many of the soil-makers had obviously not known when to stop and burrowed straight out of the soil to fall and smash themselves. When they eventually reached the hooder it seemed more like some rock formation than any beast, being over two metres wide and a hundred metres long. Wind-blown sand had mounded around it. It seemed ancient: a dinosaur skeleton in the process of being revealed. She brought the ATV to a halt in the lee of the monster.

'Let's take a look,' said Jonas.

The moment they exited the vehicle they smelt decay. Shardelle noted black insectile movement in the heaped sand; then spied one of the creatures close to her feet. It looked like a small prawn, but black and scuttling like a louse.

'Every living world has its undertakers,' Jonas explained. 'Let's just hope they haven't destroyed too much.' He pointed towards the hooder's cowl, much of which Shardelle now saw was buried in sand. 'I've brought a few hundred litres of repellant. I'll confine direct physical autopsy to the cowl and a couple of the segments behind it. I don't suppose the rest will tell me much more.'

'But you'll scan it entire?'

'Yes.' He turned to her. 'If you could dig out the tera-hertz scanner and run it down both sides a segment at a time?'

Shardelle grinned. 'I can do that.'

'Start with the cowl and those front two segments. It's going to be hard work, but I'll run a carbide cutter through there,' he pointed to a section behind the two mentioned segments, 'then we can use the ATV to haul the front end over and drag it free . . . let's get to work.'

Shardelle nodded as he headed back towards the ATV, but instead of following she walked up close to the mas-sive corpse, reached out and ran her fingers over the stony surface. Unlike the vertebrae of a spinal column, this was all hard sharp edges seeming as perilous as newly machined metal. It was not metal – more like rough flint and with the same near-translucence. Seeing holograms, pictures, film of this creature in action in no way imparted the sheer scale of this lethal machine of nature. She shuddered to think what it would mean to be this close to a living specimen. But this one was definitely dead. She sensed an aura of some awesome force rendered impotent.

The circular saw was giro-stabilized, but it bucked and twisted as its diamond-tooth blade bit into hard cara-pace. Already the disc blade had shed three of its concentric layers of teeth, and Jonas's shimmer-shield visor was flicking off and on to shed the sweat that dropped from his face onto it. He had cut only halfway through, taking out wedges of carapace just as a woods-man would remove wood with an axe. Now he was into the soft tissue of the creature, 'soft' in this case meaning

merely of the consistency of old oak rather than carbide
steel. Glancing down the length of the monster's body he
saw that Shardelle had nearly reached the tail with the
terahertz scanner. All hard work, but he was satisfied.
The scans alone, taken at close range on a static target,
should reveal masses of features not detected with distance scans. And soon he himself would be delving inside
that wonderfully complex, and macabre, cowl. He shook
more sweat from his face and continued to work.

Three replacement blades later, he had broken
through. Shardelle, bored with waiting, had manoeuvred
the ATV into position, sunk its ground anchors into the
sand, and run out the cable from its front winch to the
hooder, where she secured it through a hole diamond-
drilled through the further edge of the cowl. Jonas
backed out of the carnage he had wrought, lugging the
circular saw, which now seemed to have doubled in
weight. He gave her the signal to go ahead, and moved
aside.

Shardelle started the winch running, the braided
monofilament cable, thin as fishing line, drawing taut.
After a moment the note from the winch changed and
the far side of the cowl began to lift. Black carrion-eaters
began to swarm like ants. Sand poured from the cowl as
it came up vertical to the ground, then in a moment
turned over completely.

Jonas spotted something revealed where the cowl had
lain and walked over. Carrion-eaters were thick on the
ground there amid a tangle of bones and tatters of
leathery skin. He had wondered why they had been so
numerous around the hooder itself, for it seemed
unlikely they could feed upon its substance before time
and bacteria had softened it sufficiently. The creature

had obviously gone to its death still clutching recent prey. He returned, picking up the saw on the way, to Shardelle.

'Drag it over there.' He pointed to the cliff. 'We'll spray with repellant and set up a big frame tent over it.'

She looked askance at him.

'Please,' he added.

The cowl, with two body segments still attached, sledded easily across the sand. Jonas took a tank of the repellant from the ATV, slung it from his shoulder and using a stemmed pressure sprayer, walked around this section of the beast liberally coating it. Carrion-eaters fled in every direction. The tent, which came in a large square package, he sat on the first body segment and activated from a distance. Within seconds the package spidered out long carbon-fibre legs, stabbed them into the ground, then dropped fabric down like a bashful woman quickly lowering her skirts.

'Let's get the equipment set up,' Jonas said.

Later he was delving into the cowl: pulling up jointed limbs that terminated in scythe blades as sharp and tough as chainglass, or in telescopic protuberances that looked like hollow drills; excavating one red eye from the carapace, jumping back when it fluoresced, laughing and returning to work; running an optical probe down into one small mouth to study the wealth of cutting and grinding gear inside.

'You know, the present theory is that the hooder requires all this so it can deal with a kind of grazer living in the mountains. Those creatures feed on poisonous fungi, the toxins from which accumulate in the black fats layered in their bodies. When the hooders capture them under their hoods, they need to slice their way through their prey very meticulously, to eat only what are called the creature's white fats.' He glanced at Shardelle, who was watching with fascination.

'They don't kill their prey,' she observed.

'Apparently. When the hooder goes after a fungus grazer, the grazer immediately starts breaking down the black fat to provide itself with the energy to flee, and then its blood supply and muscles become toxic too. So any serious damage to either could release poisons into the uncontaminated white fat. The hooder dissects its prey, not even allowing it to bleed. It eventually dies of shock.'

'The same with any prey it catches,' Shardelle added. 'Including us.'

'I don't believe it for a minute,' said Jonas. 'The fungus-grazers are only a small part of its diet, and many hooders don't even range into the mountains.'

'Why, then?'

'I just don't know.' He lifted out another jointed limb, this one terminating in a set of chisel-faced pincers. 'All I do know is that when they've finished with their victim there's usually nothing left larger than a coin.'

He continued working, and did not notice till much later that the tent's light had come on, and Shardelle had gone. Looking outside he saw that she had set up her own tent, and no light showed inside. He went back to work, only stopping in the morning to get something to eat and plenty to drink, and to then sit meditating for an hour while his asomnidapted body cleared its fatigue poisons. As Calypse gazed down and the rising sun etched fire across the horizon, he experienced a moment of deep calm clarity. He knew now, felt that somewhere, deep inside, he had always known. So much confirmed it. Total confirmation had come from close nanoscopic

study of the carapace. The sun had breached the horizon
when he returned inside to package his samples. Really
he needed no more from this beast now. Others could
come here if they wished.

Shardelle wormed out of her tent, smelling coffee and
feeling a deep overpowering need for it. For a moment
she could not figure what was different, then she saw it:
the frame tent was gone, the hooder's cowl and two
attached segments were in pieces. Jonas was sitting
crosslegged on one of the limestone slabs, sipping a self-
heating coffee. He gestured to another sealed cup resting
nearby. She walked over to him.

'You've finished?' she asked incredulously.

He grinned. 'Amazing what you can achieve when you
have no need for sleep. I've been working for Taxonomy
for fifty-three years. In my last eighteen years of being
asomnidapted I've done more work than in the previous
thirty-five.'

'Perhaps I should consider that for myself,' said
Shardelle, pulling the tab on her cup. She preferred the
coffee from her machine in the Tagreb, but this convenience here was preferable. While she waited for her drink
to heat she observed that he had a piece of carapace resting on a brushed-aluminium box before him.

'Any conclusions?' she asked, leaning her buttocks
against a nearby slab.

'Very definitely.' He reached inside his coat and
removed a small handheld gun. Shardelle recognized it
as a quantum cascade, QC, laser.

'I promise not to steal your research,' she quipped.

He grimaced. 'It's not the stealing I would worry
about, but how it may well be hushed up.' He pointed

the laser at the carapace and fired. A wisp of smoke rose,
picking out the beam in the air. There was a red glow at
the point of contact, but whether from heat or simply
reflected light, Shardelle could not tell. But nothing else
was happening to the carapace.

'You know, every piece I've managed to study has
been old and partially broken down by bacteria. These
are the freshest remains I've ever studied.' Still he was
firing the laser, and still the carapace was unaffected.
'You see, a piece of old carapace would have started
disintegrating by now – that's because certain nano-
structures inside it would have broken down.' He turned
off the laser, then abruptly put his bare hand flat down
on the carapace.

Shardelle leaned forward. 'An insulator?'

'You'd think.' He poured coffee on the aluminium box
and it immediately sizzled into steam.

'Shit!' Shardelle squatted down beside the box to peer
closely at the carapace. She then looked up at Jonas.
'Conductive . . . *super*conductive?'

'Carbon fullerene nanotubes. When was the last time
you saw something like that naturally produced?'

'About never.'

'They're laced through the carapace material, which
bears some resemblance to the shock-resistant composite laminates we use in our spaceships. The interesting
part is that the nanotubes link down deep into the
hooder's body. I'll have to look closely at the scans but
my guess is that the more you heat up one of these
bastards the faster it moves.' He picked up the piece of
carapace. 'Of course, though you won't see stuff like this
naturally produced, you can find it elsewhere.'

'Sorry?'

He looked at her directly. 'Polity battlefield armour.'

'What? . . . What are you saying?'

'The genome was the first clue: so short, so concise, so exact. What I'm saying is that hooders, though living creatures, are artefacts; biogenetic artefacts.'

Ahead lay a plain of flattened flute grass, boring and level as it disappeared into misty distance. Shardelle set the ATV on automatic, monitored by Rodol, and decided it was time, as Jonas was now doing, to check into the virtual world. She took her aug from a pocket of her envirosuit and plugged it in the permanent plug behind her ear, closed her eyes and booted up.

First she checked her messages and was appalled to find over four thousand awaiting her attention. She opened only those from recognized sources. Some of it was personal; from her brother, from two of her three children, one from her third husband, another from her great-grandmother. The first were easy enough to answer with pages from her diary run through a personalizing program. The one from her great-grandmother, who was a xenobiologist of some standing, she took rather more care over. As she laid out the reply, detailing her frustrations and nascent theories, she wondered if Jonas knew her great-grandmother. She had been in Xeno for seventy years and he in Taxonomy for fifty-three, perhaps they had met at some time? Other messages updated her with news from the Tagreb. A gabbleduck's bill had been discovered in the mountains. In her absence it had been measured and analysed ad nauseam, but nothing new learnt. Still other messages were debating the merits of this linguistic theory or that one, and it was with a sinking sensation that she opened some of the messages from

unrecognized senders to find links to where papers on
The Gabble had been published. She turned her attention to the linguistic net.

The hardcore had now dropped down to below a
thousand. It seemed that most of the lunatic fringe had
dissipated, hence the appearance of all those papers.
Most serious theorists did not publish until they had
something worth publishing. That was accepted protocol
to prevent too much rubbish clogging up the informational highways. Nothing new on the net. Returning to
her messages she deleted every one from unknown
sources. Only then did she spot the message from the
haiman Kroval on Earth:

*'Every bird sings for a reason, similarly do dogs bark. Per-
haps the Anglic similarity is misleading and the morphemes
longer than we would suppose . . . maybe the length of a
gabbleduck's life. Perhaps they are all saying the same thing?'*

That made Shardelle pause. She groped for meaning
and it seemed to her to be lurking out of reach.

*'The meat is forbidden,'* the dracoman child had said.
*Something there . . . something.*

After time her frustration became too much and she
removed her aug. Once again taking up the controls of
the ATV, she noticed that Rodol had reset its course,
taking the vehicle away from the big gabbleduck. The
reason was obvious: a hooder only five kilometres away
from it. With a quick glance at Jonas, Shardelle manually
overrode that and put them back on course. She was
damned if she was going to miss seeing it on the way back
to the Tagreb. Jonas had made *his* big discovery. Maybe
she could come out of this with at least something.

A minute later, Jonas looked at her and said, 'Rodol

just informed me that you are taking us closer to a hooder than might be safe.'

Shardelle pointed at the map screen.

He nodded. 'Just be ready to run. Hooders move damned fast when they want to.'

Shardelle felt almost angered by his reasonable attitude, and felt too ashamed to analyse too closely the reason for that.

Afternoon, and they were back into still-standing flute grass. Shardelle spotted the gabbleduck when they were still kilometres away from it. It sat; a pyramid of alien flesh, its green multi-eyed gaze fixed on the horizon, bill swinging gently from side to side.

'How close would be safe?' Jonas asked when they were only a kilometre away.

Shardelle looked down at her hand gripping the joystick. Her knuckles were white. 'I'm going to approach it. I'm going to walk up to it. You can stay in the ATV if you want.'

Five hundred metres, two hundred metres. Shardelle felt her frustration increase. The gabbleduck had not even turned to look at them. It was as if it could not be bothered to acknowledge their presence. At a hundred metres she just trickled the ATV forward.

'That thing is fucking immense,' said Jonas. He had abandoned his seat to go into the back of the vehicle. Returned now she saw that he was clutching an ECS pulse-rifle.

'What do you intend to do with that?'

'I'll just keep watch. If it goes for you I can maybe drive it off, though seeing it now I realize it might just ignore this popgun.'

Shardelle nodded, and brought the ATV to a halt ten

metres away from the monstrous creature. Turning on
her shimmer-shield visor she manoeuvred past him and
headed for the door. When she finally stepped down onto
the rhizome mat and began pushing her way through the
flute grasses, she heard The Gabble.

'Umbel shockadisc po frzzzt,' gabbleduck grumbled
to itself.

A few paces took her out of the standing flute grasses
to where the creature sat. She recognized the stack of
grazer bones beside it. The gabbleduck had returned to
a previous location.

'Pthog,' the gabbleduck intoned. 'Erb scugalug.'

It just made Shardelle angry. She marched forward
and round until she was standing directly in front of the
creature. It was indeed massive: folds of flesh hanging
down from its body and almost concealing its powerful
rear limbs. When it moved through the flute grasses its
three sets of two forelimbs slotted neatly together to form
two composite forelimbs, so it seemed to run on all fours
like, as Jonas had observed, a bear. Now those forelimbs
were folded on its chest, and sat like this it seemed some
immense alien Buddha. Shardelle glared up at it.

'I've listened to over a thousand hours of that crap!'
she shouted. 'What the fuck are you saying?'

'Frogijig unth,' it observed.

All so close to meaning, but no meaning there.
Returning her attention to its fleshy torso she saw that it
had acquired a whole ecology all its own. The gabbleduck was crawling with prawnlike crustaceans. Where
these were most numerous was around wet-looking
sores, and the occasional lumpish growth leaking milky
fluid.

'Shardelle! Shardelle! Get back here quick!'

*Those crustaceans . . .*

A sudden excitement filled her. They were the very same species they had seen crawling around the dead hooder: carrion-eaters, they never fed on living flesh, but like vultures possessed an instinct for death.

'Shardelle!'

This gabbleduck was dying! She would have her corpse!

Then, through her aug: 'This is Rodol. You must flee your current location at once. A hooder approaches.'

*What?*

Shardelle turned and gazed out across the plain the gabbleduck viewed. A black train was heading towards her, weaving back and forth. The hooder bore some resemblance to a giant millipede with its segments and many paddlelike legs. It also moved with the fast oiled smoothness of that arthropod. Shardelle froze to the spot, not out of fear, but through incredible angry frustration. She could not have this taken away from her, not now. It just was not fair.

'For fuck sake get in here! Maybe it'll ignore us!'

The ATV was parked right next to her. She had not heard it arrive.

'Brogon ahul bul zzzk,' said the gabbleduck.

She suddenly realized how jealous and stupid she had been, and that both she and Jonas might pay for that. She ran for the door of the ATV and piled inside, hauled herself forward. Jonas was in the driving seat trying to get the thing into reverse. He did not take the power off and with a crunching shudder the vehicle stalled.

'Fuck fuck fuck.'

They both looked through the screen. The hooder was close, its front end rising off the ground like the striking head of a cobra. Inside its cowl was a mass of glittering knifish movement through which two vertical rows of red eyes glared. It was not focused on them. It was focused on the gabbleduck. Surely it would respond to this. Shardelle looked at the exterior intercom Jonas had been calling her through to check it was still on. No need really. She could hear the hard oily clattering of the hooder's movement.

'Brogon,' the gabbleduck repeated, waving a black claw in the air.

The hooder froze. The gabbleduck turned its bill towards the ATV. It blinked some of its emerald eyes, then returned its attention to the hooder. After a moment it reached out with one claw and made an unmistakably dismissive gesture. The hooder sank down, turned in a gleaming arc and sped away.

'How do I get this damned thing started again?' Jonas asked

'There's no need. It's gone.'

He snorted a harsh laugh. 'Yeah, right. Well when you've quit having your moment of epiphany, perhaps you'd like to take a look at the map screen.'

Shardelle did so, and for a moment could not make much of the graphics displayed there. They didn't seem to make much sense.

'About thirty of them,' said Jonas.

Then it did make sense. There were thirty hooders scattered all around them. They were moving, but seemed to be holding off for the present.

'You say the bill of a gabbleduck was found in the mountains?' Jonas asked.

'Yes.'

Jonas turned off the ATV's engine. Moving the
vehicle back into a stand of flute grass had been the best
they could do. Hopefully the hooders would attack the
gabbleduck and be too sated by that to attack them.
There was no way to hide completely. He had studied the
hooder sensorium and knew it would pick up body heat
even through the skin of the ATV. Leaving the engine
running would generate more heat to further attract
attention.

'Nothing else?' he asked.

'It's damned annoying. There should be more – bones
at least.'

They were having a perfectly sensible conversation,
sitting in the ATV, waiting to die. The nearest monitor
force had sent a transport, but that would not be here for
another hour. The hooders, it now seemed evident, were
holding off until the gabbleduck finally expired. That
could happen at any moment.

'But the tricones grind away all remains, which was
why that bill was found in the mountains.'

Jonas wondered for just how many millions of years
the tricones had been grinding stuff away. He auged
through to the Tagreb and directly into the database
maintained by those researching the molluscs. It did not
take him long to discover that the tricone genome was
just as concise and devoid of rubbish as the hooder's. He
connected then to the AI.

*'Rodol, are you listening in?'*

*'I am.'*

*'Good.'*

To Shardelle he said, 'Three ancient races, whose
physical technological remains probably would not fill
the back of this ATV.'

She glanced at him, seemed about to say something, then abruptly returned her attention to the gabbleduck. He thought she was swallowing tears.

'Tricones are biogenetic artefacts as well,' he added.

'I think it's nearly dead,' she said.

The gabbleduck seemed a sleepy old man, its head nodding, bill lowering to its chest then jerking up again. Removing his QC laser, Jonas laid it on the console before him. They both stared at it. He guessed she understood his intent. They both knew how hooders fed.

'But of biogenetic artefacts left by those races there are many: plants obviously made to refine metals from soil, worms made to accumulate radioactives in their bodies, and perhaps many others we don't recognize. You know there are theories that even some Terran life-forms are such artefacts? Why do some creatures carry a venomous punch so far in excess of that required to kill their prey? Why the chalk-builders, the coral-makers, why this why that? Much was attributed to Gaean theories. Now there is some doubt.'

'You'll be getting to a point sometime soon,' said Shardelle. 'I think we are running out of time for discussion . . . Oh hell.' She leant forward.

The gabbleduck held out a claw.

'Kzzz lub luha Brogon,' it stated, its voice clear over exterior com, then it abruptly sagged and its bill came down to rest upon its chest. The light went out of its eyes.

Jonas lowered his gaze to the map screen.

'They're coming.'

He picked up his QC laser.

A rushing hissing impinged. Jonas could feel the ATV vibrating. He closed his eyes and swallowed drily. What did his theories matter now? And even should he not state them, Rodol would have most certainly worked it all out.

The first hooder came in from the right, its front end rearing thirty metres into the air, then coming down like a striking snake on the mountainous corpse. It began feeding, its long body rippling down its length. He did not see the second approach, just suddenly there were two hooders there, tearing at the corpse. Then a crash and the ATV shifted to one side, bouncing on its suspension as another of the monstrous creatures came past. Another rose up behind the others, vertical rows of eyes glowing, eating utensils opening out in a deadly glassy array. Down. Corpse jerked this way and that. Limbs conveyed away, sheets of skin peeled, fat and muscle and sprays of milky blood. Soon there was more hooder to be seen than gabbleduck: a great black Gordian tangle, racketing with the sound of some vast machine shop. It took less than an hour. One hooder slid away, then another. Jonas waited for one to come straight at the ATV. He wondered when he would fire the first shot through the side of Shardelle's head. When it hit the vehicle, when it tore it open, or at the point when one of those cowls poised above them? One of the creatures came close, shaking the ATV and jouncing it along the ground as its carapace worked like some giant rough saw down the side of the bodywork. Then they were all gone, and he was staring down at the map screen watching their transponder signals depart.

'I guess they've eaten enough,' said Shardelle.

There was nothing solid left, only fluids spattered on ground that looked as if it had been ploughed.

'Bones as well – everything,' said Jonas. 'But then that is probably their purpose.'

She looked at him, sharp, annoyed. He stood and headed for the door and she followed.

'You want to know what The Gabble is?' he asked, standing at the edge of the churned ground.

'Of course I do.'

He gestured to the mess before them. 'Something made the hooders and the tricones. The hooders were most certainly a weapon in some war and the tricones made to digest the physical remnants of a civilization.'

'But why?'

'We'll probably not know the answer to that. Tricones and hooders possess the same planetary genome as the gabbleducks, which means the gabbleducks probably made them. But their final purpose might not be the gabbleducks' own.'

'You hinted that you knew what The Gabble is,' said Shardelle stubbornly.

'Maybe it's a language of non-meaning: words spoken by a race that has given up, withdrawn, even chosen to forgo intelligence. A race become so self-effacing it has made tricones to wipe out every trace of its civilization, and turned its own war machines to the purpose of destroying even the remains of its own devolved descendants. Or perhaps it's even worse than that.'

'How could it possibly be worse?'

'Perhaps they lost some war, and this was done to them by the victors: their civilization erased, their creatures turned upon them – just enough mind remaining to them so they always remember what happened, that scrap of intelligence just enough for them to know how to hold off the hooders until they die.'

Shardelle shivered. Jonas felt an immense sadness at the core of which grew the seed of new purpose. Calypse hung above the far horizon, etched out by the setting sun, and silhouetted came the ECS transport. Tragedy here, or choice – he did not know. He swore to himself, in that moment, that one day he would.

# Author's Notes

## 1    Softly Spoke the Gabbleduck

In my first book published by Macmillan I created a character called Mr Crane, a two-metre-tall brass android
killing machine with a tendency to rip people apart,
yet for whom many readers felt a great affection. The
upshot of this was his resurrection in the third book of
the Cormac Sequence, *Brass Man*. In the second book
of that same sequence, *The Line of Polity*, I described a
weird creature called a gabbleduck, which readers
seemed to find equally attractive. Tracing the genesis
of this monster back through my mind, I see my fear as
a child when coming face to face with an enormous
gander at Colchester zoo . . . subsequently being called
a gabble-duck by my mother when I wouldn't shut up . . .
and making something weird and duck-like out of
papier mâché when I was about seven . . . or maybe it
has nothing to do with these at all. I plan to do a novel
about these creatures because throughout the Cormac
Sequence, and stories like the one below, they've grown
into something more than mere beasts. 'Softly Spoke
the Gabbleduck' was first published in *Asimov's Science*

*Fiction*, August 2005; then was reprinted in *The Year's Best Science Fiction Twenty-Third Annual Collection* edited by Gardner Dozois (July 2006 – St Martin's Griffin Books), and has since been translated into Russian.

## 2   Putrefactors

This story contains numerous links to my Polity books. We have here Erlin, the heroine from *The Skinner* and *The Voyage of the Sable Keech*, we have a monitor from Earth who was essentially a precursor to the ECS agent, we have the idea of the Serban Kline download to corrupt the mind of a Golem. Another bit of world-building here that took its genesis from just one word that was the original title of this story: 'Shroudbeast'. Oh yeah, before I forget, we also have here the psychotic Golem that the Serban Kline download produced. Now, you just know this is going to get nasty . . . 'Putrefactors' was published only in a now defunct magazine called *Zest* (issue 7), summer 1999.

## 3   Garp and Geronamid

In my second book for Macmillan, *The Skinner*, I introduced a character called Sable Keech, a policeman so determined to catch certain criminals that he continued searching for them for seven hundred years after his own death. He was a reification: a corpse kept mobile by cybermotors, preserved by chemical and other means, his mind recorded to crystal within it. In that book I hinted that he wasn't the only one of this kind, and of course it was an idea I enjoyed too much to leave alone. The subsequent story evolved out of that and out of the various artificial intelligences and machinations at the border of the Polity. 'Garp and Geronamid' appeared in *Interzone* (issue 199), July/August 2005.

## 4    The Sea of Death

Like many other writers of short science fiction, *Interzone* was a definite target for me, in fact it was my first target. Every short story I wrote over a period of fifteen years winged its way to that magazine and a rejection letter winged its way back. They were very nice rejection letters, but still . . . Then I finally managed to break in with 'The Sea of Death', though I still wish one of my stories had broken into that market before my first science-fiction novels from Macmillan were in the bookshops. If wishes were fishes, Britain might still have a trawler industry. Published in *Interzone* (issue 169), July 2001.

## 5    Alien Archaeology

Time for another gabbleduck story. Determined, on a break between books, to keep throwing something at the short-story markets, I sat down to write a couple. That they both came out at over 20,000 words might mean I'm getting too used to writing novels, or I'm just getting waffly. I hope not. The first of these stories, 'Alien Archaeology' was first published in *Asimov's Science Fiction*, June 2007; thereafter in *The Year's Best Science*

*Fiction Twenty-Fifth Annual Collection* edited by Gardner Dozois (July 2008 – St Martin's Griffin Books).


## 6 Acephalous Dreams

In this story the artificial intelligence Geronamid appears again along with one of the artefacts left scattered about the galaxy by a long-dead race called the Csorians, who had likely been mucking about with a technology left by another dead race; the lethal Jain technology that features in many of my books and stories. 'Acephalous Dreams' appeared only once before, in volume one of the *Adventure* anthology, edited by Chris Roberson (November 2005 – Monkeybrain Books).


## 7 Snow in the Desert

An odd one here, written quite some time ago and subsequently rewritten, a lot. As anyone knows who reads my stuff, I like my super-tough heroes and lethal androids. It first appeared in Paul Fraser's sadly defunct *Spectrum SF* (issue 8), May 2002. It was then taken for *Year's Best SF*, volume 8, edited by David G. Hartwell and Kathryn Cramer (June 2003 – Eos Books).


## 8 Choudapt

This was published only in the now defunct magazine *Sci-Fright*. It was one of my ventures into playing with the idea of doctor mycelia, and familiar ideas about